# THE END IS NIGH

by

I0654053

## William Blackwell

ISBN: 978-1-7389714-6-6
Published by Telemachus Press
Second Edition

## Acknowledgements

Heartfelt thanks to my loyal and supportive friends, family, readers, and especially my editor, Winslow Eliot, who continues to help me improve my craft.

*The fourth angel poured out his bowl on the sun, and it was allowed to scorch people with fire. They were scorched by the fierce heat, and they cursed the name of God who had power over these plagues. They did not repent and give him glory.*
—Holy Bible, English Standard Version, *Book of Revelation*, 16:8-9

*It was a special pleasure to see things eaten, to see things blackened and changed. With the brass nozzle in his fists, with this great python spitting its venomous kerosene upon the world, the blood pounded in his head, and his hands were the hands of some amazing conductor playing all the symphonies of blazing and burning to bring down the tatters and charcoal ruins of history. With his symbolic helmet numbered 451 on his stolid head, and his eyes all orange flame with the thought of what came next, he flicked the igniter and the house jumped up in a gorging fire that burned the evening sky red and yellow and black. He strode in a swarm of fireflies. He wanted above all, like the old joke, to shove a marshmallow on a stick in the furnace, while the flapping pigeon-winged books died on the porch and lawn of the house. While the books went up in sparkling whirls and blew away on a wind turned dark with burning.*

— Ray Bradbury, *Fahrenheit 451*

*Multitudes who sleep in the dust of the earth will awake, some to everlasting life, others to shame and everlasting contempt...*
—Holy Bible, Old Testament, Book of Daniel

# Prologue

*You got this. Relax.* But Pastor Jonathon Brackley couldn't shake the uneasy feeling that this sermon would not go to plan. He was nervous, fidgety, and unsure about how the congregants would respond. He clasped his hands together, trying to hide the twitching of his fingers as he stepped up to the pulpit on a dark and cloudy Sunday morning. Tapping the microphone, he misstepped, staggered and swayed, and then put a hand on the mahogany platform and the Holy Bible for support. The Bible, more than the mahogany, gave him comfort and strength.

A murmur rolled through the packed church, echoed eerily, and subsided.

Pastor Jon cleared his throat. Feedback screeched from the microphone. Stopped. The worshippers murmured, a little louder this time. A baby tucked into her mother's bosom in the first row began crying. The mother, with hushed niceties, tried to silence the pinkly-clad infant. Soft sobs turned into a loud wailing cry—"Whah, whaaah, whaaaah... whaaaaaaaaah!" The mother flushed, rose quickly, and left with the baby.

As the heavy oak entrance door thudded shut ominously, the baby's cries grew faint, and Pastor Jon cleared his throat a second time. No feedback. No murmurs. No crying baby. Only silence and attentive eyes.

He looked out at the congregants, nodding fondly as he spotted some of his friends. He didn't know if they were ready, if he was even ready. But one thing he did know. This would probably be his last sermon, so they *better* be ready. He better be ready. Lately, due to the controversial nature of his sermons, his superiors in the clergy were fast becoming alienated from him. More than just alienated, actually. Downright angry and offended. The comment from senior Pastor Gary Ellington before this morning's sermon couldn't have been more direct: "If you don't tone it down, stop this doom and gloom talk, we'll have no choice but to defrock you. Keep it upbeat. That's what people want to hear. Give them what they want. And stay off the wine... at least while you're preaching."

But Pastor Jon hadn't toned downed his sermons. Nor had he stayed off the booze. It was all he could do to cope with his disturbing visions of late. And his failing marriage. Earlier this morning, in spite of admonitions from his disgruntled wife, he'd polished off a bottle of Chilean red wine. His justification—the Bible was full of wine references. Jesus had even turned water into wine at a wedding. Of course, that didn't prove He drank the wine, but it would have been perfectly normal for Him to do so. It did prove, at least to Pastor Jon's logic, that Jesus didn't condemn drinking wine any more than He condemned drinking water. Pastor Jon took his theory one step further, actually, believing Jesus was not only a wine drinker, but an excessive one. Maybe even a drunkard. *Water to wine. Never mind. Get going...*

He cleared his throat. "Thank you all for coming this morning. Today I want to talk about the *Book of Revelation*. Specifically, I want to talk about a vision I had last night that relates to Revelation." He waited for the whispered murmur to die down before continuing. "As you all know, my name is Jon. According to Revelation, one day around the year 95 AD, a man named John had a vision from Heaven. Well, last night, I too had a vision, which I believe to be a vision from Heaven. Maybe epiphany is a better word." His voice had started off as a low, slow, monotone droll. But as he talked, it gained volume, speed, passion, and conviction. "I'm guessing some of you might be curious as to what that vision might be about?" A pause. "It has to do with The Seven Bowls of God's Wrath. Revelation 15:1 – 16:21."

He paused again, listening to pages shuffling as the congregants found their reference points. "John sees seven angels with seven bowls filled with God's wrath. He hears a voice, telling the angels to empty out the disaster-filled bowls one at a time upon the Earth. Now, this is the part you might find hard to believe... but I tell you to warn you. I tell you to save you. I've been directed by God! I saw the angels, I heard the voice telling the angels to destroy the world."

Thunder boomed overhead. A few people stirred. The rain came, slow at first, then torrential, tapping on roof and windows like so many nails in a coffin. A young couple seated at the back row got up and left. Pastor Jon waited until the thunder stopped, and once the heavy wood and metal door had thudded shut a second time, he continued: "Let's talk about the bowls of God's wrath. The angel poured out the first bowl on the Earth. Ugly and painful sores broke out on the worshippers of the devil. Look at the rampant spread of disease today: Ebola, Zika, Swine-Flu, Aids, common flu viruses mutating, getting stronger, killing people, becoming immune to treatment."

He found his place in the Bible and quoted from the text: "'The second angel poured out his bowl on the sea, and it turned into blood, like that of a dead man, and every living thing in the sea died.' Look at what we do to our oceans. Reckless oil companies, irresponsible government, common people polluting and killing our eco-system. Killing us."

A middle-aged man seated near the back rose and turned to leave. "No, don't go. Stay and listen. The end is nigh. Prepare yourself."

"You're a fucking nutcase," the man said, and stormed out.

Like a rising swell in turbulent ocean waters, a loud murmur swept through the church. Then grunts, throats clearing, gasps, followed by derogatory comments. "Something's wrong with him... He's lost his mind... He never had it... I'm not gonna listen to this shit... Fucking bullshit, you ask me."

"Quiet, please," Pastor Jon said, gesturing with outstretched hands. "Hear me out. That's all I ask."

Silence settled over the church. He continued reading aloud: "'The third angel poured out his bowl on the rivers and springs of water, and they became blood.' More pollution. More human negligence. The world is full of it and God has decided we need a cleansing. I now come to the fourth angel, and the most powerful and evocative image in my vision. If you listen to nothing else I say, listen to this. 'The fourth angel poured out his bowl on the sun, and the sun was given power to scorch people with fire. They were seared by the intense heat and they cursed the name of

God, who had control over these plagues, but they refused to repent and glorify Him.'"

Pastor Jon coughed, took a sip of water—*water to wine, water to wine*—and resumed: "There are forest fires burning out of control as we speak. They will worsen. They will spread and devour our entire planet. The devil's insidiousness has permeated the very fabric of our culture. He is in our thoughts, heaven forbid, in our prayers, and in our deeds. Cast him out and save yourself."

"How do you propose we do that?" Ron Baxter shouted. Pastor Jon recognized the voice and spotted his one-time-friend-turned-acquaintance standing up in the third row. The obese, black-bearded man's brow was furrowed and he rubbed the creases with a hand in an attempt to smooth them out.

"I'm getting there, Ronnie. Sit down. Be patient. Please." Pastor Jon had planned on outlining each of the bowls of wrath in detail, referencing them with a corresponding modern day man-made calamity. Now, he realized, he was going to have to cut this sermon short if he had any hope of reaching the congregation. Too many naysayers. If he continued at this pace, he would lose half, if not all, before he properly prepared them for the end of the world. In any event, at least he had gotten to number four, the most important according to his epiphany. "Reaffirm your vows to God. Repent your sins. Go home and pray. Denounce the devil and his ways so you might be spared..."

Thunder boomed and the church trembled. A lightning bolt smashed through a large, oval-shaped stained-glass window in the peaked-roof temple of God. People started screaming, some fleeing, as shards of glass rained down on them. The lightning bolt forked and struck a white-robed Jesus statue. The lightning buzzed, circled the statue, shot through its arm, and blasted out from the pointed finger of Jesus like a well-aimed laser gun. The powerful bolt then struck a wooden church pew. It burst into flames. Pandemonium erupted and people fled en masse.

"You have one year," Pastor Jon shouted after the fleeing mobs. "One year to the day. The world will burn in one year. Dig a cave, stock it with supplies, and wait. You will be told when it's time to emerge. The end is nigh... prepare yourself!"

# Chapter One

"I'm sick of all these conspiracy theories. The world is not gonna end soon, and I'm gonna keep on doing what I do best." Even as Cray Lenning said the words, he wasn't sure what they meant, or at least wasn't sure what the latter part meant. *What do I do best?* He eyeballed his friend Mike Timble across the table of an outdoor patio in front of a Starbucks coffee shop in downtown Charlottetown, Prince Edward Island.

*I do my job best. That's what I do.*

Cray sighed. Maybe he did do his job best. But his job, a garbage collector in the small city, had become mundane. *Uneventful, unexciting, unfulfilling. Boring, actually.*

Four years ago, after discovering his long-time girlfriend Emma Thymes fucking his so-called best friend Greg Smallton, Cray had lost interest in people and relationships. *Friends and lovers... they can go fuck themselves. They burn your trust.* Burned by love, he had become cowardly concerning romance. He was unwilling to approach women for fear of rejection or, worse still, infidelity. Emma had ruthlessly ripped his heart from his chest. But never again. Never would he give someone that opportunity again.

Maybe that's why he was sick of Mike's conspiracy theories. Maybe he was sick of his own life—his own attitude—and taking it out on Mike. *It's your shit.* But no, it was more than that. Had to be more than that. Mike's theories were asinine. He had just told Cray that in his infinite wisdom the world would come to an end on Thursday, June 30$^{th}$. Today was June 1$^{st}$.

But Mike was insistent. "I'm telling you, this isn't another one of what you call my lame-brained conspiracy theories. This is the truth."

Cray sipped his coffee and gazed momentarily out at the passing traffic and pedestrians on Queen Street that sunny afternoon. "What do you mean 'truth'? It hasn't come true yet."

"No, but it will. Mark my words."

"Let's just say for a second there is a shred of truth to your theory—which frankly we both know isn't the case—where did you acquire these prophetic words of wisdom from?"

"Someone told me. Then something else happened that confirmed it. Then I had a dream that confirmed it."

"Some wacko told you? Who? A dream? You think just because some nutcase told you and you had a dream that it's gonna come true?"

Mike was becoming irritated. He squeezed his empty paper coffee cup, pushed it on the table. It tipped over and rolled onto the sidewalk. He ignored it. "Oh, forget it, Cray. You're not gonna believe me. Sometimes I don't even know why I bother."

"Bother with what? Telling me shit?"

"Even living, for fuck sakes. What's the point? The world's gonna end soon anyway and my life sucks."

"Sorry, Mike. Don't talk like that. Please."

Mike scratched his two-day stubble and adjusted his baseball cap. He always did that when he was rattled or confused. He pointed across the street to an old, scraggly-haired, disheveled man—street beggar-bum—wheeling a shopping cart. It was stuffed with all kinds of goodies; at least goodies to him. "Shit, that's him."

"Who?"

"The man. The preacher I met."

"What—" Cray didn't have a chance to finish.

The man suddenly stopped, reached into his shopping cart, and extracted a sign. He released the cart. Unattended, it careened down the sidewalk, causing two pedestrians to deftly step out of its way.

Holding up the sign, the man, with speed belying his years, ran across the street. But ten feet from the sidewalk patio where Cray sat, a newer model Toyota Camry, pulling away from the curb, struck him. He flew back, landing with a thud as his head slammed into the asphalt surface. His hands still gripped the sign tightly.

Cray ran to his aid but stopped short. The offending motorist had already stopped, climbed out of his vehicle, and knelt down beside the man. Troubled, he scanned the faces of the gathering onlookers. "Someone call 911. He came out of nowhere."

As Cray neared, he saw the pool of blood fanning out around the man's head, dark red on black asphalt. His eyes were closed, expression sullen, leathery face ashen. Dead or unconscious, Cray didn't know.

Cray turned around. Mike was frozen in his seat, expression sullen, pockmarked face ashen.

"He's moving," someone said. "Stand back."

The man's eyes opened wide. He lifted his head. His steel blue eyes locked onto Cray. He lifted the sign and repeated its proclamation scrawled in black on white cardboard. "The end is nigh! The end is nigh! Prepare yourself!"

Then he dropped the sign, fell back, slamming his head on the road a second time. His eyes rolled in his head, then closed. He grew still. Deathly still.

*The end is nigh, all right buddy. At least for you.* Cray was embarrassed and ashamed that a small smile actually played across his lips at those thoughts. He quickly wiped it away. It was replaced by a somber expression, a feeling of remorse and sadness for the poor bastard stretched out on the road, probably dead. But those feelings were intermingled with something else: a nagging, troubling, fearful feeling that something wasn't quite right in the world anymore.

*A crazy coincidence. That's all.*

Cray glanced back. Mike had disappeared.

More spectators began to gather. An ambulance siren blared. A cop car approached and stopped in the middle of the street, blocking traffic. Two cops got out. One knelt down to the victim while the other began questioning bystanders and surveying the damage.

A middle-aged woman, dressed in frumpy gray sweatpants and an oversized white sweatshirt with a pink elephant on the front, approached Cray. She had a little boy in hand who slurped an ice cream cone, white melting rivulets streaming down his chin, onto his clothes, dribbling onto the sidewalk. She touched Cray's arm. "Do you know him?"

"Know who?"

An ambulance stopped at the scene. The shrill siren died. Two paramedics got out, one removing a stretcher from the back.

She pointed to the man, who was now being carefully examined by the paramedics.

"No, never seen him before. Why?"

"He stared right at you. As if he was giving his death message directly to you."

The ice cream-carrying boy moved closer to Cray, oblivious to the bloody accident scene. He slurped the ice cream and held it up to Cray. Small white drops sprayed onto Cray's blue jeans and black tennis shoes.

"Do you want some?" the boy asked.

Cray stepped back, out of melted ice cream range. "No thanks." Morbid thoughts pressed into his mind. *White light, red blood, black dawn.* He shuddered.

"Josh, watch yourself," the woman said. "You're getting it all over him." She pulled Josh closer to her side. Ice cream drops dribbled down her already stained gray sweatpants. Oblivious, she turned to Cray. "Did you see it?"

Cray nodded nervously. "I gotta go."

She touched his arm. "Wait. You're a witness. They might want to talk to you."

Cray noticed a male cop, who had been questioning other spectators, glance curiously at him.

Without knowing why, Cray turned and ran, sprinting down the street and weaving around pedestrians on that beautiful Tuesday afternoon. A block and a half later, he stopped and glanced back, almost expecting the cops to be in hot pursuit. They weren't, but he could barely see the old man being hoisted onto a stretcher and loaded into an ambulance. *Who is he? And what does he know?*

# Chapter Two

*He knows,* Mike thought that evening as he sat in his humble apartment two blocks away from Cray in downtown Charlottetown. *He knows we're all gonna die. He knows the future.*

He had arrived home two hours ago and started taking stock of his life. Cray had called twice. He ignored both calls. *Fucker doesn't wanna believe me. I tried to warn him. He won't listen. Fuck him. He can go and fuck himself, all I care.*

But it wasn't only Cray. He had told his mother Edith the story a few days ago. She wanted to have him examined by a psychiatrist. "You're full of stupid conspiracy theories. Why don't you go out and get yourself a job instead of worrying about the end of the world? I raised you to work hard and all you do is sit around watching TV and collecting social assistance."

Easy for her to say. She grew up in a generation where if she didn't work, she would starve. So she forged a successful nursing career until her recent retirement. Now her title was cynic and potato farmer's wife. For a nurse, a career dedicated to caregiving, she certainly didn't seem to give a shit about her only son. More than that, Edith was downright abusive to Mike. At least for the last two years, when her expectations that he would become a doctor were shattered after he was caught drinking during a lecture and expelled. Would have happened sooner or later anyway. It was his first year of university and he'd only lasted four months. His marks were shit. Lack of concentration. Lack

16

of focus. "Doesn't apply himself." So they said, anyway. *Well, they can fuck themselves. And so can Edith.*

Mike moved a kitchen chair to the middle of the living room and stared up at the ceiling.

His father Thane was a little more sympathetic, but seemed equally doubtful of the veracity of the prediction. "I don't know, son. It sounds a little farfetched to me. People have been predicting the end of the world since the beginning of time, and none of them have gotten it right. And besides, we're all gonna die sooner or later. And none of us know when. So, we may as well make the best of it." Handing Mike a sack of potatoes. "Here, gimme a hand with these, will ya. Try and take your mind of that stuff. It ain't good for ya."

So Mike took the potatoes, helped his father, and dropped the doomsday prophecy. At least for the time being. But it kept rearing its ugly head. Little voices kept telling him to get his affairs in order. *Sorry, Dad. You're gonna die in the apocalypse. I'll miss you.*

Holding a small handsaw, Mike stood on the chair and cut away a small circle in the ceiling. He examined the cast iron pipe underneath. *Hope it's strong enough.*

When Mike met Pastor Jonathon Brackley a week ago, whom he now revered as a doomsday prophet, he did what few others would. He listened to the old man with the shopping cart. Bought him a bottle of rum. Sat in a park with him and drank it. Got drunk. Learned the man's story. Although his theories had resulted in the loss of his preacher job, Pastor Jon, as he preferred to be called, would not let it go. Even though the repeated prophecies also resulted in a separation from his long-time wife and an estrangement from two adult sons, Pastor Jon hit the streets of his hometown, Moncton, New Brunswick, proselytizing to anyone who would listen. "The end is nigh. Prepare yourself." Of course most people—99.9 percent—brushed him off as a lunatic and ignored him, even ridiculed and shunned him. Over time the frustration became unbearable. Hardly anyone would listen. So Pastor Jon took refuge in the bottle, drained his finances, and ended up living on the streets. When the nastiness in Moncton got too much to bear, he relocated to Charlottetown to preach his message, or "save the few who will listen."

Mike began tying a rope around the exposed cast iron pipe. He tugged it. *It'll hold.*

At first Mike had his doubts. But the reoccurring signs, signs that Pastor Jon had said would prove the truthfulness of his predictions, soon convinced him. Pastor Jon had said three things would happen to Mike after that fateful meeting in the park. The first one happened fifteen minutes after leaving the park. A crow swooped down low, circled Mike's head twice, just as predicted, then promptly shit on it. The following evening Mike had a nightmare, again, as predicted. In it, a massive fireball engulfed the Earth. Horrific screams of dying people, the terrifying shrieks of dying animals; cars, buildings, infrastructure exploding everywhere. Mike tried to outrun the flames, searching for the hole, the underground shelter that Pastor Jon had told him to dig, the one that would protect him from the massive destruction. But, when he found it, it wasn't what he remembered. It was only three feet deep, clearly not enough to protect one from such a lethal fireball. Terrified and with no options remaining, Mike took refuge in the hole, watched the Earth burn to the ground around him for a few horrifying seconds until the fireball engulfed him, fried and sizzled him like a pesky wasp.

Mike tugged on the rope, cinched it tight around the plumbing pipe. He sat down and began working the other end.

But the third sign was the clincher. The one that had made him run away scared. The one that happened only a few hours ago. Pastor Jon had been clear. "When you see me get struck down, and die, the end is nigh. Take refuge in the hole. Count the days. Stay there for ninety days and then come to the surface. My tribesmen will be there. They will help you rebuild."

"What about you?" Mike had asked.

Pastor Jon had in one large pull drained the bottle, looked at Mike sorrowfully, and said, "I don't care about me anymore. My life is over. Look at me."

Only problem was, Mike had not been able to find a hole or underground shelter; other than the shallow one in his nightmare that had become his fiery grave. Although he had tried to find one. Not wanting to wait until the final prediction, he had, stoned out of his mind one night, driven to what he thought was crown land, a government-owned forest, stolen a backhoe from a nearby farmstead, and started digging out an abandoned well in an attempt to make his refuge from the coming apocalypse. Three hours and forty feet down, he was accosted by an angry farmer, pointing a double-barreled shotgun at his head and threatening to kill him. The result, three charges: theft, trespassing, and destruction of private property.

Mike finished the noose, wrapped it around his neck, and snugged it tight. Satisfied, he climbed onto the chair and stood up.

He lit up a joint and inhaled deeply, surveying the messy living room as the reassuring buzz seeped into his brain and dulled his senses. Take-out cartons littered the coffee table. Some had spilled over onto the stained carpet. He took a few more tokes, enjoying the comforting numbness. *At least I won't have to make my court date.*

Before this moment, Mike had often wondered what his last thoughts might be. And it didn't surprise him they would return to Sybil Saunders. She, after all, had been his only true love. But when Mike couldn't hold down a steady job, nor a steady education, she had disappeared like a bat out of hell. Another toke. Exhale. *Bat out of hell. Shit, can't you come up with anything more original than that?*

But as his mind cinema replayed the two-year union with Sybil, he realized he couldn't blame her. She was twenty-eight. He, thirty-two. It was time for him to grow up and take life seriously. Toke. Exhale. For any woman to take him seriously, he would have to demonstrate the ability to provide emotionally, spiritually, and financially. Hell, he could hardly provide for himself, let alone a significant other. Toke. Exhale. *Fucking loser.*

"It doesn't matter. The world is doomed. I sure as hell can't survive in a fucking wasteland. I can barely survive here, for fuck sakes."

Toke. Exhale. He flicked the joint away. It skipped off the hardwood, landed on a Chinese take-out container and started smoking.

Seeing it, he laughed. "Typical. Burn in Hell, motherfucker! You can all go and burn in Hell, motherfuckers!"

He kicked the chair over. The pipe creaked and groaned, but held. He dropped, abruptly halted by the force of the noose tightening around his neck. His body dangled about five inches from the floor. Perfect. His neck tightened. Bulged. He gasped and emitted a gurgling sound. He felt his face redden, eyes bulge, a tremendous painful force gripping his neck, the stinging of rope burns. His world grew dark. *Yes, it's time. It's finally time to end my miserable existence.*

As life drained from his body and mind, and his vision began to blur, he surveyed the room, and saw it: a greeting card. From Sybil. Probably a birthday card, since his birthday was a week away. *Maybe she wants to get back together. Oh shit, what if she wants to get back together?*

In an instant, Mike changed his mind. He didn't want to die now, at least not until he'd read Sybil's happy birthday message. He tried to raise his arms, reach the rope, and break the goddamned pipe from the ceiling. But his weakening arms would not obey brain commands. He tried to shout out to anyone who would listen but had no voice. The rope was too tight, too constricting.

He wriggled his feet, struggling to grab the rope, struggling to shout out. All in vain. No use. As a terrible blackness encompassed him, he saw the Chinese take-out carton, the one with the smoking joint, burst into flames.

The flames fanned out quickly, devouring the old red shag carpet.

In the blackness, Mike saw fiery red. In the redness, Mike saw death.

*Pleeeease! I don't wanna die. Noooooo... nooo... noo... no...*

# Chapter Three

Six curious and probing eyes watched Pastor Jon. He slowly opened his eyes. His head ached dully. He brought his hand to it and felt layers of tight white gauze. He cleared the cobwebs. *Bandaged. But what about my vision? I should be dead.* "I'm alive."

At the foot of his bed, a male doctor stood between two female nurses. He stepped forward. "You're very lucky to be alive. Do you remember what happened?"

Pastor Jon strained the dim recesses of a memory scorched by alcohol abuse. And it came to him. "I was hit by a car."

"Yes," the doctor said. "You were hit by a car. The head impact cracked the back of your skull and you suffered a serious concussion. The chest impact caused cardiac arrest. Your heart stopped beating for about sixteen minutes."

"But I'm alive. I was supposed to die."

The medical staff exchanged confused glances. A nurse rolled her eyes. The doctor continued. "Well, technically sir, you were dead. For sixteen minutes or so. But our highly trained medical staff brought you back." He stepped closer. "I'm Doctor Daniel Ames; these are Nurses Sandra Colling and Betty Reilly. And you are?"

Grimacing, Pastor Jon scratched his head.

"Don't touch that," Doctor Ames said. "It's going to be very sore for quite some time."

Pastor Jon removed his hand. "Did you say your name is Daniel?"

The doctor nodded, puzzlement creasing his brow.

"The book of Daniel. The Old Testament. God saved Daniel and his friends from their enemies, so Daniel could save the oppressed. Daniel understands visions and dreams... you understand visions and dreams. You're the chosen one."

The doctor rubbed his temple. Frowned. "I'm sorry, I'm not a religious man. Again, do you know your name?" He made a hand symbol to Betty. She nodded and left the room.

A long silence followed. Pastor Jon opened his mouth to blurt out another religious rant, but sighed instead. "I'm Jonathon Brackley. Pastor Jon."

Daniel looked curiously at Pastor Jon. "You're a priest?"

"I was. Defrocked now. But, in God's eyes, I'm still a man of the cloth."

Sandra glanced over at a dresser in a corner of the room. On it sat a pile of Pastor Jon's stinky, tattered, booze-stained clothing. She rolled her eyes.

"I'm sure you are," Daniel said. "But right now we need to talk about other things." He held up two fingers. "How many fingers do you see?"

"Are you giving me the finger?"

"How many fingers do you see, Jon?"

"Two."

"Good. Where were you born?"

A pause. "Moncton, New Brunswick."

"Do you have a wife, children?"

"A wife. Two grown children. Estranged."

"Sorry to hear that. How old are you?"

"I'm eighty."

"What is today's date?"

"Dunno. Can't remember."

"Today is June 1$^{st}$. It's early evening."

"Oh, okay. Thirty days away from the end of the world. The end is nigh! Prepare yourself! The apocalypse is coming June 30$^{th}$. Mark my words."

Daniel shrugged. "And how do you know this?"

"All the numbers add up. The end is nigh."

"Maybe it is, Jon, and maybe it isn't, but I need to establish some things. Do you have a permanent address in town?"

"Yes."

"Can you give it to me, please?"

"Victoria Park."

"You sleep in the park?"

"I have no money. I lost my home to the bottle."

"I'm sorry." A frown. A pause.

"Do you have medical coverage?" Sandra asked.

"I don't know."

"We'll sort that out later," Daniel said.

Betty returned with a syringe and approached the bed.

Eyes widening, Pastor Jon said, "What's that?"

"It's just a sedative," Daniel said. "You need to rest. I think you're a little wound up from your accident. The police might want to ask you a few questions later. It's a miracle you're still cognitive."

"You said it. Miracle. A miracle is the work of God. I thought you *weren't* a religious man?"

"Take the sedative, please, Jon."

"I don't need a sedative. I need a drink."

"You're not going to find one here."

Betty tied off his forearm and tapped a vein until it popped. From a tray, she lifted a syringe and pressed it gently until tiny of stream of clear liquid squirted out. She lowered the needle to the pulsating vein. "Just a little prick. This will calm you down."

Pastor Jon sat bolt upright, pulling his arm away from the approaching needle. His eyes widened in horror. "Mike... you've got to save him. He's gonna die. Maybe he's already dead. Unless he's in the hole. But he said there is no hole, only the hole in his head... "

Betty stepped back, a look of concern mixed with fear on her face.

Sandra scratched her chin, studying Pastor Jon.

"Who is Mike?" Daniel said. "What's his last name?"

"For God's sake, he never told me his last name." Pastor Jon was becoming increasingly agitated. "He was there when I got hit. He knew the third sign. He disappeared to hide in the hole, as the prophecy says. But there is no hole. Only the hole in his head. Don't you get it? Maybe he's dead. If he's not, he's gonna die." Pastor Jon pulled the IV from his wrist and started to climb out of bed. "I need to get out of here. I need to save him... if there's still time."

Sandra pressed a bedside button and two male orderlies rushed into the room. One restrained Pastor Jon's arms, the other his legs.

But he struggled and shouted, tipping over a bedside tray with an errant foot. Sandra moved in and held his head with both hands, her young dimpled face flushing from the effort. Betty handed Daniel the syringe, stepped forward, and pushed down on Pastor Jon's shoulders.

The old man had suddenly developed a mountain of strength that four people struggled to contain. After a few frantic moments, his right arm was finally still enough for Daniel to retighten the knot, tie it off, and plunge the syringe into a blood vessel.

Slowly, Pastor Jon's escape efforts subsided. His extremities softened and relaxed. They released him. His eyes closed.

Sighs of relief.

"He's one strong bastard," an orderly said.

"And crazy as a loon," Sandra said.

They all started as Pastor Jon's eyes popped open. So did his mouth. "Save Mike. Please. Save yourself. The end is nigh!"

Then, just as suddenly, his eyes closed and he drifted off.

# Chapter Four

Even though he lived only two blocks away from Mike Timble, Cray didn't hear the police sirens. Or the ambulance siren. Or the massive explosion. Or the subsequent raging fire. But when he flicked on the TV on June 2$^{nd}$, while having his morning coffee before work, he saw it on the news. Mike's apartment building, still smoldering, surrounded by cops, firefighters, emergency vehicles, and crime scene tape.

Cray's jaw dropped, his hand jiggled, and he spilled coffee on the kitchen table. He steadied the cup, wiped up the hot liquid. *What the fuck?*

A female reporter stood in front of the fire-ravaged apartment building, giving the low-down. "Police and firefighters are still investigating the cause of a blaze that destroyed half of a small apartment building at 215 Victoria Street in downtown Charlottetown last night." She stepped forward, swept an unruly lock of brown hair out of her eyes, and continued. "This much we do know. Two people are dead. They have been identified as ninety-six-year-old Irma White, apparently too frail to flee, and twenty-eight-year-old Mike Timble. Twelve other residents, three cats, and two small dogs, were able to escape." The reporter went on.

But Cray didn't hear it. He spilled what remained of his coffee. Half of it landed on the floor, the other half splashed on his t-shirt and arm, scalding him. He rushed to the bathroom, peeled the shirt off, and still wearing his sweatpants, climbed into the shower. As the cold water cascaded down on him, he examined his chest and arm. Red and stinging to be sure, but he doubted the burns were serious. His coffee maker didn't produce a high enough temperature to cause serious injury, or so he surmised as he stripped off sweatpants and underwear, adjusted the temperature to warm, and washed the affected areas gingerly. He thought about what had happened.

He and Mike had been friends for three years. Aside from the conspiracy theories and mood swings that had become more evident of late, they got along well. Cray had to admit now that he loved Mike like a brother. They often commiserated on how the world was going to hell in a handbasket. The lives of many controlled by the lives of a few so-called financial elites. Corrupt politicians. Economic woes. Overregulation. Environmental destruction. Terrorists bombing innocent civilians, now threatening to attack Canada. Social injustice. Criminal injustice. The US political clown show. They even discussed ugly closet skeletons, or at least the ones they were willing to admit. Cray remembered Mike lending a sympathetic ear when he told him of his relationship woes, how he was unable to trust women after Emma's infidelity—hell, how he was even unable to trust men fully after his best friend's betrayal during that fateful, carnal encounter with Emma.

Even their family situations were similar. Although Mike was an only child, he was slowly becoming estranged from his parents, whose expectations of him far exceeded what he was capable of or at least what he was willing to apply himself to. Cray wasn't an only child. He had an older brother and an older sister, both living close to his mother and father in Moncton, New Brunswick. His brother Caleb was a criminal lawyer. His sister Darlene, a top-earning pharmaceutical salesperson. His father Glen, a retired oil and gas engineer. His mother Mary, a retired pharmacist. Cray, a garbage collector. Them, materialists; Cray collecting material waste.

Night and day.

He remembered something Mike had once said: "It's the nature of Canadian families. The bonds aren't that deep. They're fickle. People compete with one another. If you don't measure up, you get cast out. Simple as that."

Cray knew it wasn't as simple as that. Mike was making a sweeping generalization. Many Canadian families were bonded together as tight as Crazy Glue. But he had to admit, Mike had a point. There was a grain, perhaps a little more, of truth to what he'd said. Cray wasn't measuring up to family expectations, so he was slowly getting cast out. Calls would take longer to be returned, tones were changing; he had even been excluded from a recent family get-together. Of course, when mother Mary dismissed the reunion of sorts as "merely an impromptu thing," Cray didn't believe her. Her follow-up comment had only served to further widen a growing chasm of estrangement. "We knew you wouldn't want to come all the way down from Charlottetown just to spend a couple hours with your family... then have to drive all the way back home."

*Really? What about spending the night?* "Well, they can go and fuck themselves," Cray said, stepping out of the shower. The untimely passing of his friend had soured his mood. He walked into the living room and immediately picked up the phone. He called his boss at Streets and Sanitation and said he wouldn't be coming in due to a cold. He didn't have the heart to say his best friend had just died. He sat down and stared at the TV. He didn't hear the words, but he saw the picture. A picture of Mike, sitting on the patio of Queen Street Starbucks, holding up his coffee, as one might hold up a beer, and grinning. Looking at Mike's black-rimmed glasses, short-cropped brown hair, oversized belly, boyish grin, it wasn't lost on Cray how much they looked alike. Like nerds, computer geeks. Almost could have been brothers. Both five-foot-eleven, although they differed in weight. Where Cray was a slim 160 pounds, Mike tipped the scales at about 210. And the eye color different: Cray, green, Mike, brown.

He studied the image on the screen and realized that it had been cropped. He had been cropped out of it. He could see his own black-sleeved arm leaning on the table beside Mike. The unmistakable silver watch on his wrist, the one his grandfather had gifted him before his death. His hand, gripping a coffee cup. *Fuck, I was there with him. Was that picture taken yesterday?*

That's when the grief suddenly overwhelmed him. He couldn't watch it anymore. He grabbed the remote, flicked off the TV, slumped to his knees, put his hands to his face, and started crying. The tears flowed silently for a short time, but were soon accompanied by loud wracking sobs. When the sobs finally ended, Cray was hit like a sledgehammer by the second emotion. Guilt. He curled up on the throw rug. *I could have prevented this. It's my fault. I should have done more than call him. I should have stopped by his apartment and rescued him.*

Cray studied the black TV screen, as if for answers. But what if the fire was deliberate? It was still under investigation. What if it was arson? What if Mike committed suicide and took another innocent old lady with him? All the signs were there, signs that Cray had ignored, because of a selfish preoccupation with his own life. Another sledgehammer blow, one that caused him to curl up in a fetal position and put his hands to his ears, hoping to block more pain and more analysis. But it didn't work. Mike's comments yesterday—when Cray didn't believe the apocalypse prophecy—reverberated in his mind like the tolling of a church bell.

*"Oh, forget it, Cray. You're not gonna believe me. Sometimes I don't even know why I bother."*

*"Bother with what? Telling me shit?"*

*"Even living, for fuck sakes. What's the point? The world's gonna end soon anyway and my life sucks."*

An hour later, after Cray's grief and guilt had subsided to a somewhat manageable level, he went out. As he walked toward Mike's apartment, he formed a mission. Find out if Mike's death was accidental, which he seriously doubted, and figure out what happened to the wacko who predicted the end of the world and then got run over by a car yesterday. What bothered Cray the most was Mike had probably been suicidal for many months and he had either ignored or not detected all the signs.

And he wanted to find out who this old man was, maybe even try and stem the tide of his own festering guilt by leveling some of the blame at him. What had Mike called him? A preacher. Maybe the preacher had been filling Mike's head with negativity. Well, if he was, then he was responsible. Bum or preacher, he would get an earful. If he was even still alive.

As Cray approached the crime-scene-tape bordered apartment building, other questions surfaced. Why had Mike disappeared after seeing the preacher? A sign. He told him the end of the world was near. Why did Cray himself run away? *Fear. Some part of you believed it. Bullshit. It's fucking bullshit. That's it.*

The news media had left the scene. They had their deadlines. But there were still two fire trucks stationed nearby, a couple of firefighters dousing sizzling remnants of the building with pressurized water from large nozzles. A few firefighters loitered near the trucks, talking. There were also two cop cars on the scene, two cops just inside crime scene tape examining burnt debris, two more leaning against their vehicle talking. A handful of spectators stood outside the investigative line, some gawking, others filming videos with their smartphones.

Emotion welled up inside Cray as he approached a firetruck. He tried to keep his voice steady. "What happened?"

A beefy red-mustached firefighter approached. His fire-proof suit was blackened by ash. Debris particles clung to it. "It's obvious, ain't it, Sherlock?"

"I mean how did it happen?"

"We haven't concluded our investigation yet. And who wants to know?"

"Mike Timble died in that fire. He was my best friend."

The firefighter's grin changed to a look of mild concern. He stepped toward Cray. "Sorry to hear that. Hey, I think I've seen you before. Aren't you a garbage collector around town?"

Charlottetown, with forty-odd thousand residents, technically had city status. But really it was a small town. It was hard to run and hide from anyone. And, it seemed, most people knew you or knew of you. Cray nodded. "Phoned in sick today because of this."

The firefighter extended an oversized hand. "Ben Anderson."

Cray shook it. "Cray Lenning." Ben's handshake was a vice grip and Cray winced. *That fucking hurt. Fucking goof.*

"You wanna know what caused it, wait for the news. CBC will be on it."

Rubbing his stinging hand, Cray turned to leave. "I guess. It's just that Mike had been kind of depressed lately and I was wondering—"

Ben inched closer, touching Cray's shoulder. He spoke almost in a whisper. "Wondering if maybe the fire was deliberate? Wondering if maybe this was an arson-suicide?"

Cray stepped back, intimidated. "Something like that."

"You want my unofficial position? And don't say a word to anyone. If you do, I'll deny it anyway until the official report is in."

"I won't say a thing."

"I was the first man to arrive at the apartment where it started. Mike's apartment. You know what I saw?" Ben didn't wait for an answer. "I saw your friend surrounded by and being engulfed by flames."

"Was he screaming?"

"No."

"Why not?"

"He was already dead."

"Already dead?"

"Yeah, hanging from the ceiling by a rope. I can't say for sure he started the fire, but it looked to me like he hung *himself*, that's for sure, especially after you say he was suicidal. I initially thought maybe someone killed him, started the fire to cover their tracks. But now I don't believe that. He killed himself. He start the fire? Dunno yet. If he did, did he do it intentionally? Dunno yet. But, I aim to find out."

Cray's heart sank. His worst fears had come true. But, Mike wasn't an arsonist, he knew that. Mike could barely kill a pesky housefly, let alone a person. But an old woman had died in the blaze, so now it was likely being investigated as a possible arson, murder-suicide. Or arson, murder, murder. Something like that. Who knew what the cop terminology was, but Cray suspected the police would surely have this information by now; they would probably withhold it from the public until the case was solved.

"I would have been able to gather more evidence," Ben continued. "Maybe even save that old lady. But the floor caved in. I fell through it and crash-landed onto the main floor. By the time I got up to the second floor again, the fire had already engulfed your friend's apartment and was tearing through the next door neighbor's—Irma White's suite."

"Sorry."

"So was I. I hit a massive wall of flames and had to retreat." Ben sighed deeply and looked down at his blackened hands. "But I'll never forget her screams. You ever hear the sound of someone burning alive?"

Cray shook his head.

"Trust me, you don't want to. It was horrible."

This day wasn't starting out that well. "Thanks. But, if Mike did start the fire, he wouldn't have done it deliberately. I don't think he intentionally killed Irma. He could barely kill a mosquito."

Ben removed his helmet and wiped his brow. "You wanna do something for your best friend? Clear his name? Don't tell me, tell Marty."

"Who's Marty?"

Ben pointed to a plainclothes policeman picking through debris beyond the crime scene tape. "Detective Martin Strader. Transferred here from Toronto not long ago. He's a hell of a cop. Put a lot of bad guys behind bars. I'm sure he'd like to talk to you."

"Thanks. Appreciate your help."

"Sorry about your loss."

Cray moved away, watching firefighters hose down smoking debris, Marty poking at and examining evidence. He saw Ben approach Marty and start talking. Marty looked at Cray. Cray fought an urge to run. But the overwhelming tide of guilt kept him frozen to the spot. Like a swelling tsunami wave, questions tumbled through his mind. *Did they recover Mike's body? Obviously, they identified him. Where is his body? In the morgue, idiot. Where else would it be? Should I talk to Marty? I don't trust cops.*

After moving from his birthplace, Moncton, New Brunswick, three years ago, Cray remembered a nasty incident involving the cops that still left a bad taste in his mouth. He was collecting garbage on a residential street in town, had just picked up a black bin to load into the garbage truck's crusher, when a beautiful blonde dressed in red hot pants and a skimpy top strolled by. Sid Boswell, stoned out of his mind on cannabis, stood next to Cray, ogling the beauty. Randy Sindle, the driver, poked his head out the window and eyed her lecherously. Randy was also stoned on pot. Cray was the only one not under the influence of any mind-altering substances.

"Now, that's fucking smoking hot," Sid said,

Cray nodded and went back to work.

Then Sid whistled and said, "Hey, baby."

Randy also whistled. "Hey gorgeous, what ya doin' tonight?"

She looked back, glowering angrily.

The result was disastrous. Young Penny Miles not only reported the incident to Streets and Maintenance Supervisor Sal Summers (Stupidvisor, in the eyes of the garbage collectors), she also called the cops. A cop visited the three one afternoon in the staff room. Randy and Sid denied it, pointing fingers at Cray, who denied any involvement. But the cop believed Randy and Sid. "Penny plans on filing sexual assault charges." Horrified, Cray didn't know if it was a bluff or not, but he wasn't in a position to take chances. The cop demanded he make a formal apology to Penny or face sexual assault charges. Cray swallowed his pride and took the cop's advice. Believing the Penny version of events, Sal the

Stupidvisor also wrote him up for the incident. Now he had a black mark on his garbage collection career, through no fault of his own. *Fucking pussy pass. Fucking liars, those city skids. Fucking cops.*

*Yeah, but who do you trust? What about Mike? You did nothing for him in his life. At least do something for him in his death.*

"Cray?" the detective said, removing a glove and extending a hand. "I'm Detective Martin Strader. Mind if I ask you a few questions?"

Cray cautiously shook and released the hand. Firm, confident grip but not overpowering like Ben's. He sized up Marty. A hot-shot investigator presumably, although he looked unassuming enough. He stood a trim five-ten with short gray-black hair, was soft-spoken with a disarming smile, piercing blue eyes, and small facial features. He could have been the friendly and caring father of your buddy next door. But Cray suspected beyond that polished veneer there was a sharp analytical mind and a personality that could turn from good cop to bad cop in a heartbeat if the situation warranted.

"No problem, Cray said, suddenly wishing he had followed his gut earlier, ran and hid. *Yeah, right. Where you gonna hide?*

"Sorry to hear about your loss. I understand Mike was your best friend."

"Yeah."

"Look, I'm just trying to get to the bottom of this. I'm not pointing any fingers or following any specific angle of investigation until I have all the facts." He pointed to the fire-damaged building. "Two people died in there and I intend to find out what happened."

"Of course."

"What was your friend Mike like?"

Cray explained that he had noticed Mike becoming more despondent in the months leading up to his death. Suicidal, he now realized. He told the detective of the recent meeting at Starbucks where Mike had mentioned taking his own life. He told him of the car accident involving the preacher, of Mike's sudden disappearance from the Starbucks immediately after. How he had called Mike twice the evening of his death but had been unable to reach him.

"Was there something in particular you think might have driven him over the edge? Any specific event come to mind?"

*The preacher. The end is nigh. Should I tell him?*

Marty gave him a look. Tell me everything, it said.

Cray recapped, including Mike's fears about an apocalypse and details about the preacher and his prophecies. He omitted that he too, for reasons he still didn't understand, had run like hell. Didn't want to sound like a nutcase himself. There were enough of them around already without adding to the variety of mixed nuts.

Marty took a moment to process the information. He was weaving together the threads to form a cohesive and colorful quilt that would explain everything. "Jonathon Brackley?"

"Who?"

"The priest who was struck by the car. He goes by Pastor Jon."

"He's a priest? Mike called him a preacher also."

"Was."

"Is he dead?"

"No, he survived the accident. He was a priest. Defrocked. I've already done some background on him. Only this case took priority. Now, it looks like they might be connected."

After two minutes of discussion, Marty asked, "You say you went straight home after witnessing Pastor Jon get hit by the car?"

"Yeah."

"It didn't occur to you to go and check on your friend? Drop by his apartment, less than two blocks away?"

"I told you I called him twice. He didn't answer. It wasn't the first time Mike didn't return my calls. He's done that before."

"Right. Have you had any big fights with Mike lately?"

"We had a disagreement yesterday over his end-of-days theories, but I wouldn't call that a big fight."

"Okay. Do you have anyone who can verify that you were at home last night?"

Cray looked up at the sunny sky for answers. He didn't remember calling anyone. But maybe one of his neighbors had seen him come in. Most of them lived vicariously through the lives of others. "An alibi? I don't think so." *Stupid thing to tell a detective.* "But I need to think." Cray felt beads of perspiration popping on his forehead. He tried to ignore them, hoping Marty hadn't noticed. "Am I a suspect?"

"I don't rule anyone out until I have enough evidence to do so. But, frankly, I doubt it. I think Mike killed himself. But I don't know who lit the fire that killed that old lady."

"And you think I did it?"

"No, not yet. Look, I have to ask certain questions. If you become a suspect, you'll know about it."

Cray nodded, not reassured.

"One more question. So you think Jon's proclamations about the end of the world drove your friend to suicide?"

"Let's just say I think it was the proverbial straw that broke the camel's back." *Maybe the straw that broke Mike's neck.* Cray shuddered and wiped wet eyes.

Marty handed Cray a card. "Sorry, I know this must be hard for you. And I didn't mean to be pushy or point fingers. You have to understand it's my job. I just want the truth. And, if you're telling the truth, there is no defense needed. The truth defends itself."

Cray wiped his eyes. *Yeah, right. He probably says that to all suspects just to put them at ease. I don't think so. Not with you guys. The truth didn't mean shit when it came to Penny Miles. You guys wanted to charge me with sexual assault and I didn't even do anything.* He was tired of Marty and becoming overwhelmed with sadness and guilt again. He felt like going home and curling up in bed for the next twenty-four hours.

Cray nodded slowly. "Okay."

"Do you have anything else you want to tell me?"

"No."

Marty's tone grew agitated. "I need to talk to this so-called priest. If he's going around putting suicidal thoughts in people's heads, there is gonna be hell to pay." His tone turned buddy-like. "If you can think of anything else that might be important, please call me."

"Okay." Cray tucked the card in his pocket, turned and left. Walking home, he wondered what to do next. It appeared Marty was willing to mete out any punishment Pastor Jon might deserve. *Should I go to the hospital and talk to the nutcase? He's probably at Queen Elizabeth Hospital. What if Marty sees me? He'll probably become suspicious, wonder what I'm doing there. Am I a suspect? I don't have an alibi. Maybe he'll charge me for something. Arson? Murder?*

Out of nowhere, a crow swooped down, circled Cray twice, squawked, shit on his head, and flew away. "Fuck sakes!" He felt the gooey mixture drip down the side of his face and, grimacing, wiped at it. A few pedestrians pointed fingers and burst out laughing. Cray had the sudden urge to flip them the bird and give them a piece of his mind. Instead, he did what he often did when faced with confrontation or ridicule. He turned and ran.

Inside his apartment, after cleaning off the bird shit, he remembered something. A crow had shit on Mike's head a few days before he died. That decided it. Marty or no Marty, Cray had to find out what was going on. He didn't believe the end of the world predictions any more than he believed Pastor Jon was playing with a full deck of cards. But he had to find out for himself. And, to assuage his guilt, he had to learn what kind of crap the strange man had been filling Mike's head with. Whatever it was, Mike had taken it seriously.

Two hours later, he arrived at Queen Elizabeth Hospital. He hoped by that time Marty would be long gone. When he located the Intensive Care Unit where Pastor Jon was, he wondered how he was going to get permission to visit him. Didn't you have to be family or friend to visit people in the hospital? *That's easy. I'm a good friend.* At least he knew the room number. 416. Front desk administration had already given it to him, no questions asked.

Approaching the nursing station, he was stopped by an attractive nurse: long black hair, glasses, and vibrant green eyes. Young. Maybe 25. She had a look of focus and determination mixed with a hint of caution. A name tag perched atop a perky breast identified her as Sandra Colling. "Can I help you?" Her tone was more of an accusation than a question.

"I'm here to visit Jonathan Brackley." Cray rubbed his forehead with an unsteady hand. She made him nervous.

"He's sleeping."

"How's... how's he doing?"

"Are you a family member?"

"I'm a friend."

Sandra's eyes narrowed. "Really? I didn't know he had any friends. Didn't sound like it when I talked to him."

"Yes, I've known him for a long time."

She eyed Cray suspiciously. Then another nurse called her name and she turned, momentarily distracted. "Be right there."

"Do you mind if I look in on him? I won't stay long if he's sleeping."

"I don't think he should be disturbed right now. He's in precarious shape."

Cray turned to leave, but then thought of another strategy. "Did he mention the name Mike?"

Sandra paused. Her look said it all. Why should she release private patient information to this clown who didn't even know him? "You know a Mike?"

"He was my best friend. He's dead now. Committed suicide last night."

Sandra frowned, diverting her eyes from Cray. A pause. "I'm sorry for your loss. He did mention Mike yesterday. We couldn't make a lot of sense out of what he was saying. But... but Pastor Jon seemed to know your friend was in trouble."

"Shit. Was he trying to save him?"

"I... I don't know."

Cray's gut said she was hiding something. She had every reason to. She didn't believe he was a friend of Pastor Jon's and would likely tread cautiously regarding releasing private patient information. And accusations would get him nowhere. He tried a different tact. "Listen, I just want to talk to him for a minute. Mike knew him better than me. He said something to Mike before he died. Something powerful enough to make him want to kill himself. I'd like to find out what it was. Please, just for a minute."

Sandra's features softened. "Okay, but he needs his rest right now. He had a heart attack and he's got a pretty serious concussion. Frankly, I think you'll make more sense out of him sleeping than you would if he was awake. Don't stay long. The cops were just here. They kept him up when he should've been resting."

Although Sandra didn't seem particularly fond of Pastor Jon, apparently her caregiving and protective instincts were overriding any opinions she had about the man's sanity or lack thereof. Cray decided she was probably a pretty efficient nurse when you cut through that initial distrusting exterior. *But what is she hiding?*

Inside the room, Cray sat bedside and looked at a sleeping Pastor Jon. The pastor's mop of curly gray hair poked out over a gauze bandage wrapped around his head. His gray beard was long and unkempt. His face, spider-webbed with deep wrinkles, was ashen gray and jaundiced. Under his eyelids, his eyes darted back and forth in his head. He frowned. Dreaming. Something disturbing. Two IVs were plugged into his arms. Monitors and machines hummed nearby. He was shackled to the bed with leather ankle and wrist restraints.

He must have tried to escape, Cray thought. They were treating him like a lunatic. But wasn't he? Cray studied the man for a few minutes and then got up to leave. But as he reached the door, he heard a weak voice from behind.

"Wait."

He turned around. Pastor Jon's eyes were open. Cray returned and sat down. He didn't know what to say. All his anger dissipated in a heartbeat. The man already looked like death warmed over. Cray didn't want to pound the final nails in his coffin with the hammer of accusation. It sounded stupid as soon as he said it. "How do you feel?"

Pastor Jon ignored it. His eyes welled up with tears. "You're a friend of Mike's."

"Yes." Cray introduced himself. "You're Pastor Jon?"

The old man slowly nodded. "I'm sorry about Mike. I tried to tell them. They wouldn't listen. Sedated me. Maybe it was already too late, but I tried to warn them... tried to help him."

"You knew? How?"

"God sends me messages."

"He does?" *He's nuts.*

Pastor Jon seemed to read his mind. "You don't believe me. A bird shit on your head a few hours ago. *Now* do you believe me?"

*A bird shit on Mike's head. A sign. One of the signs.* "What does it mean?" Cray asked.

"It's a warning. The end is nigh. Prepare yourself."

"When is this end coming?"

"June 30$^{th}$. Coming right up."

*Same thing Mike said. Yeah, but that doesn't make it true.* "How's it gonna happen?"

"By fire, as detailed in the *Book of Revelation*. 'The fourth angel poured out his bowl on the sun, and the sun was given power to scorch people with fire. They were seared by the intense heat and they cursed the name of God, who had control over these plagues, but they refused to repent and glorify him.'"

Cray was getting tired of this charade. Even if the man was psychic, that didn't make him a prophet. His earlier sympathies were fading. "What happened to Mike? Did you say something to him to make him do this?"

"I told you. I tried to save him. They wouldn't listen."

"What *did* you say to him?"

"The same things I'm gonna tell you. I gave him three signs the world is ending. They all came true. He panicked because he couldn't dig the hole. Sadly, he killed himself. Too bad really, because he had been one of the chosen leaders."

Cray remembered the charges. Mike had tried to dig an underground shelter and gotten caught. But he could no more imagine Mike a leader than he could himself. Confrontation, for the most part, made them both put tails between legs like scared puppy dogs and run—run, run, run, and hide.

Pastor Jon continued. "And if a bird shit on your head, you've been chosen to lead."

In spite of the circumstances, Cray had to bite his lower lip to prevent from laughing out loud. This man was nuts all right. Certifiably insane. But he gave him the benefit of the doubt anyway. What did he have to lose at this point? "Is that the first of three signs?"

"Yes."

"What are the next two?"

Pastor Jon's eyes closed. They slowly opened. He yawned. "In a dream, you'll have a vision of the end of the world. The next day strange things will happen around you. Three of them, almost simultaneously. They will involve the strange and unexplainable behavior of humans. They will happen outside in broad daylight."

Cray clasped his hands together and leaned forward slightly. He couldn't believe his own mind. In spite of his better judgment, he was starting to take this nut seriously, however vague the last two signs were. "And I suppose G—"

"I'm sorry," Sandra said.

Cray turned around. She was standing inside the room, in front of the closed door. How long had she been there? Cray hadn't heard her enter.

"He needs to rest right now."

"Okay. I'll go."

"Come back after the next sign," Pastor Jon said. "I'll tell you what to do. In the meantime, find a suitable location for an underground shelter. Make it at least a hundred feet deep. Stock it with enough supplies to last for ninety days." Looking at Sandra. "When are you going to get me out of these shackles?"

"I'm looking into that. We want to be sure you're not going to bolt up and start ripping IVs out of your arm. You remember last time."

"I won't do that. I promise. I'm a man of my word, a man of the cloth. I was trying to save someone's life, for God's sakes... I need, I need a drink."

"Okay, Jon. Relax now, please."

As Cray left the room, Sandra tapped him on the shoulder. He just about jumped out of his skin.

"Sorry," she said. "I was rude back there. I'm Sandra Colling."

Cray shook her hand. Soft, smooth, warm and gentle. "Cray Lenning. Nice to meet you."

Sandra brushed back an errant lock of wavy hair from her face. "As I said, sorry for my abruptness. Things have been a little weird around here lately."

"No problem."

"It's just that I'm getting a little scared." She pointed down the hall toward Pastor Jon's room. "I'm beginning to think he knows something."

Cray wondered if Sandra had listened to his entire conversation with Pastor Jon. Probably. "Me too."

"We're not the only ones. Some guy Marty, a detective, was here earlier grilling Jon. Jon mentioned your name. He told Marty you're going to be a leader in the post-apocalyptic world. I wasn't entirely truthful earlier. Pastor Jon did predict Mike's death. And, if we'd listened to him, we might have been able to save him." Sandra diverted her eyes from Cray's and stared at the wall. "But we didn't. We shackled and sedated him; couldn't understand what he was trying to say."

*She seems to like to eavesdrop. Can you blame her? Especially if Pastor Jon is right.* "I talked to Marty earlier. Does he think I had something to do with Mike's death, or the fire that burned down half his apartment building?"

"I doubt it. He wasn't questioning him along those lines. But your name came up a few times. By the way, I know you're not a friend of Pastor Jon's, but I let you in anyway."

"How?"

"Pastor Jon described you to me. Said he knew of you, but didn't know you personally."

"Why? Why, did you let me in if you knew I wasn't a friend of his?"

Sandra's cheeks flushed slightly. "Mike was your best friend. I felt sorry for you. I'm sorry for eavesdropping, but I'm getting scared."

A few nurses at the end of the hall were starting to stare. They spoke in hushed tones. Cray felt his cheeks begin to flush. "What now?"

She discreetly produced a business card and handed it to Cray. He quickly stuffed it into his shirt pocket. "Please keep in touch. Tell me if his signs come true. I have a shelter on my property. Maybe it'll come in handy."

# Chapter Five

There she was, in the flesh and very little else. Nurse Sandra, black thong, topless, gyrating in front of Cray. He was somewhere—he knew not where—lying on a large, oval-shaped bed. He was mesmerized. An angelic luminescent yellow glow surrounded her approaching form. He couldn't take his eyes off her. *What a body! What a fucking amazing body!* Teasingly, she neared to within arm's length. Cray reached out to touch her. But she retreated too quickly.

She looked at him with seductive eyes. "Not yet. I'm not ready yet."

She resumed the dance. Cray heard music, a soft, slow romantic melody he couldn't identify.

"Come here," he said. "I want you."

She shook her booty. Her perky golden breasts jiggled in synchronicity with every thrust of her hips. She leaped in the air and with a quick flick peeled off the black thong. She twirled it in her hand and tossed it at Cray. It landed on his head. He grabbed it, brought it to his nose, sniffed, and grinned.

Nearing, Sandra smiled. "You like that?"

"I love it."

"There's more where that came from." Then she was on him, kissing passionately, embracing, touching, stroking, thrusting, and moaning.

*I'm in Heaven. There is a God.* But as the ecstasy peaked, the landscape suddenly changed. They were fully clothed, running through a forest. Running for their lives. Bullets whizzed past them and red laser beams danced in the darkness, searching for two heads to blow off.

Sandra grabbed Cray's hand. "Over here, quick."

More shots rang out. Cray heard the awful sound of bones shattering. He watched, horrified, as Sandra dropped with a moan. Shot in the back. Watching the vibrant green seep from her dying eyes, he knelt down. Then silence. Then another shot. Searing pain. Shattering bones. His bones. His spine. Cray groaned and dropped to the moist forest carpet beside Sandra.

As their last breaths ebbed in unison and the military team approached, a giant gloved military hand appeared and snatched them up. They materialized in an office, facing a steely-eyed general decorated with many medals. "The end is now," he said. "But I will protect you."

The scene changed again swiftly. They floated on a life raft on a tumultuous ocean in the middle of a starry night. A huge wave struck the vessel and it overturned, catapulting Sandra and Cray into the ocean. In an instant, they were swallowing water, getting pounded by wave after relentless wave.

Cray surfaced, coughing up seawater, and locked eyes with Sandra. Words weren't necessary. They were together in life. They would be together in death. In harmony. Through Sandra's eyes, Cray could see her soul. And he felt an unimaginable inner peace. It pacified his fear, filling him with a calm, satisfied surrender.

Then they were plucked out of the ocean by an unseen and unfelt hand. Swiftly they soared high in the sky.

Hovering slowly, they descended, landing on the busy streets of a large, unknown city. It was dark. Raining. Tires hydroplaning and water hissed. Headlights approached. Sandra grabbed Cray's hand and pulled him to safety a split-second before a speeding bus nearly smashed him into mashed potatoes. "Over here," she said.

*She knows exactly what she's doing, exactly where she's going. I like that.*

But, looking up into the crimson sky, Cray was paralyzed with fear. Bombs exploded everywhere, shaking the ground beneath him, punctuating the sky with huge expanding fireballs. Terrified screams echoed eerily through the streets. Panicked people fled. A brilliant fireworks display destroyed multiple buildings, a spectacular show of death and destruction.

"Oh my fucking God!" Cray sat bolt upright in bed, panting, sweating. It took some time for the wave of fear to pass.

\*\*\*\*\*\*

"Where are you?" he asked Sandra on the morning of June 3rd. He had showered and eaten and called in sick for work again. He hoped like hell she wasn't at work. It might be harder for her to leave.

"I'm at home. It's my day off."

"I had an apocalyptic nightmare last night." He explained it to her, saying they were fleeing the world's destruction together, and omitting the sexual details.

Silence.

"Are you there?" Cray said.

"Shit... Yeah, I'm here. I was hoping he was wrong. Hoping against my gut instincts. Shit."

"I might want to take you up on that shelter offer."

She gave Cray directions to her acreage, about fifteen minutes south of small-town Montague. Forty minutes later, he pulled his black Ford Escape into a long and winding tree-lined driveway.

Sipping coffee, Sandra sat on the porch of a yellow turn-of-the-century two-story home. She stared absently into a bright blue sky dotted with white popcorn clouds. She waved at Cray, trying a smile that didn't entirely work.

*No wonder, it's the end of days, you fool*, he thought, parking and climbing out of the vehicle.

"Would you like a coffee?" she said, standing.

"Sure."

"How do you take it?"

"Half milk, half sugar."

She nodded and went inside. Cray sat on the porch, surveying the property. Well-kept, neatly manicured lawn, bordered by trees; three outbuildings; a large barn, converted to an oversized double garage; two smaller storage sheds; a lawn tractor, an all-terrain vehicle (quad, as the locals referred to them), and a newer model yellow Ford Explorer. Cray expected a significant other to emerge with her, but she returned alone and handed him a mug of coffee.

"Thanks."

Sitting down on the porch beside him, she said, "Wow, that's some nightmare you had."

Cray nodded and took a sip. "Freaked me out, as I said."

"What about the other thing Pastor Jon said? The other signs. Did you notice anything weird on your way over here?"

"Not that I would call significantly strange. Someone in a black car cut me off on the highway. Flipped me the bird. Another old lady driver doing fifty in an eighty zone. Passed her without incident. No, not really."

"I think he was referring to something a little weirder than that. And three things, remember?"

"Right."

"Wanna hear my plan?"

"Yeah."

She pointed to a dirt road leading into the forest. "That old road goes to an abandoned well, among a few other places on my property."

"How much land do you have?"

"Ninety acres. Anyway, one of my neighbors told me the abandoned well leads to a series of caves. Some of the other older residents around here confirmed it. During Prohibition the caves were used for manufacturing and storing moonshine. Rumor has it the tunnels lead all the way to the ocean, so the boys could get their moonshine on boats, ship it to the States. I pulled the well cap off it the other day and it looks like my neighbors are right. There are metal stairs leading down."

"How deep is it?"

"Back then they didn't dig wells that deep. The water aquifers are really high around here. Maybe fifty feet. But maybe they went deeper. Maybe it was never a well, only something resembling a well to fool the cops."

"So, that's our shelter, obviously."

Sandra nodded. "The problem is, the well caved in many years back. Maybe it's even contaminated by now. But it's my best plan so far. We dig it out, open it up, and stock it with supplies." She paused, locking eyes with Cray. "I'm only twenty-seven. I'm too young to die."

Silence.

Finally Cray said, "Am I the only one included in your rescue plan?"

"So far, yes. I haven't had a lot of time to think it through. I moved to the Island a couple years ago from Vancouver and, you know, as a CFA I don't have a lot of friends."

Cray knew the acronym. CFA—Come From Away. If you weren't born on Prince Edward Island, no matter how long you lived there, you would always be considered an outsider. And this often manifested itself in a superficial friendliness and difficulty getting into an inner social circle. "I know. I'm from Moncton originally."

"You get it then?"

"Oh yeah."

"And I don't have any immediate family here." Her expression grew somber. "My parents died in a car accident in Vancouver. That's one reason I left."

An uncomfortable silence.

"Sorry. I work as a garbage man in town. Not what my folks wanted. I often feel rejected by them. They give me the silent treatment."

Uncomfortable silence.

"Sorry," Sandra said, "In any event, I can think of a few people I would like to invite—maybe you can too—but again, I haven't thought everything through yet. Besides, nobody's going to believe us if we go running around telling people we'll save them from a coming apocalypse."

Cray couldn't help a small smile. "They'll think we're nuts. Like Pastor Jon."

"Now there's a man I *would* like to join us."

"I couldn't agree more. But first things first. Let's start digging. Maybe we'll find some moonshine to drown our sorrows"

Sandra laughed, musical.

They loaded tools and other essential supplies into a trailer attached to the quad. When they were finished, Cray climbed on behind Sandra. She started the quad and pulled away.

"Thanks," he said.

"For what?"

"For offering to save me from the end of the world."

"I haven't saved you from anything yet. And besides, I have my own agenda as well."

"Which is?"

"You're a leader. You help me. I help you."

"Hate to disappoint you, but I'm more of a lost soul than a leader."

"We'll see about th—"

A beat-up white pickup truck suddenly came barreling down the driveway, kicking up a trail of dust and startling them.

"Who's that?" Cray asked.

"My neighbor, Ralph. Ralph Franks. Frankenstein."

"Oh great. We can't even get off the ground—or into the ground—and we're being invaded by monsters?"

The truck skidded to a stop and a tall, gangly man climbed out. He wore a tattered straw hat and a cigarette dangled out of his mouth.

Sandra turned the quad off and they dismounted.

It didn't take Ralph long to cover the thirty or so feet between them. A plume of dust mysteriously followed him, and slowly settled on his head, shoulders and arms as he stopped a few feet away. He removed the cigarette from his mouth and coughed, ignoring the red dirt dusting. "Sandy, how the hell are ya?"

Sandra gave Cray a look.

Cray raised his eyebrows and nodded in acknowledgement.

"Franken—Ralph, what can I do for you?"

He eyed the trailer full of equipment and supplies. "You digging a grave or something?"

"No, we're planting trees." Sandra didn't want to say any more than she had to. Living by herself on a secluded acreage, she had to keep neighbors on her side. She didn't need any Hatfield and McCoy battles. In Ralph's case, she had tried to be neighborly without being overly friendly.

Ralph crossed his arms on his chest and sized up Cray with distaste. Then he looked at Sandra and grinned. Three teeth were missing from his mouth. He puffed his cigarette and exhaled a large plume of smoke. The smoke formed a circle around his head, almost like a halo, before dissipating.

Cray and Sandra exchanged curious looks.

"Planting trees, eh?" he finally said. "You picked a good day for it."

"Sure did," Sandra said. "We need to get started."

"No problem, sweetie—"

Sandra cringed.

"—funny enough, I'm looking to do a little digging myself today. But my shovel's broke. You wouldn't happen to have an extra one I can borrow for a few days."

Sandra nodded and went to a nearby storage shed, leaving Cray alone with Ralph.

"You from around here?" Ralph asked, his black beady eyes avoiding Cray's.

"Moncton."

"Moncton?" Ralph grinned and looked directly into Cray's eyes. "They call Moncton the arsehole of the Maritimes. You know that?"

"No, I didn't."

"Yeah, got fucking t-shirts printed and everything."

Sandra returned with the shovel. She gave it to Ralph. "No hurry bringing it back."

"Thanks, sweetie, I'll return the favor one day." He spun around, walked to the pickup, tossed the shovel in the back, and climbed in. He started it, flicked his smoke out the window, and grinned. "Have yourself a great day, Sandy."

Sandra waved. "You too, Ralph."

Ralph revved up the pickup.

"What're you digging?" Cray asked.

The grin widened. "I'm digging a fucking grave, buddy. A fucking grave." He peeled away, shooting up a plume of dust that trailed him like the fiery breath of an angry dragon all the way down the long driveway.

"Pardon my language, but that guy is fucking scary," Cray said. The hairs on the back of his neck turned into prickly spears that poked through his t-shirt.

"Don't worry about language around me," Sandra said, starting the quad. "I've heard it all around here... He's a rare combination. A stoner, a drunk, a redneck, and a nut—all neatly packaged into Frankenstein."

Cray sighed. "One good thing. The signs. You notice that?" *How good are signs foretelling the end of the world, you idiot?*

"How could I not? I don't know if it's good or not, but I know I saw them. They freaked me out. Three strange things. I no longer have any doubts about Pastor Jon's prophecies."

Cray climbed onto the quad. "Me neither. Let's get this shelter sorted as fast as we can."

They drove silently through the forest, down a winding, tree-canopied road. They arrived at a clearing with a dilapidated log cabin and a small outbuilding, its roof caving in. Sandra pointed to the outbuilding. "That's the well house."

They went to work. They peeled away just enough rotten boards from the well house to gain access to the well, stacking them beside a fire pit in the middle of the clearing. It took four hands and considerable effort to slide the concrete cap away from the four-foot-wide abandoned well.

After it was removed, Cray shone a flashlight inside the black hole. It smelled damp and moldy. "Anyone home?" His voice echoed eerily.

They laughed nervously.

Sandra pointed. "You see where it's caved in?"

"Yeah." About six feet down, there was a mound of dirt, covering three-quarters of the inside diameter of the well.

They discussed the reclamation strategy and got started. Cray climbed in with a bucket on a rope and a small shovel. He reached the dirt, loaded the bucket, and Sandra pulled it up. She dumped it into a wheelbarrow and when it was full, dumped the dirt into a spot she had picked out just beyond the tree line but accessible via a small trail. After an hour of digging, they both glistened with sweat.

They took a break and sat on a nearby log, drinking bottled water and soaking up the warmth of the sun's rays. Perched on treetops, birds chirped.

"You really think he's digging a grave?" Cray said, wiping a sweaty brow.

Sandra gulped bottled water. "I don't know. He's got a weird sense of humor. And he's slow to warm up to outsiders."

"He obviously doesn't like me."

"No, and I think I know why."

"Me too."

They said it simultaneously. "Jealousy."

"Frankenstein has had a thing for me ever since I moved here. It's one-sided. I wouldn't date that oddball if it was the end of the world."

"Careful what you say."

"It's funny, it's like he has a split personality. Sometimes, he drops by and he's sweet as pie, other times he's irritated and I can sense some anger seething just below the surface.

I've tried to stay on his good side, being that we're neighbors and all, and I live here by myself. He's helped me with odd things: boosted my car one time, helped me tear down an outbuilding, fixed my toilet, and plowed my driveway a few times in the winter. But lately I haven't asked him for anything, and I even try to refuse his offers. I don't want to get in his debt and feel obligated to help him. But he's very resourceful, in spite of his obvious shortcomings."

Cray felt a tinge of jealousy. "Well, there must be a reason you're trying to limit things."

"For one, his affection for me is growing. Also, over the last few months, I've noticed him becoming more aggressive and angry. Sometimes, like today, he scares me. Maybe it's the booze or the drugs—maybe a combination, I don't know... but Frankenstein is starting to creep me out. Now he's calling me sweetie. I'm not his sweetie and never will be." Sandra looked bothered. "Always something, isn't there?"

The sound of twigs snapping nearby silenced them.

Cray started. "You hear that?"

"Probably nothing." But Cray could tell from her expression she wasn't convinced.

She stood and moved slowly toward the source of the noise.

Despite his best efforts, Cray remained frozen to the spot, unable to get his legs moving. He was convinced Frankenstein was hiding in the brush with a shotgun ready to blow his brains out. Finally his arms obeyed brain commands and he managed to pick up a shovel. But still his legs wouldn't move.

Sandra shouted from the brush. "It's only a raccoon."

Cray sighed. With some effort, he got his legs going. He walked to the edge of the tree line, just in time to see the raccoon lumber into the forest, in no particular hurry.

"Let's get back to work," Sandra said.

After an hour of digging, Cray felt the dirt he stood on loosen and begin to crumble. He grabbed a steel ladder rung for support and hung on.

"Be careful," Sandra said.

A massive chunk of dirt and concrete below him suddenly loosened and crashed to the bottom of the well. With a flashlight, Cray examined the area of the breach. The concrete well wall had cracked and broken, and there was a rough-hewn wall of dirt about three feet in diameter that had broken through the concrete. After some discussion, they propped up loose boards into the opening to block the dirt from penetrating the side; a temporary repair until they could manage a more permanent fix.

Cray climbed out and Sandra handed him a bottle of water from a cooler. They both drank.

"I'll go first," Sandra said. "My well, my idea. I'm not going to risk your life... not yet, anyway."

She began to climb down the attached ladder. From the bottom of the well, she shone the flashlight up. "Wow, it's huge down here." Her voice echoed.

Cray lowered the rope and bucket down.

"Got it."

He tied off the other end on a nearby tree—a safety line, just in case—and, grabbing a flashlight, said, "I'm coming down."

"Be careful. The last step is rusted and broken."

Flashlight guiding the way, Cray descended into blackness and slowly reached the bottom.

Shining flashlights, they examined the shelter. It was a room the size of a small living room, reinforced with steel and concrete. In one corner of the ceiling, water dripped intermittently into a small puddle. The room was strewn with empty bottles, copper tubing, large glass containers—evidence of moonshine production. In a corner were three well-built wooden doors, all of which were tightly closed.

Sandra screamed.

Cray started. "What?" Trembling, he saw tiny red eyes. Then he saw the head and body. A rat. It skittered away.

"I hate rats," Sandra said with a note of panic.

Cray's breath came in short gasps. "Maybe we should leave? We got a lot done today."

"Don't you want to try the doors?" She shone the flashlight from left to right. "Door number one, door number two, or door number three?"

*She's determined. And a hell of a lot braver than I am.* Cray found a crumb of courage and gave in. "Let's go backward. Door number three."

Together, they reefed on the door, hardened shut by old age and rust. Finally, they pried it—squeaking and groaning—open. They went inside and saw a small bedroom. There were four old dusty cots lined up, each with its own wooden bedside table, complete with antique oil lanterns.

"Wow," Sandra said. "People actually slept here."

"Guarding the moonshine, probably."

"Probably."

They shone the flashlight into a tunnel leading off the bedroom. It was the height and width of a house hallway, constructed using a mixture of concrete, steel, and wooden support beams.

Sandra stepped forward. Cray followed.

Then Sandra screamed.

Cray jerked back, shining the beam on the dirt floor. Two rats eyeballed him and scurried away. He shone the beam at Sandra. Her face had gone white. "You okay?"

"This place must be infested."

"We'll have to do something about that."

"Yeah, rat poison."

"Wanna go on?"

"Why not? We've come this far."

The hallway lead to another room about the same size as the first. It was stacked with wooden crates, with barely enough room to move. Cray removed a bottle from a crate and dusted it off. "Holy shit. We've hit a motherlode of moonshine. I'm not even much of a drinker, but all things considered, maybe it's a good time to start."

Sandra picked up a bottle, dusted it off, and grinned. "Neither am I, but maybe you're right. They used to make this stuff ninety-proof back in the day." She twisted the cap off, smelled the clear liquid, and took a small swig. She coughed and made a face, a few drops of moonshine spraying from her mouth.

Cray grinned. "How is it?"

She handed him the bottle. "Strong. Tastes kind of coppery or metallic."

Cray took a swig. He immediately felt his throat burning but managed to get it down without coughing, spitting, or spewing. He shook his head, exhaling. "That's strong all right. At least we won't need to stock booze." He handed it back to her. "Go for it."

She took another pull, this time without making a face, coughing, or spitting. "You get used to it." She passed it back to Cray, who took another large swill but couldn't help making a face.

"Uh, before we get drunk down here, why don't we throw a few bottles in the bucket and take them with us?" Cray said.

"Good idea. I'm already feeling buzzed."

"Me too," Cray said, liquid confidence coursing through his veins. "But if it's as we suspect, who gives a fuck. May as well have a good time while we got the chance."

They arrived at the foot of the well, six bottles of moonshine in the five-gallon bucket. Cray slung rope and bucket over his shoulder. Sandra took another large swallow from the open bottle and scrunched her eyes shut. She opened them. "Cheers, Cray. I never imagined this would turn into a party."

He took the bottle and swallowed a couple of ounces of shine. "Cheers, Sandra. Neither did I, but I'm glad it did. I like your company. I like you."

She laughed giddily. "I hear it works well as a lime rickey."

"What's a lime rickey?"

"I'll show you. Now get going."

Cray made a display of bowing. "Ladies before gentleman. I'll watch your ass."

Stepping onto the ladder, she smacked him playfully on the shoulder. "You better not."

By the time they returned to Sandra's house, they were both a little drunk. The mood was playful and light. They brought the moonshine inside, where Sandra mixed two lime rickeys, squeezing lime into two glasses along with carbonated water, crushed ice and healthy shots of moonshine. Cray sat in her comfortable living room, furnished with dated but tasteful furniture, his drink on the coffee table in front of him.

Cray thought, not for the first time, that the intimate parts of his dream last night involving Sandra had a good chance of coming true. Tonight. One part of him wanted it to happen, and another more pragmatic part did not. He was beginning to form a strong alliance with her, one that down the road could be lifesaving. He certainly didn't want to fuck that up. With that in mind, he hoped to steer the conversation to their future plans regarding reinforcing the shelter and stocking it in preparation for the apocalypse. *Just take it easy. Don't make any moves. As if you have the guts to anyway.*

Sandra plunked herself down in a brown armchair next to Cray, who sat on the couch. The twilight of dusk seeping through the cracks in the Venetian blinds gave the room a reddish hue. She took a sip of her lime rickey and grinned. "Tasty. Have you tried it yet?"

He lifted the glass. "Not yet." He drank and made a face. "It's tart, but good. Thanks."

She took another swig, placing the glass on an end table. "I think we should figure out our next steps."

"You read my mind."

"Good. I'm going to do some research on survivalist supplies. But right off the bat, we should get stocked with plenty of water, food, silverware, plates, cups—I have a gas generator we can bring down there. I can buy a composting toilet. Lots of clothes, candles, flashlights... wait a minute, I should be writing this down."

"Good idea."

Sandra left and returned with pens and notepads, handing one of each to Cray. She jotted several things down. "Once we have a complete list, we can figure out who brings what. Can you think of anything absolutely essential?"

Thinking of Mike's untimely passing, and Frankenstein's untimely visit earlier, he said, "Guns. Do you have any?"

Sandra shook her head. "No. I don't like guns."

"But we might need them. I think I can get some."

Sandra scribbled for a moment and then looked at Cray, her brow creasing. "You a gun fanatic?"

"No, but my father is. He taught me how to use them. I'll try and borrow some guns and ammo."

"Okay." A thoughtful pause. "How much money do you have saved up? We're going to have to buy some things."

Cray squirmed and took another sip. He was embarrassed. "Not much. Maybe a thousand dollars. But I have a ten thousand credit limit on my Visa. I can max that out. Doesn't look like I'll have to worry about paying it back."

Sandra evidently noticed the embarrassment. "Don't worry, that should be enough. If not, I have some money we can use for supplies."

"Okay." Cray wasn't about to ask her how much money she had—he didn't want any further embarrassment, and it was a rather personal question. *But things are different now. What was once personal is now essential for survival.* Nonetheless, he didn't want to pry. Old established manners die hard, and these new rules would take some getting used to. *It's only money anyway, and if Pastor Jon was right at some point money probably won't mean shit.* Which brought him to another thought. "Ninety days. We need supplies to last for ninety days, according to the preacher."

Sandra stopped writing. "Okay." She put her pen down, drank, and stared out the window at the soft orange-yellow glow of the setting sun, beginning its daily descent below the trees. She fell silent, as if the grim realization that life as they knew it would come to a catastrophic end very soon was sinking in.

Cray also fell silent, bleak thoughts of a giant fireball scorching the Earth suddenly flaring in his mind. "Are you okay?"

"This is scary shit."

"I know. Let's keep going so we don't wallow in worry and fear. We don't have time for that."

"I know."

She finished off her drink. So did Cray. She returned to the writing pad. "How long did Pastor Jon say we have before the world ends?"

Cray checked his phone. June 3rd, 8:06 pm. "He said the world would end June 30$^{th}$."

"Maybe he's wrong about the date?"

"Maybe he's wrong about everything."

"Maybe, but you don't believe that."

"No. And neither do you. And we agreed that we're going ahead on the premise that he's right. We can't start letting doubt creep in or we'll never carry this out."

"Right. I think we should bring Pastor Jon with us. His prophecies might be useful. He's the one who warned us."

"I agree."

"I'm going to talk to him tomorrow. I'll call you."

"Okay," Cray said through a developing haze. The moonshine was starting to dull his senses and heighten his emotions. Another drink, which Sandra hadn't offered anyway, and he would be too drunk to drive. He was already too drunk to drive. But he didn't want to overstay his welcome, especially since they both had to work the next day. He stood. "I should go."

"You can't drive. You've had more than four stiff drinks."

"I'll call a cab. Get my car tomorrow."

"Seventy bucks from here."

Gray winced. *Fuck it. I'll use my Visa. Won't need it much longer anyway.* "That's okay. We've done enough for one day. You have to work tomorrow too."

"I have a spare bedroom upstairs. You can stay here tonight."

Cray didn't want to impose. Although he was confused, buzzed, a little scared, and could use another drink, he thought it better to leave. They had discussed some heady stuff and he wanted time to process it. It wasn't every day you met an ally who wanted to help you prepare for the end of the world. He wanted, above all else right now, to preserve that alliance. He didn't want to slip up and make a mistake that might later return to punch him in the face. He pulled out his phone and began dialing. "Thanks, but I really should—"

The sound of an engine startled them. Sandra hurried to the window and saw Frankenstein's pickup speeding up the driveway, silhouetted by a cloud of fiery orange dust, glowing ominously in the setting sun's dying rays. Wide-eyed, she rushed to the door and locked the deadbolt. "What the hell does he want now?"

She turned a few lights off and closed the Venetian blinds part way on the bay window that overlooked the expansive front lawn. From the window, they watched. The truck stopped in front of the porch and Frankenstein climbed out. He took one step, staggered and almost fell, then regained his footing and continued.

Tentacles of fear stiffened the hairs on Cray's back to prickly spears. *Shit, not again.* "He's wasted."

Sandra's jaw dropped. Her face turned pale. "And he's got a gun." She grabbed Cray's arm. As Frankenstein approached the front door, holding a double-barreled, sawed-off shotgun, Cray and Sandra ran into the kitchen. She began looking through some drawers and produced a hatchet and a large butcher knife. She handed the hatchet to Cray and they went upstairs. Their best chance of survival would be to hide. If he came looking for them, maybe they could surprise and kill him before he killed them.

They entered the upstairs master bedroom just as Frankenstein rang the doorbell—*ding-dong ding-dong ding-dong.*

They ducked down in front of the bedroom window, waited, and listened.

The doorbell sounded again—*ding-dong ding-dong ding-dong.*

They waited in silence.

*Ding-dong ding-dong ding-dong.*

Silence.

Finally, Sandra whispered, "Maybe he means no harm."

"You know him better than I do, but what's he doing here with a gun? He ever come here with a gun before?"

"No. Never."

The doorbell sound was replaced by a loud rapping knock. Then Frankenstein's voice. "Anybody home?"

"I've had enough of this," Sandra said. She opened the window and stuck her head out before Cray could protest. "What do you want?"

"Careful," Cray said, touching her shoulder lightly. It gave him goosebumps, but in a good way. "You see that gun pointed up here, you duck down. Fast."

Frankenstein stepped onto the lawn and looked up. "Your friend's still here, I see."

"What's it to you?"

"Nothing, Sandy. Sorry, I just came by to offer you some protection."

Her voice was seething. "Protection? Protection from whom? You come by here this time of night drunk, with a fucking shotgun and you expect me to lay down the red carpet treatment or something? What's wrong with you?"

"I'm so...sooooorry, sweetie..." He raised the shotgun, barrels pointing straight up in the air. "I come bearing gifts. I want to give you my shotgun. For protection."

"Protection from what?"

"Ya never know when it might come in handy... Sandy. Lots of freaks in this world, ya know."

"Wait there."

She closed the window and turned to Cray. "I'm going downstairs."

"What? He's got a shotgun."

"I don't think he wants to hurt us."

Before Cray could respond, she was already heading down the stairs. He willed his legs to move. They wouldn't. *Come on, don't be a chicken. What's she gonna think of you?* He tried again, his breath coming in short gasps. By the time he got to the foot of the stairs, one hand concealing the hatchet behind his back, Sandra had already opened the door. She held the butcher knife behind her back.

Frankenstein, his long gray-black hair shooting off wildly in all directions, leaned against the doorframe casually like a skilled cowboy waiting for a gunfight to begin. He pointed the shotgun down, finger on trigger. He looked past Sandra and spotted Cray stepping off the last stair into the living room. His dark eyes squinted in the suffused light. He reared back, clutching the shotgun in both hands, and aimed it at Cray's head. "Stick 'em up, cowboy, or I blow yer brains out!"

Sandra reached for the gun.

Cray started to draw the hatchet, ready to attack. *This is it. It's him or us.*

But a split-second before the hatchet was revealed, and before Sandra's knife appeared, Frankenstein stepped back, cradled the gun in both hands in a non-aggressive fashion and, taking a bow, presented it to Sandra. "Here you go, dear. It's loaded, so be careful. Don't go shooting me now. I only got yer best interests in mind."

Sandra took the gun with an unsteady hand. "Jesus, Ralph... please don't go scaring me like that. Sometimes I don't know what to expect with you..."

"Sorry 'bout that, ma'am. Just trying to help."

Backing up, Cray placed the hatchet on a bureau, hiding it from view. He folded his arms across his chest and tried to slow his breathing.

"Thanks for the gun," Sandra said. "Just, next time you want to help me, try calling first."

"Not a problem, sweetie. Just thought you could use it, for, you know, personal defense and all." He turned to leave, then spun around. He looked at Cray, hatred etched in his scrunched features. "Who is your Moncton buddy, by the way? Didn't catch his name."

"Cray."

"Gay?"

"No, Cray."

"Right, Gray. He your new boyfriend?"

"He's a friend, Ralph. And he was just leaving before you scared the shit out of us."

Frankenstein shot Cray an angry look before turning around again. He walked across the porch, down the steps, and staggered to his truck. He climbed in the open door, slammed it shut, lit a smoke, and stared at them from the open window.

Cray now stood at the door alongside Sandra. The fear had turned to hot anger, coursing through alcohol-laced veins. Cray was inches away from flipping him off and telling him to go fuck himself. *Fuck it. No, fuck him.* Cray extended an arm out the open door and started extending his middle finger.

Sandra quickly grabbed his arm, whispering, "Don't."

"You folks have a good night," Frankenstein said. "I think we both know why that gun will come in handy soon." Without waiting for a response, he started the pickup and drove off, stopping once halfway down the driveway, and stepping out of the vehicle, the dark shadow of a man pissing on the side of the road visible from a distance.

Two hours later, Cray drove home. He had sobered up by drinking four coffees and eating leftover spaghetti that Sandra had nuked for them. At Sandra's urgings, and considering her level of fear, he had almost agreed to spend the night. But then they began a discussion of who else might join them in the shelter, and when Sandra said *her* name, Cray turned silent and cold, and beat a hasty retreat.

"Of all the people in the world," he said aloud, pulling into his apartment parking lot, "Why the fuck did she have to pick *her*?"

# Chapter Six

"I'm the one who should have *her*," Ralph Franks demanded, crunching a beer can and slamming it on the kitchen table. "Not that fucking faggot!"

Earlier, he had crouched in the forest on his five-acre property across the highway from Sandra, grinning at the disappearing taillights of Cray's vehicle. *Good, he's gone. Finally.* But that joy was short-lived. Later, once he'd arrived at his dilapidated trailer and consumed many beers, green jealousy transformed into seething red rage.

Kicking away empty beer cans and take-out containers littering his dusty floor, he went to the fridge, got another beer, and cracked it. He took a long pull, glancing disinterestedly at a pile of dirty dishes and rotting leftovers on the counter. He went into the living room, kicking a path through the clutter. It was lit by a single incandescent lightbulb dangling precariously from the ceiling by a four-inch electric-taped length of extension cord. He pushed away flyers and some spilled popcorn from a well-worn, tattered brown couch and plunked himself down. He scanned the room. Simulated woodgrain panel walls, circa 1960; a few panels separating near the front door; yellow, nicotine-stained ceiling tiles; a torn AC/DC poster clinging on by three pushpins; woodstove in a corner, logs piled haphazardly behind it and a fanning film of ash spreading out on the floor in front; piles of dust-covered clutter in every corner; a gun rack containing an arsenal of loaded firearms; a small TV on a cluttered stereo stand. Beside it, six fist-holes that had penetrated wood paneling.

His glazed eyes stopped at the holes, all of them bitter reminders of life's disappointments; one new one a bitter reminder of today's. He pulled on his beer, absently rubbing a cut on his knuckle from today's fist-pump rage. But if it wasn't for the fist-hole punctured wall, he thought, someone might have gotten killed. The wall was Anger Management 101.

Ralph took long, deep breaths, hoping the rage would subside, recounting the day's events that led him to this angry moment right now, a moment that might propel him upward any second to pummel one, two, three, maybe four more holes in the anger management wall. It was that fucker, Gray. Or Cray, whatever. All his fault. Ralph secretly kept an eye on Sandra, went out of his way to try and be a good neighbor. And, in two years, he had never seen her with another man.

Until now. Now, she had someone new in her life, probably more than just a friend. That meant he no longer had a chance with her, even though he thought she had been warming up to him.

"Fuck sakes!" He drained the beer in one long gulp and whipped the can at the anger management wall. It lodged in the most recent fist-hole. "Holy shit." He walked into the kitchen, returning with a six-pack—hell, no point getting up if you didn't have to—and continued to drink and think.

That morning, while he was digging the hole, his shovel had broken. Then, later at Sandra's, in search of a replacement shovel, seeing that clown Gray had started his blood boiling. Gray looked like a computer geek, a nerd and a fucking coward all in one. In the way. In the way of his success. Later that afternoon, curiosity had gotten the better of him. He had crept quietly into the forest, spying on the two while they dug out the well, listening to their conversation, wincing every time they laughed together or shared some bond-forging moment. Then there was the proverbial last straw. They emerged from the hole giddy on moonshine, laughing and joking like two long-time lovers on their merry way to a romp in the hay.

Not if Ralph could help it.

Flying into a rage-filled fit of hysteria, he barely remembered slashing his way through the forest with his machete on his way back to his trailer. He'd stabbed the machete into a woodcutting log in front of his trailer, arming himself with a loaded shotgun, and blasted over to Sandra's with murderous intentions. Most of it was still a blur—a kindergarten effort at a complicated jigsaw puzzle. Little pieces slowly fit into place.

When Sandra popped the second-floor window open and stuck her head out, her sweet face brought back his desire and snapped him out of his... what was it, a blackout... temporary insanity? He didn't know, but he now remembered, after she had yelled at him from above, he had suddenly realized he was holding a loaded gun. Not good. Not good at all. So the only thing he could think of so they wouldn't phone the cops was to offer the gun up as a gift, pretend all along that was his reason for being there.

*Did she buy it? Maybe. Maybe not. Maybe she'll still call the cops.* He sighed, drained another beer, and flung the empty on the floor. Some of the anger was draining away now and he was thinking a little more clearly. *She won't call the cops. She doesn't want any trouble. Neither will Gray. He's too chicken shit.* And then the most important reason they wouldn't call the cops fell on his head like a brick: *They won't call the cops because the world is coming to an end. That's why they're fixing the well. That's right. I remember now. I heard them say it.*

Ralph drained another beer, crushed the can, and flung it on the cluttered coffee table. He lit a smoke, trying to remember more of their conversation. But, try as he might, he couldn't. His bleary eyes wandered back to the fist-holes. Now all they reminded him of was his memory loss. When it had started. How it had started.

Now 63, he was born prematurely, one of three children to his PEI parents. When he was six, doctors said the premature birth had caused short-term, even some long-term, memory dysfunction. It became evident on that little forest hike with his older brother Walter. Walter wandered off from the trail and went missing. But, six hours later his concerned parents found him. The family had dinner that night and the mood was jovial and celebrative. The next morning, Ralph woke worried sick about Walter. He dressed quickly, getting ready to resume the search. At the door, his mother stopped him, asking where he was going. "I've gotta find Walter, Mom. He's still missing." His mother gave him a strange look; a look that, in spite of his memory problems, he never forgot. The look told him he was different, would always be different. Developmentally handicapped, or as his classmates liked to cruelly say, "retarded."

While on some occasions his memory failed, on the taunting, teasing and name-calling from his peers in Grade 5, it was crystal clear. Ralph the Retard, Retard Ralph, Ralphtard, Ralphtarded, Ralph the Reject, Reject Ralph, and on and on. Other perhaps less imaginative peers called him dumb, or often just plain stupid.

One bully in particular, Lenny Ganes, was highly adept at pushing Ralph's buttons. Often referring to him as Ralphtard, or Ralphtarded, Lenny liked to bully Ralph during recess, taunting and teasing, pushing and shoving. And Ralph would meekly take it, as would the other unfortunate victims of Lenny's bullying. But one day Lenny went too far, secretly drinking Ralph's apple juice, urinating in the empty plastic bottle, and resealing it.

As Ralph sat alone under a large maple tree that sunny afternoon, Lenny and some of his motley crew of juveniles anxious to impress their wayward leader, circled Ralph and watched. He opened a Twinkie, chomped off half of it, and then attempted to wash it down with a mouthful of apple juice. Recognizing an awful taste immediately, he spewed Twinkie chunks and urine onto his shirt and pants.

A chorus of laughter erupted from the group. A few other kids, curious about the source of the comedy, joined the circle of howlers and hecklers. "How do you like the taste of piss, Ralphtard?" Lenny asked. His query was followed by another chorus of laughter. "I pissed in your apple juice, Ralphtarded. Next time it'll be in your cornflakes, or maybe in your face, you fucking retard."

Grimacing at the jeers, snickers and outright guffaws of laughter, Ralph glared at Lenny, who was now gyrating around like an orangutan, pointing a finger at Ralph and laughing. Calmly, Ralph wiped his stained chin and mouth, resealed the bottle of urine and charged Lenny, bowling him over so fast and hard that Lenny smashed the back of his head on the ground. As Lenny rolled his eyes, Ralph jumped on his chest, pinning him to the ground, pounding him in the head, shouting, "You fucked with me for the last time, motherfucker. Now you're gonna learn to never, ever fuck with me again for the rest of your life." After he had pounded Lenny senseless, causing multiple cuts and contusions, he retrieved his apple juice, returned to Lenny, propped his blood-soaked mouth open, and poured the remains of the foul-tasting liquid into it. Then he closed Lenny's mouth tight to be sure he would swallow every last drop of the urine cocktail. Lenny did. Then Ralph glared at the circle of hushed bystanders. Even Lenny's crew of wannabe bullies were beginning to retreat.

While the incident might have led to a month expulsion from school, Ralph viewed the punishment as a small price to pay to get the bully and his motley crew to leave him alone. More than that, he saw it as a badge of honor, although it didn't serve to rehabilitate him into a model student. On the contrary, the deed only alienated him from school and his classmates, although Lenny and his crew didn't bother him anymore, and many others had become too chicken shit to hurl any insults Ralph's way.

However, Ralph started skipping classes, often wandered alone in the forest, and learned martial arts and boxing. By the age of sixteen he had a rap sheet of assault charges, even a few break-and-enter charges. Unable to deal with him, his parents placed him in the care of his strict uncle, Simon Simms. Simple Simon, as Ralph liked to call him, tolerated zero disobedience and disrespect. Disrespect to Simon also meant forgetfulness. Simon says do this. Simon says do that. Simon says, backhanding Ralph clear across the room, "I don't care if you say you forgot to do your chores. You're going to have to learn to remember. Let this be a reminder." *Simple Simon, go and fuck yourself.*

Ralph endured three years of torture with his uncle. One day when he had forgotten to take his shoes off, tracking wet mud through the living room, Simple Simon leapt up from the couch (where he had been sitting comfortably with his three essentials: beer, Cheetos, and the TV remote control) and cocked his arm back, preparing for another vicious backhand. But Ralph caught the swinging arm, twisted it behind Simple Simon's back, and plowed his uncle headfirst into the cast iron wood stove, cutting him above the right eye and severely concussing him. *Simple Simon, go and fuck yourself.*

At their wits' end, his parents bought five acres in the country and plopped a trailer and Ralph on it. Unable to hold down a job, he collected a government disability pension; enough money to keep him in booze, smokes, and cannabis. His mother and father, sister and brother, didn't visit him. He was decidedly the black sheep. They were both afraid and ashamed of him. *Helen, Mitch, Marta and Walter, go and fuck yourselves.*

The alienation spread through the community like wildfire. Local women knew all about Ralph and wanted nothing to do with him. In his entire life he had gotten laid three times, all through online-arranged meetings with Charlottetown hookers. Beneath the tough exterior, Ralph only wanted what everyone wants—love and acceptance.

He drained another beer and tossed the can haphazardly on the floor. It clinked hollowly and rolled into the wall. He picked up the remote, hoping for something to assuage his rising rage. CBC news stories flashed past, some registering, others not so much. "Lone wolf terrorist massacres at least 49 people in Orlando, Florida, the worst mass shooting in US history. Another fifty or so in hospital with bullet wounds... CBC just obtained a terrorist Kill List, containing names and addresses of at least 8,300 Canadians." He frowned, flicked off the TV, and eyeballed the cluttered coffee table. He picked up a crinkled piece of paper containing reminders of things he'd done, things he'd heard, things he needed to do. He read the words: moonshine, shelter, end of world, hole, shovel, Simple Simon. His eyes widened. *Hole, shovel, Simple Simon? Did I dig a hole? No. Yes. Who's in the hole? Simple Simon, you idiot. No. Yes.*

Confused and dazed, Ralph stood. "Where's the hole? Who's in the hole?" Reaching for his jacket, he stepped toward the door. He felt an empty beer can underfoot. He tried to kick it away, but slipped and fell, face-planting the hardwood floor fast and hard. As the lights went out, he felt warm blood trickle into his eyes, nose, and mouth.

# Chapter Seven

Saturday, June 4<sup>th</sup>. Cruising around that overcast afternoon in his unmarked brown Crown Victoria, Detective Marty Strader tried to assemble pieces of a puzzle. Mike Timble's death was obviously a suicide. Of that he had no doubt. His charred body, which had fallen through the collapsed second floor, still had ligature evidence around his neck, not to mention the strangulation marks. The structural breach provided plenty of evidence. Supporting his conviction was the metal drain pipe Mike had tied the rope onto. That ceiling pipe was bent at an odd angle. Twisted under the weight of a human body, fragments of charred rope still tethered to it. Then there was firefighter Ben Anderson's eyewitness account. Slam dunk.

But what about the fire? How was it caused? Arson or an accident? Based on what Ben had said, Marty leaned toward the latter. When Ben arrived on scene, flames had already destroyed two-thirds of Mike's suite. But, Ben had a nose for news, or at least a nose for pot. He told Marty later he could smell pot, even identified the strain. Ben would know. He was a closet pot smoker himself but loath to admit it due to possible social and professional backlash. Marty suspected there was more to it than that, but right now he was more concerned with what Ben said and, more importantly, what Ben had found. Combing through the main-floor debris in the aftermath of the fire, Ben had discovered three roaches, mixed in with the debris. And since the apartment below Mike was clean, vacant and ready to rent according to property managers, it was highly unlikely the marijuana samples originated there. *No, not likely.* Marty turned down Queen Street, already getting congested with traffic, and spotted him walking into the Starbucks. He pulled into a parking stall in front of the coffee shop. The meter was a paid meter, with no time on it, but Marty didn't bother getting out and plugging coins in. Let those fucking parking attendants try and ticket him. They would get an earful given the sour mood he was in today.

He turned the ignition off and tried to recreate Mike's death in his mind. An image formed. Mike, standing on the chair, smoking a joint, taking some time to get stoned one last time and reflect on a life not worth living. He could see Mike agonizing over his failed relationship with former girlfriend Sybil Saunders, who already told Marty earlier Mike "was a pothead and a loser." And then of course there was the Pastor Jon apocalypse theory. Mike, teetering precariously on the precipice of death, grimly realizing the world is coming to an end anyway so what's the use. He had tried to dig the hole, make a shelter, and was facing three charges as a result: theft, trespassing, and destruction of private property. Another failed attempt at salvation. Finish the joint, toss the roach on the floor, kick the chair out, and hang yourself. End of problems. End of story. End of world. They can all go and fuck themselves. But what Mike had likely not anticipated was the fire. The fire caused by the discarded roach that had ignited trash on his floor.

It could have been a neat case, easy to tie off. But, it was the apocalypse theory that Marty was still troubled about. Mike believed Pastor Jon. The defrocked priest had given

Mike signs that according to Cray and Pastor Jon had come true. When Mike couldn't fulfill the shelter instructions, everything piled up on him like an avalanche and he caved in and killed himself. Marty had initially been ready to write Pastor Jon off as a wacko but it wasn't that simple. Cray had said his predictions or signs came true, at least in Mike's mind. However, that could be rationally explained as just the delusions of a suicidal man. But again, not that simple. Pastor Jon knew about Mike's suicide and tried to save him moments before he was sedated. *He knew. How did he know?*

Marty rubbed a wrinkled brow and eyed the Starbucks. The man he wanted to talk to was sitting outside, drinking coffee alone. Perfect. He was about to get out of the car, when his cell phone rang.

"Shit, not her again."

It was Elaine Ryerson; Marty's wife, a PhD psychologist and the source of Marty's sour mood. In Toronto, they had a two-year passionate relationship that slowly went from hot, to lukewarm, to room temperature, to cold. Everything was fine until Marty's long-time partner Jake Thompson took a fatal bullet in the chest during a routine domestic dispute call. It was the guilt eating him up. Nagging questions—"Why didn't I go in first?"—that finally broke him. He lost interest in his romance, his friends, and his job. He began a devastating dance with the bottle. It was Elaine's constant analysis of his emotional state that finally drove Marty out of Toronto and estranged the two. Yet, before he left they had made an effort to patch things up. The time away would do him good, clear his head and give him a fresh start. Maybe when things settled down and he felt better, they could rekindle the romance. After all, Elaine wanted to get out of Canada's biggest city and maybe hang up a shingle in Charlottetown, away from the hustle and bustle. The call this morning was about the shrink. He knew, in Elaine's eyes, that was a potential deal-breaker to any reconciliation. Had Marty called a shrink since his arrival here? No, he hadn't. But, during his earlier conversation with Elaine he had promised her he would call in an hour. The hour came and went and he couldn't bring himself to call, didn't have the courage to re-open a can of worms overflowing with so much pain and sadness.

"To hell with it." He answered the phone. "Hi, Elaine."

"You don't sound so good. You okay?'

"I'm fine. I'm in the middle of an investigation."

"Did you call a therapist? Like you promised?"

Marty thought about lying, changed his mind. "Not yet. I've been busy."

"Marty, you've been there for almost two months. You've been telling me now for two weeks you're gonna get help. Don't you get it? It's the only thing that'll save you... the only thing that'll save us."

Marty rubbed the crease in his brow. *Maybe she's not the source of my angst. Maybe it's me.* "Listen, sweetie, I'll do it later. I promise." He was surprised he used the word "sweetie." He hadn't called Elaine that in over six months.

There was a long silence before she said, "Okay." But her tone was resigned, almost hopeless.

Marty saw the man stand to leave. "I gotta go. I'll call you later, okay? There's something I need to talk to you about."

*Yeah, right, she's gonna believe me. She already thinks I'm losing my mind.*

\*\*\*\*\*\*

Cray's mind was away. Far away. He had gone through his day mostly in a daze; silently grieving about Mike; worrying about Frankenstein and his propensity for violence; pissed off at Sandra for inviting *her*, Penny Miles, the bitch who almost had him charged with sexual assault; angry at himself for not returning Sandra's call earlier in the day and for not having the courage to voice his concerns about Penny. Then of course there was the dark depression that had accompanied thoughts about the end of the world. Just one big cluster fuck.

So distracted was Cray that he hadn't noticed the brown Crown Victoria parked nearby, the male driver eyeballing him. But when the man stepped out of the car, Cray recognized Detective Marty Strader instantly.

His first impulse was to run like hell. *Get up, get the legs going and fuck off.*

*Too late.*

In five quick strides, Marty was standing in front of him. Judging by Marty's cold stare, it didn't appear he was in the mood for social pleasantries.

"Going somewhere?" Marty said.

Neither was Cray for that matter. "Home."

"Mind if I ask you a couple more questions?"

*Now he suspects me. Fuck, how bad can this day get? Be cool. You've done nothing wrong.* "Listen, Marty, I hope you don't mind if I call you that—"

Marty nodded.

"—I'm not having the best day. I just want to go home and chill."

Marty motioned for Cray to sit. "Please, this won't take long. I've got some good news for you."

They both sat and Marty continued. "I'm convinced Mike's death was a suicide."

"Okay."

"And that he started the fire accidentally."

"How did he do that?"

"Smoking a joint. I know he was a big pothead. I think he flicked a roach on the floor and it landed on some garbage. By the time it ignited, it was probably too late for him to put it out. He was probably dangling from a rope by then."

Cray clasped his hands together and looked at them.

"Sorry," Marty said. "I'm not trying to remind you. I just wanted you to know—I still have a few loose ends—but I should be able to put the file to bed in a few days. At least as it concerns any malicious intent with regard to you or Mike."

Cray looked up. "What loose ends?"

"I don't know what to make of this Pastor Jon guy. At first I thought he was a wacko, but now I'm not sure. Did you talk to him?"

Cray was going to lie but thought better of it. It was probably a trick question. Marty probably already knew the answer and was setting the tone for the way this conversation might go. "I did, yes."

"I thought you might. I mean, if someone's good friend—best friend in your case—commits suicide they'd want to know why. More so, since it's a suicide, because of all the guilt that goes with it. Anyway, I digress." Marty recapped what troubled him about Pastor Jon: the signs about the end of the world, which in Mike's case seemed to come true; the strange fact that Pastor Jon had actually known that Mike was on the brink of death and even tried to save him, and the conviction with which Pastor Jon predicted the end of the world. "What do you think of him?"

This was the million-dollar question. To come clean would be to admit the shelter, the moonshine, Sandra's involvement, maybe even Frankenstein's crazy behavior. But how many allies did he have? He thought Sandra was one, but now her friend Penny would be invited—if she already hadn't been—to the Apocalypse Moonshine Bash and Dance. Well, if Sandra could invite Penny maybe Cray could invite Marty. *Fuck it if she doesn't like him. Tit for tat.* But Cray still hedged his bets. "I don't know what to think."

Marty didn't buy it. "Oh, come on. You must have an opinion."

"If I told you, you'd think I was nuts."

"Try me. I've been around the block a few times."

A long pause. "I think Pastor Jon might actually have something."

Marty scanned passing pedestrians. His eyes found a nearby table that had just become occupied by two twenty-something Chinese women. They chatted and laughed, eyeing the two occasionally. "Can we talk in my car for a minute?"

"Okay."

Inside the car, Marty said, "Here's the crazy thing. So do I. And you thought I'd think you're nuts, but it's probably the other way around. At first I had my suspicions, but I did some background checking on our Pastor Jon. You might be surprised at what I found out."

"Tell me."

"Three people he knew in Moncton are building fucking underground shelters and preparing for the end of the world."

"Holy shit. We're not the only ones taking him seriously."

"No. And something else. Rather disturbing." Marty paused for effect.

Cray felt his face redden and heart race. "Tell me already."

"Three more have died within the last month. Apparent suicides."

Cray let the information sink in. What was it with this Pastor Jon? You had a fifty percent chance of living by talking to him, it seemed. And then another fifty percent chance of preparing for the worst. Which category would Cray fall into? Death before or death after the apocalypse. And what about Sandra?

At that moment, she called. Cray pulled the phone from his pocket and stared blankly at it for a second.

"Aren't you going to answer it?"

It didn't take long for his concern for Sandra to override any hostility he might have felt earlier about her choice of apocalypse party guests. Maybe they would be adding another one to the roster anyway. "Sandra, hi. Listen, sorry I missed your call earlier. I was tied up."

"It's okay. Where are you?"

"Actually, I'm talking to Marty in his car in front of the downtown Starbucks."

"I know who *he* is. Are you in any trouble?"

"I don't think so."

"Can you call me when you're done? It's important."

"Are you okay?"

"Yes."

"I'll call you in a few minutes." He hung up and slid the phone into his pocket.

"Emergency?" Marty said.

"No... but I need to go."

"No problem. I just wanted to warn you, that's all. If you believe Pastor Jon and start a relationship with him, it seems one of two things will happen to you. Both of them ultimately don't end well."

Cray wiped a bead of perspiration off his brow. "That's the problem. I believe him. The signs, they happened to me. Sandra believes him too."

"Sandra Colling, the nurse?"

"Yeah."

Marty scratched his chin stubble. "Nice lady. I like her. Very professional. And smart... tell me, are you building a shelter... you know, digging a hole?" Marty's phone rang.

Frowning, he looked at it. "Fuck, this *is* an emergency. I have to go."

\*\*\*\*\*\*

At the hospital a little while later, Cray couldn't believe his eyes. Standing beside Sandra, he watched Pastor Jon pace about the room with the gait and determination of a man half his age. He had removed the IVs, broken the shackles, and dressed himself in thrift store clothes that Sandra had provided: a pair of jeans that were a little too baggy, a white t-shirt, a black and blue oversized lumberjack shirt, and a pair of bright yellow Nike jogging shoes. She had disposed of his tattered and smelly clothes. He didn't seem to mind. At least he never mentioned it. He held a Bible in one hand and occasionally glanced out the window in fear, as if the grim reaper, having been unsuccessful the first time, was about to make a return visit. Pastor Jon had even trimmed his scraggly gray beard and, after removing the bandage, had made a half-assed effort slicing and dicing his mop of Einstein-like hair. The jaundiced color was gone from his face. The bump on his head was now pea-sized, barely noticeable.

"Pastor Jon," Sandra said, stepping forward, "You need to rest."

A sharp crease formed a jagged V-shape on Pastor Jon's forehead. "Oh, no. No more needles. No more straps. What happened the last time you tried that? A man died." He pointed at Cray. "His friend."

Sandra stopped and turned to Cray. "What do you think?"

"You're the nurse," Cray said, "but he looks fit as a fiddle. Amazing really."

"He does. It is."

"I *am* fit as a fiddle," Pastor Jon said. "I want to leave. Don't you see, the longer I stay here the more people will die? I need to warn them." He stopped pacing and faced them directly. "You two don't believe me. You think I'm nuts, like most of the others. I need to tell someone who cares."

Cray was relieved about Sandra's foresight. It appeared she left no stone unturned. Before arriving at the hospital, he'd called her. She'd told him to bring a large Coke from McDonald's and a mickey of rum. Cray suspected Pastor Jon's motivations for leaving were twofold. One, he indeed wanted to warn people about the apocalypse. Two, he was suffering from alcohol withdrawal and needed a drink badly. Cray pulled out the mickey from his jacket pocket.

"Would you like a drink? We want to talk to you."

Pastor Jon's eyes lit up like a child about to get an ice cream cone. "Now you're talking."

"Sit down, please, Pastor Jon," Sandra said. She and Cray exchanged knowing looks.

Pastor Jon obeyed.

Sandra closed and locked the door, and Cray went into the bathroom, dumping some of the Coke into the sink and adding a splash of rum. He returned and handed Pastor Jon the mixed drink and the bottle of rum. He eagerly received them. Cray and Sandra sat down. He removed the lid from the Coke, poured another shot of rum into the cup, closed the lid, and took a long slurp from the straw. He tucked the bottle in his shirt pocket. "That's better. Usually I drink it straight, but I know where you're going with this. The Coke cup's a good disguise—for when I leave."

"Pastor Jon, we believe you," Cray said. "Like you said, after the bird shit there would be two more signs. The dream. That happened. The three strange occurrences. I saw them. So did Sandra. We're building a shelter. We've got a really good start on it."

His eyes widened. "You do?"

"Yeah."

"Good. I told you, you'll be a leader in the new world."

"What I want to know is what do we do now? You said talk to you after the three signs and you'll tell us what to do."

Pastor Jon took another slurp and scratched his head. "I didn't tell you what to do after?"

"Not much anyway. You said we'd have to stay down for ninety days."

"Ninety days. That's right. That's how long you need to survive in the hole. Bring weapons. Bring food. Bring booze. Bring books. Some things we'll have to relearn. When you emerge, my tribesmen will be there to guide you."

"What about others," Cray asked. "Should we invite others to the shelter?"

"I presume Sandra will be with you."

"Yes," she said. "The survival shelter's on my property."

Pastor Jon slurped. "Some of this isn't clear yet. My visions are at times convoluted." He tapped the plastic lid of the Coke cup, raised a bushy eyebrow, and continued. "But a lot of that will be dictated by how big your shelter is, and how many people it can reasonably accommodate."

"I would say six," Sandra said.

"You should consult with each other carefully before making any choices. Human beings don't do that well in closed quarters for extended periods. Sometimes they kill each other, or launch a revolt and kill the most powerful one. Backstabbing—a dangerous human trait."

Sandra looked at Cray, her face beginning to redden. She clasped her hands together, studying them.

"What about you?" Cray asked. "Sandra and I agreed that we would like you in the shelter with us."

There was a long pause. Pastor Jon's eyes welled with tears. He looked at Sandra. "Is that true... that you want me there?"

"Yes, if you'll agree."

"The other day you wanted me shackled and sedated."

"I'm sorry. It's not every day someone comes around preaching the end of the world. You were getting hysterical."

"It's okay. And I appreciate the offer. Pardon the language, but hardly anyone gives a rat's ass about me anymore except for God. Mike did, but he's dead now. I need to follow God's will and continue warning those who'll listen. And I've decided I'm gonna do that until the inferno burns me alive."

"You don't have to die. Let us help you."

"No. I'm old. My time is near. It's God's will."

"Are you sure?"

"Yes."

"Please," Sandra said. "Let us help you."

Pastor Jon shook his head resolutely.

"Think about it," Cray said. "If you change your mind let us know. I'm sure we could use your help, your wisdom, and your visions."

Pastor Jon wiped his eyes. "Thanks. I'll do that."

"Another thing," Cray said, "It's about people dying. Detective Strader says three of the people in Moncton you warned about the apocalypse are dead now. Apparent suicides. Is that what's going to happen to me? Or Sandra?"

Sandra's eyes widened. "You didn't tell me."

"I just found out," Cray said.

"I don't know. That's the work of the devil," Pastor Jon said. "I can't control that no more than I can control my drinking. God handpicks the survivors and the devil undoes it. But the devil doesn't get all of them."

"He's right," Cray said, turning to Sandra. "Marty also said three of the people Jon warned are building survival shelters."

"They are?" Sandra asked.

"They are?" Pastor Jon asked.

"They are. I didn't get all the details, but Marty's been looking into it. He believes Jon, but is probably afraid to tell too many people for fear of being labelled a nutcase by his peers."

"He's a wise but troubled man," Pastor Jon said. "But, yes, I could tell he took me seriously in the end. I wouldn't be surprised if he shows up this afternoon looking for me. But, of course, I won't be here. But he can find me at the park." He slurped his drink and eyed Cray. "Tell me about your dream."

Cray recapped it, omitting the sexual details about Sandra.

"It's exactly how I thought," Pastor Jon said. "Let me digest some of the details and I'll let you know if I get any more visions about what you need to do next." Grinning, he winked at Cray. "But you left out some parts."

"You didn't tell me everything?" Sandra asked.

"It's okay," Pastor Jon said with a grin. "He can tell you when you two are alone together."

"Is it bad?" she asked.

"No," Pastor Jon said, stretching out on the bed. "It's not bad, but it's private. I don't need to hear it... you asked me what to do now. Warn your friends and family if they'll listen. If not, say your goodbyes. Stock the shelter together, decide jointly and carefully who you want to bring, who will even come. And read the Bible, the Book of Daniel and Revelation..."

Sandra adjusted Pastor Jon's pillow. "Are you going to stay?"

"For a little while," he said, slowly closing his eyes. "For a little while. I'm tired. So tired."

# Chapter Eight

"What is that?" Cray asked the following afternoon (Sunday, June 5th), looking at a white square box tucked away in a dark corner of the survival shelter.

Sandra tore away cardboard packaging from the top. "It's a composting toilet. It uses the natural processes of decomposition and evaporation to recycle human waste. Waste coming in is over ninety percent water. The water is evaporated naturally and the leftover solid waste becomes compost which can be used for garden fertilizer. Has to be emptied about once a year."

"Cool. How did you get it down here?"

She pointed to another corner, where three bundles of rope were neatly stacked. "Roped it down. Just like I did with the generator and a few other things."

About an hour earlier, they had arrived. After leaving the hospital the previous day, Cray had been physically and mentally exhausted from recent events. The next day he had purchased some items on the list and had brought them to Sandra's house. Cray had called in sick and Sandra had taken a mental health day, reserved for employees of the health care profession. Now that they believed the end was coming, their jobs had become low priority.

With the help of the generator, extension cords, and a car battery, they had rigged up lights in the main area and the moonshine area of the shelter.

Cray stacked cases of bottled water and canned goods. "You've been a busy girl."

"We don't have much time."

"I know." Cray wondered when to broach his concerns.

As if reading his mind, Sandra stopped tearing away packaging from the composting toilet. "Let's take a break."

They returned to the entrance area, each holding a bottle of water, and sat in plastic chairs below a single incandescent light bulb dangling from the ceiling.

"I saw your look yesterday when we were talking to Pastor Jon," Sandra said.

"My look?"

"Yeah, you were pissed off that I wanted Penny Miles along without your consent. I could tell."

Cray looked at his hands. "Well, it's your shelter. I didn't know what to say."

"Listen, it's not just my shelter, it's yours. We're in this together. But there was something about your look that said something else. Did Penny do something to you? Did you have a relationship with her?"

"Did you invite her?"

"I called her and got voicemail. I just left an innocuous message, nothing about the shelter or anything. Anyway, it's not something you say in a phone message."

"I do know Penny, but not that well." Cray explained the story. "I have no idea what she told the cops, but I did *nothing,* yet I had to apologize to her or face sexual assault charges." Cray wondered how Sandra would handle this information. He had no idea of her past, barely knew her, but if her past included rape, wouldn't she tend to believe Penny over anything Cray might say? Didn't rape leave an indelible scar and create often insurmountable trust issues with men?

*If she didn't trust you, you wouldn't be right here right now, fool.*

After an uncomfortable silence, Sandra said, "You did nothing?"

"I swear to God."

Silence, but Sandra was looking at Cray suspiciously. Finally, she said, "Penny has a past, as we all do. But hers unfortunately was horrible. She moved here from Toronto maybe seven years ago. She was attacked leaving a bar one night and raped. I shouldn't even be telling you this, but the man also beat the living shit out of her and left her for dead. It's a miracle she survived, actually, but she's never been the same since."

"I would imagine. That's awful."

"If I'm going to trust you, I have to trust you all the way. I believe your story. Listen, I'm sorry for inviting Penny without your permission. She hasn't returned my message anyway, but if she does, I can tell her anything... like I just wanted to have coffee or a drink."

"It's okay. This is new to both of us. We're establishing guidelines on the fly. I didn't know her story, but if it's that bad, maybe we *should* invite her."

"You think so?"

"Can I think about it for a while?"

"Sure, but not more than a month."

"Right."

Sandra adjusted her baseball cap, brushed a lock of curly black hair away from her face, and took a sip of water. "What were you saying about people dying yesterday? You said three

Moncton residents who talked to Pastor Jon are already dead."

"That's what Marty told me. Apparent suicides. Pastor Jon says it's the work of the devil."

"I remember. Have you been having suicidal thoughts lately?"

"No. You?"

Silence.

Sandra wiped her eyes. "I had a weird nightmare last night."

Cray stiffened. "Are you thinking about killing yourself, Sandra?"

"No. But when I got up this morning the nightmare stuck in my mind for a long time... like some kind of a lead weight. "Don't you usually forget your dreams right away?"

"Yeah." His face grew pale. As he tipped the water bottle into his mouth, he realized too late it was a few inches away from his lips. He spilled water on his chin and shirt. He wiped his chin quickly. "Fuck... sorry, what was your dream, Sandra? What was it about?"

"It was pretty frightening."

"What was it?"

Silence.

Finally, "I hung myself from a rope in my living room. As I was dying, I was enveloped by a wall of flame. Pastor Jon's face appeared in the flame. He said, 'The end is now.' I woke up sweat-soaked and screaming my head off."

"Holy shit," Cray said, wondering how much Sandra knew about Mike's suicide by hanging. He decided not to mention it. He approached her.

She approached him.

Impulsively, they hugged. "I'm scared, Cray. Really scared. Will you stay with me tonight?"

"Sure. No problem."

"Let's see what's behind the other two doors," Sandra said, picking up a nearby flashlight and waving the beam across the two yet unopened doors. "One of those might be our bedrooms soon."

They approached the door in the corner of the room. It was made of oil-treated wood, bordered by steel. They reefed on it a few times unsuccessfully. Cray picked up a crowbar and pried it three times before it squeaked loudly and swung open. Inside, the room was a bedroom of sorts. Three single beds were lined up side by side, small tables with oil lanterns separating them. The room was made of concrete and sandstone and had been reinforced with wooden and steel beams.

Cray picked up an oil lantern. "Look, this even has oil and a wick. I bet it works."

The second door, its hinges fastened to rotten wood, opened easily, almost falling on them. Before going inside, they had to prop it up and place a few small support boulders behind it. This middle room was a makeshift kitchen, a table and four chairs in one corner and a woodstove in the other. There was even an old counter and cupboards, assorted dishware, pots and pans scattered about. Shining the flashlight, Cray examined the antique cast iron woodstove, noticing a steel chimney pipe was connected to an opening above another door. They tried the door, which squeaked open easily. They shone flashlights into a long winding dirt-walled hallway, about seven feet tall by three and a half feet wide.

"Black hole," Cray said. "Wonder where it goes."

\*\*\*\*\*\*

Standing in the middle of his potato field, gingerly scratching the lump on his forehead, Ralph trained a flashlight beam into a black hole about five feet deep, four feet wide and five feet long. The body of his uncle Simon Simms, Simple Simon, three bullet holes in his head, lay topside beside a mound of dirt. Nearby, a tractor affixed with a scoop, idled. Next to it, a wheelbarrow stuffed with potato plant seedlings. He tossed Sandra's shovel aside and examined the hole closer. *Gonna have to do... gonna have to.*

He brought the flashlight beam to Simple Simon's face. Mouth agape, eyes wide open. An expression of terror. *How did it happen again? Right. The element of surprise. He dropped by a few days ago, it might have been a week. Dunno. I opened the door, told him to go fuck himself, and bang, three shots to the head. With the trusty Colt 45.* "Bye-bye, Simple Simon, you stupid fuck. You should've shown me some respect."

But wait, Ralph thought, struggling to remember. A pang of guilt and remorse swept through him. *He said something to me before he died. What was it? Was it something good?* But, try as he might, the memory wouldn't surface. Finally, he gave up trying to retrieve it. *Must have been something bad.*

Ralph pulled a flask from his top pocket, removed the lid, and took a long pull. Moonshine. Strong shit. He tucked it away. He reached into his back pocket and pulled out the list, reminders of things he had already forgotten or would forget. He reviewed the items: Sandra, shovel, moonshine, apocalypse, Marty, cops.

"Cops? Were they here? Marty, who's Marty?"

As he climbed into the tractor and reversed, bits and pieces of his memory returned. Marty the detective had dropped by... was it yesterday or the day before? Didn't matter, really did it? He'd asked questions about a missing person. *Simple Simon, my uncle. Shit, he'll be back. He hadn't been convinced, didn't buy my story that I hadn't seen him in months. Better hurry.* Realizing he had stopped the tractor, Ralph quickly lowered the scoop and drove forward, pushing the body of his uncle into the hole. He stopped and examined it. It had landed in a fetal position but a wayward leg had snapped at the knee, poking out at an odd angle, the foot and heal covering the corpse's face. It would have to do. A short time later, he had the grave covered, the dirt above reasonably smooth. Smooth enough for a potato crop. He turned off the tractor and climbed down. He planted neat rows of potato plants above his dead uncle. When he finished, he took another swill of moonshine and consulted his list again. *Right. The shovel. Sandra's shovel.*

After parking his tractor, he climbed onto his quad, tossing the shovel in its rear trailer. By this time, the moonshine was creating a comfortably numbing buzz. He drove down Sandra's long driveway, frowning when he noticed *his* vehicle parked there alongside hers. The houselights were turned off. Her quad was gone. *Where to? Right. The hole. The black hole.*

He put a hand to his crotch, felt the cold steel of the Colt 45 revolver, and grinned.

******

"Did you hear that?" Sandra said, her face going pale.

Cray stopped rummaging through dust-covered pots and pans. "Hear what?"

"Up top... sounded like a motor."

"No. Want me to check?"

"We'll both go."

Arriving at the well opening, they pointed flashlights up. "Anyone there?" Sandra said.

They waited. No response.

Cray pointed to the shotgun on the ground beside the car battery. A box of shells sat next to it. "Is it loaded?"

"Yeah. You know how to use it, right?"

Cray picked it up. "Sure do."

"Is there anyone there?" Sandra said again, her voice trailing off in an eerie echo.

After a few seconds, they heard the distant sound of a motor, growing louder. Then a loud crash, followed by dust and dirt falling into the well, powdering their heads.

"What the fuck was that?" Cray asked.

"I think someone crashed into the well house."

"Holy shit. We gotta go."

"Yes, let's."

Shotgun slung over his shoulder, Cray started climbing the metal stairs, Sandra close behind. Halfway up, they heard a motor shut off and the sound of wooden planks falling on the ground.

"Who's there?" Sandra said.

Silence.

"Who's up there?" Cray said. "What do you want?"

Suddenly they were blinded by a flashlight beam from above.

A voice sounded—loud, slurring, echoing. "Well, if it isn't the little... little fucking lovebirds. Building a little shelter now are we? Preparing for the end of the world?"

"Ralph," Sandra said, "Is that you?"

"'Course it's me, sweetie. And I'm wondering why you didn't invite me."

"We're coming up, Ralph. Stand back."

The flashlight beam disappeared and there was a momentary silence as they continued climbing metal stairs. Cray reached the top and climbed out on all fours, breathing hard. He looked up and was again blinded by a flashlight beam. He pulled out his flashlight and beamed it in Ralph's eyes. Wild eyes. A silly grin. The beam caught a glint of metal. A gun. Tucked in his pants.

"Get that fucking beam away from my eyes," Ralph said.

"You first."

Sandra poked her head out and Ralph blasted her face with the flashlight beam.

Cray quickly removed the shotgun from his shoulder, clicked the safety off, and aimed it at Ralph's head. "Put one finger on your gun and I blow your brains out."

"What are you doing here?" Sandra said, looking at Ralph's quad lodged in a corner of the well house. "Why did you do that? You could've killed us."

"Watch out, Sandra, he's got a gun."

"He does?"

"Yeah. Throw it on the ground. Now!" *He'll fucking shoot me he lays a hand on it. Shouldn't I be saying put your hands up?*

Before Ralph could touch the gun, or Cray could blow his brains out, Sandra approached Ralph quickly and removed the pistol. She stepped back, aiming it at his head, even though she didn't know where the safety was, and had never fired a gun.

Ralph opened his hands in a peaceful gesture. "You folks don't need to get all excited." He pointed to the quad trailer. "I came to return your shovel is all. My gun, well it's only for protection, you know, case I get attacked by a pack a coyotes or something. Gotta be careful around here. I mean no harm to you good folks."

*This is not good,* Cray thought. *Not good at all. In the middle of the night, in the middle of the forest with a lunatic. A drunk lunatic. Shit.* He went over to the quad trailer, removed the shovel, and tossed it on the ground. "There, we've got the shovel. Now you can leave."

"A slight problem with that," Ralph said. "My quad is stuck in that there well house."

"Remove the boards, and do it carefully, and go," Cray said.

"You can't come onto my property at this hour and scare the hell out of us," Sandra said. "You should know better."

She lowered the pistol and started removing loose boards from the front of Ralph's quad.

Ralph began picking away boards. "I'm sorry. Guess I'm a little drunk."

Before Cray realized it wasn't a good idea to allow Ralph to play with planks in the forest, it was already too late. From his peripheral vision, he saw a two-by-six coming at him. He raised the gun. The board glanced off the barrel and connected hard with the side of his head. He fired the shotgun, straight in the air, then fell flat on his face, still holding the gun, as the blast echoed through the forest. Dazed, he rolled over.

Board raised, Ralph attacked. "Fucking point a gun at me, you son of bitch. I meant no harm, but I fucking well do now." The board came down hard, striking Cray on the top of the head. Cray's vision blurred. One Ralph, two Ralphs, three Ralphs. Ralph raised the board for another strike. But as he was about to bring it down, he was struck hard in the back of the head by a board. He fell face-first, landing right beside Cray. Sandra jumped on top of him, pistol-whipping him on the back of the head with the Colt 45.

Cray staggered to his feet. He aimed the shotgun at Ralph's head. "Get off him... get off him, Sandra!"

A gunshot blast rang out, echoing loudly into the night. Everyone froze. An eerie silence.

Then, the rustling of brush some twenty feet away, and a voice. "You kids done playing yet?"

Fear-induced adrenaline coursing through his body, still hazy from blows to the head, Cray staggered again, got his footing, and aimed the shotgun at the tree line, where the voice originated.

The voice. "Throw down that weapon."

Wait a minute. Cray recognized the voice. "Marty... Marty is that you?"

Sandra climbed off Ralph, who started moaning, a goose egg farm sprouting on the back of his head.

Headlights illuminated the small clearing. A shadow stepped into the clearing. "Throw down your weapon, Cray. It's me."

Cray put the shotgun down. Marty quickly advanced. He knelt down and put a knee into Ralph's spine.

Ralph grunted. "Oww... that hurts. What's... what's going on?"

Marty cuffed Ralph. "You're coming down to the station. That's what's going on."

Back at Sandra's house a half hour later, Cray, Sandra and Marty sat in the living room discussing the ordeal.

Outside, Ralph was locked in the backseat of Marty's Crown Victoria. Another cop was on route to take Ralph first to the hospital for an examination and then to the police station for questioning.

"I don't want to press any charges," Sandra said, wrapping a small cut on the ride side of Cray's head with white gauze. A goose egg was rapidly swelling on the top of his head. She had diagnosed the injuries as a minor concussion, disinfected the cut, and applied a topical antibiotic. "I mean all we have here is maybe assault, and Ralph is in a lot worse condition than Cray is." She looked at Cray. "Or maybe I shouldn't speak for you. You're the one who's been assaulted. Do you want to press charges?"

*The end is nigh. Prepare yourself.* The last thing Cray wanted was a court trial to get in the way of post-apocalyptic preparation. But, if Ralph wasn't locked up, he would be a continuing threat while they prepared. He would be back, guaranteed. And maybe with a vengeance the likes of which they hadn't seen thus far. *Well, that's fine, he threatens us again, or points a gun at me, he's gonna take a bullet and die. In self-defense.* "I don't think so."

"Are you sure?" Marty said. "I show up, hear a shotgun go off, then you get wacked with a board a couple of times. Then Sandra winds up pistol-whipping Ralph. Doesn't seem like much of a party. Refresh my memory, please. How did this all start, I mean once you got out of the well?"

"I saw his gun, so I pulled the shotgun on him," Cray said.

"Was he threatening you with it? Did he point it at you?"

"No. He said something threatening. 'Little fucking lovebirds.' Something like that. I saw he had a gun. I got scared and pulled the gun on him. I mean he was drunk, he smashed into the well house, scared the shit out of us. He's been here before, a fucking shotgun in his hands..."

"Slow down. So you pulled the gun on him, then what happened?"

Sandra finished bandaging Cray's head and sat beside him on the couch, hands on her chin, listening intently.

"Sandra took his gun," Cray continued. "So he couldn't use it on us. We told him to leave. He agreed. That's when he started taking boards off his quad, which as you saw was lodged in the side of the well house. Then he picked one up and smashed me over the head. The shotgun went off by accident. I was trying to block the board with it. So I get hit once, go down, he hits me again while I'm down, and then Sandra hits him from behind with a board, he goes down, and she pistol-whips him. You saw that part."

"I couldn't see much," Marty said, scratching his chin stubble. "But I did see you pointing a gun at him and telling Sandra to get off him. I assumed you said that because you wanted her out of the way... to get a clear shot. I think you wanted to kill him, would've killed him if I hadn't arrived."

At one time, Cray wouldn't have believed he was capable of murder. But these were the last few days before the world would never be the same. "Everything happened so fast. I was fired up with adrenaline, groggy from the head shots... I don't know, maybe I would've killed him. But isn't that self-defense?"

Silence.

Cray continued. "And, as I said, he was here a couple times in the last few days. Put the fear of God in me. Came to borrow a shovel one day, told me he was digging a grave with it. Another time he comes with a shotgun, acting like he's gonna shoot us, then he gives it to Sandra as a gift."

"Is that the one you shot in the air?"

"Yeah."

Marty turned to Sandra. "Is all this true?'

"Yes. He gave me that shotgun."

"Okay, let's go back to the first visit. When was that?"

"He came twice on June $2^{nd}$," Cray said. "Once in the afternoon to borrow the shovel, and later in the evening to give Sandra the shotgun, I guess."

The sound of a vehicle pulling up the driveway stopped the conversation. Marty's cell phone rang. "Hang on a minute. I have to take this." He went outside, answering the phone as he opened the door.

They watched silently from the window as he spoke briefly and then hung up. He then had a short conversation with a uniformed cop who'd arrived. The cop removed Ralph from the Crown Victoria, put him in the marked police cruiser, and sped away.

Marty returned and sat down.

"They took him away?" Sandra said, fidgeting with her hands.

Marty's smartphone beeped. Frowning, he stared at it for a moment and then set it on the coffee table. He turned to them. "I can't hold him for too long if you're not willing to press charges. But, there's something else I want to question him about. I want to try and scare him into a confession, that's if I can get him out of the hospital in one piece."

"Something else?" Cray said.

"I'm not at liberty to discuss it." Marty scratched his chin. "Ah, what the hell, if I say nothing I put your lives in more danger. I'm investigating Ralph Franks in a missing person case."

"Missing person?" Sandra said.

"Yeah, his uncle Simon Simms. I think Ralph may have killed him, but I don't have enough evidence for a search warrant. Not yet anyway."

"The shovel," Cray said. "Digging a grave."

"That's right. And if you don't mind, I'd like to take the shovel with me. And the shotgun. And Ralph's Colt 45."

"If you take the shotgun, we won't have any protection," Sandra said. "And if he gets released..."

"He's insane," Cray said. "We need some protection."

Marty thought for a moment. "Okay, I'll leave everything behind. I don't want Ralph looking for his guns and then getting pissed off at you guys if he doesn't find them. For all I know he might ask for the shotgun back. As I said, I just want to scare him when we get him downtown. Maybe scare a confession out of him if I'm lucky. I don't even have a body in this case yet, and that's the first thing I need to find."

"Check his property," Sandra said. "He said he's digging a grave."

"Yeah, check his property," Cray said.

"Can't without his permission or a warrant," Marty said.

"Would any of you guys like a coffee?" Sandra asked.

"Sure," Marty said.

Cray nodded, and Sandra went into the kitchen.

"I hear your friend Mike's funeral is next Saturday," Marty said.

"I heard that too."

"I imagine you'll be there."

"Yeah."

"It must be hard for you."

"Yeah, although with everything that's been going on lately, I haven't had a chance to think about it."

"I would imagine. Did you hear about Pastor Jon?"

"No."

Sandra appeared in the doorway. "Coffee's brewing. What's that about Pastor Jon?"

Marty leaned forward in his chair. "He left the hospital this morning."

"No surprise, really," Sandra said. "He said he wanted to leave."

"Where is he?" Cray said.

"I saw him on Queen Street, preaching the end of the world. I don't know how the hell he was able to recover so fast."

"It's a miracle," Sandra said. "Hold that thought."

"Is he coming with you?" Marty said, pointing out the window. "I presume that's a survival shelter you're working on over there. You bringing him along?"

Sandra returned with a tray containing a pot of coffee, three mugs, sugar, milk, and spoons. "Help yourselves."

"Thanks," said Marty, pouring a cup for each of them.

"We asked him to come," Sandra said, sipping coffee. "But he doesn't want to. Said he needs to stay and warn people. Are you saying you believe him? Do you think everything is coming to an end?"

Marty stirred his coffee, removed the spoon and set it on the tray. He sipped. "Good coffee. There's a part of me that wants to dismiss it, but as a detective, I examine evidence and probabilities based on the evidence. I combine that with gut instinct. I hate to say it, folks, but in this case my gut and the evidence says he's right."

"What are you doing about it?" Cray asked.

A pause. Marty sipped coffee. "That's damn fine coffee, Sandra. What kind is it?"

"Santo Domingo. Imported from the Dominican Republic."

"Excellent flavor. Never tasted anything this good in Canada. Anyway, I haven't done anything about it, other than to try and reconcile with my wife in Toronto. But, I've been thinking. And I don't want you to answer me right now. Think about it. I know you'll need to discuss it in private... "

"You want us to invite you to the survival shelter," Sandra said. "Along with your wife."

"You're good."

"It's not rocket science. I overheard you talking to Pastor Jon. Cray filled in a few blanks."

"Well, what do you think?" Marty said. "Imagine me telling my colleagues this. They wouldn't believe me. And anyway, I'm new here, and a lot of them still resent that I'm their boss all of a sudden. You might need someone like me. I'm resourceful, trained in combat and weapons handling. And Elaine, she's a clinical psychologist. Always good to have a nutcracker around, you know what I mean."

Silence.

Cray scratched his bandaged head. *What if he knows about Penny Miles? The trumped up charge.* Then he remembered: *You didn't do anything. The truth will speak for itself, defend itself. And these are extenuating circumstances. We could use a man like him.*

*Couldn't we?*

"Don't touch that," Sandra said, watching Cray rub the head-wrapped gauze. "Let it heal."

Cray removed his hand. "It's your shelter, Sandra."

"We agreed we would do this together."

"Right. First we have to figure out how much room we have and who else we're planning to bring. I think as it stands we have two other people we're considering. And, of course, if we figure we do have room for two more, we'll need to talk it over, meet Elaine."

"I agree," Sandra said. "Why don't we just say it's a possibility right now, detective?"

"Thanks," Marty said. "I can live with that. God, this feels almost like a job interview. Who'd have thought that two months after arriving here, I'd be applying for a position as a post-apocalyptic survivor?"

Sandra's phone rang. She stared at the incoming caller ID. "I'm gonna take this in the kitchen."

Marty's phone rang too. He answered it. "How's it going? He's okay? Right. The station. Give me forty minutes." He hung up and extended a hand to Cray. "I have to go. Ralph is being taken to the station."

Cray shook the hand and released it. "Okay."

Sandra appeared in the kitchen doorway, a hand to the phone. "Is Ralph okay?"

"Minor concussion. You didn't kill him."

"Thank God," Sandra said.

"You two have a good night," Marty said, "We'll be in touch." He left.

After they watched his Crown Victoria disappear down the driveway, Sandra sat next to Cray on the couch. "What a crazy night. That was Penny who just called."

"What did she want?"

"She wanted to make a plan to get together. I told her I'd call her back. There's something wrong."

"What do you mean?"

"She's drunk. Having a panic attack. I think something happened to her."

"You should call her."

"I will, but I need a drink stronger than coffee right now. You want one?"

"Sure."

"Lime rickey?"

"Why not?"

Sandra went into the kitchen. She returned with two drinks and handed one to Cray. They toasted and drank, neither one able to think of anything to toast to.

"How about survival in the new world order?" Cray said.

Sandra took another sip. "Fair enough... I'm going upstairs to call Penny back. Make yourself comfortable. You hungry?"

"Not yet. You?"

"No." Drink in one hand, phone in the other, Sandra disappeared upstairs. Cray heard muted conversation but nothing discernable. Didn't matter. Let them have their private girl talk. He didn't want to hear, just hoped the conversation was nothing bad about him. His name was bound to come up. What would Penny say about him? What would Sandra say? What would Sandra think? Would she believe Penny? Cray took a sip of lime rickey and shivered, partly because of the drink's potency and partly because of his edginess. He absently rubbed the growing bump on his head and winced.

The conversation continued upstairs. At one point, Sandra's voice became louder and more alarmed. This time Cray *could* hear it. "What? Some fucking asshole did that?" Then Sandra lowered her voice again and her words became incomprehensible. *Is she talking about me? Is Penny talking about me? Fucking bitch. Fucking lying bitch. She better not be. Think of something else, you fool. You're getting paranoid.*

Cray drained the drink in one long gulp and went into the kitchen. He mixed a strong one and returned to the living room, sipping it as he walked. He approached the window, pulling aside the blinds and peering out at the sliver of moon in the distance, obscured by a passing bank of gray-black clouds. Thunder rolled in the heavens and a lightning bolt snaked down and struck a power pole about a mile away. It sparked, popped, and fizzled out. The houselights flickered. Thunder rumbled and rolled. It started raining, a sprinkle initially and then torrential, tapping on the steel roof and whipping into the windows like a thousand ball-peen hammers.

Shuddering, Cray stepped back from the window, still trying to take his mind off the conversation upstairs. But he couldn't. *Something probably happened to her that doesn't concern you, you self-centered fool. Sandra said as much.*

"Sandra," he shouted, without even realizing it. The insistent tapping of the rain had drowned out her voice. He heard the stairs creak and spun around, spilling some of his drink on the hardwood floor.

Sandra stood halfway down the stairs, drink in hand, expression somber, deep green eyes accusing. Even in the dim gold light from the antique-style lamps furnishing the living room, Cray noticed the change in her color. Her once smooth olive skin was blotched red. Behind the red smudges, pale white. Had she been crying? Was she angry at him? He couldn't tell, and the confusion triggered a rush of adrenaline.

With an unsteady hand, he set his drink down and walked to the foot of the stairs. "Are you okay? What's wrong?"

Without taking her eyes off Cray, she sat on the stairs. "Penny. She's been raped."

"Are you sure?" Cray was going to move closer but abruptly changed his mind. Now was perhaps not the time nor place for consolation.

Silence.

Finally, Sandra said, "I don't know. But she was in a fit, crying, yelling, screaming, accusing..."

"Who did it?"

"I don't know. She was on the verge of telling me I think, but then she turned into a blubbering..."

"I'll call Marty. What do you think?"

"That's a good idea." She pulled out her phone, pressed a few buttons, and told Cray Penny's address.

Cray called Marty and relayed the information. Marty said he would dispatch a patrol car immediately after he finished interrogating Ralph—which would probably be sooner than later since Ralph had clammed up and demanded to see a lawyer. Marty also said he would go to Penny's house personally. By the time Cray hung up, Sandra had taken a seat on the couch. She was nervously sipping her drink and absently staring at windswept raindrops tapping incessantly on the bay window.

Cray sat in a nearby armchair. They sat silently for a moment, both watching and listening to the rain. Thunder clapped loudly and a lightning bolt streaked across the black sky, fanning out into a dozen white tentacles. Sandra shivered. So did Cray.

The lights flickered and went out.

"Fuck," Cray said.

"Shit," Sandra said.

The lights came on.

Sandra sighed. "You could never do something like that?"

Cray saw fear and doubt in her eyes, and something else—a desire to believe, to trust perhaps. It gave him hope. "I could never do something like that. I promise."

They were silent again for a moment, watching the thunderstorm, which intensified as a bank of black clouds rolled in and settled over the house.

"Everything is getting fucked up, Cray."

"Everything is getting fucked up, Sandra. We have to believe in each other."

Silence.

Finally, she said, "Come here. I want you to hold me. Just hold me."

Cray sat down beside Sandra. He set his drink on the coffee table. He slowly put his arm around her, moving closer and snuggling. He couldn't believe the euphoric sensation of skin-on-skin contact as he touched her hand. It had been so long. Too damn long.

Sandra put her arm around him. "Thanks. I need some help right now." She kissed him tenderly on the cheek. A pleasant sensation tingled through his body. An uncomfortable silence followed. It was broken by a loud thunder clap. They inched closer to one another.

"Do you have to work tomorrow?" Cray said.

"I do, but I'm gonna take another mental health day. You?"

"I'm gonna call in sick. What's the point of working now?"

"That's what I'm starting to think. Why don't we carry on stocking the shelter? That should be priority one. What if Pastor Jon is wrong about the date that the world ends? What if it happens tonight? Or tomorrow?"

Thunder clapped loudly and a strong gust of wind whipped the bay window with a sheet of rain. The house shook. Sandra hugged Cray tightly.

"It looks like the end of the world out there," he said.

"It sure does. Do you wanna put the TV on? Watch the news or something?"

"No. Do you?"

"Not really. It was just something to say. Maybe there's a warning on the news."

"Oh, there are lots of warnings out there if you look around."

"True enough."

Cray's mind kept spinning back to Penny and what she might have said. Finally, he just came out with it. "What exactly happened to Penny?"

"I'll tell you." Her tone was matter-of-fact. "Let me get you another drink first."

"Sure." *Does she trust me?*

She took his glass. "I think I'm gonna switch to wine now. It's a much mellower buzz. How about you?"

"Sounds good."

She went into the kitchen and returned with two glasses of white wine. Sitting down, she handed one to Cray. "Chilean. G7. I think you'll like it." She held her glass out. "Let's toast to no lies, no secrets, and absolute trust between us. No, wait a minute. You might have some shit you don't wanna tell me yet. I might have some shit—I do, actually—I don't wanna tell you yet. How about a toast to trust, respect, and honesty?"

"Hear-hear. I can live with that." They toasted and drank. Sandra's leg gently touched his. He liked the warm sensation. "I have another one."

"What's that?"

Cray raised his glass. "To loyalty and good communication."

"I like that."

"Cheers," they said in unison.

"I'm gonna tell you everything Penny told me," Sandra said.

Cray exhaled, realizing for the first time he'd been holding his breath. "Okay."

"Your name *did* come up." She paused, looking at him intently. "After she told me some of what happened, she said, 'Who are you with?' She could hear background voices, I guess. Anyway, I said *you*. I didn't mention Marty or what happened to us, nothing about the shelter or anything. At first she warned me to stay away from you. I immediately defended you, saying I didn't believe you were a bad person. Then I asked her what happened. Why she did that to you. She didn't want to talk about it. Said she was still in shock from what just happened to her. Maybe I was being insensitive to her situation, but I pushed. Gently at first, but then slightly more demanding. I needed to know. You're staying here tonight, for Christ sakes. She mentioned something about a physical assault. I kept pushing. Finally, she broke down and started crying. You know what she said to me in the end?"

Cray lifted his wine glass shakily to his lips. A little spilled on his hand. After taking a quick gulp, he wiped it away. "No."

"She said she was confused that day. Strung out on cocaine, amphetamines, cannabis, even drunk. She said she didn't remember who assaulted her. She said maybe her mind concocted some or all of the story. She said she was sorry..."

Cray sighed, deeply relieved. "My co-workers made lewd comments to her. Whistling, maybe someone said she has a nice ass, called her 'baby' maybe. I don't remember every detail. But I know one thing. I didn't say a thing. And I never laid a hand on her. Sure, I noticed her. She's attractive. I'm a man. I'm not blind."

"Even if you whistled at her, big deal. You know how many times I've walked by construction sites and been whistled at by construction workers, some even saying stuff like, 'You're hot, baby' or 'Marry me, sweetie.' I'm not trying to come across as full of myself, but as long as the comments don't get downright disgusting—and they usually don't—I don't give a shit. In fact, sometimes it actually feeds my ego and makes me feel good that men consider me attractive. Jesus, if I was gonna run around and charge men for every suggestive wisecrack they made I'd never get out of court. I'm a woman. Women like to be admired. Why do you think we pay ten times as much as men for a haircut, three or four times as much as men for clothes, and are constantly looking for new consumer products to make us feel younger and look more beautiful? We need to know that men find us attractive. It's the nature of being a woman. And I don't understand these women victimizing men for appreciating them."

"Wow, that's a refreshing opinion, coming from a woman."

"Don't get me wrong... if the comments are lewd and disgusting, demeaning in any way, there should be repercussions. But our laws have progressed—maybe I should say regressed—to the point where a comment like 'You look beautiful' might land someone in jail, or put a permanent black mark on their record, one that could damage their reputation and career potential for a lifetime. I mean, literally destroy them."

"Well, frankly, that's what I was worried about with Penny's allegations. That I would get put on some sexual assault watch list for something I didn't do. Have cops breathing over my shoulder day in and day out."

"Did that happen?"

"No. At least I don't think so."

"Well, I told you about Penny's background. She's got men issues."

Cray digested it in the context of his own issues. Since he'd walked in on his girlfriend cheating with his best friend, since he almost got charged for sexual assault through no fault of his own, he had women issues and trust issues. He wanted to move past them, especially where it concerned his relationship with Sandra. Seeing things from both sides, Cray suddenly felt sorry for Penny. Didn't she harbor the same issues as he, just gender-flipped? What about Sandra? The way she looked at him after hearing of Penny's ordeal. What skeletons was she hiding in her closet?

Well, that was something he wasn't prepared to pry into right now. The last thing he wanted to do was alienate her. She would tell him when she was good and ready to—on her own terms, on her own timeline. He sighed. "I guess we all have issues. I hope I can fix mine. I hope Penny can fix hers."

"I hope I can fix mi—"

Cray's phone rang, the thunder rolled, fresh sheets of rain pelted the window, and the lights flickered. Answering the phone, Cray said, "I'm putting you on speaker, Marty."

"I'm at Penny's apartment. She wanted me to call Sandra, but I don't have her number."

"How is she?"

"I'd say she's been raped... and something else?"

Cray's breath escaped in a deep gasp. "Oh?"

"She was badly beaten. I'm surprised she didn't mentioned that to Sandra, but I'm taking her to the hospital."

"What about Ralph?"

"Not enough evidence to hold him. But because of the storm, he'll probably be spending the night in jail. Half the lights are out in Charlottetown and it's too dangerous to drive. Don't go anywhere, whatever you do."

"Can I talk to Penny?" Sandra asked.

"Not now," Marty said. "I need to get her to the hospital."

"Thanks for the heads-up," Cray said.

There was a silence on the other end of the line. Marty should have hung up right away, but he hadn't. There was something else.

"Don't go outside if you don't absolutely have to," Marty said. "A man has already been killed by a lightning strike and a house just burst into flames after getting struck by lightning. Gonna be a long night."

A knot of fear tightened in Cray's throat. He swallowed. "Is that it?"

"I wish it was. There's a forest fire that started in Fort McMurray, Alberta. It's sweeping east rapidly. It's already killed 136 people and destroyed dozens of homes."

"Holy fuck," Cray said.

"Holy shit," Sandra said.

"I gotta go," Marty said.

As Cray took a long gulp of wine, Sandra went into the kitchen. She returned a short time later with two flashlights and six candles. She set everything on the coffee table. "I might be needed at the hospital tomorrow. Especially if Penny's there."

Dangerously close to the house, a lightning bolt suddenly snaked down from the sky, struck the lawn and exploded. Grass and dirt erupted into the air and a large hole appeared, burning bright orange for a few seconds before being doused by rain. Frozen, Sandra and Cray watched from the window. Another lightning bolt swept down and struck a nearby power pole transformer. There was a loud explosion and a fireworks display of sparks and flames danced across the sky.

The lights went out.

Spinning around in complete blackness, Cray bumped into a knick-knack display cabinet. It fell over and crashed to the floor, sending glass and wooden splinters flying. To avoid injury, Cray dove away from the noise, landing on the floor hard, and covering his face with his hands. "Fuck." In an instant, he felt someone kick his ankle and heard a short, shrill scream. Blindly, he held out his hands and Sandra fell right into them, head-butting Cray fast and hard.

Sharp pain. Dizziness. Stars, multiplying, dancing and twinkling. Consciousness fading. *Hang on. Don't pass out.* Slowly, the debilitating wave passed and Cray felt consciousness mount a battle for survival. "Sandra?" he said, running a hand blindly across her forehead. He felt warm blood. Now panicked urgency. "Sandra... Say something." He gently rolled her onto her back, put his head to her chest, her firm breasts pressing into his ear.

He heard a heartbeat. "Thank God."

In the darkness, he crawled toward the coffee table, cutting his hand on a glass spear as he began his journey. "Fucking son of a bitch." He lifted the hand, felt for the spear, and slowly extracted it, realizing it was perhaps an inch long and may have gone clear through his hand. He slowly removed it and continued. He reached the coffee table and bumped his head on it. "Fuck you. Fuck off." His hand fumbled for the flashlight on the coffee table.

He reached it. Turned it on, got up and raced over to Sandra, ignoring his aching head and the blood spewing from the gash in his hand. Reaching her, he bent down, shone the flashlight into her eyes. Closed. Her mouth hung open. She had a lump above her eye. A one-inch gash on it dribbled blood into her eyes, down her nose, into her agape mouth. Panicking, he brushed back a lock of her hair, realizing he was smearing her face red from his hand injury.

He removed his hand. "Sandra... Sandra?"

Nothing.

He examined her body for other injuries. A small cut on her ankle, inflicted by a small spear of glass. Otherwise, fine. Pressing his thumb against his bleeding hand, he refocused the beam on Sandra's face. She exhaled a long breath and grew still—deathly still.

"Oh my God, no. Don't die on me!"

# Chapter Nine

It was a quarter to midnight. The storm had knocked out all the streetlights in Charlottetown. Rain came down in sheets, driven by fierce winds. Occasionally lightning cracked through the blackness and lit up the sky. Marty winced every time that happened. He drove along University Avenue, Penny Miles in the front passenger seat alongside him, her rain-soaked blonde hair matted to her face, her head buried deep in her blood-encrusted hands. She had been hysterical when he'd arrived at her house a half hour earlier—sobbing, mumbling, sobbing, mumbling some more. Most of her words were panicked, fear-tinged, and incomprehensible. But the shredded blue oversized t-shirt, claw marks along her inner thighs leading to her vagina, flesh and blood clinging to long fingernails, two black eyes, a gash and two contusions on her forehead, the disarray of the bedroom showing obvious signs of struggle, and the jimmied bedroom window—clearly forced entry—told an evidentiary story where Penny's words fell short.

But from her words, Marty was able to establish that a slim, mid-40s Caucasian male intruder broke into her house while she was sleeping, put a hand over her mouth, and said, "I'll kill you if you make a sound or move." He then proceeded to tear off her clothes and sexually assault her. Apparently it was after the rape that a fight ensued, which saw Penny rake her fingernails down the man's face, tearing flesh, drawing blood, and sending him into a rage.

There was a lot of work left to do. Two cops were at the crime scene still gathering evidence. A rape kit would have to be administered. Penny would have to review photos of known sex offenders, a sketch artist needed to be called in, and Marty wanted to get the perp's DNA sample (extracted from Penny's fingernails) to the lab and eventually run it through the database. If he got real lucky, maybe he would get a match and the case would be simplified to the apprehension of a convicted sex offender. Cut right to the chase.

But first he had to have this woman examined by a doctor to insure her injuries were not life-threatening. Maybe she would be required to spend the night in the hospital and some detective work would have to wait. The last thing he wanted was for her to drop dead while describing the perp's physical description to the sketch artist. There'd been a point during his initial questioning when Penny's face had suddenly gone white, her eyes closed, and her head lolled to one side. If Marty hadn't grabbed her by the shoulders and helped her to a nearby armchair, she probably would have fallen head-first onto the hardwood floor.

As it was, the paramedics should have been on the scene after police had determined it was safe to enter. Only problem was, Charlottetown was a small city with limited resources. Existing paramedics were running off their feet dealing with other storm-related injuries and fatalities. So Marty had to play detective, paramedic, friend, psychologist, and ambulance driver.

Penny removed both hands from her face, sat up slowly, and eyed the detective. Since they had climbed into the car, not a word had been spoken. Marty had decided to give the traumatized woman some quiet time to grieve. Some time to claw her way out of shock. Let her start the conversation. Not taking his eyes off the road, he stole a glance at Penny in his peripheral vision. Wet blood mixed with rain streaked across her face, neck, and hair, giving her the appearance of a macabre circus clown.

"Do you have any kids?" she asked.

*Strange question.* "No, do you?"

"No. But I come from a family of three kids, including me. All girls. My sisters each have three kids. All girls. Isn't that strange?"

Although Marty had a close relationship with his middle-class mother and father, he didn't subscribe to their strict religious beliefs. He was an only child. He had often wished for a brother or sister when he was young, a friend to grow up with. "Coincidental, for sure."

"One day I'd like to get married and have kids. I want three boys, though. My sisters are happily married. I'm kind of the black sheep. You married?"

"Yes." *Is she hitting on me?*

"Happily?"

"Marriage is like a university that you never graduate from. Always something to learn. I'm trying to learn to at least get good grades in my class."

"That's a good analogy. I like that."

*Black sheep.* Marty tried to steer the conversation to questions that would reveal character and motivation. "You have a good relationship with your siblings, your parents?"

"I'm not really that close with my parents or my sisters. Don't get me wrong, I wasn't abused as a child or anything. My mom and dad raised me well and were very good providers."

"But something wasn't right?"

"Growing up, I always felt like I was competing with my siblings and couldn't live up to my parents' expectations. Celine and Deborah, my older sisters, got better marks in school, were more popular, and even as adults made better relationship choices, and got better jobs."

"It's tough if you feel you're always being compared to your sisters. You working now?"

"No. I just quit. I had a job as a secretary, but my boss was making inappropriate advances."

*Inappropriate advances? Another story for another time.* "Sorry to hear that. We're almost there."

"You gonna catch him? The guy that did this to me?" Penny's tone was different now, soft and pleading.

"Yes, I'm gonna catch him."

"You know, there are so many sick perverts out there."

"I know." A few things disturbed Marty about Penny. Not least of which was something Constable Bobby Briggs had said, out of Penny's earshot, just prior to leaving the crime scene. "Careful with this one. She has a history of pressing sexual assault and harassment charges. I don't know if all of them are true. Actually, I doubt it."

Penny wiped her eyes. "You might know, but not like I know. Why do they victimize me? Because I'm blonde and attractive. I don't go looking for it, you know."

"I'm sure you don't." Marty wasn't sure, actually. He had his doubts. "There's a box of Kleenex in the glove box if you want."

She opened the glove box, pulled two tissues loose, and dabbed her face and eyes.

They pulled into the hospital entrance. It looked like a war zone. Three ambulances were parked haphazardly in front of the EMERGENCY doors. Amid screams and panicked cries, medical staff rushed multiple burn victims, on wheelchairs and stretchers, into the hospital.

Marty parked. How many people were in that lightning-ignited house? he thought. Were there other homes involved? Killing the ignition, he turned to Penny. "We're going to get you some medical attention. And if doctors determine you're okay, and you're up to it, I'd like to ask you some more questions, have you view some mug shots, and get you in with the sketch artist."

Penny looked determined. "Oh, don't you worry, detective. I'll be fine for all that. I wanna catch the son of bitch who did this to me."

In pelting rain, Marty climbed out of his car, walked around, and opened Penny's door. She climbed out. He pulled his black raincoat over her head. She put an arm around his waist. He escorted her into the waiting room, in view of the carnage. He spotted Nurse Betty Reilly attending a moaning male burn victim, and tapped her on the shoulder. The man she was bandaging was one of the more fortunate victims, with only his arm burned from the hand up to his shoulder. The skin was raw, blistering and peeling.

Thank God for connections. Marty had phoned ahead and Betty had assured him she would administer the rape kit in a timely fashion, take the DNA sample from her fingernails, and get Penny in front of a doctor as soon as possible. Time was of the essence if he wanted to catch the perp.

Marty introduced Betty to Penny. "You got this?" he asked Betty.

"Yes," Betty said, her tone terse, stressed. She began escorting Penny down the hall.

The burn victim, a thirty-something man with a mop of tousled black hair, looked up at Betty. "Hey, where're you going?"

Betty turned. She looked pale, worn out. "I'll be right back. Hang in there. I won't be long."

"I'll check in later," Marty said, wanting to get the hell out of there as soon as possible. As seasoned as he was, he hated the sight of blood, particularly since his partner's untimely death.

"Please do," Penny said.

"Thanks, Betty," Marty said. He turned and left.

As he approached the door, a young cop, who didn't look a day older than fifteen, waved and approached. Marty didn't recognize the rookie.

"Detective Strader?" the young cop said.

"Yeah. What can I do for you?"

"Did you hear? There are six homes on fire on Euston Street. It's hell. Weirdest thing I've ever seen. With all this rain, I don't know how a fire could burn so fast, so ferocious. Never seen anything like it."

*Divine intervention*, Marty thought. He dismissed the thought immediately. "Presumably it's getting help from residential oil tank explosions."

"Yeah, I guess. We need as many bodies as possible. You heading there?"

"Shortly. I have a few other priorities first." He turned and left.

Inside his vehicle, he tried to decide what to do next. A rare moment in his lengthy career, he was undecided, discombobulated. Things were happening too fast. The raging inferno in Alberta, aided by strong winds and hot, dry conditions, was advancing much faster than anybody had imagined. He turned on the radio: "Emergency responders claim they have never before seen a fire behave like this. The worst disaster in Alberta's history, it seems to have a mind of its own, suddenly changing directions, sparing some homes while decimating others." A firefighter's comment: "This fire is moving faster than anything I've ever seen. We simply don't have the resources or even the know-how to stop it."

He turned off the radio. *A mind of its own. The storm here seems to have a mind of its own.* After all, it had downed selected power grids, spontaneously combusted selected homes, caused flash flooding in selected areas, and blocked cell phone reception wherever and whenever it damn well pleased. *What the fuck is going on?*

Lightning cracked from the heavens and Marty watched it snake down about a half mile away, explode into a ball of white sparks and orange fire, ignite, and slowly start to burn.

*Death by fire. Was Pastor Jon only wrong about the date? Is this the beginning of the end?*

He considered returning to the rape scene to gather more evidence, then changed his mind, even though the two cops there would probably fuck up the evidence. But there were other more important issues. He could go to the Euston Street fire, where at least six homes were burning. How many more homes? How many more victims?

The rain suddenly slowed to a drizzle.

"Shit," he said. "Fucking shit. What the fuck do I do?"

Then it occurred to him. The shelter was his only chance of survival. If Ralph got out of jail tonight, and Marty didn't have enough evidence to hold him, what would he do? Would he go to Sandra's, house, kill her and Cray, and destroy the shelter? Maybe a stretch, but Marty didn't put anything past the freak. He called the holding cell cop, Peter Myers, to ascertain Ralph's whereabouts. With any luck, Ralph would be passed out, giving Marty more time to think things through. Myers didn't answer. "Shit."

Marty started the car, reversed quickly, and spun tires on wet pavement with one mission in mind—find out if Ralph was still in lockup. Penny was going to have to wait. The most important thing he could do now was to survive and preserve the lives of those necessary for that survival.

He turned the police siren on. He weaved adeptly in and out of traffic. *Preserve the lives of those necessary to my survival. Elaine. I'm sure as hell gonna need her.* He *had* included her in his end-of-days planning, but she hadn't consented. He checked the time—1:36 am—and dialed her number anyway. *Pick up, honey. Pick up.*

She did. "Marty, is something wrong?"

"Something is very wrong. I need you here."

"What's the matter? You sound panicked."

"Things are going from bad to worse, fast. I need you here."

"I know. We have a bad storm here, but not as bad as there from what I hear. I'm watching the news right now. So many natural disasters happening everywhere. Are you okay?"

"I'm okay. Listen, this is a matter of life and death. Do you have power?"

"Yes."

"Pack what you think is important and book a plane ticket for tomorrow There's a flight that arrives at six. Maybe you can get on it. I'll pick you up at the airport."

"What?"

"You heard me, Elaine."

"I can't do that, I have patients... "

"Fuck your patients. The end of the world is coming!"

"What?"

"You heard me... "

"I don't know... I can't just..." Her voice was drowned by static and then the connection dropped.

He was about to call back, but saw a man in dark clothes step off the curb, fling his arms out, and dart in front of him. As Marty approached, the man suddenly fell onto the road, in his path. Marty slammed on the brakes. His phone flew out of his hands, hit the windshield, and bounced along the dashboard. He skidded to a stop, hoping he wouldn't hear the sound of tires crunching human flesh and bones.

Opening the door, he heard an agonized cry. He stepped out and rushed to the front of the car. The man was lying face-first on the asphalt. He looked vaguely familiar. But who? He bent down and tapped the man's shoulder. "Are you okay?"

The man lifted his head and looked at Marty, wide-eyed and horrified. "The end is nigh," Pastor Jon said. "Prepare yourself!"

# Chapter Ten

Sandra held Jake Hamilton's hand as they strolled down the street that sunny afternoon. She squeezed it. He turned to her, his deep brown eyes dazzling and mesmerizing her as they often did. Then he gave her that million-dollar smile. "Everything okay, sweetie?"

She stopped, squeezing his hand a little tighter. "Everything is more than okay. It's amazing. It's excellent. I love you so much."

Jake moved in closer, enveloping her tightly in both arms and planting a long, passionate wet kiss on her lips. "I love you, too."

They continued on, oblivious to the lookers and the gawkers in the downtown core. Sandra couldn't be happier. Her nursing career was going well, her relationship with her parents was close, intimate, and loving, and her romance with Jake had blossomed like a red rose, naturally, into a passionate love affair. One that contained all the elements for longevity: honesty, respect, trust, good communication, and of course, love, the glue that securely bonded everything together. They hadn't gone too fast, starting off as friends after that first chance meeting in a coffee shop. The friendship lasted three months, until one night during a candle-lit dinner at Jake's downtown apartment, they both fell passionately into each other's arms, practically tearing each other's clothes off and making love on the kitchen table, untouched spaghetti Bolognese plates simmering beside them. That first time left Sandra with a warm tingly sensation every time she thought about it. And the warmth turned into hot molten lava after the second, third, fourth times. With Jake, it just kept getting better and better.

Now, three years into the union, she was ready for the next step. Living together. She had no doubt Jake felt the same way. An electrical engineer, he had an uncanny ability to know what she was thinking even before she did. He would often complete her sentences, say what she was about to say, or suggest a plan for the evening that she couldn't have scripted any better.

They approached a busy intersection and stopped at the crosswalk. Jake released her hand and pressed the pedestrian button. They stood and waited, eyeing each other fondly. "You know, I was thinking of something," he said.

"Oh, *you* think?"

"Occasionally, but I try not to do it too often. It makes my head hurt."

Sandra laughed. "What were you thinking, baby?"

He turned to her with those penetrating eyes. "That we should move in together. Sell our places and buy something together. Not yours, not mine. Ours."

"Oh my God," she said, hugging him tightly. "You read my mind again. I love you to death."

The pedestrian crosswalk light turned green. A grizzly-looking man nearby scowled at them. "Get a room, for fuck sakes."

Sandra released Jake's hand. She threw her arms up in resignation to the man, as if to say, "Hey, we're in love. Give us a break."

She reached for Jake's hand again. But he had already stepped off the curb. That was when a speeding bus plowed into him. Sandra froze in fear. The blood-curdling sound of bones snapping. A short, shrill scream. Jake flew through the air and landed in the middle of the busy road. Then a pickup truck ran him over, killing him instantly.

Sandra screamed. "No, no, no, no... please God, nooooooo... "

She opened her eyes and bolted upright in bed. It was 7:36 am on June 6$^{th}$. Her heart pounded in her chest. Beads of sweat dribbled down her face. Her breath came in short, panicked gasps. She tried to steady her breathing. *A dream. Only a dream. Jake isn't real. You are... where am I?* Her throat was parched and her head ached dully. She touched it and felt a large goose egg and blood-encrusted bandage gauze. *What happened?* She looked around the room, saw the familiar floral-patterned sheers covering the two windows facing her bed, rays of sunlight streaming in, and it came to her. *I'm home. I fell. I hit my head.*

But the next question was even more disturbing. *Who am I?* Peeling blankets back quickly, she examined her clothes: black bra and panties, a black oversized t-shirt. *Who undressed me?* She noticed a bandage on her ankle and examined it. *Someone got me to bed, took care of me. Who? More importantly, who are you?* She touched the ankle bandage as if tactile sensation would stimulate memory.

A knock on the door.

"Who is it?"

"It's me. I've got coffee."

"Who's me?"

"Sandra, it's Cray."

"Wait a minute."

"Are you okay?"

"Yes." But she wasn't. Her memory was selective. She didn't know who she was, who this man calling himself Cray was. *This isn't good at all. Concussion. This man helped me. He must be good. Maybe his face will bring it all back.* "Come in."

The door opened. Cray held a tray of coffee and condiments. His head was wrapped with blood-stained gauze and most of his right hand was bandaged. He wore A PROUD CANADIAN t-shirt. He entered the room and set the tray on a bedside table. "How do you feel?" His brow was creased with worry, intense concern etched into deep green eyes, enlarged behind black-rimmed glasses.

"You look like a post-apocalyptic survivor," Sandra said.

With that observation, the memory of who *he* was, who *she* was, where everyone fit into the grim picture, suddenly flooded back in like a giant tidal wave. The thoughts were dizzying. She laid her head back down on the pillow. Her mind swam as it assembled the pieces, clicking them into place a hundred times faster than words could explain. The fog cleared a little. She sat up in bed. Cray quickly tucked two extra pillows behind her back and head.

"Easy," Cray said. "You had quite a fall last night. You want some coffee?"

"Thanks. One cream and one sugar, if you don't mind."

Cray fixed it and handed her a cup. "Do you remember anything? You looked at me like I was an alien."

She sipped. "Sorry, I didn't remember anything for a while there. That was terrifying as hell."

"You remember me?"

"Yes, but after the fall everything went dark. What happened?"

He explained the story, saying he had carried her up to the bedroom after disinfecting and bandaging her head and ankle. "You were in and out of consciousness. I was panicking a bit. Power was down. Called 911. Hospital staff overwhelmed. No one would come. I had no choice but to put you to bed and hope for the best."

She tugged on the oversized t-shirt. "I see you got me a nightdress."

Cray's cheeks reddened. "Sorry about that. Your jeans and your other shirt were full of glass particles. And blood. I didn't peek."

"That's okay. Thanks for looking after me."

"It's okay. At least the power is back on."

"It is?"

"Yeah, came on at 5:36 this morning."

"You were up all night?"

Cray nodded. "I didn't know what else to do. I didn't want you slipping into a coma, although I guess I couldn't have prevented it. I just felt more vigilant at your bedside keeping an eye on you."

"Did I say anything, you know, when I was conscious?"

"A few things, but not many."

"What?"

"You said, 'We're all gonna die... I don't wanna die.' Sometimes you would wake up, look into my eyes and ask, 'Who are you?'"

"Holy shit. I was really far gone."

"One time you called me Jake. Do you know a Jake?"

*Jake? Do I know a Jake? Of course I do.* "I don't know."

"It might come to you. Anyway, you did eventually doze off. Your breathing was even. I started to think you'd be okay."

"After I hit my head, it was complete black-out."

"Shouldn't you get your head examined?"

As a nurse, Sandra knew that diagnosing the severity of head concussions was inconclusive at best, totally inaccurate at worst. But that was medical science when it came to the human brain. So many mysteries, so much unexplainable and unpredictable. Yet her training said yes, she should have a CAT scan done. At least get some kind of assurance that she didn't have any serious brain damage. But, on the other hand, sometimes nurses make the worst patients, and she wasn't exactly an exception. She thought of Penny, Ralph, other unknown storm victims. "Can you get me two Tylenols? They're in the bathroom in the medicine cabinet."

Cray got up, went to the bathroom, and returned with two Tylenols and a glass of water.

She swallowed them. "Tell me, what happened to Penny?"

"Last I heard, Marty was taking her to the hospital."

She started to get up. The room spun and swept her back down. She waited for the dizziness to pass. "I should go into work. See if Penny is okay."

"I don't think you're fit to work, but I'll drive you in for a head X-ray. I'm definitely not going to work today. We have more important things to do."

"Let me think for a bit. Did you hear more about the storm?"

Cray's brow creased, the head gauze floating up with the lines. "Not good. Heard on the radio earlier that eighteen homes were destroyed, sixteen people burned to death, two more struck by lightning and killed. Another eighteen survivors being treated in the hospital. Some homes are still burning."

"Shit, they need me."

"Sandra, you're in no shape for work."

"Maybe you're right. What about Ralph?"

"Marty doesn't have enough evidence to hold him, remember?"

"No." *Jake? Who is Jake? Jake's dead.*

Cray's gaze shot across the room to an armchair. She followed his eyes to the shotgun on the chair. "He's probably at his house across the highway," Cray said. "Or at least on his way there."

"What should we do?"

"How about you stay in bed, get some rest, and I'll make breakfast? Bacon and eggs sound good?"

"I feel like a fool, Cray. Charlottetown is burning."

"Well, first things first. You can't help others if you can't help yourself."

She threw up her hands. Cray rose from his bedside perch, grabbed the shotgun, and turned around when he reached the door. "How do you like your eggs?"

"Sunny-side up. I want some hope."

"Sunny-side up it is." He disappeared down the stairs.

Sandra sat up slowly and sipped coffee. Part of her wanted to rest, the other natural caregiving part said go and help the storm victims. She saw her blood-stained clothes in a clump on a throw rug. She set her coffee down, shifted and slowly got up. She carefully went to the pile of clothes, picked up her jeans, and searched through the pockets. She found her phone, threw the clothes in a laundry basket, sat on the bed, and turned it on. Two missed calls from Penny Miles; one at 2:36 am, another at 7:15 am. She went into the bathroom and examined herself in the mirror, the appetizing aroma of sizzling Canadian back bacon drifting upstairs. Her stomach growled. Hungry. A good sign.

There was a black circle below her right eye. The eye was bloodshot and partly closed, unlike the left eye, deep green iris contrasting with a bright white sclera. Good sign. At least in one eye. Strands of her long black hair poked out from the gauze and were matted to her face with crusted blood. She tried a smile in the mirror and it came off as posed, plastic, in spite of her straight white teeth. At least none of those had been knocked out in the fall. She moved closer to the mirror, noticing a small cut on her lower lip that had already scabbed over. She washed her hands in the sink, dried them, and slowly removed the gauze around her head. She wanted to get a better look at the injury, evaluate Cray's medical care. He wasn't a doctor. Maybe she needed stitches. But what she saw when she removed the gauze was encouraging. On her forehead was a small goose egg, marked with a clean, one-inch-long cut. Not large enough for stitches, certainly. It should heal on its own nicely, probably wouldn't even leave a scar. It was crusted with blood and a topical antibiotic. She would remove the gauze, clean and disinfect it, and replace it with a small adhesive bandage after showering.

Her nightmare flooded back. She realized with sudden clarity who Jake was. He was real. He was her boyfriend. He was dead, killed three years ago after stepping off the curb at the wrong place at the wrong time. She bent down, put a hand to her head, and tried to suppress the tears. They came. And as they flowed, she remembered the other deaths a short two weeks after Jake's untimely passing.

One evening her loving parents, Lester and Simone, had been returning to Vancouver from a short weekend vacation in Whistler. The roads on Highway 99 were wet and slippery, visibility low—the result of a torrential thunderstorm. Rounding a hairpin turn, her father had lost control of the vehicle. It had smashed through the guardrail and launched missile-like in the air. It landed in the forest and exploded into a ball of flames, killing them instantly. So much misery in such a short time—the reason for her sudden exodus from Vancouver and her new life on Prince Edward Island.

*What new life? It's exploding into a ball of flames. Just like theirs.* The thought of self-preservation stopped her tears. She towel-dried her face, realizing for the first time she was sitting on the toilet. She stood.

A wave of dizziness swept over her and she put both hands on the vanity sink, steadying herself. The room spun and her vision blurred. Looking at her image in the mirror, she watched it slowly come into focus. She took a couple of deep breaths and plodded on, slowly undressing.

She closed and locked the bathroom door, then stepped into the shower. *Don't get overcome by emotion. Forward, not backward.* So many things to do. So little time. This Charlottetown blaze was just a small spark in a massive fire that would destroy the world. One chapter of her life was ending, and a terrifying chapter was just beginning. She willed herself to be strong, be brave... *fight for your life. Go to the hospital. Get your head examined. See Penny. Discuss the details of the shelter with Cray. Stock it. Solve the Ralph problem...*

******

Cray started to rush upstairs when he heard the shower going, but the phone stopped him in his tracks. He carefully lifted two fried eggs from the frying pan, set them on a plate, and answered the phone.

Marty dispensed with social niceties. His tone was agitated, almost desperate. "The city is burning. The wildfire in Alberta is out of control and heading east rapidly. I need to know now if you want us."

"Can I call you back in fifteen minutes? Sandra's in the shower."

"Please, no longer than that. I'm trying to get my wife over here tonight."

"Okay."

"Be careful. You need to know Ralph left the holding cell with his lawyer twenty minutes ago. He'll be home soon."

Cray bit his lip. "Okay. How's Penny?"

"They kept her in the hospital overnight for observation. I think she'll be fine. I've been up all night dealing with burn victims, and haven't had a chance to follow up with the investigation. It's low priority now."

Cray could hear faint but agonized shouts and screams in the background. "Are you okay?"

"Yes... something else. I have Pastor Jon with me. He's locked in my patrol car, watching the city burn."

"Shit... what a fucking nightmare." Cray was about to tell Marty about Sandra's accident, but he heard a loud, painful shriek on the other end, and then Marty's desperate voice mixed with loud static.

"I gotta go... call me in fift—"

Cray helped Sandra downstairs after she showered and dressed. She had insisted she could manage independently, but in light of her recurring dizzy spells, he vetoed that idea. He tried to kybosh the notion of Sandra leaving the bedroom at all but that had gone over like a lead balloon. She was a determined woman.

In the kitchen, they ate breakfast and listened to the radio. Cray picked up a piece of crispy bacon and bit into it as he eyed Sandra. In spite of the fall, she was looking a lot better. Her shiny black hair was tied back in a ponytail, a small bandage on her head. She wore a black CANADIAN FORCES baseball cap. Her white Nike t-shirt proclaimed JUST DO IT! A new pair of tight Levi's blue jeans and black and white Nike joggers completed the look of preparation and determination.

The radio squawked and came to life: "Officials are asking local residents to avoid travel to Charlottetown today.

A house fire that started last night as a result of a lightning strike now covers a two-block radius. Twenty-seven people are dead, twenty-six people are being treated for burns in local hospitals, and twenty-two homes have been destroyed. Firefighters from New Brunswick and Nova Scotia have been called in and the city mayor is close to declaring a state of emergency..."

Cray frowned and got right to the point. "Marty called while you were showering. He wants to know if he and his wife can join us in the shelter."

Sandra crunched into a piece of bacon. "I think so. What do you think?"

"I got a good vibe about Marty now. I say yes to both of them. If he's good, I'll bet Elaine's solid."

Sandra twirled her egg yolk with a fork, dabbing a piece of toast into the liquefied result. She took a bite. "Okay, done."

"A state of emergency has been declared in Alberta resulting from a forest fire that is now burning out of control. The fire, which started in Fort McMurray, has sparked massive evacuations, killed two hundred and thirty-six people, and injured another hundred and forty-seven. Officials say the fire is moving faster than anything they have ever seen and is threatening to cross the border into Saskatchewan..."

"I'll call Marty," Cray said.

"Do that. And if he asks what we're doing, tell him we're going to Charlottetown to get the last of our emergency supplies and say our goodbyes."

Cray reached Marty. "You're in. We're heading to town to stock up... " After a moment, he hung up. "He says he'll meet us at the shelter at nine tonight. He's bringing guns, ammo, and other stuff."

"In world news, a terrorist group has claimed responsibility for a suicide bombing that claimed the lives of over a hundred and fifty people in a busy shopping district in Baghdad last night. This marks the latest in a series of coordinated suicide bombings around the world in the last two weeks that have claimed over seven hundred lives..."

Finishing the last of her breakfast—she wolfed it down like it was her last day on Earth—Sandra tried to stand. She wobbled slightly and grabbed the table for support. She regained her balance. "I'm gonna make a few calls. Let me look at your hand before we leave."

Cray tried to help her but she dismissed him with a wave, turned around slowly, and went into the living room.

Cray stared at the gooey egg mixture on his plate, beside a half-eaten piece of toast and two pieces of bacon. He lifted a piece of bacon to his mouth.

"Terrorists threatened today on social media they will begin systematically executing Canadians on a kill list that contains about eighty-three hundred names..."

He threw the bacon on the plate. He picked up both plates, emptied the leftovers into the garbage, and hand-washed the plates, careful to keep his bandaged hand away from the hot water.

"A heat wave in India has caused temperatures to flare to fifty-five degrees Celsius, sparking a dozen fires, and killing thirty-seven people. Officials say..."

Cray clicked the radio off. Enough already.

Sitting in his Black Ford Escape an hour later, Cray looked at Sandra, his face tight with concern. "Are you sure you want to do this? Are you sure you're up for this?"

"Get going. We don't have a choice."

He glanced in the backseat, the barrel of the Colt 45 revolver, the double barrels of the shotgun, glowing a molten gold hue in the sun's rays. "You sure we need these?"

"Cray, the rules have changed. Can't you see that? I don't give a fuck about Ralph or the murder investigation anymore. If he tries anything, I'll put a bullet right in his stupid fucking head."

"You're right. What the fuck am I thinking?"

"You're not."

As they turned onto the highway, they saw Ralph's pickup parked diagonally across his front lawn, fresh skid-tracks leading to the rear tires. The truck bed was stuffed with assorted supplies: a chainsaw, foodstuffs, bottled water, pots and pans. Wearing dirty coveralls and a shit-eating grin, he stood beside it. One hand gripped the handle of a pitchfork, one work-booted foot resting on the sharp metal of its business end.

As they passed, his grin widened and he waved to them.

They waved back.

"Do you know why we did that?" Cray asked.

"Keep your friends close, your enemies closer."

"You believe that?"

"I don't know. But it's all I could think of to say."

They were silent for a few minutes, alone with their thoughts. Finally, Sandra pointed up. "Look at that plume of smoke over Charlottetown. Nasty."

"I know. But see something else in the distance? There's a bank of clouds rolling in. Maybe it'll rain again."

"I sure hope so. This day hasn't started off so great."

"No, it hasn't." Cray examined the new bandage Sandra had applied to his hand after he'd showered. He flexed the hand. It stung a little. "You say it'll be okay?"

She nodded. "It doesn't looks like it penetrated bone or flexor tendons. You say you can move it all right?"

"Yeah."

"You're lucky." She had also re-examined his head wounds before they left, and cleaned and re-bandaged the small cut near his ear. "How's your head feel?"

"I'm okay. You?"

"Occasional dizzy spells. Dull pain."

"Are you gonna get a CAT scan?"

"We'll see."

By the time they arrived at the hospital, weaving around panic-stricken drivers, the sky was completely overcast, a gray-black mixture of smoke and rain clouds. Instead of the dawn of a new day, it looked like the dusk of an old day. The plan was for Sandra to get a CAT scan and visit her friend Penny. Despite her urgings to have his injuries examined by a specialist, Cray refused. It was a death zone in there, and he wanted no part of it. His plan was to collect some things from his apartment; shop for some necessities; call his family and return to the hospital to pick up Sandra when she was done. He doubted any of it would go to plan, but at least he had one.

Cray parked a good seventy feet from the EMERGENCY doors. Any closer would mean getting trapped by a parade of incoming and outgoing vehicles. Two ambulances were parked out front. Other vehicles sped in, one Volkswagen Beetle bumping over a curb, driving over the lawn, and coming to a skidding stop a few feet from the building. Amid pained screams and shouts, medical staff unloaded the dead and wounded. An ambulance siren blared as the frantic driver attempted to leave to collect more burn victims. The carnage was being directed by an agitated finger-pointing police officer attempting with marginal success to impose order on chaos.

"I'll call you," Sandra said, climbing out of the car.

"Do you want me to walk you to the door?"

"Not if you're not coming in. Don't you want to meet Penny?"

"I met her."

"You know what I mean. What if she wants to come? What should I tell her?"

Current circumstances dictated they weren't in a position to have a board meeting on the matter. They had covered some ground last night, but Cray wasn't sure how much of it Sandra remembered in light of her injury. He made a snap decision. "Your call. You want her to come, she comes."

Sandra looked annoyed. "Jake... I mean, Cray... that's not what we agreed."

"Sandra, the rules have changed. Besides, I feel sorry for her... "

# Chapter Eleven

Frantically rummaging around inside his apartment an hour later, Cray was surprised he couldn't find his parent's house phone number. It had been, what, a month since he'd spoken to them? It must be in his smartphone somewhere then. In the bedroom, he stopped fishing through a drawer of miscellaneous papers, and dug his phone from his pocket. He scrolled through the call log. It was not readily apparent. He stopped scrolling. "You fucking idiot."

In the anxiety of gathering up his worldly possessions before his world came crashing down, he had overlooked the obvious. Look the number up on the internet. He did that and soon found the right Lenning on the right street.

He sat on the bed, breathing deeply, and thought about how to word it. Deciding there was no easy way to say it, he made the call.

His father Glen answered on the second ring. "Hello."

"Glen, it's me." After turning twenty, Cray had stopped calling his father Dad. Maybe it was revenge for how his father referenced *him*.

"Cray, are you okay?"

He knew his father scorned profanity, but he said it anyway. "I'm okay... but we're in a world of shit."

"I watch the news, Cray. I know what's happening. You talking about the fires?"

"Yes, the fires. But there's more to it than you might think."

A pause. "What's that supposed to mean?"

Cray sighed deeply before continuing. "The world... the world is coming to an end."

"Have you lost your mind? How would you know?"

"Never mind that now. Listen, Glen. Fire will burn everything. And everybody. And it looks like it'll happen before June 30$^{th}$. Get Mom and take cover in an underground shelter if you can. Stock it with supplies... "

"I will do no such thing."

"Please do it... or you'll die! Warn Darlene and Caleb for me. I'm not gonna keep you. I don't have time. I wanna thank you for raising me. I know I have a hard time saying it, but I love you. I wish I could have turned out more to your liking."

Glen's voice was calmer now, tinged with emotion. "I love you, too... son. Don't go doing anything stupid. Maybe you should consult a psychologist... "

"I don't have time. Glen... uh, Dad, can I speak to Mom, please?"

"She's gone shopping. I'll tell her... " The line went static. The call dropped.

"Shit. Fucking shit." Cray was becoming overwhelmed with emotion and it took a moment for him to calm down. When he did, he called his brother Caleb and left a message on his professional-sounding voicemail. "I don't know any other way to say this, Caleb, but the entire planet is gonna burn to ashes soon. Find a shelter and get underground with supplies. I love you."

Another voice message to his sister, Darlene: "Sis, it's me, Cray. I know we haven't been that close lately, but if ever there was a time to put differences aside, the time is now.

The world is burning to the ground. Right now! Get supplies and get to an underground shelter. Now! Please, take me seriously... I'm not crazy... please!"

He called his mother Mary's cell phone and got voicemail. He left a message: "Mom, it's me. Glen's probably gonna tell you I'm crazy, but I'm not. The world is burning to ashes. Get supplies, find an underground shelter, and hole up... I love you."

As emotion threatened to overcome him, Cray began scrambling around the apartment, stuffing clothes and other essential items into a small knapsack. *Do. Don't think. Do.* It took some time to decide what he would and wouldn't need on a trip such as this. A trip into a new existence, possibly devoid of technology. He finished stuffing the knapsack, and began filling plastic bags with dried food items: beans, Kraft macaroni and cheese, instant oatmeal, coffee, canned tuna, and the like. After filling three bags, he surveyed the apartment and, beginning to panic, thought of what he might have forgotten. *You always forget something. Goes without saying.* He returned to the bedroom and, rummaging through a bedside dresser, found what he was looking for—the remainder of his identification, including his passport, social security card, health care card, birth certificate, and a few credit cards. He stuffed them into a zippered pocket of the black travel pants he had changed into. He would definitely need the credit cards. He planned on maxing them out on supplies before returning to Sandra's shelter. Credit meant a lot right now. Credit rating, that didn't mean shit.

About to close the dresser drawer, he spotted a picture of Emma Thymes, his ex. Picking it up and examining it, he sat on the bed. It had been taken on Panmure Island beach at the beginning of their three-year union. That was seven years ago. They had asked a Japanese tourist to snap the photo. A beaming and in-love Cray, wearing shorts and a yellow t-shirt, stood backdropped by the red sandy beach, bright blue cloudless sky, calm water, and his arm around Emma. Clad in a yellow polka-dotted bikini, she smiled brightly. Her resemblance to Pamela Lee Anderson was uncanny, right down to her sensuous curves. The photo was torn halfway down the middle, stopping at the tip of Emma's blonde hair. After that fateful day of infidelity, Cray had planned to tear it to shreds and burn it, but emotion and a bitter conviction had gotten the better of him. He had instead tossed it into the dresser drawer, looking at it every few months to serve as a reminder of why not to wear your heart on your sleeve; why not to open your heart to a woman; why not to forge a bond of deep intimacy; why not to develop too many close friends, male or female.

A small wave of anger, hatred, and resentment rose up in Cray, broke, and fanned out on the ocean of emotion. Unexpectedly, the deep blue waters became calm and serene. He no longer wanted to kill Emma for cheating on him, or murder his so-called best friend Greg Smallton for betraying his trust. Brought on by horrific circumstances, Cray felt a change taking place in his heart. Instead of hating his betrayers, he suddenly felt only sorrow and pity for them. Would their relationship last? How successful could a relationship based on betrayal possibly be?

For his part, he had never cheated on Emma. Sure, he had admired other beauties. He was a man after all, and certainly had eyes. But he had been careful not to let Emma catch his sometimes wandering eyes. He had never betrayed her trust and bent over backwards to treat her with kindness, love, and respect. If anything, he now realized, perhaps he'd been too good to her. Didn't women get turned on by bad boys? The opposite of Cray, the modus operandi of Greg. That, and let's face it, Greg was a much better-looking guy than Cray. People had often said Greg resembled a young Marlon Brando; Cray, a studious and nerdy computer geek. *Black and white, black and gray, Greg and Cray...*

Before he even realized what he was doing, he found Emma's number in his phone. He dialed it. *What the hell am I doing?*

She answered on the first ring. "My God, Cray. It's been so long."

It had indeed been four years. "Yes."

"How are you?"

"I'm okay. And you?"

There was a long pause. "No point in bullshitting you now. I tried that before and it didn't work for very long. I caught Greg cheating on me about a week ago. We're through. I guess Karma's a bitch, eh? When you least expect it to, it bites you right in the ass. In my case, the heart."

"Sorry to hear that."

A long pause. "I don't think you are, Cray. You have no reason to be after what I did to you."

"I don't want to talk about that now. I *am* sorry to hear it. I forgive you. I've been harboring anger and hatred for too many years. The only person who it's fucked up is me. I'm done with it, or at least I'm trying to be done with it."

There was a long pause. Emma's response was heavy with sadness. "I'm sorry for what I did to you. You didn't deserve it. You deserve better than me. It took this for me to realize that..."

"I appreciate that, Emma. I really do. But I didn't call you for an apology, or even offer my forgiveness, although, as I said, I *do* forgive you."

"Why *did* you call?"

"I called to warn you. Don't ask me how I know. I don't have time for that right now. But the world is burning to the ground. If you want to survive, you need to get to a shelter, stock it with supplies, and stay underground until..."

The connection went static.

A loud explosion rocked the apartment building. Through the bedroom window, Cray saw a flash of fiery red flames fan out and flare up an otherwise black sky. A bedside lamp flickered and popped. The light bulb turned black.

"Emma, can you hear me?" The static stopped, replaced by a dead silence.

Cray called Emma again but received voicemail. He clicked the call dead without leaving a message, grabbed his knapsack and three plastic bags of supplies, and headed for the door. No time to waste. The city was burning.

As he locked his door, thinking it would be the last time he ever saw his apartment, his ninety-six-year-old neighbor approached. Miss Smith, as everyone called her, held a mop in her hands. Her gray hair flew in all directions, as if she had stuck her finger into an electrical outlet. Her gray dress drooped on her boney frame. Black sockets framed hollow eyes. Like cracks in a dry riverbed, deep creases lined her face.

"You going somewhere?" she asked.

Another explosion, more distant this time, shook the building. She put a hand on the wall to steady herself and, in doing so, dropped the mop. Cray set down his bags, picked it up, and handed it to her. It was heavy, dripping with water.

"The city is burning," Cray said. "I'm evacuating. You should leave here."

She took the mop. "I'm not going anywhere." Her voice was weak, hoarse. "News says stay inside until further notice. There's no evacuation order. I'm an old hag. If it's my time, it's my time. All there is to it."

"I'm going underground. You would be well-advised to do the same."

"I'm staying put." She waved the mop. "Besides, my toilet's overflowing and I'm mopping up shit creek and ass wipe. You got a plunger, by the way? Up shit creek without a paddle. You know the saying."

Cray picked up his bags, studying her resilience. *Up shit creek without a paddle. She doesn't know how right she is.* "No, I don't. Sorry. I gotta run, Miss Smith. Hang in there."

As he reached the exit door at the end of the hall, he heard her mutter, "I always hang in there. Better than hanging from my neck, like your buddy."

Cray's face tightened, casting her a sideways glance as he opened the door. *Insensitive bitch.* He heard her knocking on another apartment door as he hurried down the stairs.

Fucking city was burning and all she could think about was cleaning up shit.

Stepping out onto Victoria Street, he grimaced at the pandemonium. Like a caged rat, his heart pounded in his chest and his throat became parched. Amidst wailing sirens, the panicked screams and shouts of fleeing pedestrians, and hum of rapidly exiting vehicles, he looked up at the sky. It was just before one in the afternoon, but it could have been midnight. In the distance three blazes burned, flames licking higher and higher into an ominous gray-black mass. It had stopped raining and a large circle of ash and hot embers swirled in the air. Like a possessed demon, a small black and red apparition separated from the mass, fanned out, swooped down, and chased a man down the street. Mesmerized, Cray watched as it engulfed the man, swirling around him furiously as he screamed horribly. Man and hot ash apparition morphed into a black and red tornado, spun violently, and disappeared down the street. Was it burning him up? Cray didn't wait around to find out. He quickly located his vehicle, popped the back hatch, tossed the supplies haphazardly inside, and approached the driver's door. Opening it, he was startled by a whooshing sound and spun around.

A beach-ball of fire, about thirty feet away, hurled toward him, accelerating rapidly as it attacked. "Holy fucking shit." Cray quickly climbed into the vehicle and slammed the door shut. He felt a hot flash engulf his back, arm and neck as he started the vehicle. He smelled burning clothing. Glancing to his left, he saw a small fire ignite on his shoulder, just a candlelight, really. He quickly patted it out and watched as the flame ball swirled above his vehicle for a moment, then attacked a young woman who had just exited her home. Screaming as it approached, she turned quickly and fled to the safety of her home.

As he pulled out onto the catastrophe-ridden street, he saw it circle her door momentarily, hover above her bay window, and then crash right through it. He heard another terrifying scream and then the house exploded into a massive ball of flame, raining burning debris onto his vehicle as he turned left onto Spring Park Road. A loud thump startled him and he jerked the wheel spasmodically, narrowly missing a gushing fire hydrant. He leveled his trajectory, turning on the windshield wipers and washer spray to clear the windshield of ash and debris. When the windshield cleared, with widening terror-filled eyes, he saw it—a severed arm burning brightly on the dented hood of his Ford Escape.

There was no time for Walmart, no time for more supplies, he quickly realized, jerking the wheel again. The flaming arm—*Was it the woman's arm?*—bumped along the hood and flew off, landing on the neatly-trimmed hedge of a quaint white Victorian home. A small fire ignited on the hedge. The flames quickly spread, becoming a wall of flame that raced toward the home. A fat, bald man emerged, flipping Cray the bird and running for his nearby garden hose.

Cray arrived at Kirkwood Drive, barely stopped, turned right, and sped along in the enveloping black haze and ash, with only one goal in mind—get to the hospital, get Sandra, and get the fuck out of here.

Stopping briefly at the Queen Street intersection, he looked both ways, barely able to see anything in the reduced visibility produced by the fires. He accelerated into the black haze, glanced right, and noticed—too late, he realized—two luminous white eyes approach. The crunching of metal, a loud smash. His head jerked, slamming into the driver window, and his vehicle spun around in the intersection as it was struck.

Entangled, both vehicles spun to a stop. Cray heard shouting as he lifted his head, trying desperately to clear the cobwebs. "Goddammit, not another concussion." He heard a car door click open and slam shut. The angry, incomprehensible voice grew closer in the darkness. Then he understood the words loud and clear: "Get outta the car, motherfucker! You're gonna pay for your stupidity."

******

Contrary to all her years of medical training, Sandra felt a nervous anxiety bordering on panic as she stood over Penny's bedside watching the woman sleep. The grim landscape outside the window didn't help—black and gray, punctuated by fiery red bursts, advancing closer as the clock ticked. She took a few deep breaths, trying to still her mind and body. *What a world of shit.* Her CAT scan had indicated a somewhat inconclusive result. A concussion that was somewhere between moderate and severe. Some gray zone that defied textbook definition. But the symptoms were there; temporary loss of consciousness, confusion and fogginess, amnesia, dizziness, ringing ears, sensitivity to light and noise, nausea, and vomiting. Doctor's orders were to go straight home and get some rest. Only problem was, she couldn't reach Cray. Three recent calls had gone straight to voicemail.

So, against the doctor's orders, she had gone to work. She had quickly changed into green surgical scrubs and had begun bandaging burn victims, calming them, and administering doctor-prescribed medications. Exhausted and queasy from the effort, she'd just left the chaos of the main-floor burn unit and taken the elevator up to the third floor, still sporting blood-soaked surgical garments. Victims were filling the hospital so fast that staff were sending people home who weren't critical. The beds were almost full and some of the injured were even being taken to nearby hospitals.

Penny, on the other hand, had been earmarked for discharge. Her chart revealed only a mild concussion, two black eyes, a small cut on her forehead (requiring six stitches), some bruising around her vaginal area, and psychological shock trauma. But there wasn't time or resources for a hospital shrink now; they were running ragged, breaking tragic news of death by fire to grieving family members.

With black sockets around both eyes, Penny resembled a raccoon, Sandra thought, as she bent to touch her friend's arm. But before she reached it, Penny stirred and opened her eyes.

As she did, Sandra's vision grew foggy and the room spun. Harsh overhead fluorescent lights flickered. Given the chaos erupting around town, Sandra didn't know if it was her condition causing the flickering or the natural disasters. She grabbed the arm of a nearby chair and slumped into it.

"Are you okay?" Penny said.

After a moment the room stopped spinning and the lighting stabilized. "Yes, I am. How are you?"

Penny brushed a clump of matted hair away from her forehead. "I wanna go home."

Sandra nodded. "Were the lights just flickering?"

"No. Not that I saw."

*Shit, I'm not doing so well. May as well come right out with it.* "The city is burning, Penny. They're discharging everyone who isn't in dire straits. You *can* go home. They want you to go, need you to go. People who are in worse condition than you need your bed."

Penny got out of bed. "What are we waiting for? Let's go."

Doctor Daniel Ames appeared at the door with a man in a wheelchair. The man's arms, chest, and head were wrapped in bandage gauze. Small holes in the white and blood-red gauze delineated eyes, nose and mouth. A pink froth dribbled from the mouth hole as did a slow, pained wheezing sound.

"You ready?" Daniel said.

Sandra nodded. Arms wrapped around each other's shoulders, she and Penny staggered aside as Daniel quickly wheeled the man bedside. A nurse and a porter followed him in and they began carefully helping the man onto Penny's bed.

He moaned loudly. "I don't wanna die." His voice was weak and hoarse, his tone defeated.

"You're not gonna die," Daniel said. "Calm down, please." He turned to Sandra. "Get out of here. Now! You're in no condition for this."

Amidst the chaos, the women wandered down the hospital hallway, arm in arm. Sandra couldn't help feeling like it was a case of the blind leading the blind. She had no idea how to get home. Then it came to her. The obvious.

*Marty.*

******

Of all the things Detective Marty Strader imagined doing on this day, training a gushing fire hose on a burning building wasn't one of them. But two firefighters had already been killed battling the blaze, and firefighter Ben Anderson, whose hose Marty now held, had just been rushed to the hospital with third-degree burns covering most of his body. Ben's horrific screams still echoed in Marty's head as he doused the remainder of small flames that had decimated a house, and quickly refocused the hose to another, larger fire that was rapidly inching toward him. He removed a muscle-cramped hand from the hose and wiped a small tributary of sweat from his sizzling forehead. Then he quickly clamped the hand back on the hose and resumed his new firefighter duties.

Twenty feet beside him, another firefighter brought the gushing stream of his hose in line with Marty's trajectory. Beside him, another cop-turned-firefighter, armed with a blasting hose, did the same. Others were positioned on the far side of the blaze, trying to circle and corral it with their hoses.

Behind them were two firetrucks, two ambulances, and ten cop cars. A few spectators had stayed to watch and film the action, but most of them had fled.

"Over there," someone shouted. Marty glanced back and saw where the firefighter was pointing. Screaming in pain, a fire-engulfed man staggered out of a wall of flames. Marty blasted him with water, quickly dousing the flames. The pressurized water knocked the man on his ass, skidding him back toward the flames.

Marty handed his hose to the firefighter. "Cover me." He ran over to the downed man, picked him up, and hoisted him over his shoulder in a strong and single motion. As the man screamed, Marty, smelling burning flesh, feeling the intense heat from the wall of flames, carried him over to an ambulance and set him carefully down on the road.

He looked down at the man. Half of his face had been burned away and a large flap of bloody and burnt flesh hung from his chin. Where his eyes, nose and mouth had once been, now only a maze of blackened facial muscles, tendons, a protruding eyeball, and a macabre, twisted grin remained. "You're gonna be okay," Marty said, not believing his words.

He stood, wiping blood, flesh, and singed hair from his shoulder.

Two paramedics approached with a stretcher. Their mouths were agape with horror. "We'll take it from here," one said. "Good work."

The man's screams had subsided, replaced by pain-filled groans.

Throat parched, Marty retreated to his Crown Victoria, where he had a cooler stored. He opened a rear passenger door, opened the cooler, and removed a cold bottle of water. He popped the top and drained the contents in six quick swallows. He belched loudly, breathing deeply as he gasped for oxygen. He realized he was the only one fighting the blaze without oxygen. Suddenly feeling dizzy, he sat down on the backseat, shoving over a few hastily gathered supplies, and reached for another bottle of water. Coughing, he retrieved one, popped it open, and drained half of it in two long swallows.

"Get your vehicles back," someone shouted. "The fire's advancing."

Still dizzy, Marty got up, went around to the driver door, and opened it. Pastor Jon was slumped over in the front seat, passed out drunk, an arm curled around the steering wheel. Marty climbed in, gently removing his arm, and sliding him into the passenger seat. Pastor Jon's head bumped the passenger window. He stirred for a moment, then drifted back to sleep, snoring loudly. Marty spotted his cell phone on the seat as he closed the door. Picking it up, he scanned the missed call list: his wife Elaine, Cray, and Sandra, in that order. He started the car, began pulling away from the flames, and then got caught in traffic gridlock as the ambulance containing the man he had just rescued flashed lights, activated a wailing siren, and cut him off.

He spotted an opening in a dark alley, lit by leaping flames on both sides, and turned in, calling his wife. But the call was interrupted by an incoming call from Cray. Marty answered.

Cray's tone was panicked. "I'm stuck at the intersection of Kirkwood and Queen. I had an accident. Some angry fuck is smashing the windshield with a baseball bat. He... he's trying to kill me."

Marty was only a few blocks away. "Hang on. I'll be right there."

******

Terrified, Cray watched the baseball bat smash the windshield a third time. He could see the man's squinty red eyes, hear his angry voice with each blow. "Come on, chicken shit, get your ass outta there. Be a man."

He put the vehicle in reverse, trying again to dislodge himself from the vehicle sandwich. *What is this guy thinking? He hit me, not the other way around.* He heard the crunching of metal as the tires began moving. But his Escape stopped and the tires spun. Cray slammed the vehicle into drive, inching forward as the baseball bat smashed down again on the windshield. Again, the vehicle stopped, and the tires spun. Cray floored it, but the tires only spun some more, screeching and burning rubber. *Maybe I can smoke the fucker out.* But another idea occurred to him. He put the vehicle in Park and reached into the backseat, grabbing the Colt 45 handgun and a flashlight. Shining the flashlight through the smashed windshield, he pointed the gun at his attacker.

In the flashlight beam, he saw the menacing man clearer. Face tight and twisted. A mop of tangled dark hair, crazed eyes, frothing at the mouth. *Frothing? Foaming at the mouth?*

*No, it can't be.* "I've got a gun pointed at your head, asshole. Clear outta here now or I'll shoot your fat fucking ass."

Blinded by the light, the man stepped back. "What did you say?"

"I said I'll shoot you if you don't stop."

The bat came down, smashing the windshield with such force that shards of broken glass flew into Cray's face. If it weren't for his glasses, he would've taken a few slivers right in the eyes.

Cray aimed the gun slightly left of the man's head, removed the safety, and cocked the barrel. *Fire a warning shot. Scare the fuck.*

But as he gripped the weapon in both hands, he heard a crash and was jolted sideways by a hard impact. As the gun flew out of his hands and into the backseat, he heard a car door open and close, and then a deep, commanding voice.

"It's the police. Drop it and put your motherfucking hands in the air," Marty said.

"Fuck you," the man said.

Seeing that the man was distracted, Cray seized the opportunity and climbed out of his Escape. Cray could see that Marty had struck the offending pickup in the rear quarter panel, dislodging it from his Escape. He saw the man moving toward Marty, the bat high in the air.

"Drop the weapon," Marty said.

The man continued to advance. "Cops. I hate fucking cops."

Drawing on courage reserves he never would've believed he had, Cray said, "Hey, fat man, it's me you want. Come get me."

Waving the bat menacingly, the man spun around.

Marty seized the moment. He holstered his handgun and charged, hitting the man square in the back and sending him flying face-first into asphalt. By now other vehicles were weaving around the accident scene, none of the motorists bothering to stop and film the event. Marty landed on top of the man, whose outstretched hand still held the bat. Marty struggled to grab the bat hand, but the man gripped it tightly in both hands.

Cray stepped forward and slammed his foot down on the man's wrist. He quickly brought his other foot down and landed another wrist-crunching blow.

"Yeeeeoooww," the man shouted. The bat squirted free and rolled along the road. Cray snapped it up and, gripping it tightly in both hands, raised it over the man's head. Getting up, Marty twisted the man's arm at an awkward angle.

"Ouch," the man said. "You'll break my arm. That fucking hurts."

"Not as much as that bat would have if you wacked me over the head with it," Marty said, planting a knee in his spine, and tightening the arm submission. "What's your name?"

The man stopped struggling suddenly. "I'm Craig. Craig Burns. I'm sorry. My wife left me for another fucking loser. I've been a little crazy lately." He began sobbing like a little baby.

"If I release you, don't move. You do, you'll get a bullet in your head. Understand?"

The sobbing ebbed. "You're hurting my arm. I won't do anything. I promise."

Marty drew his gun and aimed it at Craig's head. "Tell you what. Today is your lucky day. I'm gonna let you go. When I do, I want you to get in your truck and fuck off. I wanna arrest your ass, but the city is burning and people are dying. Wasting time booking you will likely mean more innocent people will die. I'm not gonna risk it."

"I'll go," the man said. "I promise."

"You better. You don't, you die. I don't have time to fuck around. Okay?"

"Okay."

Marty released Craig's arm and removed his knee from his spine. Backing up, Marty aimed the gun at Craig's head.

Craig rolled over and sat up. Rubbing his wrist, he eyed Marty and Cray, bewildered. After a moment, he said, "What just happened?"

"You snapped," Cray said.

"Yes, you snapped," Marty said. "Now get in your truck and fuck off. I don't have time for social pleasantries or small talk."

Craig quickly did as he was told, forgetting all about his bat.

As Craig pulled away, Cray turned to Marty. "Thanks. You saved my ass."

"Forget about it. You did pretty well yourself, grabbing that bat and all. You okay?"

"Hit my head again, but I think I'm all right. You?"

Marty nodded. "You can put the bat down now."

Cray still had it raised over his right shoulder, gripping it tightly with both hands. He sighed, transferred it to his right hand, and lowered it to his side.

"Cell phones are intermittent," Marty said.

"I know. What's the plan?"

"I've gotta get to the airport. My wife got the last flight here. I hope it lands safely."

Cray examined his vehicle. Both right side doors were jammed shut from the collision and the right front fender was badly damaged. But the tires and frame appeared undamaged as well as most of the left side. Although the windshield was spider-webbed with cracks and a few baseball-sized holes, he could still see out of it. He thought it would get him to safety. "Okay. I'm going to the hospital. Then straight to Sandra's. I gotta go."

Marty nodded. "I missed her call. I'll meet you at the shelter—with any luck, with my wife. You know I've got Pastor Jon?"

Cray nodded. "Bring him along. Good luck."

"Same to you."

# Chapter Twelve

In the suffused light of the black-gray afternoon, Cray thought he recognized the silhouette of Sandra sitting on a bench about fifty feet from the chaos of the Queen Elizabeth Hospital Emergency entrance doors. She had her arm around another woman, presumably Penny, whose head was slumped over on Sandra's bosom. As he neared, Cray noticed—yes, it was Sandra—occasionally caressing the woman's long blonde hair, patting her like one would a feline pet.

As he climbed out of the Ford Escape, she recognized him and waved. On route, he had managed to send her a text message, informing her he was on the way, to which she had responded, saying she would be waiting outside. It was as if God was controlling the cell reception, providing two-way communication only when He deemed it necessary.

Cray got out, recovered the handgun, and tucked it under his belt. He turned to the approaching women and opened a rear passenger door on the driver side since both doors on the passenger side were stuck shut from the accident.

"Here you go," Cray said, gesturing for them to climb in. Sandra helped Penny in and turned to Cray. Impulsively, he hugged her warmly. She reciprocated and he felt both the warmth of her skin and a shiver shoot through her body. He stepped back, taking in the bloody surgical scrubs. "You look like you've been through a war."

Sandra shrugged. "So do you. What happened to the car? Are you okay?"

"I'm fine. A little accident. A little more head trauma. What else is new?"

Sandra bent down and peered in at Penny. "You okay back there? I'm gonna sit up front."

"I'm fine."

Sandra slid across the driver seat and into the front passenger seat.

"How's your head?" Cray said, pulling out of the parking lot and onto Riverside Drive.

"It's somewhere between a moderate and a severe concussion. I'll be fine. How's *your* head? You've got another bump."

"I think I'll be okay."

"You don't look okay."

"Thanks for the vote of confidence."

"Sorry... I didn't mean it that way."

"I know." In the rearview mirror, Cray studied Penny, who was staring vacantly out the window. "How are you, Penny?"

Penny's vacant eyes turned from the fireworks of a burning, ash-fallen city to the back of Cray's head. "I don't know if you care. And you'd have every right not to. Listen, I'm sorry I did that to you. You didn't do anything and I almost had you charged with sexual assault. Sometimes I'm so fucking mixed up I don't know which way my head is screwed on."

"Don't worry about it. Life is too short. Are you okay?"

"Thanks. I'm not, but I hope I will be."

"I tried to reach Marty when you didn't answer," Sandra said. "I couldn't. Is he okay?"

Cray recapped events leading up to the present, abridging some of the more horrific moments. "I just hope her plane lands safely. I think they'll declare a state of emergency."

"It *is* a state of emergency," Sandra said, pointing to a distant explosion rocketing flames and debris high into the ashen sky. "Whether they declare it or not."

\*\*\*\*\*\*

*Thank God I have lots of guns,* Ralph thought, caressing the cold trigger of his Glock 17, the most widely used cop gun in the world. For fun, he aimed at a small sapling twenty feet away, fired, and blew the top four inches off it. The blast echoed through the forest and slowly faded away. He liked the action of the Glock: smooth, reliable, easy to use, accurate within a short range, and the nine-millimeter handgun had good stopping power, especially with a seventeen-round magazine. He tucked the Glock in his holster, picked up a bottle of moonshine, and took a long swill. Setting the bottle on the forest floor, he studied the two fires; one, a small fire he had built in the clearing near Sandra's shelter; the other, a fanning orange haze, surrounded by black clouds that engulfed the city of Charlottetown some thirty miles west.

Picking up a stick he had fashioned as a poker, he pushed some hot coals into his fire and prodded a few logs into place. The flames spread and grew. Satisfied, he sat down in the tall grass, took another pull of moonshine, and crossed his legs. Arriving earlier in his pickup, he had ventured down into the network of caves to do some exploring. He had brought along a knapsack of supplies, spread them out in his new bedroom, filled the knapsack with six bottles of moonshine, returned topside, lit the fire, drank, waited, and plotted.

With or without their agreement, he would be spending a lot of time in the shelter in the very near future. The plan was simple, really. Kill that fucker Gray—or Cray, whatever the nerd's name was—and bring Sandra into the shelter with him. If they arrived with anyone else, well, they too were destined for death. While Sandra might not appreciate Ralph's rough and redneck exterior, he was sure over time and with some gentle coercing she would not only come to like him, she would fall in love with him.

Feeling in his pocket for his trusty flashlight—it was where it should be—he rehashed the plan in his mind. The fire was a sort of decoy, a distraction that would draw their attention, so he could attack from behind. He checked his other pocket. Good. The other seventeen-round magazine was there, although he doubted the job would take more than five or six bullets. But, always better safe than sorry, better to be more prepared than less prepared. You never knew what kind of curve balls life might throw at you. He felt for his hunting knife. It too was sheathed and strapped to his belt, next to the Glock. Everything looked good. Now it was just a matter of waiting.

He swallowed another three or four ounces of moonshine, coughed, and spewed a fountain of the potent hooch into the fire. It ignited instantly. Flames fanned out and attacked him. He blocked them with his forearm, lost his balance, and somersaulted backwards. "Not gonna get *my* ass," he said, checking the bottle and grinning when he realized he hadn't spilled a drop. "Not gonna get *my* ass, you fucking fire."

For that matter, he thought, neither was Detective Strader. Maybe the end of the world was divine intervention. He was sure the detective, like a crafty bloodhound, had his scent and wouldn't stop until he had his hungry fangs firmly embedded into Ralph's neck, dragging him like some unfortunate Raggedy Andy to a term of incarceration of no less than twenty years, maybe even life in prison. But not now. The detective would be preoccupied trying to save his own ass and the asses of his friends and family. Marty was smart. He would be planning and plotting how he would survive this upcoming apocalypse. Earlier, Ralph had watched the news, understood the dire nature of the situation. Sandra had been right. The end of the world was coming. Thank God he had made a note of it, or he might have forgotten.

*Speaking of notes.* He inched closer to the fire, found his worn patch of ground, and crossed his legs. He fished into his front shirt pocket. Nothing. Grimacing, he checked his two front pants pockets. Only the flashlight and extra magazine. *Fuck. What did I do with it?* He reached back and checked his right back pocket. A few coins, nothing else. Starting to panic, he quickly checked the left back pocket. The familiar crunch of paper. And something else. A pen. Deep breaths. *Thank God, if there is one.*

Absently rubbing the bump on his forehead, the result of the recent drunken face-plant with a hardwood floor, he shone the flashlight on the list, reviewing its contents: moonshine, shelter, end of world, hole, shovel. Simple Simon, Sandra, Cray or Gray, Strader. Taking another pull on the moonshine, he crossed out moonshine. Plenty of that now. He also crossed out shelter, hole and shovel. But when he got to Simple Simon he paused for a moment. It took some chin-scratching before the memory returned. Yes, right, he had put an end to that miserable old fuck. Gunshots. Dead. Dead and buried. He crossed him off the list, feeling a mixture of satisfaction and a sudden rush of sadness. He tried to wash the now palpable grief down with a couple of shots of moonshine. It didn't work. It only made him more melancholy and he wondered what would have become of Simple Simon if he had just been more accepting of Ralph. Might they have formed a solid bond?

Love and acceptance, what everyone wanted, and many people found. But not Ralph. Everywhere he looked, he found rejection. It was a cruel world out there. All it had dealt him was a black cloud of rejection. A cloud that over time had wrapped itself around him like a cloak of many dark emotions: fear, disappointment, sadness, grief, a bitter sense of isolation and aloneness, resentment, and finally, a bitter loathing, disgust, and anger toward humankind. Anger that had boiled over months ago and was fast becoming a bubbling hot geyser of murderous rage.

"Fuck with me, I'll fuck with you," Ralph said. But a disturbing thought from the more rational recesses of an unbalanced mind popped into his head: *But if you don't fuck with them, they won't fuck with you, moron. Kill your enemies with kindness. That's how you do it, nimrod. That's how you get acceptance... "*

The sound of an engine in the distance shattered the blatant logic of the thought and he discarded it. He reached for the gun. "Fuck kindness. I'd rather kill them with bullets through their heads."

******

Peering in the rearview mirror as he turned into Sandra's driveway, Cray saw that Penny had drifted off. Her head was slumped over in her hands and she snored lightly. Glancing over at Sandra, it appeared she too had fallen asleep, her head resting on the cracked passenger window. About ten minutes earlier, the conversation had ground to a halt. Everyone, it seemed, had become absorbed in their own thoughts and, maybe, prayers. For his part, Cray had tried to keep a calm demeanor throughout the trip and as the conversation died down, he too had become absorbed in his own thoughts; about Emma, his ex, about his parents, about an impending sense of doom and, yes, despair. Fiery images appeared in his mind. Emma, engulfed by fire, screaming horribly, going to an excruciating death. His parents, holding hands calmly, stoic, while flames ravaged them. An image of Mike, a noose around his neck, standing on a chair, smoking a joint, grinning, welcoming a combination of death by fire, death by hanging. At the last minute, changing his mind, struggling, failing, screaming, shouting, and finally succumbing to death.

Hot tendrils of fear inched up Cray's spine, turning ice cold when they reached the hairs on the back of his neck. Looking at his white hands gripping the steering wheel, Cray realized they were shaking. Something was happening. He was losing control. Fear was taking hold. No, it would render him useless. He couldn't let it happen. "We're here," he said, wanting and needing to hear a response, a reassuring voice. The women did not stir. He parked and killed the ignition. He breathed deeply. Slowly, his heart rate slowed, but the jitters remained.

Thinking about Sandra's concussion, he realized it may be dangerous for her to sleep. How long had she been out? No more than ten minutes, that was for sure. Could she slip into a coma and not come out of it? "Sandra, we're here."

Sandra stirred and slowly opened her eyes.

From the backseat, Penny's head moved. Her eyes opened quickly. "I'll kill you, you son of a bitch."

"Penny," Sandra said, reaching back and touching her arm. "It's okay. It's okay. You were dreaming."

Penny's faraway gaze found focus. She blinked, looking around. "Where are we?"

"At my house," Sandra said, squeezing over toward Cray. He took the cue, opened his door, and climbed out. Sandra slid out and opened Penny's door. "Come on, let's go inside."

Inside, Cray was surprised the power was still on. As Sandra and Penny went upstairs to freshen up, change clothes, and collect some last-minute supplies, Cray hurried into the kitchen and turned on the radio. It dawned on him that he could have done that in the car, but his mind had been so preoccupied he hadn't even thought of it. The radio was all static. He played with the tuning dial and found a clear voice:

"A state of emergency has been declared in Charlottetown and officials have ordered an evacuation, effective immediately. The Confederation Bridge is gridlocked with fleeing traffic and five fatal traffic accidents have already been reported. The Charlottetown airport will be closed shortly for commercial flights, allowing only emergency flights as military planes and helicopters prepare to assist in the worst disaster in this small city's history. City Mayor..."

The radio squawked static. Cray searched for another station. More static. He reached into his pocket, retrieved his cell phone, and speed-dialed Marty. No signal whatsoever. "Shit. Where the hell is he?"

******

All airport protocol had been abandoned. Order had turned to chaos. Pastor Jon and Detective Marty Strader stood on the tarmac, watching and waiting. The perimeter of the airport was surrounded by fire trucks, many that had rushed in from neighboring Nova Scotia and New Brunswick. Like a giant sprinkler, this man-made barrier sprayed jets of water outward, soaking the ground around them and creating a large lake of water that it was hoped would block the destructive fire as it inched closer. A handful of anxious people were also on the tarmac, some hugging each other tightly as they waited for what would be the last commercial flight permitted to land. Most airport security personnel, and there were few in the small airport, had been hastily converted to firefighters. Anxious people had hurried out onto the tarmac after security had broken down.

"Don't worry," Pastor Jon said, putting a hand on Marty's shoulder. "She's gonna make it. She's a strong woman."

"How would you know?"

"Sometimes, I just know things."

"Well, you're right. I'll tell you something. When she was eight years old, her mother, father, and brother were murdered. She was raised by her grandmother, thankfully a caring woman, who did a good job."

"I'm sorry. How did that happen?"

"Home invasion and robbery. Shot by gangsters. The only thing that saved her life is she hid under the bed. Must've heard everything though. Imagine what that would do to an eight-year-old psyche."

"Must have been horrible."

"Yeah, but she bounced back. Dedicated her life to helping others who've been traumatized. Could've gone the other way, the wrong side of the tracks, you know what I mean. I've seen plenty of that. But she didn't."

"I think she's an amazing woman. I think you've been blessed by God."

"She is. I guess I am a lucky man. Sometimes, I just don't realize how lucky." Marty often wondered why he couldn't deal with his demons as well as his wife could. Supposed to be a tough cop. But some shit, particularly the death of his partner, still fucked him up. Maybe, in time. At least that was the hope.

Pointing to the dark sky, Pastor Jon said, "There it is. The plane."

"I see it." Marty watched as the jet emerged from a bank of black clouds, wobbled in a strong gust of wind, and dropped another two hundred feet or so. Stabilizing, it descended and approached the runway. Closer, closer, the wheels lowering; a thump, a loud shriek, a small plume of smoke, a few sparks, and the tires gripped tarmac, engines suddenly roaring like a high-powered vacuum cleaner; then there it was, slowly taxiing toward them.

The gatherers clapped loudly. Marty and Pastor Jon walked toward the plane. A few others started running.

"Wait," a panicked controller holding two orange flashlights said. "Let me guide it in."

Most people stopped. But one man continued sprinting toward the plane, yelling, "My son, my son... he made it."

Marty realized the man was running right for the rushing wheels of the jet. "Fucking clown." He ran after him.

Shaking his head, the ground controller glanced over, but quickly turned to the plane, guiding it closer with his orange flashlights.

"Stop. You're gonna get run over," Marty said, flailing his arms in the air.

Oblivious, the man neared the plane. Marty closed the gap and tackled him on the tarmac. They rolled and stopped. Marty saw the wheels coming right at them. "Holy fuck."

Some bystanders started screaming and pointing while a few others produced smartphones and started filming.

Marty scrambled to his feet. The wheels rushed toward them.

Thirty, twenty, ten feet away.

He grabbed the man's wrist, dragging him to safety a fraction of a second before the wheels rushed past, missing them both by inches. Marty smelled burning rubber and felt a strong gust of wind. He helped the man to his feet. His eyes narrowed, spraying the rescued man with spittle as he spoke. "What the fuck do you think you're doing?"

The man looked at him blankly. Eyes wide. Petrified. "I don't know. I lost my mind."

Marty released him as the plane finally came to a stop about a hundred feet from the terminal. "You could have killed yourself, you fucking moron."

"Thanks," the man said. "Thanks for saving me."

But Marty was already gone, running toward the plane as crews wheeled staircases to the front and rear exit doors.

Among other anxious people, they waited at the foot of the stairs at the front of the plane. By now, airport personnel had given up even bothering to warn people about standing too close, breaching painted do-not-cross lines, and running around the tarmac. From the strained looks on their faces, it was evident all they wanted to do was safely de-plane passengers and luggage, then beat a hasty retreat to their own families and their own struggles for survival.

"I'm sorry. I was wrong," Pastor Jon said.

Marty looked at him. "What do you mean?"

"Wrong about the date. It's not June 30th. It's June 6th. Today... today is the end of the world. It's not the end is nigh anymore. The end is now!"

"Just stay with me, will you. Don't go wandering off. And please, no preaching right now."

Pastor Jon dropped his head and fell silent.

Marty watched exiting passengers, trying to spot Elaine. As he looked for her long brown hair, small dainty features, and her bookish eyeglasses, Marty had a million thoughts swimming through his troubled mind. Watching passengers, he tried to categorize and prioritize these thoughts, tried to make sense out of them. How did this mysterious priest beside him know so much? What was his story? How had he miraculously recovered from the terrible car accident, an accident that would have likely put anyone else in a permanent coma, damaged their brain irreparably, or killed them? Was Pastor Jon, as the *Book of Revelation* said, a modern-day servant of God, sent here to deliver God's message, to warn some so they might be saved, while others perished and suffered terrible deaths? Growing up in Toronto, Marty's parents were strict practicing Catholics. Although he had wavered from the Bible's prophecies and moral guidelines (What kind of a God would allow sickos and psychos to walk around, inflicting all manner of brutal murders on innocent people?), he still remembered many of its parables, particularly the *Book of Revelation*. Were Pastor Jon's prophecies going to go to the letter of that book? Seven angels, seven plagues? The bowls of God's wrath? A scorched Earth? Earthquakes? Giant hailstones? All sea life annihilated? Sea turning red with blood? Severe drought? Attacking locusts? Destructive dragons? A beast rising out of the sea? Ten horns, seven heads? 144,000 spared, so they might start...

"I can't tell you that," Pastor Jon said, grabbing the staircase rail for support. He suddenly looked drained, jaundiced, and haggard, as if he was battling some mysterious unseen force. "Not yet anyway."

"Tell me what?"

"If the end of the world will go to the letter of the *Book of Revelation*. Lately, my visions have been jumbled and confused."

*Shit, did I say that out loud? No, surely not. Better watch what I think. Fuck. He can read my mind?* "It might have something to do with all the booze."

"I don't know. When I get a clear vision, I'll tell you. I know this much. We've got to get to the shelter. And fast."

"Marty," Elaine shouted from the top of the stairs.

"Thank God," Marty said. "You're here."

"You're a believer?" Pastor Jon asked, as Elaine, being pushed from behind by panicked passengers, jostled her way down the stairs.

"That's just an expression. I don't know," Marty said, stepping forward to receive his wife. He had changed out of his debris-coated, fire-and-smoke scented clothing before heading to the airport. Now he wore a black Canada Day baseball cap, multi-pocketed blue travel pants, hiking boots, a black t-shirt, and blue lumberjack shirt, attire more suitable to an apocalypse than an investigation. He looked more like a redneck than cop, particularly with his chin stubble.

"Slow down," Marty warned the exiting passengers. "Someone's gonna get trampled."

Wearing a navy-blue jumper, blue-jeans, and hiking boots, Elaine also looked ready for war. A camouflage knapsack slung over her shoulder, dark hair tied back in a neat pony-tail, and a determined expression added to the look of military preparedness. She was mid-way down the stairs now, and doing some shoving and jostling of her own, one anxious male passenger shoving her from behind and receiving an elbow to the head for his efforts.

"Watch your fucking elbow," the disgruntled man said.

But Elaine was in no mood for bullshit or brawn. Expression tight, she glared at the perpetrator. "Then don't push me down the fucking stairs."

She reached the bottom. Marty stepped on stair number one and reached a hand out. She took it eagerly and he pulled her to safety. The crew-cut man who had pushed her from behind paused, contemplated a retort, saw the no-nonsense look on Marty's face, and quickly thought better of it. He turned away and ran.

"Better run, asshole," Marty said, hugging his wife warmly. It felt comforting being back in her arms, welcoming her affectionately after pushing her away for so long. Maybe this time it would be different, he thought. Maybe he could embrace his demons now and stop blaming Elaine. After all, she had nothing to do with his problems. Nothing to do with him being unable to accept the death of his partner and blaming himself for it.

He released Elaine and introduced her to Pastor Jon. They shook hands. She smiled politely. "Nice to meet you."

"Let's go," Marty said, taking her hand.

As they hurried off the tarmac, the heat from the surrounding flames growing nearer and more intense, now accompanied by distant shouts and screams, a man on a loudspeaker barking out commands, Pastor Jon turned to Marty. "Elaine's emotionally intelligent. I can tell."

\*\*\*\*\*\*

It was almost midnight by the time Cray, Sandra, and Penny started out down the winding road leading to the shelter. Just before the power went out and cell and internet reception disappeared entirely, they had managed to gather some supplies, eat TV dinners, and freshen up. Penny and Sandra, before coming down for dinner, had had a long talk upstairs, the contents of which Cray was oblivious to but once again curious about. When they emerged, both women had one concern on their minds—that Ralph would be waiting for them at the shelter. Passing his house earlier in the evening, it was Sandra who had noticed (evidently she hadn't been sleeping after all) that Ralph's houselights were on, but nobody was home. His beat-up pickup was not there. You didn't have to be a detective to determine where he might be. So, after Cray had showed Sandra how to use the Colt 45, they'd discussed strategy. In the end, it was decided that Cray, loaded shotgun on his lap, would drive Sandra's yellow Ford Explorer. Sandra, in the passenger seat, would pack the Colt 45, and Penny would be ducking down out of view in the backseat. In this battle-ready formation, and stocked with supplies, they neared the clearing, nerves taut and frayed.

About a hundred feet away, surrounded by total blackness, Cray spotted the orange-red flames. He stopped the vehicle and whispered, "Someone's there. Look." He turned to Sandra. "Stay here. I'm gonna check it out."

"No, I'm coming with you." She turned to Penny. "You stay here."

Eyes wide with fear, Penny quickly nodded.

Cray opened the door. "Okay, but stay about ten feet behind me. Shoot first, ask questions later. We don't have the luxury of fucking around."

"Okay."

Armed with the shotgun and a flashlight, Cray slowly moved down the road. *Is this a stupid plan? I'm in plain sight.* He turned to Sandra. "You go through the forest. We're exposed here."

Nodding, she slipped into the trees, Cray wondering dumbly why he wasn't taking his own advice. Too late now. He picked up his pace, hearing twigs crack and snap a short distance behind him as Sandra made slow but steady progress. Entering the clearing, he saw Ralph's pickup near the fire. The snap, crackle, and pop of Sandra's progress grew fainter.

He hurried to the pickup and shone the flashlight inside. A mess of empty beer cans, food wrappers, a cigarette-butt stuffed ashtray, a rotting-fish stench, but no Ralph. He shone the flashlight toward the fire. In the darkness, he thought he saw a body. He hurried over to the fire, frantically shining the beam around the perimeter. He accidently stepped on something hard and looked down. A steel-toed boot. Ralph's steel-toed boot.

Empty moonshine bottle in one hand, handgun in the other, Ralph was passed out by the fire. His face slicked in sweat, he grimaced and snored lightly. Cray quickly found the apparent reason for the grimace. The sweet smell of burning flesh assaulted his nostrils. A hot ember had popped out of the fire, landed on his pant leg, and ignited. Ralph was on fire.

Cray put the flashlight in his pocket, set the shotgun on a nearby log, removed his shirt, rolled it up, and began pounding out the flames. "He's on fire. Help!"

A loud explosion nearby rocked the ground under his feet and, off balance, Cray spun around. He felt intense heat and saw a giant crimson mushroom cloud fan out, not a half mile away. Burning debris rocketed skyward and came showering down. *A house explosion? Oh my God.* With the ground continuing to tremble underfoot, he turned to Ralph, almost fell into the fire, caught his balance, and continued pounding out the flames. The earthquake-like ground shake subsided. The Ralph fire was almost out.

Ralph opened his eyes, clamped his hand tightly around his handgun (Cray had forgotten to kick that loose before he started Operation Save-Ralph's-Life), and began raising his arm.

Sandra appeared and crunched a hiking boot down hard on his wrist. Ralph screamed in pain. The gun squirted free. Sandra picked it up and pointed both guns at Ralph's head. "He saves your life, all you can think about is killing him? No you don't, you worthless piece of shit."

Ralph tightened his grip on the empty moonshine bottle. Sandra shattered it with a bullet from the Colt 45. Shards of glass sprinkled the air as the blast echoed through the forest. A three-inch glass spear lodged right between

Ralph's eyes. Blood squirted down his nose, a small red circle forming around his open mouth, giving him a ghoulish appearance.

Ignoring the blood dribbling down his face and his smoking pant leg, Ralph sat up and extended a hand and a toothless grin to Cray. "I was wrong about you, bro. I'm sorry. You saved my life. Thanks for that."

Cray was unwilling to accept the handshake. He did, however, nod politely to Ralph.

Sandra still had both guns trained on Ralph. "Should we kill the useless scum?"

Cray grabbed the shotgun and aimed it at Ralph, ready to do just that should the bleeding man attempt to get up. "I... I don't know. Your call."

Sandra stepped forward and brought the guns closer to Ralph's head.

"Please," Ralph pleaded, bringing both hands together in a gesture of prayer. "We don't have much time. Take me with you. I'll be good from now on. I promise."

Twenty feet behind them, it was Penny's squeaky, uneven voice they heard. "Don't kill him. You do, you're no better than him."

# Chapter Thirteen

In a corner of the cave, a small oscillating fan wired to a car battery whirred. Hooked to the ceiling, a battery-powered lightbulb dangled back and forth, casting giant menacing shadows behind those seated cross-legged in the circle. Periodically, the network of caves trembled with the sound and force of distant explosions. A faint but steady whooshing sound whispered topside as flames on the Earth's surface decimated everything in their path. A thermometer haphazardly nailed to a nearby wall tracked the rising mercury; eighty, ninety, now one hundred and two degrees Fahrenheit, all in the course of one hour.

Watching the small flame from the candle positioned in the middle of the circle dance in the grayness of this new and terrifying reality, Cray thought it had probably been Penny's words that had spared Ralph's life. Wiping away sweat from his brow, he knew Sandra had been willing and able to plug his head full of bullets. Cray too had snapped, his pent-up tension and rage boiling over, bringing the shotgun closer to Ralph's head and demanding, "Give me one good reason to spare his life?"

Stepping closer, Penny had said, "Two wrongs don't make a right."

And as corny as that overused cliché had sounded, it had precipitously taken the wrath out of Sandra and Cray's rising tide of fury. They had lowered their guns and looked at Penny curiously, wondering what she had in store for Ralph.

It was then that Pastor Jon, Elaine, and Marty had arrived. After some heated discussion, they'd agreed to handcuff Ralph and bring him along. Seconds after that decision, the wind had intensified and a giant wall of red-hot flame launched an all-out assault at them. It had been all they could do to gather half of their supplies and escape beneath the Earth's surface.

Upon reaching the bottom of the cave, they had propped up Ralph in a corner, watching him closely as his fear-filled wide eyes finally closed and, handcuffed, he drifted off into an alcohol-induced sleep. Penny had removed the small glass spear from his forehead, cleaned the minor injury, and covered it with a Band-Aid.

He snored suddenly—sputtering like a poorly-maintained chainsaw—and broke the tense silence.

"What are we gonna do with him?" Cray said, eyeing the others, who were alone with their thoughts. Either way he sliced it, Ralph's presence here didn't sit well with him. Somehow bringing an attempted murderer—hell, probably a murderer—to a post-apocalyptic party didn't register on the sound-logic Richter scale.

Wiping a sweat-soaked cheek and removing his gaze from the candle's flame, Marty said, "I think he's a killer."

"I know you do," Cray said. "That's the problem."

"He's obviously got psychological issues," Elaine said, turning to Marty. "But tell me, what was this Simon Simms like, the man you believe he murdered?"

"Frankly, all the information I've been able to gather says he was an abusive asshole."

"Maybe it was self-defense?' Elaine said. "Maybe Ralph's just a lost soul looking for love and acceptance."

"Well, this isn't the psychiatric ward of a hospital," Cray said. "We're not here to reform him. We're here to survive and get along. And I think he's a detriment to that game plan. And I have every reason to think that. Shit, he was planning to kill us, probably would've if he hadn't gotten so drunk."

"Are you suggesting we kill him?" Penny said, her voice tinged with emotion.

The sputtering chainsaw started, croaked, died.

"You got a better idea?" Cray said.

"We shouldn't be having this discussion when he's right here," Marty said. He stood.

Penny stood too, waving him off. "I got this."

Before Marty could move, Penny approached Ralph and tapped his shoulder lightly, interrupting the beginning of a new chainsaw sputter. He opened his eyes slowly. "Whaa... "

She lifted him by an arm. "Come on. I'm taking you to bed." Ralph didn't protest, even found his legs, as she lifted him slowly and escorted him into one of the makeshift bedrooms.

"Put him in there," Sandra said, pointing to door number three, the one that led to the moonshine. "Door number one is my room."

Penny returned a minute later, closed the heavy door, and took her place in the circle. They were silent for a minute, waiting for the chainsaw to begin sputtering. It didn't take long before it started again, this time gaining momentum, finding a sporadic rhythm. If it weren't for the door muffling the noise, the white noise of the whirring fan, and the hissing inferno above, it would have been downright annoying.

"I'm with Cray," Sandra said, finally, removing her hands from her face, scanning the other faces. "I don't think we're in a position to gamble with our lives right now. Who knows how long we've got. Look at the mess we're in."

"Killing is not God's way," Pastor Jon said, waving his arms dramatically and then taking a long pull on a bottle of moonshine.

"Really?" Cray said, pointing to the trembling ceiling. Small cakes of dirt and pebbles occasionally fell to the floor. "Who the hell brought this on then?"

"That's for sinners, non-believers, idolaters, and evil-doers."

Cray balled his fists. "What do you call Ralph? A Bible-thumping model of Christianity at its ever-loving finest?"

"Maybe he can be redeemed," Elaine said. "Please, let's not argue at a time like this. Why don't we keep Ralph around for a few days and keep an eye on him? If he threatens any of us or tries to kill us, we'll revisit the issue."

"I don't know," Sandra said. "At one time I might've agreed with you, but all the rules of civility have suddenly changed. The protocol of human decency and humanitarianism is not the same as it used to be, probably never will be now." She was getting worked up. "I mean, look at me, a nurse, a natural-born caregiver, a preserver of human life, telling you this. This is so screwed..."

"Why don't we vote on it?" Marty said. "Let democracy decide."

They fell silent. It was punctuated periodically by Ralph's sputtering snore, the occasional rumble from above, the whirring of the small fan, and the steady whooshing whisper of annihilation above.

*We're fucked now*, Cray thought. Phones and internet were completely cut off. Power was down. They had meager supplies. Fierce winds fueled walls of flame, destroying what remained of humanity, not to mention other life forms. Prince Edward Island was burning. The entire world, if Pastor Jon was right, was being razed to the ground.

"What time is it?" Pastor Jon said. "What day is it?"

Marty checked his digital watch. "It's two-thirty-six in the morning. June 7th."

"I was only wrong about the date," Pastor Jon said. "But it's here. The Seven Bowls of God's Wrath are here." He took a long pull. Wiping dribbling drops of moonshine from his chin, he raised the bottle to the others. "So sorry. I've been rude. Anyone like to join me?"

One by one, heads shook. When they got to Marty, he hesitated for a second, glanced at Elaine, and slowly shook his head. "Maybe later."

"I'll have one later," Cray said. "A nightcap before I go to bed." On one level, he couldn't believe that here he was, contemplating drawing the Glock and putting three bullets into Ralph's sleeping head. Fuck democracy. Fix the problem right now and let the chips fall where they may. But on another—more political—level he understood the need to tread cautiously. After all, Pastor Jon was in favor of preserving Ralph's life. Had he been wrong before? A few minor details maybe, but not really. Elaine, a psychologist, believed Ralph could be redeemed. Penny, a sexually abused victim or a conniving con artist, was vying for the preservation of human life. Maybe she had some sort of perverse attraction to Ralph. Sandra was on Cray's side. Good to see. But where was Marty? Sitting on the fence, maybe trying to maintain some political correctness in front of his wife, also a caregiver of sorts. But wasn't Marty right? Shouldn't democracy rule? Shouldn't they set the standard now for future negotiations, future relationships, future cooperation? It was hard for Cray to fathom they were thinking about voting on saving or killing someone and a sudden wave of sadness swept over him as he realized how much he had changed. All of their lives would never, could never, be the same anymore.

Sandra touched his arm lightly. "Are you okay? You look white."

"Not really," Cray said, hot flashes ebbing and flowing through his body, a wave of dizziness settling in. The heat was getting more intense and he felt like he was slowly cooking to death in a large, covered frying pan. *Out of the frying pan, into the fire.* "I'm a little dizzy, maybe heatstroke, but thanks for asking."

Sandra searched his face concernedly. "I agree with Marty. Let's vote on it."

"Okay," Marty said in a low voice. "All those in favor of killing Ralph raise your hand."

For a moment no one moved. Or spoke. After the dizziness had passed, Cray began to think even Sandra's support had vanished. But, raising an eyebrow, she eyed Cray and slowly raised her hand. He did the same. Sandra and Cray looked at the others.

Marty raised a hand but it wavered slowly and scratched his head, then his slicked back hair, and finally wiped sweat from his brow. "Two votes in favor of killing him. Is that it?"

No other hands raised.

"All those in favor—for the time being— of keeping Ralph alive, raise your hand," Marty said. Four hands raised: Penny first; Elaine second; Pastor Jon third, and finally Marty, slowly and less than confidently, raised his hand. "Four to two to keep him alive. That settles it then. Is everybody okay with that?"

"He gives us any grief, we revisit this," Cray said. "Is that agreed?"

"Definitely," Sandra said. "To survive, we have to get along." She scanned the other faces. They nodded.

"I'm tired," Sandra said, rubbing her bandaged head. "And a little dizzy." She turned to Cray, touching his arm lightly. "I'm going to bed. You should get some rest."

"Where do I sleep?"

She pointed to door number one, her bedroom. "There's more than one bed in there, remember?"

"Right."

She took his hand and helped him up, the majorly concussed leading the minorly concussed.

"Do you not want a nightcap before bed?" Cray asked.

"Don't worry," Sandra said, leading him to the door with a flashlight. "I've got some in the bedroom." She turned to

Marty and Elaine. "You two can sleep in door number two if you want." They nodded. "Penny, I'm not sure about you."

"I noticed an extra bed in Ralph's room," she said. "I'll sleep there. Keep an eye on him."

Sandra raised an eyebrow. "You sure about that?"

"Don't worry about me," Penny said. "Get some rest. You need it."

Beside the bathroom in the main area, Sandra had rigged up some blankets to the ceiling, creating a makeshift bedroom that offered only a modicum of privacy but the best bathroom access. Looking at Pastor Jon, Sandra pointed to it. "Guess that puts you there."

"I'm fine anywhere," Pastor Jon said, patting a case of moonshine. "As long as I have this." He pulled out a fresh bottle, popped the cap, and offered the first sip to Penny. Initially she shook her head, but finally she gratefully accepted, took a pull, and passed it to Elaine.

Sandra and Cray didn't wait around to see if Elaine would partake. They were already at the door, pulling it open. As it creaked fully open, Cray and Sandra bid their guests good night, entered, and closed the door behind them—two flashlights illuminating their dark and dusty sleeping quarters.

Inside, Cray sighed, realizing the bedroom was quite a few degrees cooler than the sweltering hot common area. With any luck, he could manage a few much-needed hours of sleep. But, shining the flashlight beam around the room, he thought maybe Sandra had other plans. She had pulled two single beds together to make a double, replaced the old dusty linens with fresh flowery-patterned ones, added several decorative pillows and cushions, and had rearranged the night tables; one on each side of the bed, both adorned with oil lanterns and disposable lighters. A bottle of moonshine with two silver wine goblets sat temptingly on a wooden chest at the foot of the bed. A little less romantic, she had placed peanut-butter baited rat traps in each corner of the room.

Sandra sat down on the bed, fidgeted with the oil lantern, and lit it while Cray peeled his sweat-soaked clothes off, down to his underwear and t-shirt. He placed them on the chest, lit his oil lantern, and sat next to her. Sandra stripped down to pink panties and a white t-shirt, plopped her clothing next to Cray's on the chest at the foot of the bed, and picked up the bottle of moonshine. They had extinguished their flashlights and the room was illuminated by the soft yellow glow from the oil lanterns.

A mischievous grin pursed her lips as she twisted the cap off. "Care for a shot?"

Cray approached and extended a hand. "Don't mind if I do. It's been a rough day."

She poured a healthy shot into a goblet and handed it to Cray. After pouring herself a drink, she set the bottle down and raised the goblet. "Can you think of anything to toast?"

"How about that we're still alive. And still together?" Cray thought his comment sounded as if they had been together as a couple for a long time. Meanwhile, they were just establishing their friendship, although there had certainly been signs of chemistry, seeds of an intimacy deeper than friendship. *Dumb comment. Too late now.*

But Sandra didn't seem to mind. She moved closer, clinking her goblet with Cray's "I like that. To our union."

Taking a large pull, Cray couldn't help noticing the nipples on Sandra's perky and well-shaped breasts begin to harden and poke through the sheer fabric of her t-shirt. He saw the dark brown roundness of her cherry-sized areolas contrasting with the fabric's whiteness. He felt the stirrings of sexual desire. An all-encompassing passionate hunger and longing for physical love swept through his body like a tingling tidal wave. It had been so long. He had been so hurt, so depressed, he never imagined he would feel a sensation this powerful ever again in his life. Conflicting thoughts swirled through the tidal wave. *Take it easy. Go slow. No. Take this beautiful woman. Now. There might not be a tomorrow.*

As if reading his mind, Sandra wrapped her arms around Cray in a passionate embrace. She kissed him softly on the neck.

"Ooohh," Cray said. "That feels so good. Should we do this?"

She smiled, her lips full, pouty, and red. She smelled of lavender and honey. "I don't do would've, could've, should've. Not anymore... I don't have time for that."

Cray looked into her soulful green eyes, searching his hungrily. "Neither do I, baby. Neither do I."

As they kissed, long and passionate, Cray felt his member stiffen, tingle, and rub against her naked leg. The wave of desire was a tsunami now, unstoppable.

They peeled each other's clothes off slowly and retreated to the comfort of the bed, leaving their drinks on the chest. Cray kissed Sandra as his hands roamed over her erect nipples, tweaking them softly, kneading them lovingly. She moaned, found his erect member, and stroked its sensitive hardness. Emitting a soft moan of pleasure, his hand caressed her tight stomach and slowly found its way down to her soft mound. As he touched her wetness, she moaned, slow, long, and loud. Cray lowered his lips to her rock-hard nipples, gently sucking them before sliding his tongue down to her honey-scented genitalia. He reveled in the fragrance, the taste, the aroused smoothness of her dripping clitoris.

The intense foreplay lasted about twenty minutes—to Cray it felt like hours—before Sandra gently rolled him over on his back, mounted him cowgirl style, and began a slow and steady rhythm. They rocked back and forth, slowly at first. As their mutual ecstatic moans grew more acute, the pace of their lovemaking quickened, reaching a steady, even pace. Suddenly they both exploded with powerful, intense, shuddering orgasms.

Locked in a post-coital cuddle a moment later, liquefied in sweat and breathing in short gasps, Cray was incredulous. The passionate lovemaking session was leaps and bounds more powerful than his sexual dream about Sandra. Not only that, it appeared now, it was a premonition dream; finally he had consummated the sexual fantasy that had, like clockwork, churned through his mind ever since he had met her. *My God, what a one-track mind men have.*

Yet there was something here more powerful than mere sexual fantasy, Cray knew. He really liked Sandra. Maybe a stronger emotion was taking root. Was this love?

"Do you think they heard us?" Sandra asked, caressing his arm and chest.

Cray listened. But for the steady, muffled sound of the whirring fan and the intermittent, deathly whisper of the destructive inferno topside, the makeshift shelter was quiet. The unintelligible murmurs of conversation that were audible before their explosive sex session had started, had died down. "Does it matter?"

"Maybe at one time. But definitely not now."

Cray's thoughts swirled, finally finding a home at their current horror movie and the supporting actors. "Don't you think it's strange that Penny slept in Ralph's room?"

"Yes. Especially since she's just been raped. She obviously sees something in him that we don't."

"What does she see in him?"

After a moment's pause, Sandra said, "If you think about Frankenstein, Ralph's nickname, it's rather fitting. In Mary Shelley's gothic novel, Frankenstein's monster is mistreated, maligned, and misunderstood. He's rejected. He wants what most people want, a mate. He wants love and acceptance. When he doesn't get it, he becomes violent, murders his creator's brother and his bride-to-be."

Cray was impressed with the analogy as it applied to Ralph. Fitting. Insightful. Sandra was obviously more than just a pretty face with a hot body. "So if you connect it to current events, Ralph murdered his uncle, or allegedly murdered him, because he was rejected by him."

She pecked Cray on the cheek. "You got it. You're more than just a pretty face."

Cray laughed. "I was just thinking that about you. Great minds think alike."

"I won't entertain the flipside of that."

"Me neither. Did you invent Ralph's nickname?"

"As far as I know."

"With that interpretation in mind?"

"Yeah. Did you ever read *Frankenstein*?"

"No."

"Well, at one point the monster admits to murdering William, his creator's brother, but says he did it because Victor Frankenstein, his cruel creator, wouldn't make a female companion for him. Basically, Victor rejected his creation. The monster is even remorseful about the murder, claims it was revenge for being shunned and rejected."

Cray felt a pang of guilt for being so willing to kill Ralph. Perhaps they had been too hard on him. "That makes me think we made the wrong vote."

"I've been thinking the same thing. When it actually came down to the vote, I had my doubts, but listening to what you'd said, I didn't want to abandon you. I knew you'd vote for his death."

Cray snuggled closer to her warm body. "Thanks for that. Maybe I was wrong, but it's nice to know you're on my side."

"I've got your back. And maybe I was wrong, but I'd like to know how Ralph would react to questioning about his uncle."

"What, like, if he'd admit to it and show remorse?"

"I wonder if he's to the letter a symbol of Frankenstein's monster. In the book, the monster actually weeps over the death of his creator. The monster didn't kill him, by the way, but when he finds out Victor Frankenstein is dead, he weeps over his body, admitting his own suffering, loneliness, hatred, and remorse."

"What happens to the monster? I mean, in the book. I've seen the movie. I guess it's the same result. Is it?"

Sandra yawned, her eyes rolling back in her head. "That's another chapter for another day. I'm so tired, and still a little dizzy. Let's get some sleep."

Cray too felt the dense fog of fatigue settling over his eyelids and into his bones like a fine but powerful mist. He kissed Sandra on the cheek, said good night, rolled over, extinguished the oil lantern, and closed his eyes. But in spite of the fatigue, sleep did not come easily. Too many thoughts about the uncertain future. In an attempt to promote sleep, he began silently counting backwards from a hundred. When he reached eighty-seven, Sandra extinguished her lantern.

"Thanks for being by my side. It means a lot," she said.

"No. Thank you. It means the world to me."

# Chapter Fourteen

Leather belt in hand, Simon Simms stood over Ralph, his weathered face so tightly knotted, the crow's feet fanning out from his squinting black eyes resembled water-starved crevices in a bone-dry river bed. Scowling, he raised the belt. "You forgot to take the garbage out? How many times do I have to tell you and you still forget?" With a quick flip of his wrist, Simple Simon snapped it down. It made a leathery slapping sound as it struck Ralph's face so hard it left a thin two-inch gash above his right eye.

Ralph groaned in pain, feeling warm blood dribble into his eye, down his nose, into his gaping mouth. "I'm sorry. I forgot. It won't happen again. I promise."

This angered Simple Simon even more and he raised the belt again. "You know how many times you told me you forgot?"

Paralyzed with fear, Ralph said again, "I forgot."

The belt came down hard, snapping into Ralph's forearm, which he had raised over his face for protection. Stinging pain shot up his arm and into his hand. He covered his face with his other arm and silently curled up into a fetal position.

"You fucking forgot," Simple Simon said, raising the belt. "You fucking forgot. That's all I hear from you lately is you fucking forgot. Well, I don't *forget* disrespect. I remember it. And I punish it." The belt snapped down, striking Ralph's exposed leg.

He groaned, curling tighter, thinking, *How do I get out of this?* He studied the room, looking for something, any implement of salvation. But other than the fiery orange silhouette highlighting Simple Simon's formidable bulk, everything was black. The belt came down again, striking his leg. He bit his tongue so he wouldn't cry out in pain, determined to not let this bastard know he was hurting. He knew this beating well. It was the fourth time Simple Simon had imposed his vicious behavioral modification techniques, attempting to instill recollection and respect into Ralph. But Ralph had a bad feeling about this beating. Simple Simon's rage was worse than he had ever seen before. This would be the most brutal beating, even though the last one had been so severe he had almost wound up in the hospital.

As the painful lashes continued, Ralph wondered if this time Simple Simon might actually kill him. *I can't take that chance. Fucking faggot.* He scanned the blackness again. Nothing. But then, something. A yellow glint, about three feet away, on the cold floor. What was it?

Another lash struck his wrist. A leathery slapping sound. More stinging pain chasing up his arm and into his hand. Ralph bit his tongue so hard he drew blood, determined not to show his punisher any more weakness.

"Say something, you imbecile... say something other than you fucking 'forgot,'" Simple Simon said.

In a lightning swift movement, Ralph rolled over, grabbed the yellow glint, grinning when he realized it was his trusty Colt 45. Gripping it tightly in both hands, clicking off the safety, he aimed it at his tormentor's head.

Eyes widening in terror, Simple Simon stepped back.

"You want me to say something... other than I fucking forgot?" Ralph said. "How about you fucking faggot?"

Simple Simon didn't have a chance to respond. Ralph quickly fired three bullets—with a neat pattern a marksman would be proud of—that struck Simple Simon right between the eyes.

With a soft moan, Simple Simon dropped to the floor like a sack of potatoes. Although Ralph might have been celebrative, a sudden and unexplained wave of guilt and sorrow flooded through him. He brought both hands to watery eyes. "No, no, no. Why did it have to come to this?"

He felt a soft, warm hand on his shoulder and heard a voice. "Easy, easy. You had a nightmare."

Opening his eyes wide, he woke up abruptly and looked at the woman staring down at him. *Worried. She's worried about me.* Dark brown eyes, framed by black sockets. Someone had punched her good. Long blonde hair, a few strands matted to the side of her head. Two small bumps and a small cut on her head. Yellow shirt, medium-sized gravity-defying breasts. Tight red shorts. Hot pants. The soft yellow light of an oil lantern on a bedside table cast an angelic glow over her. *Not bad. Not bad at all.* Who was she? For a moment, Ralph only remembered his terrifying nightmare, nothing else. He exhaled, long and whispery. "Where am I? Who are you?"

\*\*\*\*\*\*

"You're in a shelter," Penny said. "I'm Penny. Don't you remember me? From a few hours ago?"

"No. What time is it?"

"It's four-thirty in the morning." Looking into his dark, fearful eyes, Penny wondered why she had decided to watch over this strange man, by all accounts a danger to himself and society at large. A loser and a psycho. But really, she knew why and was just trying to suppress it, unwilling to fully admit her weakness even to herself. Ralph reminded her of Jimmy Stieger, the man who had recently beaten and raped her. There was much more to the story than Detective Strader knew, much more to it than he likely even suspected. Jimmy was Penny's boyfriend, had been for the last three months. He was obsessive, compulsive, and controlling, not to mention violent and volatile. And when he learned Penny had posed as a prostitute at a dental convention in downtown Charlottetown, actually lured in and fucked an eighty-two-year old orthodontist, he snapped, punishing her in the only way he knew how. But she couldn't help her sexual addiction and, truth be told, it was this addiction that had brought her to Ralph's bedside. Oh sure, she could have justified it by saying she was a humanitarian, concerned about a fellow human being's safety and sanity. Could have rationalized it by saying that it was Ralph's panicked screams and shouts that brought her rushing to his bedside. But that would be a lie. Really, the stirrings of sexual desire, accompanied by the distant moans of pleasure next door, had prompted her to approach Ralph's bed, sit down, and study him a full hour before the anguished sounds and panicked contortions of his nightmare even became apparent.

Penny wiped Ralph's sweating forehead with a towel, feeling a faint stirring of desire as she did. He didn't object. What Detective Strader would also never know, likely never even suspect, is Penny actually enjoyed the sex when Jimmy had raped her. In the bedroom, she liked being dominated to a certain degree; needed a certain amount of pain; craved a certain amount of violence and tough talk. Years of being victimized and sexually abused had created an insatiable beast. And maybe, just maybe, now that life had become so uncertain, Ralph was just the monster to feed the beast in her; as long as it fell somewhere within her wide limits, limits that, unfortunately for Jimmy, had been overstepped. Penny's limits fell just short of wanting to get the shit kicked out of her and suffer a minor concussion.

"Are you okay?" she asked, noticing a weird mixture of sadness and anticipation in Ralph's expression.

Ralph tried to scratch his head, and showed surprise when both hands raised, one being lifted by the handcuffs. He frowned. "Can you take these off? Why am I handcuffed?"

Penny recapped events leading up to this point as best as she could remember them, filling in the names of the actors involved. "Some of them think you're a killer. But I voted to save your life. They fear you might try and kill them." She pointed to the cuffs. "I'm sorry I can't take them off. I don't have the keys, don't even know where they are."

Disappointed, Ralph lowered his arms. He searched her face. "Do you think I'm a killer?"

"I don't know. I hardly know you. Are you?"

There was a telling pause before he answered. "No."

"You need to think about it?"

"I need to think about a lot of things. My memory's fucked."

A tingling sensation started below Penny's waist, spreading up to her bosom. She felt hot flashes. Red splotches sprouted on her neck and chest. Her cheeks began to burn. *Dear God, what's wrong with me? I get aroused by a killer?* This was a thus-far unrealized level of depravity. It made her slightly uncomfortable. She crossed her legs, folding her arms across her chest, trying to will away the burning desire and anticipation. *Where did it come from? What made me so... so sick?*

But, as she studied Ralph's face, weathered lines fanning out from beady black eyes, a mass of tangled hair poking out in odd directions, pronounced lump resembling a small rhino horn right between his eyes—*Why does everyone here have bumps on their heads?*—his toothless grin, patchy facial scruff, the way he put his teeth together, grinding them after every second or third sentence, it dawned on her like a nuclear explosion. While Ralph vaguely resembled her ex, Jimmy, he more closely resembled Gideon Waulking, the man who had beaten and raped her seven years ago, late one night in Toronto as she was leaving a pub near her small apartment. With lightning speed, the entire ordeal flashed through her mind. Gideon had come up from behind her as she cut through a small park, put a knife to her throat, and said, "Shut your mouth and cooperate or I kill you."

Penny bit her tongue, remembering the initial terror that had seized her. But something had changed. In the interest of self-preservation, she had slowly taken her clothes off, laid down in the dew-coated grass that warm summer night, and spread her legs. As Gideon had entered her, she was careful not to resist, but began sobbing, tears streaming down her cheeks. He had pumped her vigorously—and it had hurt badly—for about five minutes, falling just short of blowing his load. But when he extricated his member and glided his tongue down to her vagina and began slurping voraciously, something inexplicably strange happened. Her tears dried up, the soft sobs turned to pleasurable moans and she had exploded with a shuddering, powerful orgasm. And despite repeated efforts, she had been unable to repeat its intensity or level of enjoyment for the next seven years.

What had tipped Gideon over the edge and sent him into a hysterical fit of rage was exactly that enjoyment. He was the type of psycho who relished in others' pain. A serial rapist, he had probably never encountered a woman who had actually enjoyed it, let alone climaxed with such intensity. Their pain and suffering was his pleasure. On the flipside, their pleasure was his pain and suffering. Seeing her shudder to a screaming orgasm, he had jumped up quickly, his dick as limp as a dishrag, hot anger contorting his Ralph-like features, and began punching her in the face repeatedly. To this day, Penny had never forgotten his sob-laced words, repeated over and over, until she lost consciousness: "You're not supposed to like this, bitch. I'm the one who gets the pleasure... you're not supposed to like this, bitch. I'm the one who gets the pleasure..."

She remembered what the police detective had said while visiting her in the Intensive Care Unit three weeks after Gideon's violent assault. "We got the fucker. Shot him in the head five times. You're lucky you survived. After you, he beat two other women to death, the first two times he's actually killed."

"A penny for your thoughts," Ralph said, snapping her out of it.

"What?"

"Isn't that your name? Penny?"

"You remembered," she said.

"I remember sometimes," Ralph said. "My mind works in mysterious ways. What were you thinking? You got all... I don't know, all flustered"

"You won't hurt me, will you?" Penny said, trying but not entirely succeeding to suppress the memory of Gideon, the man who had given birth to her dark masochistic tendencies, the monster who had in his violent wake created another insatiable beast, the beast in her who frequently wanted sex; hard, fast, and laden with verbal and physical abuse.

"Not if you don't want me to."

Penny was about to say, "Maybe I do," but stopped herself. Too much, too early. "Can I get you something?"

"Do you have a smoke? I need one badly."

"Okay." Earlier, she had removed Ralph's smokes from his pants pocket and placed them on a pile of wooden crates. She had done a little more than that, if memory served. Removing his jeans, she had reduced him to boxer shorts and a t-shirt. And, just before she had pulled the covers over a snoring Ralph, she had pulled down his boxer shorts and snuck a peak at his member. To her delighted surprise, it was large and swollen. And circumcised, her preference. She couldn't resist caressing its hardness for a moment before covering him with blankets and returning, giddy with arousal, to her nearby single cot.

Her path lit by the oil lantern, she went to the table and retrieved Ralph's smokes and lighter. Being watched attentively by Ralph, she returned, sat down, put a smoke in his mouth, lit it, and suddenly became confused about why she was being so nice to this alleged murderer. Had he become Gideon? Did she want to punish him? Was her compassion beginning to rule her behavior, driving her to reform him? Or was it simply the sex-addicted, throw-caution-to-the-wind beast overpowering all rational thought, needing to be fed, and craving new heights of dark and depraved ecstasy?

Never mind that now, she decided, watching Ralph blow a row of tiny blue smoke rings that slowly dissipated. "A penny for my thoughts? Is that what you said?"

Ralph exhaled a cloud of smoke that destroyed two smoke rings, another two drifting up and away to temporary safety. "Yeah. Were you thinking that you're afraid of me?"

"Yes," Penny lied. "But I was thinking something else also."

"What?"

"Why were you crying? What was your nightmare about?"

\*\*\*\*\*\*

Ralph paused, rolling his eyes up into his head in an attempt to retrieve the memory. Unlike other, often irretrievable memories, the dead face of his uncle instantly appeared, close-up, three horizontally patterned bullet holes between his eyes, mouth wide with horror, blood dribbling down his nose, around and into his mouth, down his chin, tie-dyeing his white t-shirt blood-red. *She likes me. Nobody's ever liked me like this before. If I tell her the truth, she won't like me anymore. I want her to like me, need her to like me. What does it matter? Everyone's gonna die anyway. You've reached the end of the line, brother. There's nowhere to go but up.*

"My uncle, Simon Simms, used to beat, belittle, and insult me all the time," he began slowly, searching her eyes for a sign of rejection.

She inched closer, worry lines creasing her brow.

Encouraged, Ralph continued: "My parents couldn't handle my forgetfulness, I guess, so my brother and sister got all the attention. I was the misfit, the under-achiever, not what they wanted. The rejection made me act out and things only got worse. They believed Simon would be a good role model so they shipped me off to live with him, calling me a detriment to the family, a detriment to the healthy upbringing of my brother and sister. Basically, a loser. Things didn't improve with Simon. I think he was abused as a child and took it out on me." Ralph wiped a wet eye.

Penny wiped his forehead with a towel, gently stroking his chest as she removed it. "That sounds awful." She handed Ralph the towel.

"He used to hit me with fists, boots to the head, sticks, bottles, a two-by-four, whatever he could get his hands on. When I was real young, the belt was his favorite. But as I got older, the other objects replaced the belt. One day I snapped and knocked him out, slammed his head right into a cast-iron wood stove. I almost killed him. That's when my folks bought me five acres right across the highway there, set up a double-wide trailer, and moved me in." Ralph wiped his eyes with the towel, looking at her sadly.

There was something building.

"Did he keep beating you after that?"

"No. I think he got scared of me and that's the only thing that stopped the beatings. Maybe even saved my life. But he would visit me sometimes and the verbal abuse continued. Things like, 'Why don't you be a real man and get a job?' Or, 'With your attitude you're not gonna amount to shit.' Sometimes he'd say, 'Ralph, you might not be the stupidest man in the world, but you're certainly in the top three.'" Noticing Penny's legs open, her hand gliding up her thigh toward her genitals, Ralph stopped. "Are you okay?"

She blushed, crossed her arms around her breasts. Then, as if realizing this posture was negative body language, rested them on her legs. "Yes, I'm okay. Go on, Ralph. Let it out."

"Over time, the insults, my memory of all the beatings, started to take their toll on me. Booze, drugs, a fuck-you attitude toward everyone. Hey, that reminds me, we got booze here?"

Penny was thankful to distract herself from the tingling feelings of arousal. "There's a pile of moonshine in the other room."

"Get a bottle, if you don't mind. I'm gonna need a drink for this last part."

She grabbed a flashlight, shone it toward the door, and then swept the beam at Ralph's face. "Give me your butt. I'll stub it out." He did and she dropped it on the dirt floor and stepped on it. Unable to locate glasses or cups, she returned with two bottles of moonshine, opened one, and handed it to Ralph. He took a long swill, swallowed without making a face, and pointed at his smokes, sitting on a bedside table. She lit one for him, opened her bottle, and took a small swig. Grimacing, she swallowed it.

Smoking and swilling moonshine, he continued. "Where was I?"

"Simon's abuse taking its toll on you."

He exhaled a thick cloud of smoke. "Right. Every time he left my house, I felt like killing myself. It reached the point where I felt I had to do one of two things. Either kill him or kill myself. Or both."

Penny took a large swallow of the moonshine. "So what happened?"

"I think the original plan was to kill *him* and myself. Put two misfits out of their misery."

"You're not a misfit. You're misunderstood."

Ralph fixed his gaze on her. His weary, hardened features softened. "Thanks. Nobody's ever said that to me before."

She put a hand on his leg and squeezed.

Ralph felt something stir below the sheer fabric of the blanket. "Anyway, he came by one day and all my rage boiled over. I opened the door, told him to go and fuck himself, and plugged three bullets into his head." Ralph's tone changed, defensive. "So, yeah, I did kill him. Do you blame me?"

"It sounds like an act of self-defense and self-preservation, you ask me."

"But, when it came to killing myself, I chickened out. Couldn't go through with it. So I buried his body in my potato field instead." Suddenly, another memory invaded Ralph's mind like a sword penetrating his heart. It was the one he had struggled with, but couldn't retrieve while he planted Simon in the potato field. It was the reason he had awoke from the nightmare, crying. Flicking the cigarette on the ground, setting the moonshine bottle down, he brought both hands to his face, being overcome by intense grief. Between soft sobs, he said, "Shit, I remember. You know what Simon said to me just before he died?"

Penny moved closer and hugged Ralph. She glided her hand down to his member, grinning as she began slowly massaging its stiffness. "What?"

"He said, 'I came to apologize. I'm sorry for abusing you.'"

\*\*\*\*\*\*

"I'm sorry for pushing you away," Marty said, his ear pressed to the door, listening to soft moans of pleasure coming from not one but—*What?*—two of the other occupied rooms. *Everyone fucking like rabbits and us arguing. What the fuck is that?*

Elaine stirred slightly but didn't turn around, didn't answer.

*Is that what psychologists do? Give you the silent treatment? Give you their back. Some therapy. Rejection therapy. Works great.*

After two or three drinks with Pastor Jon, he and Elaine had decided to turn in, both becoming slightly annoyed at the preacher's repetitive biblical phrases about the end of the world. The prophecies had started off coherent enough, with Pastor Jon detailing The Seven Bowls of God's Wrath. But, the drunker he got, the more repetitive he got, until finally all he kept saying was, "The end is now. Prepare yourself. Ask for forgiveness while you can."

*But isn't that what I'm doing? Asking for forgiveness?* Marty thought, surveying the dusty kitchen that he and Elaine had transformed into an impromptu bedroom. Earlier, the discussion had started off light and playful. But the problem was, Marty had started too amorous, too fast, for the refined and clinically analytical sensibilities of his psychologist wife. He should have talked more, touched less, or at least last, after the discussion had ended. Marty had told Elaine how he wanted to improve, wanted desperately to put the death of his partner, Jake Thompson, behind him, and start bridging the gap his morbid obsession had created in his marriage. But the mere mention of his partner's name recreated the terrible moment when his partner was shot in the chest by an angry housewife, venting her anger at her abusive husband on the entire male species.

Elaine had paused when Marty brought up Jake's name, watching his eyes well with tears, seeing his pain, searching his eyes intently, giving him that clinical-psychologist-diagnosing-a-patient look that so annoyed him. So, he had stopped talking and fell silent. "You can't let it go and can't talk about it, Marty," she'd said. "So how am I supposed to help you?" And that was it. He had been given the coldness of her back.

After lying silently next to her for a few minutes, the sounds of heated sex filling his ears, he had put an arm around her and, without thinking, slid his hand under her t-shirt and began fondling her left breast. That was met with another cold response. "You don't want to talk to me, but you want to fuck me?" she had asked, firmly removing his hand from the object of his apparently subconscious desire.

He approached the queen-sized air mattress where Elaine was curled up, staring at an exposed shoulder where part of the blanket had slipped away. Somehow, without him seeing, she'd managed to remove her t-shirt. *The heat, nothing else.*

Thinking of a way to solve this impasse, he remembered the death of Jake Thompson, and his convicted murderer, sixty-three-year-old, bat-shit crazy Martha Bates. Then it dawned on him. Martha was taking her anger at her husband out on the entire male population—if she'd had her way, she would've killed a half a dozen or more men before being incarcerated. But wasn't that kind of what he was doing now? Taking his anger at Martha Bates out on his loving wife Elaine?

*Fucking idiot. I should have known better.* He sat down on the corner of the bed, beside a wooden crate serving as a bedside table, lit by two candles. "Honey, did you hear me? I said I'm sorry for pushing you away. I want to change. I want to talk. Will you help me? Please."

Elaine turned around, exposing large, pendulous breasts. The burning candles cast a soft yellow glow on them. Strands of her long black hair fell on her chest, covering the right breast and part of the left one, leaving an exposed thimble-sized nipple standing at attention. Her deep brown eyes were filled with concern and compassion. She opened her arms. "I'm sorry. I'm supposed to be a therapist and I'm giving you the cold shoulder. Since when did that work? Come here, baby. I love you."

Marty fell into her arms, feeling the intense stirrings of a long unsatisfied desire. Her warmth felt comforting. It felt like home. Suddenly nervous, he said, "We can discuss this now if you want."

But her look said something else. She kissed him softly at first, then aggressively, passionately. "I know you're trying to change, baby. I appreciate it. I really do." They joined lips again, long and intense.

Through his jeans, she began softly stroking his swollen member.

"Are you sure you don't want to talk about my problem?" Marty said, wanting to play it safe, not wanting to fuck it up a second time, but also not wanting to talk at all. He would never understand how his wife could go from serious therapist to sex-starved goddess in a matter of a few seconds. Venus and Mars. *Get used to it.*

"Tomorrow's another day," Elaine said, moaning softly as Marty glided his hand expertly to her waiting, wet mound. "And it might be our last."

# Chapter Fifteen

As the pained and terror-filled shouts and screams of death and destruction permeated the dark afternoon sky, as the province of Nova Scotia burned to the ground, twenty convicts, led by Crass Muldoon, aka Killer Crass, boarded a diesel-powered, fifty-foot fishing boat bound for Prince Edward Island. The men scrambling aboard the boat represented the most malignant cancer known to humankind. All macabre manner of serial killers, child killers, thrill killers, those who specialized in bomb-building, those who were highly proficient in what they liked to call the "art of torture," sick arsonists, perverted pedophiles, predatory rapists, nasty necrophiliacs, even a few calculating terrorists. Earlier in the day, after panicked guards had fled, they had escaped a super-max prison a few hours away on the outskirts of the city of Halifax.

Calmly standing on the bow, Crass, a bald-headed hulk of a man with a thick black beard, removed a flask from his breast pocket, took a swill of the prison-made moonshine, wiped his chin, grinned, and began barking out orders to two men on the dock of the bay. "Pick up those crates of ammo and guns and load them in. Now!"

The men, who had stopped for a short breather, immediately snapped into action as Crass regarded them with sinister black eyes. He pointed to a man on deck, seated on a canvass lawn chair, while others around him furiously packed away supplies. "You. What the fuck are you doing?

You think this is a cushy union job or something? Get your ass in gear and help them."

Leaping to his feet, the man rushed over to the edge of the boat, jumped onto the dock, and almost fell into the swelling sea in his haste. He immediately went to work, lowering his gaze, avoiding direct eye contact with Crass.

Satisfied, Crass watched the progress. He knew they knew his rap sheet and wouldn't dare disrespect him. Twelve others who had tried that, including two in the joint, had paid with their lives. Two days ago, the most recent victim, the "Boss" of the prison hierarchy, had died at Crass's hands, brutally strangled in front of all the others while having lunch in the prison cafeteria. While he strangled Boss Standon, some watching in shock, others in fear, still others in admiration, Crass began his lecture. "How do you like these apples, Boss? Looks like you won't be the boss for long, you low-life child molester. You disrespect me, disrespect the seeds of generations to come... " But then a powerful black rage boiled over and the lecture stopped. When the uncontrollable rage had subsided, Crass looked down at Boss and realized there was no point in continuing. His beady brown eyes bulged from their sockets. His face was purplish red. Blood dripped from his open mouth. With brutal, vicious force, he'd crushed Boss's windpipe, snapped his neck like a ragdoll. Coming to his senses, Crass realized there was one more exclamation point left. He poked Boss in the eyes and watched his bulbous brown eyes pop from their sockets.

Then he did what in his view any revolutionary leader would do. He released Boss, watching his limp body drop to the concrete floor with a thud, and turned to the others. "You got a new leader now. Anyone got a problem with that, speak now or forever shut the fuck up." The cafeteria was stone-cold quiet for a moment. Then the applause started, slowly at first, and then erupting into a loud chorus, some inner-circle inmates even approaching Crass, patting him on the shoulder, and offering congratulations for his violent rise to the top.

Although Crass understood the need for knives and guns, he preferred killing with his bare hands. Much more intimate. Every single one of his victims had died from those powerful hands. He took great satisfaction in strangling his victims, lecturing them while the life ebbed from their sorry-ass souls. But, in most cases, they wouldn't get to hear much of the long monologue on his moral code. A black rage would boil over and their necks would snap like little twigs.

Crass watched as the men finished loading supplies onto the boat, released the dock ties, and climbed aboard. Looking up in the sky, he saw red embers being whipped by furious winds swirl around and land everywhere. At times, the embers would ignite small fires that would rapidly fan out and spread into destructive infernos of death. *A new world order*, he thought. *One where the strong survive and the weak perish. One where rule by fear and intimidation becomes the new law of the land.* He took another swig from the flask and grinned. *A land where I'll be king.*

Turning to his second in command, Nerves-Of-Steel Nelson Pry, Crass said, "Start the engine, Steel. Let's get the hell out of here."

Steel, a tall, muscular man with a red Mohawk and tattoos covering most of his body, saluted his leader. "You got it, Crass." He knew better than to call him boss.

The engine rumbled to life as the ocean began to swell and a shower of hot embers dusted the exiting boat. Crass turned to the others. "Wet some towels. Get those embers out." The men hastily complied.

A few minutes later, approaching the rough open water, Crass spotted a small vessel. It was getting pounded by growing waves and, unlike Simmering Heights, his stolen craft Simmering, the small vessel was making rather slow progress. He instructed Steel to change course and approach the boat. They neared to within twenty feet. Three men on the boat waved to them. Crass waved back. As they got closer, he said. "Having a little trouble?"

As per his instructions, three of Crass's men trained their rifles on the wayward vessel. Two men aboard the small boat looked nervously at their visitors while a third went below deck. Crass pointed to a wooden crate. Steel opened it and removed a bottle of clear liquid with a cloth wick.

"Where you off to?" Crass asked.

"Anywhere that's not burning. You?"

"Same story, my friend. Same story. Tell me, you got any women and children aboard?"

"No," a man answered. "Why?"

Crass flicked his thumb like a lighter. Steel lit the wick on the Molotov cocktail and tossed the improvised bomb into the air. As it descended onto the boat, Crass said, "I wouldn't wanna go killing any women and children, now would I? That just wouldn't be right."

The fire bomb landed on deck a few inches from one man and instantly burst into flames, turning him into a screaming fireball. Another man dove overboard and his flaming friend tried to follow, but was hit by another cocktail and began rolling around the deck, screaming horribly, trying in vain to extinguish the flames. Two more cocktails followed. As the man below deck emerged, one hit him squarely in the head, shattered, and turned him into a human fireball. Before he had a chance to dive overboard, the small boat burst into flames and exploded, showering flaming debris into the ocean and on Simmering Heights.

As his men scrambled to put out small fires erupting on deck, Crass stood calmly atop a makeshift wooden pedestal and pointed at the man in the water. His head surfaced, bobbing in the fierce waves. Gasping for air, he began swimming for his life.

"Put him out of his misery," Crass ordered. They riddled him with bullets. He uttered a muffled moan as the sea swallowed his sinking, quite dead body.

As the men doused the remainder of small fires, Crass looked out to sea and noticed a small southeast patch of Prince Edward Island apparently untouched by the raging inferno. Turning to Steel, he pointed. "Over there. Maybe that's our salvation."

# Chapter Sixteen

The serene yet deathly image was unlike anything Pastor Jon had ever seen. A beautiful woman, with long, flowing black hair and massive black wings filling up the fiery sky. Dressed in a long elegant white gown, she hovered above a tumultuous ocean, arms folded across her chest. Her frown deepened. She removed her arms from her chest, held out her hands, and a bowl magically appeared in them. Her blue eyes resonated intense sadness as she poured out the liquid contents into the swelling sea. In an instant, it turned blood red. Hundreds of seagulls dropped from the sky, slapped the ocean, and lay still. Sharks, whales, sea lions, and fish large and small leaped out of the water. They landed with loud slapping sounds on the ocean surface, wriggled in agony, and lay still.

The scene was presented to him as if he was not in it; he was floating surreally outside a giant fish bowl—a macrocosm of sorts—looking in. But he recognized it instantly, even though it was a female angel, and not a male as outlined in the *Book of Revelation*. It was the second angel, pouring out one of the seven bowls of God's wrath, killing every living thing.

The angel raised the bowl in both hands and held it up to the heavens, a look of deep sadness furrowing her delicate features. The bowl disappeared. A small boat appeared on the ocean. The young couple aboard appealed desperately to God to spare their lives. "I repent my sins," the woman said, kneeling in prayer, tears streaming down her face. "I killed my brother. But it was an accident. I swear to God. Please forgive me."

The man knelt down beside the woman. He put his hand gently on her shoulder, then kneeled beside her in prayer. Pleadingly, he looked up at the angel. His face tightened in anguish. "I committed adultery. But it was a one-night thing. It meant nothing. I swear. I'm sorry. Please forgive me. Save me. Save us!"

The woman turned to him—shocked, saddened, hurt. "You did what?"

Tears streaming down his face, the young man put a hand on her shoulder. "I'm sorry."

Her blue eyes welling with tears, the angel looked down at the young couple floating helplessly on unforgiving waters. "I'm sorry. It's too late for that now."

The boat burst into flames. Pain-filled screams punctuated the night sky. The boat exploded with a thunderous boom that echoed loudly through the heavens. An eerie quiet settled on the vast seascape. Rough waters grew still, calm, glass-like.

The angel's head turned. Her eyes suddenly widened. Her mouth fell open.

Following her gaze, Pastor Jon quickly realized why. A black vessel, Simmering Heights emblazoned on its bow in glowing white, glided through the smooth waters. As it neared, he saw a giant man, sitting on a glowing white throne fastened to the bow's deck. The man had a torn muscle shirt, exposing huge, hairy, muscular arms, and a chiseled chest. His black eyes seemed to cast a shadow in front of the boat.

Worse, Pastor Jon saw the personification of evil in those menacing eyes.

"It's the devil," Pastor Jon said, trying to warn the angel. "Kill him. Kill the devil."

But his words went unheard by the angel, unheard by Crass. The boat glided directly below the angel and stopped. Pastor Jon watched the other men on the boat stand up.

Crass pointed to the angel, his black eyes squinting, his mouth contorting. "Are you the angel of death? Did God send you?" The angel shrank as he spoke. "You have no power over me. You can go straight to Hell. Or, better still, go back to that pussy you call God, tell him to grow some stones and come and get me himself instead of sending his goddamned disciples of death. I'm the new grim reaper around here."

The angel's features tightened. She pointed a finger at the boat. "I cast you down to the bowels of Hell, where you'll suffer intolerably and live a life of trapped misery forever and ever."

But nothing happened. The ocean remained calm. A fine white mist settled over and enveloped Simmering Heights. Crass's face turned white with rage. He pointed at the angel, waving his finger threateningly. "I cast you out, you fucking bitch. Go and suck the cock of your spineless creator."

The silence was broken by a thunderous boom from above. A powerful lightning bolt sprang from the sky and struck the angel. She exploded into a million pieces and vanished in an instant.

With a wickedly satisfied grin, Crass pointed ahead. "To the red island, men. We've got work to do."

"No, no, no," Pastor Jon shouted. "No, no, nooooo..."

\*\*\*\*\*\*

Both hands on his shoulders, Cray shook Pastor Jon. "Wake up... wake up."

Horrified, Pastor Jon opened his eyes slowly. Befuddled, he looked around the room, seemingly unaware of where he was. A look of recognition crossed his face as he spotted two empty moonshine bottles nearby. His troubled, wide eyes turned to Cray. "He's coming."

"Who's coming?"

Although most of the group were awake that afternoon, it was eerily quiet in the shelter. The steady hissing of the fire-breathing dragon above had subsided. With the exception of Ralph, who was still passed out, all of them had washed themselves as thoroughly as improvised facilities would allow, and eaten from a variety of canned goods. Some curious yet knowing looks were exchanged as they went about their respective morning rituals. Now, most of them sat around in a circle, watching and waiting for Pastor Jon to wake up, anxious about what might emerge from his mouth after seeing him toss and turn for the last two hours, muttering a litany of largely incomprehensible biblical phrases.

Pastor Jon's bloodshot eyes darted around the room. "I had a vision. The second angel. Evil is coming. The devil is coming."

Cray knew better than to doubt Pastor Jon. The others eyed the odd preacher attentively. "Does the devil have a name?" Cray said. "Is he a person?"

Pastor Jon's twirling gaze found the nearby case of moonshine and locked on it momentarily. His intense blue eyes refocused on Cray and he nodded, his pupils dilating, then expanding. "His name is Crass. Killer Crass. And he's such a powerful force of evil that even God's disciples are powerless in his wake." He gouged sleep from his eyes, sat up slowly, and stared at the moonshine.

Cray broke the silence. "No, later. We need you coherent right now. What happened in your vision?

Sandra handed Pastor Jon a bottle of cold water. "Here, you must be dehydrated."

He drained half of it in two long gulps, wiped his chin, and told the story of his vision, everyone listening with rapt attention. Finishing, he said, "So you see, we have a new world order. One in which Crass will rule by fear and intimidation."

"Will he succeed?" Marty asked, turning away from an arsenal of weapons he'd inspected and cleaned earlier.

"He *is* succeeding," Pastor Jon said, wiping a hand through his tangled mass of hair. Two fingers got stuck in the steel wool and he removed them with a "tsk" sound. "As I said, the second angel vanished at Crass's command, powerless against him. And I won't repeat the vulgarities Crass said to her."

"What I wanna know is, will this evil force rule the world, conquer all good?" Marty asked.

"I'm sorry," Pastor Jon said. "I can't say right now. We have to wait until I have another vision. But he has about twenty men with him, all rotten to the core. His disciples of death."

"When is this Crass guy coming?" Sandra asked.

Pastor Jon scratched his head, polished off the bottled water, eyed the moonshine, and looked at Sandra. "Thirty days."

"Are you sure?" Cray asked. "You missed the date on the end of the world. Today isn't June 30$^{th}$. It's June 7$^{th}$."

Pastor Jon's hands began trembling from alcohol withdrawal. He clasped them together. "Give or take a few days, thirty days. I need a drink."

"What do we do now?" Penny asked, nervously eyeing the others.

"We stay here for ninety days."

Penny glanced at the door from which Ralph's muffled, chainsaw-like snore began a slow rumble. Her eyes found Pastor Jon. "We can't stay down here for ninety days. We don't have enough supplies, and look at the sanitary conditions around here. Last night while I was sleeping, a rat scurried over my head."

"I didn't think you slept at all last night," Cray said, biting his tongue so as not to elaborate.

A nervous laughter erupted and subsided.

"Really," Penny said, standing. "By the sound of it, you and Sandra were fucking like rabbits. If there was an Olympic competition for intercourse, you two would have been guaranteed a spot on the podium, probably a gold medal."

More embarrassed laughter.

Cray couldn't prevent a small smirk. Sandra also tried unsuccessfully to stifle a grin. *You asked for that one. Walked right into it like a chicken with its head cut off.*

Penny looked at Marty and Elaine, now sitting side by side, holding hands. "And you two probably would've won silver."

"Marty and I have been separated for many months," Elaine said. "This is our reunion."

"Never mind that," Marty said. "No need to justify it, sweetie." He pointed to the door containing Ralph. "You would sleep with the likes of that?"

"He's misunderstood," Penny said, not denying it. "Like I am." She went over and stood in front of Ralph's door.

"I understand him quite well," Marty said. "He's a cold-blooded killer."

Slightly annoyed, Elaine looked at Marty and put a hand over his mouth.

"He killed his uncle in self-defense," Penny said, then put her hand over *her* mouth, suddenly embarrassed about repeating something said to her in confidence.

Marty removed his wife's hand. "So he *did* kill Simon Simms."

"You don't know his story," Penny said. "He's been abused and rejected from a very young age. He's a victim of societal rejection. If you were in his shoes, you would've done the same thing. Do you know how often and how brutally his uncle beat him? How many times he verbally abused him?"

There was an uneasy silence as they digested this information. Pastor Jon tried to stand up, wobbled, and plunked down on his butt. On all fours, he crawled over to the moonshine crate, opened a bottle, and took a long pull, unable to contain the powerful demons of alcoholism. He wiped his chin. "I'm not going to judge your indiscretions. It's up to God to do that. And He's got too much on his plate right now... " He trailed off, taking another pull on the powerful hooch.

"Yeah," Penny said. "Why don't you let God judge Ralph's indiscretions? Don't be so quick to write him off. Give him a—"

"Hey," Ralph said, pounding on the door. "Let me outta here. I gotta piss like a racehorse for fuck sakes."

Penny fumbled with the metal catch, finally released it, and opened the door. With his hands cuffed in front of him, pants falling down, dragging his boxer shorts down with them, Ralph stepped out into the dimly lit open area. Looking at the others with a wry grin, he said, "Morning, folks. Another beautiful day in paradise, ain't it?"

Cheeks flushing, Penny adjusted his boxers, pulled up his jeans, cinched his leather belt, and buckled it. Leading him by the arm, she went over to the composting toilet semi-privatized by three shower curtains affixed to the ceiling.

Ralph looked at Pastor Jon, already well into his first bottle of moonshine. "Now there's a man after my own heart. If we're gonna go, may as well go out in style."

Smirking, Pastor Jon raised the bottle.

"Don't mind if I do," Ralph said. "But I gotta take a dump first."

Penny pointed to the handcuffs. "How are you gonna do that with those? I'm not wiping your ass. I'm not a nurse."

A blush crept across Sandra's face.

Penny turned to Marty. "I think you need to take those off."

Marty stood, looking at Ralph hesitantly. "You're a cold-blooded killer. You murdered your uncle. I'm not taking them off."

Turning to Penny, Ralph cocked an eyebrow. His face tightened. "You told them?"

"It was an accident," she said, clasping her hands together and staring at her fingers.

"Now you've just confessed," Marty said, turning to the others. "You think we should un-cuff a murderer?'

Silence.

"Let the man take a shit in privacy," Pastor Jon said. "Then put the cuffs back on. Everyone should be entitled to wipe their own ass if they're capable."

A few grins. Some eyes rolled. Everyone nodded. There was no formal vote required this time. Drawing his gun, Marty motioned to Cray and approached Ralph. While Cray held his outstretched hands, Marty extracted a key from his back pocket and unlocked the cuffs. He stuffed the key in his pocket, hooked the cuffs to his belt, and pointed the gun at Ralph's head. "Try anything at all, I'll blow your fucking head off."

Ralph rubbed his wrists. "Listen, I didn't kill my uncle for the thrill of it. It was self-defense. I finally had enough.

Finally snapped. He abused me so often and for so long, I thought it was all I could do to save my own life. I mean you guys no harm." He pointed to Cray. "You saved my life, partner. Why would I want to kill you?"

"You remember murdering Simon, then?" Marty said, the gun still leveled at Ralph's head. "Not the story you gave me."

Ralph approached the bathroom. "For the longest time I didn't. Blocked it out, I guess, but yeah, it came back to me." He dropped his head. "I meant to kill myself also but chickened out." Then he crossed his legs and began squirming. "Can this wait?"

"Go ahead and relieve yourself," Marty said.

A few fingers plugged noses as they listened to a chorus of farts and the splattering sounds of Ralph's bowel movement.

Sandra stood, waving a hand around her nose and grimacing. "I'm going to put some things away in the kitchen." She looked at Elaine. "Anyone want to help?" Nodding, Elaine got up. They went into the kitchen and soon the clanging of pots and pans, glassware and cutlery, foodstuffs finding homes, could be heard, along with muffled conversation.

Ralph emerged from the bathroom with a sheepish grin. Eyeing the others, he said, "Sorry about that. Not a lot of privacy." He stretched his arms out cooperatively and Marty fastened the handcuffs. Penny led him over to a corner of the room where some bottled water, soap and towels were stored. She wiped him down with a soap-and-water soaked towel as the others watched. When she was finished, she led him over to a table with two plastic chairs. They sat down.

"You hungry?" she asked, putting a hand on his arm.

"I need a smoke. And I'm thirsty." He pointed to the crate of moonshine. "Get me one of those."

From her jeans pocket, Penny removed Ralph's smokes and lighter. She put one in his mouth, lit it, and put the smokes and lighter on the table. "You should eat first. I'll get you something." She went into the kitchen.

Cray unpacked some plastic chairs stored in another corner of the makeshift main area and brought them near the burning candle. He arranged five chairs as Marty examined a cache of weapons and ammo stored in another corner. Cray brought three wooden crates over and set them between the chairs to serve as makeshift tables. He sat down, motioning for Pastor Jon to join him. Pastor Jon tried to stand up, but stumbled. Cray rushed to his side, grabbing his arm, pulling him up, and sitting him down.

Cray pointed to the two-thirds full moonshine bottle that Pastor Jon was clutching like it was the elixir of life. "You should take it easy on that. We need you to make sense."

Pastor Jon took a swill, spilled a few drops on his chin, and wiped it with his shirtsleeve. "The second angel poured out her bowl in the sea, and it turned to blood like a dead man, and every living thing in the sea died... except for Crass, the personification of evil. And he's coming. He's coming here. Prepare yourself. The evil is near..." Pastor Jon trailed off, staring at the flickering candle with a lost look.

Tucking another handgun fastened with a silencer under his belt, Marty carried another piece over to Cray and handed it to him. It was a Colt 45. Ralph's Colt 45, the murder weapon used on his uncle. Cray took the gun and tucked it between the small of his back and his jeans.

"You still got the Glock?" Marty asked.

Cray pointed to the bulge in the crotch of his pants.

"So you're not just happy to see me then?" Marty said.

Cray laughed, a nervous chuckle.

Pastor Jon's vacant eyes watched the candle flicker.

"Those are *my* guns," Ralph said.

"Correction," Marty said, pointing the silenced firearm at Ralph. "Those *were* your guns."

"Hey, no need to get hot," Ralph said, pointing to the moonshine. "I just want a drink."

"Get it then and sit your ass back down."

Ralph complied, popping the cap off the bottle and taking a long swill as he sat down. "You guys should learn to trust me. I'm not your fucking enemy. From what I can understand from the preacher, the enemy is out there."

"We don't know you're not the enemy," Marty said. "For all we know, you *are* the enemy." He leaped up suddenly, aimed the silenced weapon toward Ralph, and fired. Ralph twitched spasmodically, and, still holding the moonshine, fell back in his chair.

The rat's head exploded, blood and brain matter splattering the wall. Headless, it scurried along the ground, stopped a few inches short of the candle, twitched for a second, and then lay still, leaving a thin trail of blood.

Cray leaped up, drawing his gun, pointing it, first at the dead rat, then at Ralph. Marty also had his firearm aimed at Ralph.

The kitchen door opened and three terrified female heads poked out. "What the hell's going on?" Sandra asked.

"A rat," Cray said, picking it up by the tail. A few drops of its blood dripped onto the candle and sizzled. Pastor Jon's mouth opened, horrified.

"Marty killed a rat," Cray said. He carried it over to a plastic garbage bin.

"They carry diseases," Marty said.

Holding up the moonshine bottle, Ralph got up, bringing the fallen chair with him. He watched Cray drop the rat in the wastebasket. He looked at Marty. "Nice shooting, Tex. You scared the shit outta me, though. And look, I still got the moonshine. Didn't spill a drop. One thing you don't want to do is spill moonshine. At any cost. That's taboo no matter where you're from."

"I'll drink to that," Pastor Jon said, holding up his bottle to Ralph. Grinning, they drank.

With opened cans of beans and tuna in her hands, Penny approached Ralph, set them on the table in front of him, and said, "You should eat before you drink. Don't drink on an empty stomach."

Ralph looked at the food, disinterested. "I don't wanna ruin my buzz."

"Please," Penny said.

Ralph set the bottle on the table and looked at Penny, his black eyes filling with affection. "Okay, sweet-cakes.

Whatever you say." With a spoon, he began picking away at both dishes.

Marty holstered his weapon, sat down, and stared at the flickering candle. Pastor Jon's now somber gaze also focused on the candle. A few drops of rat's blood sizzled on the flame as a few more dribbled down the candle, the dark red contrasting sharply against its whiteness.

The ensuing silence was broken only by the muffled clattering and conversation from the kitchen, the whirring of the fan, and the occasionally clinking of metal on metal and open-mouthed chewing as Ralph ate.

Becoming acutely aware of his dimly lit surroundings, Cray realized the temperature had dropped to something approximating room temperature. Also, the steady hissing of the fire-breathing dragon above had abated for about the last hour. It was eerily quiet topside and Cray wondered if this was a good or bad sign. Had the fire stopped? Or had it decimated the area and just moved on to greener pastures? Was everybody dead? Was the malignant cancer that Pastor Jon had predicted on its way to destroy them? If so, when? Thirty days? Maybe a lot sooner.

Penny sat down beside Ralph. He grinned and winked at her. A small smile pursed her cut lip as she touched his hand gently. He resumed eating.

Snapping out of his mesmerized trance, Pastor Jon pointed to the candle. "That blood dripping down there is a symbol of death. It represents the blood of our enemies. We kill our enemies and we put out the fire. You see, look, the flame flickers, boiling the blood of our enemies, weakening as it does. It's a message from God."

"I thought you said we need to stay down here for thirty days?" Cray asked. "Or was it ninety days? I don't even know anymore." Cray was becoming confused by Pastor Jon's contradictory revelations.

Clenching her fists, Penny leaped to her feet. "I've heard enough. I've *had* enough." Spittle shot from her mouth. "I can't stay down here for thirty days and listen to that drunken preacher rant and rave like this. It'll drive me nuts before whatever is gonna kill me, kills me. I wanna leave here, and I wanna leave now." She turned to Ralph. "You wanna come with me?"

Ralph drained the juice from the tuna can and slapped it down on the table. "Damn right I do, baby. Long as I get treated like a fucking prisoner here, I wanna fuck off. I wanna take my chances up there. I can't hear the fire. It's out. And, like the preacher says, we got enemies to kill. Why should we wait here like sitting ducks for them to come get us? Wait for them to kill our motherfucking asses?"

# Chapter Seventeen

Standing on the bow of Simmering Heights in the smoke and fire-filled afternoon haze, Crass focused his binoculars on the southeast corner of Prince Edward Island that appeared untouched by the destructive fire. It was a small island, just off the coast of the bigger Island, but still in the province's jurisdiction, he believed. He put the binoculars down on a wooden throne affixed to the bow and glanced around at the other men. Most were sitting around on deck, drinking, playing cards, talking in hushed tones. None of them were looking at him. Good. He disliked people staring at him unless he was personally addressing them. Then, his intimidating scowl demanded they look him right in the eye. Hanging the binoculars around his neck, he went into the cabin.

Steel was busy steering the boat through rough waters, following the fanning track of a large fog light affixed to the roof of the cabin. His steely gray eyes squinted as he wrestled with the helm, trying to keep the boat on course. He was a devil-worshipping serial killer with twenty-seven murders notched in his black leather belt. He took great pride in torturing his victims and branding many of them in the forehead with a molten hot pentagram. He disliked quick kills, preferring slower and more intimate methods. He enjoyed watching his victims suffer terribly before they died. From his periphery, he saw Crass enter.

"You know where we're going, right?" Crass said, pointing.

"Sure do," Steel said. Fleeing the law, Steel had lived on Prince Edward Island for six years before authorities had nabbed him. He knew the lay of the land well, frequently taking boat trips off the Island to kill victims in New Brunswick, Nova Scotia—anywhere but PEI, in an effort to avoid too much heat from the Pigs. "That's Panmure Island. That's where we're heading."

"What's there?" Crass asked, pulling out his flask and taking a pull.

As they neared the shoreline, Steel dug out a pack of Colts and a lighter from a breast pocket. He opened the pack and offered one to the boss who he dared not call boss. Crass took one. Steel lit it for him, lit one for himself, took a long drag, and exhaled a thick cloud of blue smoke. The smoke cloud was caught by the wind and dispersed quickly. "Not much, really. Bunch of homes. Nice beaches. An old lighthouse. Provincial park. Trailer park campsite. Bar and restaurant."

Crass exhaled a cloud of smoke and belched loudly. "Do you think there's any trouble there?"

"Don't think so, Killer. Nothing we can't handle." Steel grinned sheepishly. "Might even find us some nice sluts who need their brains fucked out. Been a long time, you know what I mean."

Crass ignored the comment. "How long before we get there?"

"Fifteen minutes tops."

Crass nodded. "You let me know if you see any boats."

Steel grinned and a dimple appeared on his pock-marked face. He pointed out to sea. "Boats? One right there—look."

Looking through his binoculars, Crass saw the light first, then a small vessel bobbing in the waves. "Head for it."

"Already on course," Steel said, running a hand through his gravity-defying Mohawk.

"You got the Molotov cocktails ready?"

Grinning, Steel tapped a nearby wooden crate with his boot.

"Good. When we get there, I want you to send Rick and Ron on board." Crass made a thumbs-up. "Then wait for my orders. You got that?"

"Got it."

Crass left the cabin and returned to his throne at the bow. He sat down, took another pull on the flask, and snapped his fingers. Sammy, the prison whipping boy and unwilling anal sex victim, quickly grabbed a bottle of Jack Daniels from a case and ran it over to Crass. Without making eye contact, the skinny man, who looked no older than nineteen but was actually thirty-six, handed the bottle to Crass, spun around, and returned to his place beside the liquor stash. He had been ordered to guard it from the other inmates, only allowing them five out of its twenty-four bottles. If the rations were breached, the men knew there would be hell to pay.

Crass returned the flask to his breast pocket, opened the bottle of Jack Daniels, and took a long pull, grinning as he envisioned what would become of Rick and Ron in very short order. Fuck them, he thought. In his eyes, they were the lowest form of criminal. Both pedophiles, young boys being their victims of choice. Rick had sexually molested and then murdered six young boys, all of them less than twelve years old, the youngest being a mere five years old. Detestable. Ron had sexually molested and subsequently murdered four young boys. He was the worst in Crass's eyes: all of Ron's victims were between the ages of four and six. The worst kind of bottom-feeding scum sucker. Well, fitting for the scumbag to meet his end on the ocean floor. Ironical even.

The boat was in sight now, maybe fifty feet away, but turning away from Simmering Heights, speeding up, as if sensing impending danger. Crass saw the black silhouettes of two people aboard the tiny craft. "Hey, wait a minute. We mean you no harm. Stop, please!"

The driver killed the outboard engine and pointed a handgun at Crass. Simmering Heights drifted to within twenty feet before Steel calmed its engine. Crass spoke. "You can put that piece down, young man. We're just wondering if you need any food or water." Steel trained the fog light on the occupants of the boat. It appeared there were only two. Crass realized it was a young woman who stood next to the nervous, gun-toting man. *Oh well*, he thought. *I hate to do this, but she'll just have to take one for the team.*

"We could use some water," the man said. His gun didn't waver from its focal point—Crass's head.

"No," the woman said, her voice tight. "We don't know them. Start the engine."

Crass picked up a case of bottled water and stepped forward. "You want this? I'll toss it on your boat, and off we go. Just let us get a little closer, okay?"

"Let's go," the woman demanded, pulling the man's arm. "I don't trust them."

But Steel had already pulled Simmering Heights to within five feet of the wobbling boat. The man, perhaps realizing his female companion had been right all along, handed the gun to her and started pulling the cord on the outboard motor. One, two, three pulls. It sputtered but wouldn't start. "Fucking cocksucker."

Crass pointed to Rick and Ron. "Jump aboard. Now!"

Rick ran to the edge of Simmering Heights and drew his gun. He fired it at the woman and a bullet whistled past her head. She screamed and shot him three times in the chest. As he dropped into the ocean, quite dead, Ron leaped aboard and tackled the woman. The gun flew out of her hands and into the sea as she fell down, Ron landing on top of her. As the man charged Ron, he quickly throttled the woman with one hand and shot him in the face. The man moaned in pain and toppled overboard, splashing into the ocean and floating alongside Rick's corpse. Still throttling the woman, Ron pulled her to her feet. "What do you want me to do with her?"

Crass gave the thumbs-up to Steel, who quickly launched a Molotov cocktail onto the small boat. It was a perfect shot, shattering on Ron's head and drenching him and the struggling and screaming woman with flames. On Crass's signal, Steel tossed another flame bomb aboard, this one exploding just in front of the two victims. Locked together in an embrace of fiery death, they fell on deck, screaming horribly. On Crass's command, Steel accelerated and veered toward Panmure Island.

Crass pointed at the screaming victim. "That's what you get for molesting and murdering little boys, you dick-sucking bottom feeder. Return to the bottom of the ocean where you belong, you sick fuck."

About a hundred feet away, Crass glanced back. The engine noise was drowning out most of the screams now. He watched the boat explode; red embers, flesh and blood, and burning debris lighting up the dark sky like a fireworks display. He permitted himself a small grin, then turned and scowled at a few of his men who had dared observe him. "What the fuck are you looking at? Just be thankful you ain't pedophiles, or you'd be next. Now take your fucking eyes off me."

# Chapter Eighteen

Tuesday, June 21. Two weeks exactly had passed in the small shelter. Using a pen, Cray had marked off the days on a calendar pinned to the wall of the bedroom he shared with Sandra. She slept comfortably beside him now, breathing slowly and evenly, as he reflected on past events and their plans for the future. In spite of the grim circumstances, Cray had many things to be thankful for. He was still alive, for one, and his wounds were healing nicely, with no sign of infection in the cut to his hand, or his head. Initially, he had been worried about Sandra's concussion, as periodically she would slip into a daze and was unable to remember things: what she had eaten for dinner, what day it was, what she had done the hour before. But over time, her memory grew stronger and the memory lapses became less frequent. There were still the occasional lapses, but overall Cray felt she was pulling out of the concussion admirably. Due to their dire situation, he might well attribute her memory lapses to their cramped living conditions and their uncertainty, even dread, about the future.

Of one thing he was certain, however. He had become much closer to Sandra, opening up to her about his family and the incidents that had caused his distrust and dislike for humankind. She, too, had confided in Cray about the tragic death of her Vancouver boyfriend and gone into great detail about the terrible car accident that had killed both of her loving parents. This openness and vulnerability had created a strong bond that had blossomed into something much stronger. Love. Maybe it was in part due to circumstances; there was no longer an abundant supply of mates to choose from. But Cray didn't care, and didn't give a lot of thought to the reasons. This was the here and now and he had no choice but to make the best of it. She loved him. He loved her. That was all that mattered. Well, maybe not all that mattered, he thought, but still a much better way to endure an apocalypse. Their relationship was not without some friction, being forced into a situation of cohabitation. Sandra sometimes commented on Cray's untidiness, and she considered some of his comments, particularly those concerning Penny and Ralph, to be at times insensitive. But at least he and Sandra discussed problems as soon as or soon after they arose. Wasn't communication the core of any successful relationship?

The other couples in the shelter had also bonded remarkably well. Against their better judgment, Ralph and Penny had decided to stay; the condition, which they had democratically voted on, was to release Ralph from the handcuffs. As long as he wasn't being treated like a murderer, although he was one, he had agreed to stay on. And his behavior, although characterized by Elaine as being that of someone developmentally handicapped and having intermittent explosive disorder, had improved dramatically; Penny's unusual love and affection for him had curtailed his fear, loathing, and hatred for humankind. Even his memory had improved somewhat, and he now consulted his reminder lists less frequently. *A little love can go a long way*, Cray thought, although he often wondered if what Penny exhibited toward Ralph was really love. Elaine had one or more labels for all of them, and Cray had heard her refer to Penny as "a sex addict and quite possibly a sadomasochistic sexual narcissist, who derives pleasure from pain, both verbal and physical."

Was Elaine right? Did Penny have a grandiose sense of her sexual prowess which she felt entitled her to emotionally and physically manipulate Ralph at his expense? Was there a lack of true intimacy in the relationship? Was Ralph merely being exploited to fulfill Penny's twisted needs and desires? Sandra had also said Penny suffered from post-traumatic stress disorder as a result of her abusive upbringing. Mix those ingredients with a developmentally handicapped man with intermittent explosive disorder, and what do you get? A ticking time bomb? A powder keg of turbulent emotions that could explode at any time? Cray didn't know. He wasn't a shrink. Best to stay out of it; don't meddle in other people's affairs, particularly affairs of the heart, if that's what they were. *It's their thing. Their love affair, or whatever it is. Let the chips fall where they may.* At least whatever Penny had with Ralph seemed to be working, turning him into a better and more loving person.

At one time Cray feared and hated Ralph, had voted for his cold-blooded execution. Was afraid that at any moment, Ralph would storm into his bedroom and riddle them with bullets. But now Cray had a rapport with Ralph, morphing ever closer into an unlikely friendship. They occasionally exchanged witticisms, shared a drink together, and often called each other bro. A one-eighty degree turn. An unlikely paradigm.

For their part, Marty and Elaine had also become closer, although occasionally Cray heard argumentative exchanges coming from their room. Often the muffled words sounded like Elaine applying her therapeutic skills to help Marty through the trauma and guilt of his partner's death. And while Marty had dipped into the moonshine a few times with the guys, and some insults had been flung around—a few directed at his wife—for the most part they did not air their dirty laundry in public. Instead, they retreated to their bedroom to resolve disagreements. Cray could see in Marty's eyes that he loved Elaine dearly, and was trying hard not to push her away; trying hard not to get obnoxiously hammered and subsequently withdrawn; trying hard not to repeat the same destructive patterns that had led to their initial    split.    Elaine    even    had    a    label    for Marty—post-traumatic stress disorder.

But as much as Elaine had tried to label Pastor Jon, his odd behavior defied characterization; he defied a textbook definition that would place him neatly into a box of lunacy. She tried paranoid schizophrenic, manic-depressive, PTSD, bipolar disorder, and attention deficit disorder, among others. Finally, she settled on "a rambling, confused alcoholic who nonetheless exhibits true and prophetic visions of the future."

And it was just those visions of the future that had begun to worry Cray. Lately, Pastor Jon had been hitting the bottle hard, some of his ramblings becoming less coherent. But at times, his tired, drunken eyes would become alert, and he would convey with remarkable clarity and detail the murdering, raping, and pillaging being committed by Crass and his gang of evildoers. According to Pastor Jon, Crass planned on starting an evil polygamist cult. And perhaps most frightening of all, "the devil and his disciples," as Pastor Jon called them, were slowly inching their way toward the shelter. At times he could even place their geographic locations. He was sure the ruthless murderers would stumble on their shelter sooner rather than later.

The issue had been discussed ad nauseam and up until last night the result had always been the same. "As long as we have supplies, we stay put," Pastor Jon had warned. But that was no longer the case. They had run out of water, numerous rotting rat corpses were creating an unbearable and unhealthy stench, and two days ago the compost toilet had broken and methane gases had begun seeping into the shelter, making them dizzy, clogging their minds, slowly robbing them of rational thought, ridding them of the ability to make sound judgments.

Necessity had forced their hands. They had to go topside. And they had to go today. Cray stirred, checking the time on his wrist watch. 6:53 am. Close enough, he thought. They had agreed to an 8:00 am departure and for the last four hours he had lain awake, thinking, reflecting, and worrying about the forces of evil that may now rule the world.

Sandra stirred, rolled over, opened her eyes, and faced him. Overwhelmed with emotion, he kissed her forehead. "It's time."

\*\*\*\*\*\*

Cray was the first one out of the hole. As the backpack-toting others filed out, he surveyed the landscape. The sky was a mixture of gray and black with a fiery orange haze in the distance, a grim picture of the sun struggling to rise. The forest had been razed to the ground, with a smattering of black skeletal forms poking up, sad monuments of former living trees. Scattered plumes of smoke rising up from the ash dotted the bleak wasteland. It was deathly quiet and intensely hot. Ralph's pickup had been reduced to charred metal remains, all window glass shattered. Marty's Crown Victoria was a twisted metal tombstone marking a former motor vehicle.

Cray stumbled forward, stiff joints protesting angrily after a sedentary existence in damp, cramped quarters. He found his legs just as he found something else. Sandra's yellow Ford Explorer sat in a perfect circle of green forest carpet, untouched by the savage beast. Cray turned to Sandra. Her face was tight, worry lines etched in her brow, as the grim realization of the massive scope of the destruction sank in. "Look. I can't believe it," Cray said. "Your SUV."

Her face brightened somewhat—though nothing approximating her normal room-illuminating smile—as she approached it. "My God." She opened the door. "The keys are still there."

The last one out of the hole, Pastor Jon, half-full moonshine bottle in hand, staggered around, eyes wide with incredulousness. "Divine intervention. God is watching over us."

Ralph and Penny stood by Ralph's burnt pickup, looking distraught and sad. Ralph looked in the driver window, tried the door and jumped back, wincing and clutching his hand. "Fuck, it's still hot. Real hot."

Marty and Elaine, hanging their heads near the charred remains of the Crown Victoria, turned away and approached Sandra and Cray.

"We have no communication," Marty said. "No cell signal whatsoever."

Cray removed his cell phone from his pocket and tried calling Marty. Same story. Zero signal. "You're right. Nothing."

"Let's go for a ride," Marty said, peering inside Sandra's SUV. "Try and start it."

Sandra climbed in and turned the key. It rumbled to life. They climbed in, Pastor Jon opting to sit in the rear cargo area along with his knapsack of moonshine. Halfway down the road, Cray's face brightened as he pointed ahead. "Look, is that your house?"

"Holy shit," Sandra said, as they neared. "It is."

"Divine intervention," Pastor Jon said, slurring his words slightly. "There's hope."

She pulled in front of the house and parked. She turned to Cray. "I'm going to get water."

The house and outbuildings had been spared by the fire. Although covered with a thick carpet of ash, most of the lawn around the buildings showed signs of green beneath the ash.

They climbed out. While the others walked around the property, taking stock of the situation, Sandra and Cray went inside. They walked through an undisturbed living room and into the kitchen. Everything was where it should be.

"I can't believe this," Sandra said, reaching into a kitchen cupboard and removing a case of bottled water. She handed a bottle to Cray and he drained it in a few quick gulps. Sandra finished half of hers in three gulps.

"Amazing," Cray said, "that the fire could destroy everything else and save your property and vehicle."

She took his hand. "Let's bring some water to the others. Maybe there's hope."

They went outside and handed out bottled water. Pastor Jon was reluctant to take one, but Sandra insisted, finally stuffing a bottle into his unsteady hand, scolding him with a waving index finger, "You drink that."

Thirsts properly quenched, they sat down on the porch steps of the large wraparound deck. Pastor Jon sat on a steel bench beside a nearby fire pit. Drinking moonshine, he started muttering in a low, largely incomprehensible voice.

There was a moment or two of silence as they adjusted to the gravity of the situation, the general mood somber as thoughts of deceased loved ones occupied grief-stricken minds. Consulting his to-do list, Ralph finally broke the silence. "I see your ATV is in the barn. Mind if I borrow it? If it starts, I wanna see if my house survived."

"I'll come with you," Penny said.

"Go ahead," Sandra said. "We should try and get the well going." She pointed to an outbuilding. "I have a spare generator in there. We can run the house off that."

Ralph nodded, and he and Penny walked off hand-in-hand toward the barn.

Cray noticed that for a rare change Ralph hadn't started off his day with a few belts of moonshine. The bottled water was the only drink Ralph had put to his lips, unless of course he had taken to secretly drinking. No, not his style, Cray decided. "Hey, Ralph." Halfway to the barn, Ralph turned around. Cray continued, "If you find any gas, bring it back. And, if your house survived, at least come back and let us know, so we don't have to come looking for you."

"Will do, bro. Will do. I appreciate that."

The quad rumbled to life. Ralph and Penny disappeared down the charred driveway surrounded by a gray, black, and bleak landscape. Even the distant fiery orange sunset was fading, as if surrendering its battle to brighten the day.

Marty and Cray agreed to fetch the generator and try to wire it to a porch outlet while Sandra and Elaine went inside the house to clean out the kitchen, rid the fridge of rotting food, and try and fashion a breakfast of sorts from what remained.

"I don't believe this," Marty said, as they lifted the generator. "Everything looks destroyed, but her house survived. I wonder if my house survived."

"Maybe we can check," Cray said, as they carefully squeezed the generator through the open doorway of the outbuilding, a slim one-inch clearance on either side. "But I don't think now is a good time for that."

"I agree," Marty said as they carried it across the ash-coated lawn. They climbed the steps, brought it over to the porch outlet, and set it down. Cray removed the gas tank cap and, with the aid of his flashlight, peered inside. "Got gas. Half a tank."

Marty plugged it into the electrical outlet, which was wired to six essential interior outlets, a backup power supply Sandra had wisely thought to install shortly after purchasing the property. Marty grabbed the handle of the starting cord, then stopped, eyeing Cray with anticipation mixed with dread. "How are you holding up?"

"Not bad, considering. You?"

"The same. But I'm starting to worry about those savages Pastor Jon has been on about."

"I'm worried about them too." Cray knew Marty was going somewhere with this. Marty's mind was methodical, systematic, calculating.

"When we get this going, I think we should install motion detector lights around here."

"Good idea."

"I don't want to be a sitting duck."

"But there's more on your mind than that?"

Marty nodded, tired, bloodshot blue eyes widening. "I think we should launch an offensive." He pointed to Pastor Jon, who had removed himself from the bench and now sat cross-legged by the fire pit, alternately sipping moonshine and bottled water. "He says they're on Panmure Island. That's maybe thirty minutes away. I say we reinforce our defenses here, then go there. Try and size up the enemy and then return."

"Who goes?" Cray asked, wondering if he had the courage for such a mission.

"You and me."

"You wanna leave Ralph with the women?"

"It looks like you're starting to trust him."

"I don't know if I trust him *that* much. Do you?"

"Dunno. Can you think of a better idea?"

Cray thought maybe he and Ralph alone should go. Leave Marty, a capable shooter, with the women. Or maybe Sandra, Marty, and himself? No, that could potentially put Sandra in more danger than she was in now. Finally, the only idea that made sense formed. "I think we should vote on it. Maybe it comes down to you and me, and we have to trust Ralph a little more than we already do, but we don't really have a lot of options. If we're going to succeed in fighting off any enemies, we gotta be able to trust one another all the way, gotta be able to form a tight bond."

"Let's do that, then. After we eat, after we reinforce our defenses, after Ralph returns." Marty adjusted the choke on the generator and pulled the cord. It sputtered and stalled. After three more tries, it fired up.

Sandra and Elaine appeared at the door, clapping and offering encouraging smiles. They came off as hopeful, but falling well short of overjoyed.

"Way to go," Sandra said.

"Good work, boys," Elaine said.

They disappeared inside. Marty and Cray moved away from the hum of the generator so they could hear each other speak. Standing on the lawn, they began discussing plans for the defense perimeter.

*****

The skeleton head poked up from the ash, black eye sockets boring into Ralph. Its mouth was agape in an expression of part terror, part macabre, maniacal grin. The blaze that had decimated Ralph's house and property had also burnt through the thin layer of dirt covering Simon, torched his corpse, swept away the soil, and blanketed it in ash, exposing only boney head, hands, and feet. Simon appeared to be digging himself out from the tomb, resurrecting himself so he might seek revenge on his murderer. At least, that was the first thought that popped into Ralph's head as he killed the ignition on the quad, climbed off, kneeled down, and covered his eyes with both hands. Shame, guilt, and remorse raveled tightly together like a rope and formed a painful knot in the pit of his stomach.

"I'm sorry, Simon," he said, his voice cracking with emotion. "I'm so sorry."

"It's too late for that now," Penny said, kneeling beside him and putting a comforting hand on his shoulder. "He's dead."

After a moment of silence, Ralph slowly removed his hands from his face and looked at her with a grimace. "What should we do?"

"Cover him with dirt, mark it with a cross if you like, and say a eulogy—if that makes you feel any better." Her tone was nonchalant. She pointed to a nearby metal shovel. "We can use that."

Ralph picked up the shovel. "It's still warm."

"But not too hot?"

"No, not like the truck." He approached Simon's skeleton and began shoveling black dirt and ash over it.

Penny wandered off for a few minutes and returned with a small metal garden trowel and a small metal boat anchor.

She set the trowel beside the grave and pointed to the top t-shape of the boat anchor. "Here's his tombstone."

Ralph continued working, amassing a mound of black dirt and ash over Simon's remains. Penny set the anchor down, kneeled down and, using the garden trowel, began digging. Fifteen minutes later they had a mound of dirt neatly covering the gravesite. Penny stuck the anchor in the middle.

They stepped back and stared at it for a moment. Penny broke the silence. "Can you think of anything to say? I mean, he treated you badly."

"He apologized." Ralph's voice carried a note of anger.

"One apology doesn't absolve a lifetime of abuse."

Defensively, Ralph stepped away, his hand tightening reflexively on the handle of the shovel. "What do you want me to say? He was an asshole and should rot in Hell?"

Penny's eyes widened, fixing on his tightening grip. She stepped back, an arm instinctively raised above her head. "Say what you want. I never knew the man, but he doesn't sound like a very nice one. You forgive him, say something nice. You don't, then don't. I don't know."

Ralph's beady black eyes squinted. He closed his mouth tight, grinding his teeth. He lifted the shovel in the air.

Penny retreated another step.

He whirled suddenly, pitching the shovel high into the air, well behind them. He turned to her and his expression softened. "I don't know if I forgive him. But I'd like to try."

Penny slowly relaxed. "I was just trying to help."

"I know. I'm sorry. I'll say something and we'll leave. Okay?"

Penny nodded but remained where she stood, a good ten feet away from Ralph. He stepped closer to the metal cross and clasped his hands together in prayer. "I don't know how much you suffered in your childhood to have caused me so much pain. I never liked you enough to ask. But I guess you must have been terribly abused to abuse me as cruelly as you did. I'm sorry I killed you, Simon. I'm sorry for your pain. I'm sorry you didn't know any better than to take it out on me. I... I'll try and forgive you. I'll try and accept your apology. I'll try not to become the same person you did." Ralph paused, wiped moist eyes, and continued. "I hope you're in a better place in death than you were in life. Rest in peace."

Penny had moved beside him. She put her arm around his shoulder. She wiped a dry left eye and looked at the anchor tombstone. "Rest in peace." She turned to Ralph, opening her arms. "That was good. Come here."

They hugged, a loose embrace that slowly tightened with emotion. "Let's go," Ralph said. "I can't be around here too long."

Pulling out onto the road, Ralph saw something a short distance down what was once a two-lane highway, but was now a fire-blackened, burnt-debris strewn path. Instead of turning into Sandra's driveway, he turned left toward the whitish object. He stopped beside it, turned off the quad, and examined it. It was the skeleton of a woman, he presumed, curled up in a fetal position, clutching to her chest the smaller skeletal remains of what was obviously a child. The woman's head was twisted upward, mouth wide open in terror. Oddly, the child, arms wrapped tightly around the mother, looked almost serene in death, mouth closed tightly in an expression of resignation, even peace.

"My God," Ralph said. "What a terrible way to go."

"Yeah. I'm sure there's more where that came from. Imagine driving into Charlottetown. Or even Montague."

"Do you want to see what's in Montague? You know, check for survivors?"

"No. Remember, they want us back for breakfast, and to let them know we're okay."

Ralph pulled a list from his top pocket. "Right. Later maybe." He looked at it. House, Simon, gas, food, guns, moonshine. He turned to Penny. "Guns. I forgot. I've got weapons buried in the back. Let's get them."

She tightened her grip around his waist. "Later. We should check in with the others."

"Okay." He started up the quad. "Good idea. I could use a fucking drink right now anyway."

"So could I," Penny said. "So could I."

\*\*\*\*\*\*

Three hours later, the survivors gathered in Sandra's living room, preparing to vote on what Marty called a discovery mission. With the help of the generator, they had gotten some electric lights going, gotten the water well pumping, and had tried to no avail to get radio reception. They had eaten a breakfast of scrambled eggs, canned beans, hash browns, sliced tomatoes, and orange juice from concentrate. Sandra and Elaine had even managed to shower. Marty and Cray had installed motion detector lights and some trip wires around a portion of the property and erected a plywood watchtower platform atop the barn, giving them a 360-degree view of the surrounding wasteland.

Pastor Jon had woken up long enough to eat. After finishing his meal, half of which was spoon-fed to him by Sandra, he had promptly passed out again. They sat on an L-shaped sofa set while Pastor Jon slept in a comfy armchair. He snored lightly. At times, he would bob his head and mutter something, but his words were incomprehensible. They had tried to wake him by shaking him, nudging him, and calling his name. It wasn't working.

"I got this," Cray said finally. He went into the kitchen, returned with a glass of cold water and a towel, and threw the water into Pastor Jon's face.

"Whaaat?" Pastor Jon snapped his head back, opening his mouth wide, and quickly bringing both hands to his face.

Cray threw the towel on his lap. "We need you awake. You can sleep later. We're voting now."

Pastor Jon removed his hands from his face, studied the faces watching him and, ignoring the towel, reached for his moonshine bottle.

Cray snapped it up. "Later. Give us five minutes of your attention. Please."

With sad puppy dog eyes, Pastor Jon looked at Cray. But he didn't make a move for the bottle, instead drying his face with the towel and resting each hand on an arm of the chair.

Marty began. "I'm not sure how this is gonna go, but we need to do a discovery mission to size up our enemy." He pointed to Pastor Jon, who had begun listening intently. "Based on what you say, we have to be proactive, go after them before they come after us. Some of us should go. But some of us should stay behind, in case we don't return. I guess I should first establish who wants to be a part of this mission. Raise your hand."

Cray and Sandra raised their hands. So did Ralph. So did Pastor Jon. So did Marty.

"Wait a minute," Cray said. "We can't just leave Penny and Elaine behind."

"I would go," Elaine said. "But as Marty says, someone should stay behind. I'll stay and guard the fort."

"Me too," Penny offered. "Maybe Ralph can stay with us."

"No, no," Ralph said, taking his eyes off the bottle of moonshine that he and Penny had begun sharing. "I want to go, I want to kill some motherfuckers before they kill us." He looked at Penny. "But I don't want to leave you behind either." He paused for a moment. "Okay, tell you what, I'll stay and guard the girls."

Cray had envisioned this scenario and wasn't sure he trusted Ralph enough to have him guard Penny and Elaine. Maybe Ralph would snap, black out, rape and kill them. But if Sandra came along, at least she wouldn't be in a position to find herself in the wrong place at the wrong time. Cray could protect her, or at least try to. Maybe it would work itself out. However, he didn't like the look on Marty's face, nor did Elaine's somber expression convey that she agreed with Ralph's suggestion. But in this new survival-of-the-fittest existence, there would be many more leaps of faith they would have to take if they were to survive. Better to get it out in the open.

"How about this?" Cray said. "What do you guys think of me, Sandra, Marty, and Pastor Jon going? And Ralph staying behind to guard Penny and Elaine?"

Marty's eyes narrowed. Then he turned to Sandra. Cray suspected what he was going to say. "Are you well enough to travel? Are you sure you *want* to come along? Wouldn't you be safer here?"

"I don't want to leave Cray," Sandra said. "My concussion is better every day. I can feel my memory improving. Besides, I'm a nurse. If someone gets injured, I can help." She shifted her gaze between Ralph and Marty, stopping at Marty. "I think we should get this out in the open. I don't think you trust Ralph enough to leave him with your wife."

After a moment of tense silence, Marty said, "Would you? Do you trust him enough to leave Cray behind with him? Or stay behind yourself with him?"

"Hang on," Ralph said, before Sandra could answer. "I'm not gonna hurt any one of you guys. We're all in this together now." He lit a smoke, took a long drag, and blew a gray cloud into the air. He put his arm around Penny. She snuggled closer to him. "She saved my life. She made me look at life in a different way. I'm not the same man as I used to be."

"You've got intermittent explosive disorder," Elaine said. "That's not something that goes away overnight."

Ralph threw up his arms. "Well, help me then. You're the shrink."

"Ralph won't hurt any of us," Pastor Jon said. "He was once on a dark and lonely path. Once had dark storms brewing in his head. Now he's on the path of redemption. Give him a chance. You'll see. I promise."

Marty locked eyes with Ralph. "You so much as lay a finger on my wife, I'll kill you with my bare hands. I promise."

Something, a flash of anger maybe, flickered through Ralph's squinting black eyes. But in an instant it was gone, replaced by a silly, toothless grin. He flipped his palms open resignedly. "Cross my heart and hope to die. I won't touch her. Better, I'll give my life for her, it comes to it."

Marty put his arm around Elaine. "Before we even bring this to a vote, I wanna know, honey, are you okay with staying behind with *him*?"

Elaine sighed, opened her mouth to speak, and then closed it again. Everyone waited patiently for her response. "I guess we have to trust him sometime," she said softly. "Okay. I'll stay."

"You sure?"

"Yes."

"All right. Let's vote," Marty said. "All those in favor of me, Cray, Sandra, and Pastor Jon going on a discovery mission first thing tomorrow raise your hands."

All hands raised.

"Carried. Unanimously," Marty said, pounding his fist on the coffee table for affect.

"I need a drink," Pastor Jon said. "Can I have my bottle back now?"

Cray handed it over. "Don't overdo it. We need you sharp tomorrow."

"I need a shower," Penny said, handing Ralph the moonshine bottle and rising.

Turning to Cray, Marty said, "I need to finish some work outside. You wanna help me?"

"Sure."

"Anyone else wanna help?" Marty said.

Sandra stood and touched Elaine's hand. "I need to clean the kitchen. You wanna help?"

"Sure."

As Penny climbed the stairs to the upstairs bathroom, Ralph consulted his list. "Guns."

Cray and Marty stood at the door. Marty turned around. "What?"

"Guns. I got more guns buried on my property. I'll help you guys, but we should get my guns before nightfall."

"Okay bro," Cray said. "Give us a hand. Then we'll get your guns."

They left.

"I'm waiting for a vision," Pastor Jon said to an empty room. He stared at the clear moonshine, swirling inside the bottle like the swelling of the sea. "Waiting for a vision of what tomorrow will bring."

# Chapter Nineteen

Although it was only 9:36 am that Wednesday, June 22$^{nd}$, the thick black clouds blocking out the sun and the blowing black ash made it seem like the middle of the night, Cray thought, as they headed to Panmure Island. Marty drove, Pastor Jon sat in the front passenger seat, and Cray and Sandra were in the back, armed with AK-47s. Last night, after reinforcing the watchtower atop the barn and setting up a series of trip wires and motion detector lights around the property's perimeter, Ralph had told them the whereabouts of his weapons cache (he didn't have the stomach to accompany them). Marty and Cray had unearthed a good selection of firearms and hauled them back to the house. For the next two hours the twisted skeletons of trees had become targets as most of them developed close and intimate bonds with their new firearm friends.

Searching for food, fuel, and survivors, they had made a few stops on the way. All they had discovered were a multitude of animal and human skeletal remains, razed homes, vehicles and outbuildings, and a bleak, fire-blackened landscape that grimly harkened back to T.S Eliot's critically-acclaimed poem *The Wasteland*. That had set the stage for a somber mood and for the last ten minutes none of them had spoken a word. Even Pastor Jon, known for his spontaneous proselytizing outbursts, had fallen silent. Perhaps more importantly, Cray thought, today marked the first day Pastor Jon had woken up, albeit fuzzy-headed, and not gone straight for the bottle. *Good. We're gonna need him coherent. Today of all days.*

"How much longer?" Cray asked, finally breaking the uncomfortable silence.

"I think it's about ten minutes that way," Sandra said, pointing. She removed a hand from the trigger of the AK-47 and touched Cray's leg.

"That sounds about right," Marty said.

"I can feel it." Pastor Jon said.

"Feel what?" Marty asked.

Pastor Jon pointed to one o'clock. "Over there. A powerful evil presence." He looked at the others. "Do you feel it?"

"I don't feel shit," Marty said.

"Me neither," Sandra said.

Cray was about to agree when a fleeting image of screaming burn victims shot through his mind. Multiple terror-filled faces of men, women, and children crying out in agony as a giant flame ball smothered them, sucking them down into a black pit of death and despair. Was it a vision? Probably just a shell-shocked mind playing tricks. He shook his head slowly, unsure of the image, sure he didn't want to panic the others. "I don't think so."

With windshield wipers scraping away black ash, the field of vision steadily shrinking to a small ragged oval shape, Marty continued down the road. He made a right turn, a left, and then stopped. He pointed to four o'clock. "Over there. Look."

Cray studied the image. The distant sky had turned a fiery orange as a bank of gray-black clouds, aided by strong winds, drifted out so sea. Sunlight, largely obscured by dark cloud cover, blanketed the landscape in an orange haze. In the background, he saw Panmure Island, surrounded by a black swelling sea. It appeared untouched by the devastation. *Why would a God spare that? For them?* In the foreground, the causeway connecting the 800-acre red sandstone island to PEI. At the entrance to the causeway, three lights flickered. *Lights from a fire? Or houselights? The light is on and... and somebody's home...* Cray released the safety from the machine gun, put his finger on the cold and comforting steel of the trigger. *I never thought I would say this, but it's... it's killing time.* He pointed to a debris-strewn bluff near the flickering lights. "Pull up there, Marty. It'll give us some protection. And a good vantage point to see from."

In the rearview mirror, Marty glanced at Cray and Sandra. "You ready?"

They nodded, wide-eyed with nervous anticipation and fear.

Marty turned to Pastor Jon, who, in spite of numerous urgings, had flatly refused to learn how to use a firearm or carry one for that matter; insisting, in so many words, that he was in God's protective custody. "Are you sure you don't want a weapon?"

"I've never been more sure of anything in my life," Pastor Jon said, stoic.

Marty put the SUV in drive. "Let's go then. Roll the windows down."

Slowly, he approached a bluff consisting of blackened Earth and the scorched remains of a residence. He parked behind it. Even before he killed the ignition, the painful screams became audible, mixed with shouts of joy. They climbed out of the SUV, crouched behind the small jagged hill of protection, and watched.

Cray recognized the oceanfront Sandbar & Grill and surrounding parking lot immediately—it was untouched by the apocalyptic devastation. He had enjoyed a drink there on a few occasions, had even eaten a delicious lunch on the picturesque oceanfront patio. Pleasant memories. But what he saw now was the furthest thing from pleasant he had ever laid eyes on. In fact, the heinous nature of the crimes would come to haunt his psyche for the rest of his life. Beside the Sandbar & Grill, six men danced around a naked man, who was tied to a pole surrounded by branches and twigs. Kindling. Three men carried flaming torches. As the captive writhed under his ankle and wrist ties, they circled him, shouting, taunting, and drinking. At times a man would separate from the circle, approach their prisoner, shout an obscenity, "You fucking faggot," or "You're gonna rot in Hell, motherfucker," or "How do you like your wifey bitch now?" then spit a mouthful of alcohol in his petrified face.

And that wasn't the worst of it. A few feet away from the struggling man, a naked woman lay on the asphalt parking lot, grunting, groaning, and struggling; her extremities pinned to the ground; a man standing on each hand, a man standing on each leg; a man on top of her in the missionary position, pounding her senseless—violently sexually assaulting her.

Sandra removed her hand from her mouth. Her face had gone white. "We can't let this happen."

"He's not here," Pastor Jon said.

Marty moved closer, his eyes small slits. "Who's not here?"

"Their leader. Crass." He pointed to the far end of Panmure Island, where now more lights were visible. "He's there. With more disciples of the devil."

Marty clicked the safety off his AK-47 and aimed it at the crime scene. "I don't care where the fuck he is. I couldn't live with myself if I stood idly by and let this happen." He looked at Cray and Sandra. "You with me?"

They nodded, slowly, uneasily.

Pastor Jon folded his hands together and began praying.

"No," Marty said. "Not now. Can you drive?"

"What? I need to call God. For your protection."

"Not now. Get in the SUV. Watch. When you see us ready, I want you to drive down and pick us up. You got that?"

"I'll try."

"Don't try. Do it and don't fuck up." He turned to Cray and Sandra. "Go for the girl. I'll go for the guy."

Marty led the ambush, running down the hill to the parking lot, staccato bursts of machine gun fire leading the charge. Three men dropped instantly as others reached for their weapons. One man tossed a flaming torch onto the kindling surrounding the pole-strapped prisoner, drew his gun, and returned a shot that whizzed past Marty's head. Marty riddled his chest with a V-pattern of bullets. The man groaned and dropped dead as the captive man burst into flames and starting screaming horribly.

Cray shot two men pinning the woman. Two more dropped from Sandra's well-aimed gunfire. As Marty reached the bottom, one man ran for a Black Ford Expedition, jumped inside, and slammed the door. Another retreated inside the bar. As the Expedition started, Marty riddled it with bullets. It exploded, rocketing flaming debris into the sky.

Marty cautiously approached the bar as Cray and Sandra reached the woman. A large shirtless tattooed man with a mop of tangled hair yanked her up by the throat and put a gun to her head.

"Heeeeelp me... heeeeelp me," the burning man shouted in between screams. "Pleeeease!"

"Take another step and she gets it," the man holding the woman by the neck said.

Guns leveled at the man's head, Sandra and Cray stopped.

The woman's blonde hair was wet with blood and sweat and matted. Scratches snaked down from her eyes to her bruised and blood-soaked mouth. Her large breasts were cut and bruised. Blood from her assaulted vagina flowed down her legs. She pointed to the raging fire beside her, where the once piercing screams had subsided to barely audible moans and groans of death. "My life is nothing without my husband. Kill him."

The man pressed the gun to her head and tightened his grip on her throat. His eyes were fiery with rage and evil. His victim struggled. "You want her to die," he said. "Go ahead."

A vehicle fishtailed into the parking lot and screeched to a stop, headlight beams blinding. The man's attention was diverted. The woman, with supernatural strength, spun around and kneed him hard in the nuts. "Oww, oh, oh." He released his grip and doubled over in pain. She ran toward her burning husband.

Sandra and Cray riddled the man with bullets—head, neck, and chest. "Take that, you sick fuck," Cray said.

As the man fell on his back, he raised his gun, fired, and shot the fleeing woman in the back. Cray plugged three more bullets into his head. The man moaned loudly and died. The woman fell face-first on the edge of the fire. As Pastor Jon climbed out of the SUV, Cray and Sandra ran toward the fire and pulled her out of the rising flames. Luckily she had landed on the perimeter, escaping major damage. They turned her over on her back as gunshots erupted inside the Sandbar & Grill.

As Pastor Jon and Sandra kneeled over the woman, her face and naked chest fire-blackened, Cray tapped Sandra on the shoulder, pointed behind him, and hurried to the bar's entrance door. Two more gunshot blasts echoed inside the wooden structure. Cray, fueled by a rush of adrenaline, ducked and dove inside, not knowing what to expect.

Breathing in short gasps, he felt a hand tap his shoulder. He rolled over quickly and pointed the machine gun at the dark face above.

"Put that down," Marty said, smoking gun in hand. "I got him."

Cray got to his feet. "Are there any more?"

"I thought I saw someone running down the beach. I'm not sure. But we don't have time." Along with his machine gun, Marty had three handguns tucked in the belt of his jeans. One was a new addition, presumably stripped from the dead man lying somewhere inside the bar.

Cray produced a flashlight, turned it on, and looked around. He saw a rustic seating area with five round wooden tables, four chairs at each one, and large windows facing what was once a peaceful ocean view but was now black and gray. The view was tinted orange by two fires burning: one a funeral pyre, the other a four-wheel-drive metal coffin, both emitting the sweet smell of burning flesh. Thinking of the essentials—food, booze, weapons, and fuel—Cray went into the small kitchen. "I'll be right out."

"Okay." Marty went outside. As Cray rummaged around, he heard Marty bark out orders to the others. "Is she alive? Okay. Get her in the car, strip all the guns and ammo off them, and let's go."

"Where's Cray?" It was Sandra, her voice breaking with emotion.

"He's okay. Looking for supplies."

In the kitchen, Cray almost tripped over the dead body of a skinny but muscular man wearing a blood-spattered FUCK OFF AND DIE muscle shirt. He had a mop of frizzy black hair, two bullets in his forehead, and two in his chest.

Cray spotted some stacked cases in a corner and went to investigate. A case of Scotch, a case of vodka, and two cases of canned goods. Behind it, two red five-gallon jerry cans. Even with the lids securely fastened, he could smell gasoline. Jackpot. He slung his machine gun over his shoulder, and lifted a container of gas and a box of Scotch. He went outside and loaded them in the SUV, turned around, and approached Pastor Jon and Sandra, who were helping the burned, bleeding woman into Sandra's SUV.

"What can I do?" Cray asked.

"Get the door," Sandra said, pressing a hand to the woman's blood-soaked chest, just above her breast. "I've gotta stop the bleeding."

Cray opened the rear passenger door, and Pastor Jon and Sandra began helping her in. As her gaze passed over Cray, she locked eyes with him. Her eyes were gray and pleading, tears streaming down her bulbous purple cheeks. "Thank... you." Her voice was weak and broken.

They got her seated and Sandra turned to Pastor Jon. "Gimme your shirt. I need a tourniquet." He peeled off his long-sleeved denim shirt and handed it over.

Marty was at the back of the SUV, loading in guns and ammo he had stripped from the dead. He set the last handgun down. "That's everything. Anything else inside?"

"Yeah. Come on," Cray said.

He and Marty went inside the bar, returned with the supplies, loaded them up, and clicked the rear hatch closed. Pastor Jon had already climbed into the front passenger seat, closed the door, and was busy muttering what sounded like both a prayer and a condemnation. "Forgive them, for they have sinned... God have mercy on their souls... wipe the evil scourge of society off the face of the Earth... send them to the bowels of Hell... amen, amen..."

Cray heard the distant rumble of an engine and saw the lights at the same time Marty did—two menacingly white, evil eyes, halfway down the causeway that joined the islands together, barreling toward them.

"Time to go," Cray said.

"Fucking cocksuckers," Marty said, starting the SUV and peeling out into the darkness. "Open your windows and point your guns." Sandra and Cray complied. Marty pulled a piece from his jeans and handed it to Pastor Jon. "Take it."

Pastor Jon cringed, looking as if he were being handed a venomous snake. "No. I don't even know how to use it."

Marty released the safety. "I'll show you."

Pastor Jon folded his arms across his chest in defiance. Marty got the body language, checked the rearview mirror, saw the evil white eyes gaining ground, and put pedal to metal.

"I'm Sarah," the wounded woman said. "And I want a gun." Her voice was stronger now, a determined tone mixed with a survival instinct and a need for vengeance.

"Here," Marty said, passing a gun to Pastor Jon. "At least pass it back to her, for fuck sakes."

Pastor Jon hesitated briefly, then took the piece and passed it back to Sarah, who snatched it up with an unsteady hand. "Don't worry. I know how to use it. And I won't hesitate." Pastor Jon's denim shirt was wrapped around her shoulder, stemming the blood flow. Her left breast was exposed, bloody, slashed and bruised. She held the gun up, covering her exposed breast with the other hand, gritting her teeth, her gray eyes squinting. "Come and get it, you fucking sons of bitches."

"They're gaining," Sandra said, hanging halfway out the window. "Go somewhere. Hide..."

A loud explosion rocked the vehicle and both rear wheels shot airborne for a second or two before slamming hard onto the road.

"Hang on," Marty said as the SUV fishtailed and careened dangerously close to a black mass of mangled trees.

A split-second before slamming into it, he regained control, found a side road, and made a sharp left, spinning out debris and burnt asphalt, jerking passengers, banging heads.

His ears ringing like tolling church bells, Cray pulled himself inside the vehicle. The explosion had almost launched him into the blackened wasteland. "Where the fuck did they get a rocket-propelled grenade launcher?"

"The Lord works in mysterious ways," Pastor Jon muttered, rubbing a contusion on his forehead.

Sandra pulled herself inside, along with her machine gun. "I don't see any lights. Maybe they missed the turn."

"You okay?" Cray asked, listening to a chorus of clanging bells.

She nodded, turned, and repositioned her upper torso and the AK-47 outside the window. "I see any more lights, I'm firing."

"Over there," Marty said. Maybe seventy feet off the highway, alone in a blackened field, sat the remains of a steel building that had survived the brunt of the fire's wrath. Marty didn't wait for a democratic vote, taking a sharp left, racing down the driveway, and skidding to a stop directly behind the building.

"Everyone okay?" Marty said.

Three heads nodded.

"I'm dying," Sarah croaked.

Marty turned the lights off and killed the ignition. For a moment they were silent, except for the whooshing sound of deep, gasping breaths and thumping heartbeats.

Marty opened the door and curled a finger to Cray. "Stay here," he said to the other tight faces. Then he climbed out and walked briskly to the edge of the oval-shaped steel building. Cray followed.

Twitchy fingers caressing triggers, they peered down the driveway to the access road. Silence. Then the distant rumble of an engine and headlights silhouetted by black and gray, slowly but steadily approaching.

"You ready?" Marty whispered.

"I better be."

"If they come down the driveway, we wait until they get about twenty feet away, then ambush them. Like we did before."

Cray wiped a sweaty brow. "Got it."

The dark-colored Ford Expedition stopped just past the driveway, reversed to the driveway, and turned in.

"Shit, fucking shit," Marty said.

Moving at ten or so miles per hour, it neared.

A hundred feet, ninety, eighty, seventy...

Cray readied the AK-47, intending to fire a small burst before leaping up and attacking. *Goddammit, what a fucking life.* Though not a religious man, he began praying, a slight contradiction given his earlier blasphemy. *Please God, hear us, help us... hear us, help us... please...*

Sixty feet, fifty, forty...

"Get ready," Marty whispered. "We're not gonna live forever anyway."

Thirty feet, twenty-five...

The Expedition stopped, its driver killing the ignition just as Marty and Cray were about to spring from their metal cover.

Marty stepped forward. Cray grabbed his arm. In a low voice, he said, "Wait! Until they get out."

The front passenger door clicked open.

With trembling hands, Cray gripped the machine gun tightly. *Everything's going in slow motion. Fuck, this is it. This is really it.*

A monster of a man stepped out. "I can't see shit," Crass said.

"There's no one here, Killer."

"Gimme a fucking flashlight and let me check over there." The voice was deep, guttural, tinged with pent-up rage and aggression.

Suddenly, in the distance, an engine rumbled. Then flashing headlights, momentarily blinding, passing quickly on what remained of the highway.

"Fuck sakes," Crass said, spinning around and spraying a burst of machine gun fire. He got in the vehicle. Its engine rumbled to life. It backed up quickly, spinning gravel, turned around, and sped away in hot pursuit.

Cray waited a full minute before speaking. He sighed deeply. "Fucking lucky we are."

"Holy shit," Marty said. "Fucking lucky we are."

A satisfied grin on his face, Pastor Jon hung his head out the window as they approached. "Divine intervention. It has nothing to do with luck."

They climbed into the vehicle. Marty fired it up. "I'm taking another way back. I don't want to run into them again."

Cray looked at Sandra. Her face was tight, white. A lone tear sprouted under one eye and glinted in the vehicle's interior light. She closed her eyes. The tear snaked down her dimpled cheek. She wiped it away.

"How's Sarah?" Cray asked.

"She's dead."

# Chapter Twenty

"That's not them," Steel said as they neared the vehicle. "That's a small pickup. They drove an SUV."

"I don't give a fuck who it is," Crass said, enraged that he had just lost almost a dozen men, a vehicle, and more than likely guns, ammo, booze and food supplies to a group of violent opportunists. "Shoot out the tires."

Two of the three men sitting in the backseat complied, hanging their heads out the window, aiming their handguns, and firing multiple shots, two of which blew the rear tires from the vehicle with a loud pop.

Up ahead, it fishtailed violently before careening into the ditch, flipping over and crunching down hard upside down on its roof. Steel slowed and came to a stop right behind it. Smoke swirled up from its still-running engine, all four wheels spinning.

Crass was the first one out of the Expedition. He hurried over to the driver's door, a burst of adrenaline coursing through his body, excited at the opportunity for vengeance, however misdirected it might be. He had one goal in mind. Drag these fuckers from the vehicle and throttle them with his bare hands, the only method that would assuage at least some of his boiling rage, now mixing with the adrenaline and producing a powerful high. Kneeling down next to the driver door, a handgun in one hand, he extracted a flashlight with the other and shone it into the cab, frowning at the gruesome sight that beheld him.

By all appearances, the young male driver had mashed his head first into the windshield, second into the dashboard, and third into the steering wheel. The crunched roof had squashed his skull into the steering wheel, mangling his face beyond recognition. Blood, shattered skull bone, and gray brain matter oozed out. One bloody eyeball clinging to its socket by a thin elastic muscle stared at Crass defiantly.

"Fuck sakes," he said, reddening. Denied one kill. He went around to the passenger door, shoved Steel out of the way and knelt down, shining the light, thinking, *I saw someone move. I heard someone moan.*

He saw a woman, her body folded at an odd angle, her bloody face pushed into her crotch as if she was performing some odd acrobatic sex act on herself. Her long brown hair was splayed out on her legs like a mop.

"Are you okay?" Crass asked, reaching into the shattered window and touching her twisted arm. His mantra, "Spare the women, spare the children," had been for the moment forgotten, replaced by the seething rage, the need for any kind of vengeance. All he wanted to do now was drag this woman from the wreckage and strangle out of her what little life she still had in her.

With a loud snapping sound, she twisted her head toward Crass, looked him straight in the eye contemptuously, raised a crooked "fuck you" finger, and reiterated the universally understood salute. "Fuck you, asshole!" Then she closed her eyes, opened her mouth, moaned softly, and died.

The rage boiled over. Crass began kicking the truck door, yelling, "Fuck you, you fucking cunt" repeatedly. He began slamming fists into the door, the fender, any metal body part his unbridled rage took him.

His men stood on the road watching him fearfully and silently.

When the black rage had subsided, Crass examined his bloody fists, then noticed a swirl of smoke rising above the overturned vehicle. He saw a lick of flames snake across its underbelly. He scrambled out of the ditch and slowly opened his clenched fists. "Let's go. It's gonna blow."

Once they were fifty feet down the road, a loud explosion erupted behind them, breaking the dark brooding silence that had settled over the Expedition. It rocked Crass back to reality and the tasks at hand. "To the beach bar first. Then home. We'll get them later." In stark contrast to his earlier tone, his voice had become calm and composed.

As they drove, Crass lit a cigar, swallowed a shot of whiskey from his metal flask, and tried to compose himself, slightly ashamed of his earlier outburst. He understood that to be successful he would have to display more leadership qualities. The temperament of a leader. That included not flying off the handle at every failure. Failure was a part of success, he reminded himself, shifting his thoughts to the positive instead of dwelling on the negative. He tried to think of his successes rather than his failures.

Since arriving on Panmure Island just over two weeks ago, there had definitely been more triumphs than disappointments, the first being that the tiny island was for the most part untouched by the destructive blaze. In the days to follow, Crass had managed to root out a half a dozen survivors, commandeer three strategically located waterfront homes and an assortment of outbuildings, and amass a cache of weapons, generators, various foodstuffs, fuel, and a handful of vehicles, utility and otherwise.

Sure, ten men and three women, non-believers, or apostates as he liked to call them, had been murdered in the process, but he had also spared the lives of five women and six children, setting aside a large guarded home for them within easy reach of his compound. His recruitment efforts had also produced four new male followers who understood that to disobey meant death, but also that he, Crass the King, offered them a better way of life. If they subscribed to his new religious order—brainwashing cult might be a better description—they would be assigned certain duties, be allowed to survive, be permitted a few indulgences and maybe, just maybe, be assigned a number in the hierarchy of the Order.

If Crass had done anything right in the joint, besides murdering his predecessor and becoming king, it was to do plenty of reading. He had thoroughly researched the Utah-based polygamist religious cult known as the Kingston Clan, or the Order. Under the guise of religion, the Order, a deviant faction of Mormons, practiced incest, marrying much younger family members, including daughters and cousins. Young women who had escaped the Order reported numerous acts of sexual abuse wrought upon them, typically by their fathers, uncles, or other male family members of the polygamist cult.

Founded by Elden Kingston during the Great Depression, the Order, according to law enforcement officials, ran a multi-million dollar organized crime operation in the state of Utah. With thousands of members, the secretive and insular nature of the Order allowed it to operate largely with impunity from the law.

On the surface, the Order's far-flung business empire seemed legitimate. But, according to its defectors, it skirted the edges of the law, exploiting brainwashed members as slaves and hiding profits from the tax man. Much of the labor force was made up of children born into the Order, and teenage brides. Remuneration for work came in the form of an arcane credit currency called scrip that can only be used in the Order's stores.

Brainwashing starts young, teaching children to be polite, but to never make friends with outsiders. To avoid detection by law enforcement, the Order avoids doctors, believing them to be evil and unnecessary. High-ranking Order members believe they have a hidden knowledge of health, directly from God. The Order also avoids banks and police, preferring to mete out its own brand of justice, at times violently, to wayward, insolent, or disobedient members.

Order leaders preach to followers that they're descendants of Jesus and as such a race of chosen people. Since they believe they are part of a master race, all marriages are arranged within the original four founding families. Members are taught that the prophet, Crass's new identity as defined by himself, demands absolute loyalty and they should be prepared to defend the Order at any cost.

As Steel pulled into the parking lot of the Sandbar & Grill, it occurred to Crass, not for the first time, that he didn't buy all the Order's religious bullshit. *Let's be serious. It's all a guise for the pursuit of money, sex, and power.* And while perhaps money no longer had any value in this new world, it could easily be replaced by labor, perhaps sexual favors, or even a version of the scrip currency used by the Order. This needed to be thought through. But the Order served as a reliable and efficient model on which he could base his new-and-improved world Order. His order, a society the way He wanted it, catering to His demands, His needs, His innermost desires. *How sweet it'll be. Oh, how sweet.*

Seeing the carnage in the parking lot, Crass grinned in spite of the obvious losses. The other Expedition still smoldered and skeletal remains of the funeral pyre victim swirled small black plumes of smoke into the dark sky. But, at this moment, it mattered not to Crass. During the journey, he had thought himself into a much more positive frame of mind.

"You want us to check it out?" Steel asked.

"Go ahead," Crass said, a calmness settling over him. "I doubt you'll find much."

Four men climbed out of the Expedition. Steel followed one man inside the bar while the other two checked dead bodies. Crass watched, silently plotting. A pretty twenty-something woman by the name of Maria Martinez popped into his head; she had flowing brown hair, bright green eyes, perfectly proportioned nubile young body. Upon first arriving to Panmure Island, they had raided her house and taken her and her six-year-old son captive. Crass had made sure no one had laid a hand on her, or her son. Now he believed it was time to meet with Maria privately. Time to groom her to be his new bride. He would clean himself up, even change out of his grubby clothes, request the pleasure of her company, and prepare for a romantic evening. The rest of the shit, the vengeance he wanted on the bastards who had dared breach his perimeter and slaughter his men—well, that would just have to wait until tomorrow. The first Order of the day—start the Order. *With my first wife.*

The men returned to the Expedition. "Only a container of gas and a few bottles of Jack Daniels," Steel said.

"Load them in and let's go," Crass ordered.

Steel pointed to the dead bodies. "What about them?"

Crass pointed to the smoldering skeleton bound to the funeral pyre. Some of the fire had extinguished itself and some fresh kindling still remained at the foot of the crucifix. "Drop me off, come back, throw them in a pile with him and torch them all. We don't want rotting corpses lying around. They'll spread disease."

"Okay," Steel said. He climbed in. He started the engine as the others climbed in. "Homeward bound, Crass."

"I have a favor to ask you—two favors, actually," Crass said a few minutes later as Steel pulled up and parked beside a large white two-story Victorian-style home with a large ornate wraparound deck. It was built a hundred and thirty years ago and in its day housed aristocracy, a lavish home for the upper class.

"What's that?" Steel asked.

"Can you call me King Crass?"

"Sure," Steel said.

"Even just King. Either one will do."

"No problem, King Crass."

Crass turned to the others in the backseat. They nodded, almost in unison. "After you return from burning the dead, fetch Maria for me, please."

# Chapter Twenty-One

"Does anyone wanna say anything?" Cray asked as they stared solemnly at Sarah's dirt-covered, shallow grave located next to Simon's anchor tombstone. Black clouds blanketed the late evening sky of June 23$^{rd}$. A cool, gentle breeze whistled through dead, tangled trees.

They had spent the last hour digging her new resting place in the improvised cemetery. A white wooden cross poked up from the mound of dirt covering her body.

"I didn't know her," Ralph said. He adjusted his shoulder-slung AK-47 and lit a smoke. He stood holding hands with Penny.

"Neither did I," Penny said.

"Don't look at me," Elaine said. She stood beside Marty, who only shrugged and looked at Sandra.

Sandra began to speak but was interrupted by Pastor Jon, who had rejoined the bottle—Scotch, his new drink of choice—after returning from the discovery mission late last night. The bottle was half full. He was well on his way. "I have something to say."

"So do I," Sandra said. "You go first."

Pastor Jon took a sip of Scotch and cleared his throat. "We give thanks to you, Lord God Almighty, who is and who was, because you have taken your great power, and have begun to reign." Pastor Jon kneeled down, set the bottle of Scotch on the ground, folded his hands in prayer, closed his eyes, and continued. "The nations were angry, and your time has come. The time has come for judging the dead, and for rewarding your servants the prophets and your saints and those who revere your name... I pray to you, Lord God Almighty, that you find it in your heart to forgive Sarah her sins and welcome her with open arms into the kingdom of Heaven. May her future days with you be filled with joy instead of the terrible suffering and pain she endured during her last days on Earth. Thank you for hearing my words, oh Lord... amen."

A few of them muttered "amen." It was followed by a moment of silence. Finally, Sandra said, "I'm sorry I didn't get the opportunity to get to know you better, Sarah. But, from what I saw, you were a strong and courageous woman, who seemed nice enough. I'm not a religious person, but I'm gonna say this anyway. May God be with you in your new life in Heaven. Rest in peace." Sandra lowered her head and wiped moist eyes.

"Rest in peace, Sarah," Cray said.

"Rest in peace," said Marty, Elaine, Penny, and Ralph.

"I need to get out of here," Ralph said, leading Penny by the hand to the quad. They climbed on. "This shit fucks me up."

Pastor Jon stood, his hands precipitously trembling, as the others turned to leave.

"Too much booze," Cray said, helping him back to the SUV.

"No," Pastor Jon said, wide-eyed. "I can feel it. The seeds of evil. Growing, festering. We're in danger."

"We've been in danger ever since the fire," Cray said, trying to reduce his own uneasiness as well as calm the preacher. "What else is new?"

"Imminent danger. We need to batten down the hatches tonight and stay vigilant."

Pastor Jon was right, Cray thought. As much as he hated to admit it, they couldn't expect to slaughter eleven members of the Crass clan with impunity. They would be seeking revenge, hunting for blood.

Ralph pulled up beside the SUV as the others climbed in. "We're gonna take a little ride. See if we can spot any signs of trouble, maybe find some more supplies."

"You sure that's a good idea this late at night?" Cray said.

Ralph shrugged. "What else we gonna do? Wait for them to come and get us?"

"You got a watch?"

Penny pulled up her sleeve, exposing a neon green, luminescent wristwatch.

"All right. Don't be gone late."

Marty stuck his head out the open window as the SUV rumbled to life. "Two hours. Don't be gone longer than two hours. And if you spot trouble, let us know as soon as you can."

Ralph massaged the trigger of the AK-47. "I'll let those fuckers know first."

Leaving what was now a cemetery road and entering the highway, the SUV went one way, the quad the other.

\*\*\*\*\*\*

"You okay?" Penny asked, tapping Ralph's shoulder as they barreled down the dark, winding road.

Ralph slowed, wiped his brow, turned around, and glanced at her, fire in his beady black eyes. "I took Pastor Jon's speech to heart. I feel like I gotta atone for my sins. You know, make it right with the eye in the sky."

"Don't be doing anything crazy."

"Oh, I'm gonna get right medieval on those bastards. You want me to take you back? Go it alone?"

"No." After a moment, she grinned. Something about the word "medieval" was making her squirm. "But where're you going?"

"Into the eye of the tiger. Panmure Island. You up for that?"

"I don't know."

Ralph pulled into a driveway leading to the remains of a decimated house and fire-flattened barn. He drove to the end, parked beside a mound of debris representing the former home, stopped, and turned off the quad. He climbed off, took Penny by the hand, and helped her dismount. His eyes searched hers. "I've got a chance to make things right. Finally do something good in my life. I need to know if you're in this or not. You gotta be sure. Because if you're not, I'm taking you back right now. I don't wanna put your life in danger."

Penny stepped in closer, caressing his chin stubble. "I'm with you, baby—hook, line, and sinker. You had me at 'medieval.'"

Ralph hugged her and kissed her tenderly on the lips. He felt all tingly and knew he had to stop before it was too late. "Okay, let's get going. Otherwise, I'll tear your clothes off right here."

"I wish you would."

"Later. I promise." He shone a flashlight in the trailer of the quad, removed an AK-47, and handed it to her. "Put it on your shoulder."

She did.

"You got a handgun?"

She lifted up her shirt, deliberately exposing half of her breasts. Ralph's eyes wandered up. "Down here," she said. Two handguns poked from the waist of her jeans.

He scratched his head and adjusted his baseball cap as she readjusted her shirt. He dug into his pocket, retrieved the list, and shone a light on it: Stock and repair shelter, new home, gas, food, guns, Crass. Somehow Crass had made it to the bottom of the list, normally reserved for low-priority tasks. But in this case, the order didn't apply. Crass had become priority one, and it was time to execute the mission. The others had done their job, wiping out eleven of his men. Now it was Ralph's turn; time to prove to everyone, especially his new girlfriend, not only that he wasn't a chicken shit, but that he would become their new hero, bravely putting his life on the line for theirs. His new friends meant something to him, more than they would ever know, and he felt the only way to prove that was through action. Action spoke much louder than words. He climbed onto the quad, extending a hand to help Penny on. He turned and kissed her on the cheek. "You ready?"

"Now or never. Let's do it."

Ralph started the quad, exited the driveway, and turned onto the highway, more determined than ever to prove his self-worth. About twenty minutes later, he saw a small, flickering flame in the distance and, after being reminded by Penny, recognized it as the Sandbar & Grill, the killing site, where the others had made their mark of death. A sliver of the moon poked out from black clouds, illuminating the lone bonfire. Ralph turned off the quad lights and approached slowly, skirting the perimeter.

"Look," Penny said. "That bluff over there. Must be the same one."

He turned toward it, pulled up on top, turned off the quad, and climbed off, stealthily approaching the raised edge, a sheltered vantage point from which to see but not be seen. Penny followed.

Reaching the edge, he pulled out his binoculars and examined the fire. The first thing he noticed was the smell—the sweet smell of burning flesh, the coppery, metallic smell of fresh blood. He wrinkled his nose, focusing the lenses on the fire. It was a cremation sight with multiple bodies burning, and many bones scattered about the perimeter. Atop a large steel pole erected in the center, a human skull grinned macabrely, a powerful deterrent to any post-apocalypse survivors who might think about taking the narrow two-lane causeway leading to Panmure Island.

"Are there people there?" Penny asked.

"No." He handed the binoculars to her. "No live ones, anyway. See for yourself. He's one evil son of a bitch."

Looking through the binoculars, Penny gasped and handed them back to Ralph. "What do we do?"

Before Ralph could respond, they saw vehicle headlights on the causeway, driving slowly toward the Sandbar & Grill. They both ducked. And watched.

A few minutes later, peering through binoculars, Ralph saw a dark-colored pickup enter the parking lot, back up near the outdoor crematorium, and stop. The engine went silent. Two men climbed out, walked around to the truck bed, and began loading fresh cadavers onto the fire. In the still of the night, they heard voices.

"Grab his legs. He's fucking heavy."

"Why couldn't we just bury him back there? Or toss him in the ocean, for that matter?"

"Don't cross King Crass. He wants them cremated. And you know why."

"Yeah, well, why do we have to do all his dirty work?"

"Have faith, brother. You will be rewarded."

"Yeah, when? He's the one getting all the pussy."

"Your turn will come."

"Sure. When Hell freezes over."

"It already has."

"You're right. Fucking heavy. Where do you want him?"

"Right there. On three. Ready."

"Yeah."

"One, two, three."

Ralph watched them toss a fat dead man onto the flames. There was the snapping sound of breaking twigs, or breaking bones, and then fanning flames engulfed his body.

"Two more guys. Skinny fucks."

"Good."

They loaded two more bodies onto the pyre, threw some dead tree branches onto it, and doused it with gasoline. The blaze shot up about ten feet high and fanned out with a whooshing sound. Both men stepped back, grinning at the result, their beady eyes turning fiery red in the flame's reflection.

"Now that's a fucking fire, Clyde."

"That's a fucking fire. Now what?"

"We have to fetch Maria. And the new girl, Belinda. King Crass wants them both tonight."

"He gets all the fucking pussy."

"Shut up and get in."

One man pulled out a flashlight, beaming it around the perimeter, then up at the bluff where Ralph and Penny watched. As the beam neared, they ducked, Penny's heart fluttering, Ralph beginning to sweat profusely, his throat becoming parched as he held his breath. They stayed quiet, waiting. Ralph removed the safety on the AK-47, preparing to rain down hot lead on them.

Penny touched his arm. "Wait. Not yet."

The beam stopped directly in front of them, a sliver of light catching Ralph's black baseball cap.

Penny pinched his arm hard. "Stay still."

Voices from below.

"I can't believe four cocksuckers ambushed us from there and killed eleven of our fucking men."

"Who cares? I don't miss any of them. You?"

Silence. Finally, "I guess not. Come on, let's go."

They heard the clicking of vehicle doors opening, then the metallic crunching of doors closing. The engine started, the pickup turned onto the causeway, and began its journey onto Panmure Island.

Exhaling deeply, Ralph took Penny's hand. "Come on. Let's follow them with the lights off. They'll lead us right to King Crass."

"You're remembering more. I like that."

To avoid detection, Ralph veered off to the beach after leaving the causeway and entering Panmure Island. He saw a number of houselights fronting the ocean. The size and scope of them said compound. Sure enough, as he drove along the beach at low tide, he saw the pickup—driving on the road fronting the homes—stop at a small house that was set apart from a cluster of three homes, one a large two-story turn-of-the-century house. Parking in front of some brush, Ralph was amazed. It appeared Panmure Island in its entirety had been untouched by the fire. He turned the quad off, climbed off, and crouched down along with Penny.

Lit by a porch light, the two men got out of the pickup, went inside the small bungalow-style home, and emerged with two women. One went along willingly, while the other protested, kicking and screaming, finally clinging to the pickup door so she couldn't be loaded in.

The metallic click of a handgun's cocking hammer eventually convinced her to get inside. "Just shut your mouth and get it."

"You won't kill me."

"Wanna try me?"

As the pickup pulled out of the driveway, driving the short distance to the apparent headquarters, Ralph and Penny left the quad and, hidden by a neat hedge line, followed the truck's progress. It parked in front of the large home and two men led the women inside at gunpoint.

Another man received the women at the door. The door closed and the two men returned to their truck. Before Ralph moved, he waited for them to finish speaking.

"What now?"

"Three more bodies. You forgot?"

"Yeah. Fuck sakes, it's late. Is that it?"

"Yeah."

"Okay... then after, what do you say we grab a bottle and take a little cruise? Do some drunk driving. Maybe fuck some people up. Just because we can."

"We'll see."

The doors closed. The truck pulled out of the driveway and drove off.

Along with the intermittent crashing of waves on the shoreline, the only other sound was the steady hum of a generator, muffled somewhat by the nearby outbuilding that housed it. Ralph finally moved. He peered out, noticing stairs that led up from the ocean entrance to a large deck. Inside the screen-enclosed deck, the back door of the house. He pointed.

"I see it," Penny whispered.

"Let's go in there."

They crawled alongside the brush.

******

Inside the spacious, dimly lit house, decorated in 1950s furniture and art, Nerves-of-Steel Nelson Pry, armed with an AK-47, guarded the front door. Skinny Sammy Farnsworth,

Crass's go-to gopher in the joint, armed with a shotgun, guarded the back door.

Sipping a glass of Scotch on the rocks, dressed in a black suit with white bowtie, Crass sat on a floral-patterned armchair across from the women, who sat together on a floral-patterned couch with a plastic liner.

Belinda's gray eyes were wide, darting around the room nervously. Her short red hair was matted with perspiration to her freckly face. Her drink, Scotch and water, sat untouched on the coffee table. At times she tugged at the white lace on the sleeve of her blue, full-length evening gown—as if trying to tear it off.

Maria, in contrast, sat relaxed and radiant in a dark red evening gown, her long, flowing brown hair neatly combed back and arranged in a bun just the way Crass had told her last night that he liked it. "Formal when we talk, informal when we fuck," he had said.

Maria drained her Scotch on the rocks, picked up the bottle, and offered some to Crass, who waved her away. Then she offered some to Belinda, who dismissed her with a waving index finger. Maria topped up her own glass.

Finally Crass began. "What I am about to say is very important. I want you both to listen carefully. You got that?"

Maria smiled, plastic, and nodded.

Belinda fidgeted with the lace. Her brow furrowed and she pressed her thin lips together.

At the front door, Steel cocked his ear and raised an eyebrow.

Sammy pulled the back door curtain aside, peered out, and then turned around, satisfied that no intruders were nearby.

Crass continued. "I've been chosen by God to build a master race of people. The reason I survived the apocalypse is because I am the chosen one. The prophet. God's prophet on Earth. God needed a leader for this master race so He chose me, King Crass. I've been instructed to marry eighteen women, and each woman is to bear several children. Exactly how many children, God only knows. But through slow and steady procreation, we will build this super race of people, a race that is above all others, above all the evil that God has erased from the world."

Crass paused and sipped Scotch. "For my first two wives, I want you two. You don't have to answer me right away. Take your time. Think about it. But one thing I can tell you is that my wives will receive the most luxurious of accommodations, the pick of the crop for food, and the finest lifestyle this new existence will afford." He pointed to Maria. "I know you have a six-year-old son. Adam. He too will be moved to privileged and private quarters, and will be given the best education once the school is up and running..."

A hollow thumping—footsteps—startled Crass and he turned toward the back door. Sammy tried to open the door. Five bullets shattered its small window and struck Sammy in the face. As his limp body dropped on the floor, the door burst open and Ralph stepped in, aiming the machine gun at Steel, who fired multiple shots.

Maria screamed and dove behind the couch for cover. Belinda bolted upright, ran across the room, and dove right through a window, shards of glass trailing her descent.

Crass calmly extracted a handgun and aimed it at Ralph. He fired.

But Ralph, tripped by the last dying effort of Sammy's outstretched hand, face-planted the floor, groaning in pain as bullets sprayed past his head. As Ralph struggled to get up, still locked in the steel grip of Sammy's not-quite-dead grasp, Crass ran over, knelt down, and pistol-whipped him twice in the head, knocking him unconscious.

Penny, advancing into the house, was grabbed by the neck from behind by a man who had heard the commotion, spotted the intruders, and had decided to act. Curling an arm tightly around her neck, the man twisted the AK-47 from her grip and slammed her hard in the head with its buttstock. She fell to the floor, not quite unconscious, but seeing plenty of dazzling, dancing stars.

As consciousness ebbed and blackness closed in, Penny saw the rage-filled face of Crass, his black, hate-filled eyes boring into her. "Put them in the dungeon," she heard him say before unconsciousness won the battle and her world went completely black.

# Chapter Twenty-Two

Maybe Pastor Jon had been right after all, Cray thought, checking the date on a wall calendar that afternoon. Friday, June 24$^{th}$, seven days before the wayward proselytizer had predicted the world would officially end. Maybe in seven days they would all be dead and, for all intents and purposes, it would be the end of their world. After all, Ralph and Penny had not returned from their drive in the country the previous night. There had been much discussion about what to do about it. The others were still sitting in the dining room, considering their options, plotting a course of action. In the absence of a consensus, they had not acted, voting instead to sleep on it, and decide today. However, thus far, they could not come to any agreement on what to do about the missing persons list.

That would come, Cray thought, refilling his coffee mug, and re-examining the calendar. *Seven days. Would Crass launch an assault and kill them all off within that timeframe? Were Penny and Ralph already dead?* Like sands through an hourglass, dark thoughts bombarded him. *Not a single animal left? Why haven't I seen a bird, even? Not even an insect. All dead. The oceans, dead too? Food. We're gonna run out of food. What about the rest of the world? Everyone dead? Panmure Island spared. Sandra's house spared. Why? Charlottetown? Spared? Burned to the ground? My apartment? My parents, brother, and sister? All dead? What kind of a God would spare Panmure Island so someone like Crass could start an evil cult? Is this God's vengeance for man's*

*sins? Is this some epic battle between the forces of good and evil?*
*Was what remained of humankind just a malignant cancer,*
*the only cure being complete annihilation? How do we fit in?*
*Are we really the good guys fighting the bad guys? Or is it*
*the other way around? Had civilization become a rotten apple*
*whose only value was to be fed to the pigs? Maybe so. Maybe it*
*had. What have we done with our lives? What have we done*
*with the planet? Fucked it up. Give a man enough rope, he'll*
*hang himself. This is fucked up. Pretty fucked up.*

Cray wiped tired, bloodshot eyes, and sipped coffee. He
was a rat on the treadmill of existence; running, racing,
wheezing, but only going in circles. Last night the predatory
insomnia beast had attacked, opening its dreaded jaws and
swallowing up most of Cray's sleep, leaving him sleepless,
restless, tossing and turning most of the night. He'd been
plagued by dark thoughts, the same ones bombarding him
now. Every so often he would stare out the window, hoping
to see the stars, the moon, but all he saw was blackness,
broken occasionally by the beam from Marty's flashlight.
Marty, who had volunteered to do sentry graveyard shift
atop the barn's watchtower, would every so often illuminate
the flashlight, focusing its tiny beam on the ground at some
audible but unseen noise; the snap of a dead tree branch
falling, a creak from the old house, the faint sound of the
whispering wind. Each time the light came on, Cray would
reach for his gun, tucked underneath his pillow, slide it out,
and click the safety off. And each time Marty turned the
light off, Cray would carefully slide the safety on and put the
firearm back under his pillow. The repetition of black, white,
black, white, had left him terrified and jittery—frayed nerves

clinging by tiny threads—but more aware than ever of the ever-present danger, of the fragility of an existence in a glass menagerie. *Sticks and stones will break my bones, but names will never hurt me. Stop it. Get a grip.*

"Are you feeling all right?" Sandra, looking fresh and alert in a happy face t-shirt and tight blue jeans, had entered the kitchen. Her jet-black hair was neatly tied back in a ponytail by a bright yellow ribbon matching the yellow happy face.

Cray had become so lost in his thoughts he hadn't even heard her open or close the kitchen door. He'd even tuned out the muffled conversation drifting in from the other room. That was bad, he thought. To survive, reaction time had to be good. Better than good. Lightning fast. He lifted his head, also realizing for the first time he had been leaning on the kitchen counter, resting his head in his arms. "I'm a little worried. I didn't sleep well last night."

"I know." She stepped closer, putting a comforting hand on his shoulder. "We're all worried, Cray. Me too. But we don't have the luxury of wallowing in worry."

*She's so strong. Such a caregiver.* He looked into her deep green, mesmerizing eyes. They gave him hope, a tiny white life preserver floating in an enormous, rising black tide of death. "They reach a decision?"

She took him by the arm. "Yes. Come on. We need your vote."

Inside the dining room, Cray surveyed the faces sitting around him. Marty, too, looked haggard after his sentry graveyard shift. He had black sockets under his eyes and his normally slicked back hair was flopped in front of his worn face, a few strands poking off in odd directions.

Elaine, by contrast, was composed and poker-faced, her long hair combed back and tied in a ponytail, business-like yet ready for war.

Pastor Jon, signature bottle in hand, sat with his arms folded on the table, his head resting in them. He appeared to be sleeping.

Outside, the day was still gray-black, as it had been all morning. Maybe even the sun, the great life giver, had abandoned them, Cray thought. "What are you guys thinking?"

Marty wiped a few strands of hair from his eyes. "My best guess is that Penny and Ralph have been captured by Crass and his men. It stands to reason that they'll torture them to get our whereabouts. The question is, will they give us up. I think anyone will give anything up if the right torture methods are employed." Marty spoke with an air of authority in spite of his worn-out appearance. "The reality is, whether they give it up or not, Crass and his men will find us. We're out in the open, sitting ducks." He looked at Pastor Jon and suddenly snatched the Scotch bottle from his hand. "Give me a shot of that." Pastor Jon didn't bat an eye or move a muscle.

Eyes narrowing, Elaine shot Marty a look.

"Excuse me, dear," he said, taking a drink. "I'm not returning to my old ways. I don't *need* a drink right now. But I *want* one."

Elaine folded her arms across her chest and said nothing.

"You think we should go after them?" Cray said, starting to feel the urge for a stiff drink himself.

Marty nodded. "I say you and I go." He waved at Pastor Jon. "We leave him here with the women."

"You okay with this?" Cray asked Sandra.

"Yeah. At first I wanted to go, but some of us should stay behind. And I think it'll be good luck for us if Elaine and I stay close to Pastor Jon."

Pastor Jon raised sleepy eyes. "What?"

"Stay awake," Sandra said. "We're gonna vote."

Cray didn't need to ask Elaine. Agreement was written all over her face, along with a look of disappointment at Marty's mid-afternoon relapse. Cray didn't have the energy, will, or courage for such a mission, but to decline would label him a coward among the others. That would be worse than the alternative, particularly in light of his recent bravery and courage. "All right, then. Let's vote."

The quiet afternoon was suddenly interrupted by a buzzing sound—not quite mechanical, not quite natural. Faint and directly overhead. All heads turned up to the ceiling, as if they could see through it and into the sky from where the strange sound originated. Even Pastor Jon looked up. The sound intensified, so loud that Cray covered his ears with his hands. He rushed outside. The others, including Pastor Jon, followed.

Standing on the front porch, they all looked up. Black and gray clouds. Nothing else. Then the buzzing sound intensified; one buzz becoming ten, twenty, thirty, until it was a cacophony of ear-splittingly loud noise. Cray dropped to his knees, along with Sandra, wincing and covering his ears. But then the noise faded and suddenly stopped entirely. Cray removed his hands from his ears, examining the dark sky for a sign of life. Nothing. "What the hell was that?"

Pastor Jon's eyes became clear, alert and resolute. "It's not about Hell. It's about Heaven. A message from God. Divine intervention. It's a sign. Abort the mission."

# Chapter Twenty-Three

"Here, take this," Simon said, offering Ralph a glass of clear liquid. His uncle had appeared as a dime-sized white light at first. Then it fanned out and morphed into an angel, touching Ralph's dark world with a comforting glow.

Ralph's throat was dry, parched, aching. He took the glass. He put it to his mouth and stopped. "What is it? You trying to poison me?"

Simon frowned. "No, dear Ralph. It's water. I'm trying to save you. I'm trying to atone for my sins."

"I forgave you."

"I know. And your forgiveness has saved me. For that, I have a gift for you. Drink the water and you'll remember. You will forget no more."

"Really?"

"Trust me. Drink."

Ralph hesitated for a moment, then drank. It was cold and refreshing. But something gritty—dirt, maybe, or poison—poured into his mouth and he coughed, spitting out a mouthful. "What've you...?"

Still coughing, he opened his eyes. The white light of Simon the angel disappeared, and once again his world became pitch-black. He was lying on his stomach, he realized, in a puddle of water. Thinking the puddle was Simon's amnesia cure, he had put his lips to it and sucked up a mouthful of dirt-filled, probably bacteria-contaminated, leaky basement water.

He spit out dirty water. "Fuck sakes." His head ached dully. He tried to move his arms. Tight. Sore wrists. Tied behind his back. He tried his legs. Tight. Sore ankles. Bound with what felt like rope scraping against raw flesh. His mind raced. His memory retrieved the events quickly and vividly. Crashing through the back door, filling a guard's face with lead, then tripping, falling, and blackness. *Penny? What happened to Penny?* "Penny? Penny?" Louder, desperate. "Penny, baby, are you here?"

Silence. Total and complete. Ralph searched the darkness. In the distance, a pinprick of light. Panicking, grunting, and sweating, he bent his knees, straightened his legs, and inched forward on all fours. He repeated this procedure, watching the pinprick widen as he neared, becoming a pencil-sized ray of incoming light. His head bumped into something soft, fleshy. He brought his cheek up to it, trying to get a tactile identification. A leg. "Penny? Is that you?"

Silence.

He inched closer, moving his cheek along the leg, up the torso, across the chest—*breasts, good*—up to the head. He moved his mouth along her neck, tonguing her cheek, feeling wetness, tasting coppery blood. His heart thrashed spasmodically, trying to tear through the prison bars of his rib cage. He ignored the sour taste of blood, continued to her mouth, kissed her.

"It's you, baby. Thank God."

Then, thinking, *She's dead*, his heart sank, a million octopus tentacles of panic tightening around his body, choking him, restricting all movement. He tried speaking her name again, but even his vocal cords were constricted. The heartache and panic were so intense Ralph thought he would die. He knew life without Penny was no life at all. But a moment later, the panic and heartbreak-induced paralysis was replaced by something else—a fiery, intense rage. The octopus tentacles unraveled slowly and Ralph tugged hard on the ropes binding his hands. A snapping sound. They loosened, but not enough to free him. He tried again. Another snap, more movement, but still not free.

A cough. A deep gasp. A voice. Penny's voice. "Ralph? Ralph? Is that you, baby?"

"Yes, honey. Are you okay?"

\*\*\*\*\*\*

Penny wrestled with the cobwebs in her aching head. Slowly they broke, dangled, and withered away. Her wrists and ankles, rope-bound, were sore and raw. And, something else, she remembered. A low-grade pain deep in her vagina—throbbing oh-so satisfyingly. When she had woken up this morning at 4:26, according to her neon green wristwatch, she was in a room next door, well-lit by ceiling fluorescent lights, lying naked on a queen-sized bed, spread-eagle, each extremity rope-bound to bed-posts. The man who had stood naked above her with a chiseled, tattooed body and red Mohawk, had introduced himself simply as Steel, adding, "I'm gonna fuck the living shit outta ya, bitch. It's been way too long."

Steel had slapped her breasts hard, leaving pink handprints. He had slapped her face twice, flushing her cheeks with more pink handprints. Then, guiding his mammoth erect member, he lowered himself and entered her. He pounded her hard, fast, and furious, his musky smell engulfing her senses, his salty sweat dripping on her face and into her open mouth. And, in spite of her best efforts to contain the beast, the sadomasochistic sexual narcissist was unleashed. Penny had begun moaning with intense pleasure. Seconds before she exploded into a powerful orgasm, she had cried out: "Fuck me, baby. Fuck me like that... I love it soooooooo muuuuuuuch!"

But Penny knew she couldn't tell Ralph that. She would tell him—when the time was right—that she had been beaten, violently raped, and only feigned pleasure as an act of self-preservation. If he knew otherwise—well, who knew what he was capable of? What had Elaine said? "Intermittent explosive disorder." *But that might be fun, too.* Remembering Steel's cold, hard steel, his precision drilling, his vice-like grip, and his powerful, metallic slaps, Penny grinned, a soft moan escaping her lips. *No wonder he's called Steel.* "I'm a little sore. You?"

"My head hurts."

"Me too."

"But I remember."

"You do?"

He explained the dream. "For my forgiveness, my uncle gave me a gift—my memory."

"That's great, baby. You remember what happened last night?" She hoped he hadn't heard her pleasurable moans before Steel had put her in captivity with Ralph.

Ralph brought her up to speed with no mention of hearing pleasure-filled moans. "I'm getting free. My ropes are loosening."

"Loosen them then. Let's get outta here."

Ralph grunted. *Snap*. He grunted again. *Snap*. "I got it. My hands are free."

"Untie me."

"Wait. Gotta untie my feet." After a moment, he said, "There. Got it."

Penny felt his warm and calloused hands untying her ankles. Her body tingled with anticipation. A moan escaped her lips.

"You okay?" Ralph asked.

"Yes. I'm fine."

He freed her ankles and moved over to her wrists. She felt erotic juices oozing from her genitals. He freed her wrists. "There you go."

She rubbed her wrists. She fought the urge to rape Ralph. *Later. Later, you insatiable demon.*

Ralph helped her to her feet.

A door was flung open and bright white light blinded them.

"Where do you think you're going?" Steel said, the barrel of his AK-47 a few inches from Ralph's sweating face. Another man entered, grabbed Penny roughly by the hair, and began hauling her out of the room.

Ralph's eyes narrowed as he stood up. "Take your fucking hands off her."

"No you don't," Steel said. With one hand, he grabbed Ralph by the throat and squeezed hard enough to make his point. "Don't panic. King Crass wants you changed and washed up. He requests the pleasure of your company."

As they were led down a dark, narrow corridor, Steel tapped the shoulder of the man pulling Penny along by her long hair. "Hey, not so rough. She's my special little peach."

Ralph's blood began to boil.

\*\*\*\*\*\*

"We can do this one of two ways," Crass said, sitting on a chair positioned a few feet away from his two orange prison-coverall-clad prisoners. "The nice way. Or the nasty way."

"What do you want?" Ralph asked. He sat handcuffed on a couch beside Penny, who wasn't handcuffed. A few feet away, Steel stood guard, training an AK-47 at Ralph's head.

Crass rubbed his hands together. "What do I want? I want many things. I want power. I want control. Guided by God's divine will, I want to create a master race of followers. But first I want to know where you came from, who you were with?"

"We're... we're by ourselves," Penny said, flicking her gaze at Steel, who responded with a mischievous grin.

"That's right," Ralph said. "By ourselves."

"Where's your house?"

There was a moment's hesitation as Ralph and Penny made eye contact.

"No, no," Crass said. "Not like that. Look at me and tell me where you lived, where you survived the holocaust."

There was a moment's hesitation, before Ralph said, "Montague," but Penny blurted out "Charlottetown" at almost exactly the same time.

Crass paused, stood and moved closer, his formidable bulk towering above them. He lowered his face to within a few inches of Ralph's and locked his meat hook of a hand around Ralph's neck. "Which is it then, Einstein? Montague or Charlottetown?" He squeezed. Ralph's face turned pink, then dark red, and then splotches of purple appeared on his cheeks as he gasped for air. His eyes bulged.

"Don't," Penny said, squirming, crossing her legs. "It's Montague. He's right. I was lying."

Crass loosened his grip. Ralph's breath returned in short gasps. Then Crass backhanded Penny hard across the face. The blow toppled her over onto the floor. She landed on her knees, bringing both hands to her swelling cheek. "Speak when you're spoken to, bitch. And not before."

Steel rushed to her side, helped her up, and sat her on the couch, pointing the gun at her head.

Ralph struggled. "Don't... don't touch her. I'll... "

Crass brought his other hand to Ralph's throat, applying a tight, two-handed vice. "You'll what, you little twerp? Kill me? Is that what you were gonna say? Now, once more, where was your house?"

Between gasps, Ralph said, "Monta... Monta... Montague."

Crass released him. Ralph slumped over, wheezing and coughing, fighting for breath.

Steel backed away, aiming his gun at Ralph's head.

Crass sat down, the hot red anger draining from his face. He took a moment to compose himself. "I said we can do this one of two ways. The nice way or the nasty way. Up to you."

Ralph finally caught his breath, feeling his neck redden and begin to swell. The same words kept going through his mind. *Don't rat, don't rat, don't rat... find a house, describe the house. Don't rat, don't rat.* The image of his Uncle Simon's two-acre property in Lower Montague popped into his head. It had a root cellar that gave way to a bomb shelter fifty feet below ground. Simon had locked him down there a half dozen times, punishment for his "bad behavior." Where once he had blocked the memory, now every detail was crystal clear. Simon, from the grave, helping them? Ralph had no idea if the house had survived the blaze, but it was worth a shot. It would buy them some more time, if nothing else. If only Penny didn't blow his cover and blurt out a different story. "The house is on two acres in Lower Montague. We survived in a bomb shelter during the holocaust. The house was destroyed." He looked at Penny with pleading eyes.

"Keep your eyes on me," Crass snapped.

Ralph continued. "We ran out of water, so we had to come up. My uncle had the quad and weapons buried. He was a survivalist. We went looking for food and water... "

"Stop there," Crass said. "So it was just the two of you?"

"Yeah. I swear."

Crass pointed to Penny, who was rubbing her cheek gingerly. "Is this true?"

"Yes. I cross my heart and hope to die."

"You better not hope to die. You might get your wish." Crass's black eyes bored into Ralph. "Why did you kill Sammy? My man at the back door."

*Don't fuck up, don't rat, don't rat, don't rat.* "We saw your men burning dead bodies. Heard them talk about murder. Saw the skull on the steel pole. A deadly threat. They led us here. We're trying to survive. What would you do?"

Crass clenched his fists and stood. "I'm not here to answer your questions. You're here to answer mine. Is that clear?"

"Yeah. Very clear. Sorry."

Penny folded her arms across her chest. Her expression had become calm and composed. Her gaze alternated between Ralph, Crass, and Steel.

Crass stepped closer to his prisoners, knelt down, and locked eyes with Ralph. "You didn't slaughter my men the other day?"

He could finally answer honestly. "No."

Crass's eyes bored into Penny. "Is that true?"

"Yes," she said quickly.

"Do you know anything about who did?"

"No," she said.

"Is that true?" Crass asked Ralph.

"Yeah," he said, dropping his eyes, then quickly reestablishing eye contact.

Crass slapped Ralph hard across the face, sending him flying into Penny, who screamed and wrapped her arms around him. "Leave him alone. He's telling the truth."

Crass gripped Ralph's neck in both hands. "Tell me again. Do you know who killed my men?"

*Don't rat, don't rat... look him straight in the eye.* "No. I don't have a clue."

There was a knock on the front door. Crass released Ralph and sat down. He waved to Steel. "Who the fuck is that? I said no disturbances."

Steel went to the door and pulled it open a crack. He turned around. "It's Belinda. The one that got away. They found her. They thought you'd wanna know."

\*\*\*\*\*\*

Crass's gut said his prisoners were lying. Ralph wouldn't look him in the eye, and they couldn't get their stories straight on the house's location. His gut wasn't wrong. Ever. The realization came to him that his interviewing tactics were a little rusty. Best to interrogate them separately, ask them to describe the bomb shelter and details of the house, and then compare notes. He was sure they wouldn't square.

But right now his need to reacquaint himself with his bride-to-be, Belinda, overrode his anger and need to get to the truth. Besides, wouldn't it be easier to organize a hunting party, bring Ralph and Penny along, and have them show him what was left of the house and bomb shelter? Then, if it wasn't there, he'd simply torture them until they led him to the other killers who had slaughtered half his army and stolen his supplies. He suspected they were in cahoots. And, if Ralph and Penny still wouldn't budge, well then they could easily be disposed of like yesterday's trash.

"Bring her in," Crass said.

Two men led Belinda into the room. Her long blue dress was tattered, torn, and blood-smeared. An errant breast peeked out from a circular rip in the gown. Her face was a wash of tears and blood. A few shards of glass were stuck in her cheeks, one in her forehead and a half a dozen others protruding from her ankles and legs. She stared down at the floor silently, her expression sad.

Wearing an oversized white t-shirt, Maria walked down the stairs, stopping halfway down. Her jaw dropped, and she looked wide-eyed at Belinda. "Oh my."

With a flick of his hand, Crass motioned to the two men holding her. "Take her upstairs."

Crass looked at Maria, remembering the eroticism of the consummation of their union. He couldn't help feeling a stirring in his loins. She had performed surprisingly well. Even appeared to have an orgasm. But Crass couldn't help wondering whether she harbored a secret agenda, one that included his murder. *Never mind. She doesn't have the courage. She likes me. More than that, she likes what I promised her. A position of power and control, at my side.* "How are you doing, honey?"

Maria yawned. "Good, dear. I slept in. You wore me out."

"Clean her up and get her changed," Crass told Maria. "I'll be up in a minute."

"Of course, my love," Maria said. The men led her to Maria and released her. Maria took her by the hand and led her upstairs as the two armed men followed close behind. "Come now, my dear," she said. "We'll get you cleaned up and put a smile on your face. Everything's gonna be all right. I promise... "

Crass faced his prisoners. "Tonight we're going to visit your house. I don't have to tell you what's gonna happen to you if I find out you're lying."

They looked at him silently, Penny still calm and stolid, Ralph frowning slightly.

"Get some food into them and lock them up," Crass told Steel. "Bring them back at eight."

# Chapter Twenty-Four

If Pastor Jon was right—Had he ever been wrong?—tonight would be do-or-die time, Cray thought as he knelt down at a front window of the house, poking his AK-47 through a hole in a piece of plywood that had been fitted to the window. He peered through the sight hole that Marty had cut. He saw nothing but blackness and heard nothing but terrifying silence.

Pastor Jon sat in total darkness on the couch behind him, still swilling Scotch. He was on his third bottle, and Cray had never seen him so tense and so intent on getting pie-eyed out of his mind.

Marty was on the watchtower atop the barn, occasionally sweeping the perimeter with a flashlight, signaling to Cray with two quick flashes that the coast was clear. Three flashes meant trouble was in sight. One meant he'd been hit. Four meant the enemy had breached the perimeter and were attacking. Elaine was in an upstairs bedroom, armed with a machine gun, waiting for trouble to arrive. Sandra was fifteen feet away from Cray at another plywood-fitted main-floor window on the far side of the entrance door—armed and dangerous. Motion sensor lights—wired to a series of batteries—had been installed all around the perimeter of the property. Once an intruder got within four hundred feet in any direction, they would be blasted by light. As the theory went, it would blind the enemy, giving Cray and the others an advantage. *That's the theory. We'll see how it goes in practice.*

Cray turned on his flashlight, sweeping the beam over to Sandra. "You ready?"

"Yeah. Are you?"

"Yeah. Are you okay?"

"Yeah. You?"

Cray's hands trembled but he thought better of mentioning it. *Don't want to get her riled up. She must be feeling the same way.* "I'm fine."

"That means you're scared."

*Ahh, what the hell.* "Yeah."

"So am I. We use the fear to our advantage. It's fight or flight."

Cray wiped away beads of sweat that had started dripping in his eye. "If there is a God, I hope He's on our side."

\*\*\*\*\*\*

*God help me,* Ralph thought, as Crass shone the flashlight beam into what was left of the bomb shelter in Lower Montague. About twenty feet from Simon's fire-destroyed home, there was a large crater where the bomb shelter once was. The intense heat from the apocalyptic blaze had evidently reached an accelerant, igniting it and blowing the underground room to smithereens. There was no way in hell anyone could survive in that. Furthermore, there was no evidence that an ATV or firearms had been buried beneath the surface and recently been unearthed.

With both hands, Crass grabbed a handcuffed Ralph roughly by the throat; his eyes narrowed and red rage swept across his cheeks as he squeezed tightly. "What did I tell you about lying to me? I'm gonna kill you right fucking now."

"No," Penny said, raising her handcuffed arms in a gesture of prayer. "Don't. Please. I'll show you where they are."

"Where who is?" Crass asked, still squeezing while Ralph gasped and gurgled, trying to speak but unable to.

"The people who killed your men."

Crass released Ralph. Ralph fell to the ground, coughing and gasping for breath, almost rolling into the crater. He stopped just short of it, extending a leg to stop his sideways momentum. "Don't," Ralph said through deep breaths. "He'll... he'll kill us anyway. Don't you see?"

Crass kicked him square in the nose, producing a fountain of gushing blood. "Shut your fucking mouth, twerp, and let the woman speak."

Crass waved to Steel, who stood nearby, alongside five other men, watching. "Put him in the car." He dismissed the others with a wave. "Give me a minute with her."

Along with another man, Steel picked up Ralph and led him to one of two Ford Expeditions parked nearby.

"Don't," Ralph said. "Don't tell them, please. They'll kill all of us... "

Steel punched Ralph in the face, a quick hard right. "I thought he told you to shut up?"

Ralph did.

They loaded him in the backseat and got in alongside him while the other four men climbed in the other vehicle and closed the doors.

Stepping closer to Penny, Crass turned off his flashlight. Now they were in the evening's complete blackness. He grabbed her by the throat, gently at first, then slowly squeezed tighter. "You gonna help me?"

She moved a hand to his leg, gliding it up to his crotch. "Keep Ralph alive. He's trainable. I swear, if you do, I'll become one of your wives. I'll marry you."

"You would?"

Penny gently tugged on Crass's nuts. "Yes. I like things... well, a little rough. I like these handcuffs even. But I would prefer to be handcuffed to your bed with them."

"Take me to them. You do that and we'll see."

"Okay."

\*\*\*\*\*

Cray saw three short flashes of light coming from the watchtower—Marty's warning—and scanned the dark horizon; four headlights barreling toward them at high speed, trailed by a plume of gray dust. "They're coming. It's showtime."

Using a broomstick, Sandra tapped three times on the ceiling. Above, Elaine tapped three times in response. "She's ready."

Pastor Jon stood, staggered, and crashed onto the coffee table, collapsing it and shattering his bottle of Scotch.

"Stay down," Cray said. "You okay?"

"If anyone is to go into captivity, into captivity he will go. If anyone is to be killed with the sword, with the sword he will be killed," Pastor Jon said.

"Shut up," Sandra said. "Not now, please."

Watching the approaching lights grow brighter, Cray rehearsed the drill. Once the motion sensor lights lit up, it was time to fire. Exactly four hundred feet. Not before, although his machine gun loaded with the right cartridge had an effective range of about 1300 feet. They wanted the highest and best use of their limited ammunition. He tried to gauge the distance, closing fast.

Eight hundred... seven hundred... both trucks slowed, turned into the driveway, and accelerated, coming straight at them. Were they planning on using the vehicles as battering rams?

"Sandra, honey, If I don't get outta this alive, it was a pleasure knowing you." *How stupid does that sound? Isn't that something you'd tell a casual acquaintance?*

Six hundred... five hundred...

"How about you love me, numbskull?" Sandra said.

"I love you."

"I love you, too."

Pastor Jon began muttering: "Therefore rejoice, you Heavens and you who dwell in them! But woe to the Earth and the sea, because the devil has gone down to you! He is filled with fury, because he knows that his time is short... "

As the vehicles closed in on them, Cray realized that four headlights had morphed into two, occasionally flashing back to four. He understood what it meant. One vehicle had dropped behind, using the first one as a high-speed metal battering ram. It appeared they had no intention of stopping. Were they really planning on crashing into the house?

Four hundred feet. Lights positioned on the property and affixed to the house flashed brightly, illuminating a dark-colored SUV, another one about seventy feet behind, gunning for the house at about eighty miles an hour.

Gunfire erupted, bullets flying everywhere. Cray, Sandra, Marty, and Elaine sprayed the first vehicle, bullets tearing through the windshield, shattering headlights. Approaching fast, the vehicle returned fire, bullets tearing into the house, shattering windows, splintering wood.

\*\*\*\*\*\*

Marty was firing prostrate when he saw the head pop out the open rear window of the first vehicle. Then a body, two arms and—*no, fuck no*—a grenade launcher, aimed right at Sandra's house. He scrambled up, knelt down on one knee, and aimed the AK-47. Two bullets caught him in the chest—in the heart area. "Ugh, fuck sakes." He staggered back, regained his footing, aimed the assault rifle, and sprayed bullets.

The man with the grenade launcher, a split-second away from blowing up the house, took three bullets to the head, two to the chest. "Aaaaah," he said, losing his grip. The grenade launcher swayed down to the ground, then up. The man fired the weapon, then dropped it and fell out the window, dead.

Marty heard the blast and saw the missile coming right at him. He looked at the second-floor house window, where Elaine was perched, also firing. *This is the last time I'll see her alive. Goddammit, I love her so much. It's not supposed to end like this. Not supposed to end like this.*

She spotted Marty, her face tight with panic and worry. "Marty, Marty, get out of there! Please! Now!"

"I love you, baby. I'll always love you."

He scrambled down the roof of the barn, toward the edge, away from the missile's trajectory. *Too little, too late.* A loud explosion rocked the barn. Flames and debris fanned out and flew through the air. The explosion rocketed Marty, still conscious, into the air. As he soared skyward, he saw Elaine take two bullets to the head, moan in pain, and fall from the bedroom window, somersaulting onto the porch roof below and coming to rest on her back at the edge of the roof, expression calm and serene, eyes wide open, staring into the dark sky.

"No, no, you fucking assholes." He didn't know if it was shrapnel, flying debris, or a bullet, but Marty suddenly felt a sharp pain in his head as it entered. His world went black. *I'm dead, she's dead. That's it, that's all. No, no, no, not Elaine. Not my baby. Not supposed to end like this. Please God, no...*

Then all thoughts disappeared and Marty's world descended into black nothingness.

\*\*\*\*\*\*

"Fucking hell," Cray said, feeling the house shake, hearing pictures falling from the walls, glass shattering on hardwood floors. Through the gunfire, he watched the barn explode, saw Marty hurling through the air amidst the flaming debris, heard Elaine's pain-filled moans, heard the *thunk* of her body falling out the window, rolling down the porch roof and coming to rest, somewhere up above them, quite dead, he was sure.

"They're dead," Sandra said between staccato bursts of machine gun fire.

"I know." Cray gritted his teeth, his blood beginning to boil, a hot rage starting to overcome rational thought. *No, control this. You got this. Make them pay. Kill these fucks. Kill them now.* "The tires. Take out the tires."

Aiming low, Cray and Sandra resumed firing. He heard a loud pop, then another. The Expedition skidded, careened wide, adjusted, and came straight for the house.

He continued firing, bullets crunching into metal, piercing the front grill of the SUV as it fishtailed out of control again, but then found its intended path of destruction—the front door of the house.

Still firing, Cray remembered Sandra's SUV, parked behind the house behind some bushes. "We gotta go. Out back. Now!"

The fishtailing vehicle neared.

Cray stopped firing, turned his flashlight on, and ran over to Sandra. She was still firing. He didn't think she had heard him. He tapped her shoulder and she stopped and stared at him, eyes wide with fear. He pointed to the back door. "Let's go. Now!"

For a second, they locked eyes—intense, soul-penetrating eyes. They turned, fixing frozen-in-fear gazes on the metal cannonball flying toward them. A flame suddenly snaked along its hood and enveloped the windshield as it neared.

Fifty feet, forty, thirty, twenty...

Grabbing Sandra's hand, he led her quickly across the living room to the back door. "Go. Start the SUV. I'll be out in a minute. Gotta find Pastor Jon."

"I'm not leaving you."

"Get out of here, now," Cray demanded, angrier than he intended.

Sandra saw the look, turned, and ran out the back door.

Cray shouted, "Pastor Jon. Get out!"

The SUV crashed into the house, smashing through the door and barreling through the living room. It veered left and smashed into the kitchen, where it stopped, lodged into the refrigerator and the far wall, its tires spinning, antifreeze spewing, pumping out fuel and exhaust fumes, debris raining down on it.

Cray stood at the open back door, frantically searching. "Pastor Jon?" He heard a grunt and a moan. He inched forward and was hit by a hailstorm of falling debris. "Pastor Jon? Is that you?"

He heard a metallic click and the driver door of the flaming SUV opened. A bald man with a goatee stepped out and pointed an AK-47 at Cray. His head was cut and bleeding badly. He staggered. He fired.

Cray dove onto the floor, feeling broken glass gouging his arms.

He tried to scramble to his feet but the man was already upon him, stepping on Cray's AK-47 as he tried to raise it.

Cray looked up, seeing the gun barrel pointed a few inches from his face.

"You're dead," the man said, the house now lit by yellow and orange flames that snaked along the floor and up the walls.

But as the man fired, Cray rolled over, the deafening sound of machine gun fire ringing in his ears as a spray of bullets narrowly missed his head. As the man followed his rolling body with the barrel of the gun, Cray stopped and kicked both legs into the air.

He connected hard with the man's head and a spray of bullets riddled the ceiling above, covering him with a plume of drywall dust.

"Fucking bastard," the man said, staggering back.

Cray grabbed his weapon, leapt to his feet, and pulled the trigger. Nothing. It jammed.

He swung the assault rifle, the buttstock slamming into the man's head.

Staggering, the man groaned as flames began to engulf the house. A staccato spray of machine gun fire erupted into the ceiling as Cray attacked, dropping his gun and grabbing the hot barrel of the man's machine gun. He felt his fingers burning on hot steel. He winced, gripped it tighter in spite of the pain, and shoved the man back. The man inched toward the flames, tightly gripping the AK-47.

They did the AK-47 shuffle for a moment before Cray wrenched it loose and aimed it at the man. The man bent down and charged, driving his head into Cray's chest, winding him. The AK-47 went off, bullets spraying around the house as both men hit the floor. On impact, the gun squirted loose and the man mounted Cray, gripped his throat tightly with both hands, and began strangling him.

Cray gasped for breath, bringing his hands up and raking his fingers over the man's face, gouging at his eyes and poking a thumb directly into one eye. He felt the eye pop, gripped it, and ripped it from the man's head, tossing it away like yesterday's trash.

"Oww, you fucking slime," the man said, tightening his chokehold around Cray's neck.

The flames licked closer. The house grew hotter. Cray struggled frantically, but felt the life ebbing from his body. His arms grew weak. His hands grew weak. He could no longer breathe. He dropped his arms to his sides. Blackness closed in and the silhouette of the killer against a fiery backdrop blurred.

*No, not like this. It's not supposed to end like this. Where the fuck is Pastor Jon?* He opened his mouth to cry for help but no words came. *Where's Sandra? Help me...*

"Poke my fucking eye out, will you, motherfucker? You'll pay with your life."

The powerful flesh-and-bone noose tightened around Cray's neck.

Blacker still. And as his last reserves of life drained, a golden light suddenly appeared. Starting as a tiny dot, it quickly grew to a life-sized beautiful female angel, her glowing wings fanning out and surrounding Cray's dying body. The angel said two words: "Your gun."

*The Colt 45. Ralph's Colt 45.* With a divinely inspired last burst of energy, Cray brought his hand to his waist, slid out the Colt 45 he had tucked away and in his panicked fight for survival had forgotten about, pointed it at the side of his would-be killer's head, and fired.

*Kaplow!*

"Aaaaaaaah," the man said, gray matter exploding out the side of his head. He loosened his grip, his hands went limp. He dropped dead, his head falling on Cray's chest.

"Come on," Sandra said. "The house is gonna blow."

Cray saw an angel standing above him, fiery golden wings fanning out. She pulled the dead man off him, grabbed his arm, and helped him up. "You okay?"

His vision cleared somewhat and he realized it was Sandra. He coughed a few times and finally caught his breath. "You?"

"Who do you think? An angel from Heaven?" She put an arm over his shoulder and helped him to the back door as the flames inched closer, the home rapidly turning into a pressure cooker.

"Pastor Jon?" Cray asked.

"I don't know."

As they stepped off the porch, the house was completely engulfed by flames and then rocked by a loud explosion that lit the black sky fiery red as the flames fanned out. Heat-singed by the sudden fireball, Cray and Sandra ran, both diving onto the ground and rolling. On all fours, they crawled toward the idling SUV.

\*\*\*\*\*\*

It wasn't just the flames that made Ralph see red as the trailing SUV skidded to a stop about thirty feet from the inferno. Nor was it the dark red blood dribbling down his face from Steel's sucker punch and Crass's boot to the nose.

No. It was something else. The agitation had started with Penny's betrayal of the whereabouts of his friends—slowly unleashing the uncontrollable fury of the intermittent-explosive-disorder monster lurking inside him. Then it was the rejection demon intertwined with the green-eyed monster of jealousy that had begun to untangle the ties that bound him to a semblance of sanity. Frankenstein's monster had begun to unravel. He first noticed it during the interrogation, but had dismissed it as tricks of his imagination. A look Penny had exchanged with Steel. A look of affection. *Nothing. My mind playing tricks on me.* But on the way to Sandra's house, he had seen it again. Not once, but twice. And, to rub salt in the wound, he had also watched her exchange a weird look of affection with Crass.

That might have been enough to unleash the monster's blind rage. But it wasn't just one thing. It was everything combined. And the proverbial straw that broke the camel's back was witnessing two murders. First, Marty's limp body somersaulting through the air after a rocket-propelled grenade blew the barn to smithereens. Second, Elaine taking two bullets to the head and falling dead from the bedroom window onto the porch roof below.

Not how Ralph planned it. He wanted to prove to his friends that he was worthy of their trust, wanted to impress them, win their favor and loyalty with heroic acts of bravery. Show them he was willing to risk his life for them, die for them. Now what had he become? A chicken shit prisoner leading the enemy to the only people who had shown him a modicum of love.

What had he become? A coward. And a jealous and rejected one at that.

The red rage boiled over.

Ralph head-butted the man beside him fiercely, knocking him unconscious. Then with superhuman strength he wrapped his handcuffs around Crass's neck tightly, squeezing, watching the evil man's face redden and swell.

Crass struggled furiously, opening the driver door and dragging Ralph, still clinging to his neck, outside of the vehicle. As Crass thrashed violently, tossing Ralph around like a rag-doll, Penny opened the front passenger door, and got out to watch.

Steel pointed a handgun to the head of the unconscious man beside him and fired two bullets into it. "Fucking asshole, terrorist. You're not really a team player. You'd turn on me on a dime." Then he calmly got out of the SUV and watched his leader fight for his life.

Riding Crass piggy-back style while strangling him with the handcuff chains, Ralph locked his legs around the man's waist. Crass thrashed about forcefully, but Ralph hung on for dear life. Slowly, the leader's strength began to wane and he dropped to his knees. Gasping for breath, he turned to Steel, black eyes frightened and desperate. "Do... do something."

"Fuck you," Steel said, pointing his AK-47 at him. "Your time has come."

Ralph winced, tightened his grip on the handcuffs, and jerked. With a loud snapping sound, Crass's neck broke. His head lolled to one side and blood dribbled from his open mouth. Ralph released his death lock and the big man slumped to the ground.

\*\*\*\*\*\*

As Cray opened the passenger door for Sandra, he heard a scream, spun around, and saw Pastor Jon, his lower torso on fire, staggering out of the basement of the burning house. Sandra grabbed two blankets from the vehicle and they ran toward him, tackling him to the ground, patting out the flames with the blanket. They smothered the flames. Much of his legs were burned and flesh had begun to peel off in different spots above and below the knees.

"You okay?' Sandra asked.

"They're coming," Pastor Jon said. "God's other plague."

"What happened to you?"

"Must've passed out. In the basement."

\*\*\*\*\*\*

After killing Crass, Ralph wasn't even breathing hard. He was on fire with energy. He scanned the property for any surviving friends. Looking at the barn, he frowned, seeing the flames rapidly destroy it. He eyed the house, also being quickly decimated by the fire. He spotted Elaine's dead body, burning on the roof of the wraparound deck. *So much fire. So much pain. So much death.*

He turned to Penny, looking at her with hurt eyes. "You... you betrayed me."

"No. I tried... tried to save you."

Pointing a handgun at Ralph, Steel said, "I think she likes my dick better. Probably because it's a fuck of a lot bigger than your pencil dick."

Blind rage overcame Ralph again and, shouting obscenities, he charged at Steel as Sandra's SUV pulled around the burning house and neared. Before they could stop or fire, Steel shot Ralph three times in the head.

Ralph's forward momentum knocked Steel to the ground, Penny watching calmly from a safe distance. As they pulled closer, Steel pushed a dead Ralph off him, stood, and aimed at the SUV.

Ralph got to his feet, stretched his hands, and snapped the cuffs off. Instead of attacking Steel, or Penny for that matter, he turned, spread his arms to the heavens, and walked casually toward the flaming house. Stopping a few inches from the flames, he turned around, facing the incredulous onlookers. Turning to Sandra's SUV, he said, "Now you can say I died a hero."

His face an expression of serene calm, he turned around, folded his arms in prayer, and walked silently into a growing wall of fire. Orange flames billowed up, fanned out into fiery angel wings, and slowly faded away into the dark sky.

Armed with a machine gun, Cray stepped out of the SUV. *How the fuck did Ralph get up with a head full of lead?*

"The Lord works in mysterious ways," Pastor Jon said, stepping out of the vehicle and pointing skyward.

Steel sprayed them with bullets. As Cray dove to the ground, bullets whizzed past, none of them hitting him, Pastor Jon, their SUV, or Sandra.

Pastor Jon knelt down and prayed. "The Lord works in mysterious ways."

Penny grabbed Steel's gun hand. "No more killing. Enough for one day."

"What?" Steel said. "I wanna... "

Cray got up, apoplectic after the murders of Elaine, Marty, and now Ralph. He aimed the machine gun, readied to fire, wanting to seize the moment since Steel was momentarily distracted.

"No," Pastor Jon said. "Listen. They're coming."

Everybody froze.

Cray heard the buzzing before he saw anything. Starting off low, it erupted into an ear-piercing chainsaw. Then they swarmed in—human-sized angry wasps, thickening, threatening, hovering, hissing.

One split from the swarm and nose-dived directly for Steel. As it neared, he blasted it with machine gun fire. It exploded, showering him in a gooey yellow liquid. Waving to Penny, he scrambled to the Expedition, climbed in, and closed the door.

Penny jumped into the passenger seat and slammed the door as another nose-diving wasp smashed into the windshield and splattered—blood, guts and insect body parts flying into the air. In spite of the danger, she rolled down the window and stuck her head out. "I'm sorry. I've gotta do what's right for me."

Cray helped Pastor Jon to his feet as the angry wasps swarmed around their heads. Quickly, they climbed into the SUV and closed all the doors and windows.

"It's the locusts as predicted in the *Book of Revelation*," Pastor Jon said "They'll kill the enemy. Don't worry. Stay here."

They watched Steel and Penny hightail it out of the driveway. As the Expedition reached the main exit road, the swarm of yellow and black wasps began pursuit. By the time it turned onto the main road and began accelerating, it was covered in a thick mass of deadly poisonous insects.

"I think it's time to go," Sandra said a moment later.

"Let's go," Cray said.

As the SUV entered the driveway, she stopped. Wiping wet eyes, she turned to Cray. "Anything you want to say?"

"Later," Cray said, overcome with grief. "Let's get the fuck out of here."

"You sure?"

"May God have mercy on their souls."

# Epilogue

Draining the juice from a can of tuna he had just eaten, Cray watched the man wrapped in a sleeping bag curled up on the grass in front of him. *Such a mystery. Why won't he wake up?* The man's fingers suddenly twitched—the first sign of life in twenty-four hours. In the mid-afternoon gray haze, Cray rose from the plastic chair in a grassy field on the outskirts of Charlottetown, tossed the can into a nearby garbage pile, and approached the man. *Should I tell Sandra? Should I tell Pastor Jon?* But they were sleeping in nearby tents and Cray thought it was best to leave them be for now. For what lay ahead, they would need energy.

As he neared, he saw the man's eyelids flutter. *He's coming out of it. Please, God, help him.* Cray knelt down beside the man and touched his shoulder.

Miraculously, the man opened his eyes. Slowly at first, but then wide and panicked. He jerked up, but Cray put a steadying hand on his shoulder. "Easy. Not so fast."

"Where am I?" Marty asked.

"You're safe. You're with us, near Charlottetown."

"Elaine?"

"I'm sorry. She didn't make it."

Marty grimaced and brought both hands to his face. "Sandra?"

"Sleeping."

"Pastor Jon?"

"Sleeping."

"Penny?"

"I don't know. Dead, I think."

"Ralph?"

"He's dead, Marty. I'm sorry. If it's any consolation, he died a hero. He killed Crass."

Marty turned over and shrank into a fetal position. He began to sob softly. "Leave me alone for a minute. Please."

"Okay. Call if you need anything."

Cray walked to the edge of the field and surveyed the bleak landscape that lay in front of him. Twisted metal ruins of buildings, fire-ravaged vehicles, razed homes, the skeletal remains of people who had been burned alive. Carnage. A war zone.

*Marty is one lucky guy.*

Lucky to have been wearing his Kevlar vest when he took two bullets to the chest. Lucky the bullet that hit his head only crazed his skull, knocking him unconscious but not entering fatal territory. Lucky that when the rocket-propelled grenade blasted him into the air, he landed on a small outbuilding, breaking through the roof, but also breaking his fall. Other than the head injury, inducing a twenty-four hour coma, and a few minor cuts and bruises, Marty was unhurt. He had not even broken any bones during the fall.

At least, Sandra's diagnosis had indicated as much. Just before they were ready to leave the property forever, it had been Pastor Jon who'd said, "Stop. Check that outbuilding." When they did, they found Marty, unconscious but still breathing, stretched out on a pile of broken boards. So they loaded his comatose body into the SUV and went in search of greener pastures.

*One tough son of a bitch. One lucky son of a bitch. But is it luck?*

"Do we have anything to eat?" Marty asked.

Cray turned around and saw Marty rummaging through one of the tents, the same one he had slept in last night. It had been Pastor Jon who had insisted earlier in the day they put him in the middle of the field to get some fresh air "so God can heal him."

Cray pointed to a nearby cooler. "Over there." He approached Marty, who had found a bottle of water and was busy guzzling it down. He finished it, tossed the bottle away, and went fishing in a plastic bag. He pulled out a can of beans, found an opener, and began working the can.

"How do you feel?" Cray asked.

"A little stiff. A bit of a headache. But damn thirsty. And damn hungry."

"That's a good sign. You're one tough son of a bitch."

"I guess I'm lucky to be alive," Marty said, smiling weakly. His face was jaundiced with a smattering of small cuts and purple and black bruises.

"At one time I might have agreed with you," Cray said. "But now, I'm not so sure. Maybe Pastor Jon was right all along. Maybe it *is* divine intervention that's keeping us alive."

\*\*\*\*\*\*

For six days they hadn't spoken about the deaths of Ralph or Elaine, or Penny's surprising change of heart, preferring to grieve silently and by themselves. Even Pastor Jon, known for his prophetic outbursts, religious rants, and touching eulogies, had stayed silent on the subject. Instead they had thought only about survival, about new beginnings, about a better life away from Prince Edward Island.

Normally so clairvoyant, Pastor Jon had come up dry when Cray reminded him of the so-called tribesmen Pastor Jon had predicted would arrive after the apocalypse and guide them to safety. "I don't know. I haven't had a vision about it yet."

The preacher had also answered vaguely when Cray pulled him aside one day and said, "I thought you said I'm supposed to be a leader in this new world. I haven't led shit during this ordeal."

Pastor Jon had scratched his head confusedly and responded, "Our journey isn't over yet. When I know the time for your leadership, I'll tell you."

So Cray had forgotten about it for the time being, concentrating his efforts on tangibles—searching for supplies and survivors. They had driven through Montague, seeing only glass, steel, concrete rubble, human and animal skeletons, and scorched blackness, a town completely decimated by the holocaust. So too was it devoid of any human, animal, or insect life. Even the giant wasps had disappeared, although Cray wondered if they had indeed devoured Penny and Steel and decimated the polygamist cult Crass had tried to start.

They had also discussed returning to Panmure Island, as Marty still wanted revenge. So did Cray. So did Sandra. But after many heated debates, in the end it was Pastor Jon's prophetic words that had convinced them otherwise. "The locusts are a sign from God to stay away. The locusts will devour the evil polygamist cult. It's in God's hands now."

In the days to follow, they had also ventured into Charlottetown. But all they found was a city in ruins, devoid of any life whatsoever. It was on the outskirts where they stumbled upon the grassy field next to a small underground shelter untouched by the blaze.

Pastor Jon's burns appeared worse than they actually were. Sandra had diagnosed them as only first-degree and had gone to work nursing him back to health, disinfecting the wounds daily and changing the dressings.

From the shelter, they had removed foodstuffs and tents, living above the surface in darkness for six days, before they had finally decided to try and get to the mainland. Moncton, New Brunswick, Cray and Pastor Jon's place of birth. Cray liked the idea. So did Marty. So did Sandra. So did Pastor Jon, who claimed the so-called tribesmen might be there, might be interested in working together and building a new community, one based on honesty, trust, loyalty, love, and goodwill toward neighbors. What did they have to lose? Anything was better than this mere survival existence.

Maybe Cray's parents were alive. Maybe they had heeded his warnings and survived. Maybe he could strengthen his relationship with them, now that money meant shit. Maybe there was life there. Maybe some of Pastor Jon's former congregation, the so-called tribesmen, had heeded his warnings and survived. Maybe they could rebuild, start anew. Maybe Pastor Jon could find a church and start preaching again, as lately he had withdrawn into periods of long brooding silence. Cray thought it might help the man out of his silent misery if he could once again find his proselytizing calling.

In the ominous gray haze, Cray stood on the dock that afternoon, examining the boat. It was a white converted fishing boat, New Beginnings painted in black on its stern. There it was, floating on the dock of a bay in North Rustico, the only vessel they could find that had not been razed by the death-producing flames.

Marty loaded supplies into the boat.

Sandra put an arm around Cray. "Do you think it'll start?" she asked, a glimmer of hope in her green eyes.

Pastor Jon was in the cabin, fidgeting with controls.

"I don't know. Why don't you ask the captain?"

Marty stopped, pointing to Pastor Jon. "He's the captain? He's always drunk."

"Wait a minute," Pastor Jon said. He turned the key. It sputtered and stalled. He tried it twice more with the same result. On the fourth try, it rumbled to life. He emerged from the cabin, grinning ear-to-ear; it was the first time Cray had seen him smile in a long time. "There we go. Thank you, Lord."

They loaded in the rest of the supplies, including what was left of their ammunition and guns, and climbed aboard.

In the cabin, Pastor Jon steered while Marty kept a watchful eye on him. Cray and Sandra sat on deck, on folding chairs, watching Prince Edward Island grow smaller and smaller. Occasionally they would pass floating dead fish, sharks, sea lions, and birds.

They were silent for a long time.

Sandra touched Cray's hand. She wiped away a tear. "I... I miss them."

Cray put his arm around her, pulling her close. The warmth of her body felt comforting on a day that had turned slightly chilly, one of few days the heat had abated significantly since their ordeal had begun. "Me too. A lot. I never thought I'd say this, but I think they're in a better place."

"What, like Heaven?"

He kissed her. She smelled of roses and honey. "Yeah, like Heaven."

"Maybe you're right. Maybe you're right."

"Why don't we have a drink in their honor?" Cray asked. Without waiting for a reply, he reached down and pulled out a bottle of Glenlivet single malt, one they had been saving for a special occasion. He handed it to Sandra and located some plastic cups. He pulled two out, then remembered Marty and Pastor Jon, and grabbed two more.

He sat down beside Sandra. She opened the bottle and filled both of their cups.

"To our friends, whom we loved so dearly," Cray said. "We wouldn't be here today without their courage, and I'm including Penny in this, however misguided she might be. Rest in peace. May God look after you in Heaven—if that's your final destination."

"Amen," Sandra said. They toasted and drank, and then hugged each other tightly, their eyes becoming moist as they remembered their friends and tried to find some closure to a tragic chain of events that would deeply scar them for the rest of their lives.

"Wait a minute," Sandra said, wiping her eyes. "We forgot Marty and Pastor Jon."

Plastic cups and bottle in hand, they went inside the cabin. Pastor Jon was at the helm, steering, concentrating intently on the route ahead. Marty watched him. "He's better than I thought. Actually knows how to drive this thing."

Cray filled a cup and handed it to Marty. "Want a drink? I hope you don't mind, but we wanted to have a toast in honor of Ralph, Penny and Elaine."

Marty paused for a moment. His face stiffened, then softened. He took a cup. "Why not?"

Cray filled a cup for Pastor Jon and handed it to him.

Wide-eyed, Pastor Jon scowled as if he were looking at the devil himself. He slowly held out a quivering hand, and then withdrew it, reaching instead for a bottle of water in his shirt pocket. "I better not. I wanna try and keep my wits about me for a while. I've seen too much. Maybe I've been scared straight."

It occurred to Cray that Pastor Jon hadn't had a drink in almost two days—a milestone for a hard-core alcoholic like him. He was trying to beat it, and Cray wanted to respect that. He liked Pastor Jon better sober anyway. He made a hell—*or is that "a heaven"?*—of a lot more sense.

Cray raised his cup. "Use your water, Pastor Jon. We wanted to include you in a toast to our heroic friends."

Marty and Sandra raised their cups.

Pastor Jon's brow furrowed, then his face brightened. He raised his water bottle. "They are in Heaven. They are in a better place—in God's hands." His aged eyes suddenly glassed over. "I loved them all dearly. Friends, rest in peace."

They toasted and drank.

"I hope you find peace where you are, Elaine," Marty said. "I love you so much. Rest in peace."

A chorus of "Cheers" followed.

"You are all heroes," Cray said. "Ralph, Elaine, even Penny. I love you dearly."

"Me too," Sandra said. "I'll always remember you fondly. I love you all."

After an awkward silence, they wrapped their arms around Pastor Jon in a group hug. "We love you too, Pastor Jon," Sandra said. "Thanks so much for saving our lives. We're deeply in your debt."

"She's right," Cray said, wiping moist eyes. "I love you. Thank you so much. You're our brother for life."

"I'll second that," Marty said. "I love you all. And it's high time I said it."

Pastor Jon wiped wet eyes. "Did I ever tell you I have an estranged wife and two estranged sons?"

"You might have mentioned it when you were in the hospital," Sandra said. "But I don't remember."

Marty shook his head.

"You never told me," Cray said. "I was probably too concerned about surviving to ask."

"They live in Moncton. Maybe they're still alive. Maybe I can make amends."

"I hope so," Marty said.

"What are their names?" Sandra asked.

After a pause, Pastor Jon said, "You won't believe me if I tell you. But it's true. I swear to God."

"Oh, I think we know better now," Cray said. "Whenever you swear to God, talk to God, have visions from God, or pray to God, almost everything comes true. Try us."

"My wife is called Sandra, and my sons are Marty and Cray."

Three mouths dropped open and they stood incredulous for a moment.

"Now that *is* fucking weird," Marty finally said. "But I think it calls for another toast. I'm ready to get hammered."

They toasted and drank, then moved in for another group hug.

Pastor Jon was overcome. "I love you, my children. And thank you. As much as I may have saved your lives—which I believe was God's doing—you've saved my life. You've probably gone a step further and saved my sanity." He stepped back, a little flustered. "Now, please, let me captain our boat."

"Aye, aye, Captain," Cray and Sandra said in unison, releasing him.

After a moment, Cray said, "I just realized, today is June 30th, the day you said the world would end."

"Shit," Marty said. "I was looking forward to getting drunk."

After a long silence, Pastor Jon looked up into the sky. They followed his gaze. He opened his arms to the heavens. A bank of black clouds suddenly split, revealing brilliant yellow sunshine and a wedge of bright blue sky—the first sign of light after so many dark days and nights. Out of nowhere, a white seagull swooped down in front of the boat, squawked, shot them a curious sideways glance, soared high in the air, and vanished into blue sky.

Tears began streaming down Pastor Jon's face. "I was wrong. I'm only human. June 30$^{th}$ is a day for new beginnings. Our new beginnings."

The End

## Also by William Blackwell

*Phantom Rage, Poison Rage, Infected Rage*
*Nightmare's Edge*
*Resurrection Point*
*Brainstorm*
*A Head for an Eye*
*Rule 14*
*Assaulted Souls*
*Assaulted Souls II*
*Assaulted Souls III*
*Blood Curse*
*Black Dawn*
*The Strap*
*Orgon Conclusion*
*The Dark Menace*
*The Witch's Tombstone*
*Freaky Franky*
*Macabre Alley*
*Tales of Damnation*
*In Your Dreams*

## *Freaky Franky* Preview

When an enigmatic town doctor saves the life of Anisa Worthington's dying son, she abandons Christianity in favor of devotion to the cult of Saint Death. Some believe the mysterious skeleton saint will protect their loved ones; help in matters of the heart; provide abundant happiness, health, wealth and justice.

But others, including the Catholic Church, call it blasphemous, evil, and satanic.

Anisa introduces Saint Death to troubled Catholic friend Helen Randon and strange things begin happening. One of Helen's enemies is brutally murdered and residents of Montague, a peaceful little town on Prince Edward Island, begin plotting to rid the Bible belt of apostates.

Anisa suspects Helen is perverting the good tenets of Saint Death but, before she can act, a terrible nightmare propels her to the Dominican Republic in search of *Freaky Franky*, her long-lost and unstable brother, who mysteriously disappeared without a trace twenty years ago.

To her horror, Anisa learns *Freaky Franky* is also worshiping Saint Death with evil intentions. As a fanatical and hell-bent lynch mob tightens the noose, mysterious murders begin occurring all around Anisa. Unsure about who's an enemy and who's an ally, she's thrust into a violent battle to save her life as well as the lives of her unpredictable friends and brother.

"Blackwell's descriptive writing style allows us a personal glimpse into the minds of his characters to a point where you will feel as though they're lifelong friends. My only dislike is that it ended!" -Amazon

"The suspense builds as we follow several characters as they worship Saint Death, receiving both miraculous cures and the curse that often befalls the Saint's worshipers. Some violent scenes but an entertaining read." -Amazon

"If you're looking for a horror with a slice of religion, I recommend this book. It's one of the greatest horror novels I've ever read and it's not a cliché plot. I rate this book 10/ 10." -Goodreads

## Author Comments

Thank you for reading this book. I would be eternally grateful if you would post a book review on your favorite book retailer website. A positive review is the highest compliment a writer can receive. Reviews also help readers discover new books.

In other news, I have a gift for you. Complete the signup form below with your name and email address to get a FREE download copy of *Resurrection Point*, a dark tale about the horrifying consequences of experimenting with death and resurrection. You're only agreeing to be kept up to date on blog posts, new releases, and freebies. I promise I won't spam you and you can unsubscribe at any time.

http://www.wblackwell.com/free-ebook/